THE WOLF WHO
SWALLOWED THE SUN

OTHER WORKS BY DONALD NEWLOVE

NOVELS

The Painter Gabriel

Leo & Theodore

The Drunks

Sweet Adversity — *Embodying the author's final revisions*
for Leo & Theodore *and* The Drunks

Eternal Life

Curranne Trueheart

Blindfolded Before the Firing Squad, or The Brothers Kirkmaus

Beautiful Soup & Other Works of Memory

Starlite Photoplays: A Hollywood Trilogy, embodying

The Welles Requiem — *A Symphony*

Together at Last: A Village Fantasia

Archie: A Screwball Tragedy Starring Cary Grant

Downpour: A Love Story

The Goddess Clarissa

NONFICTION

Those Drinking Days: Myself and Other Writers

First Paragraphs: Inspired Openings for Writers and Readers

Painted Paragraphs: Inspired Description for Writers and Readers

Invented Voices: Inspired Dialogue for Writers and Readers

Passion: Ardor and Desire in Great Writing

Perfection: A Guide to Revision and Finishing a Work to Be Abandoned Forever

Helen's Ass Strikes Homer Blind! or The Great Memory

Trumpet Rhapsodies & Other Pieces of Time

The Three-Headed Pet Dog

PLAYS

Pleasures of the Night, Four Plays:

Beautiful Soup

Between Lives

The Doll's House

The Whiffle Hen

SCREENPLAYS

Beautiful Soup

Archie

THE WOLF WHO SWALLOWED THE SUN

A Jungian Fable of Family and Finance
Across the Twentieth Century

Donald Newlove

Tough Poets Press
Arlington, Massachusetts

Cover design by Rick Schober.
Back cover photo by Keith Guenthardt.

ISBN 978-0-578-51296-9
Tough Poets Press
49 Churchill Avenue, Floor 2
Arlington, Massachusetts 02476
U.S.A.

www.toughpoets.com

To Nancy
Ageless starlight

To Erika
Constantly surprising music

This novel deserves a dedication to Robert O'Leary, late husband of Erika O'Leary. Without his background in undercover work for the CIA and his skill with skulls dug up in world finance, this novel would not exist. But Robert's background cannot be spelled out by me, since he kept stringent secrecy about it and even to me would not speak about or reveal what he thought must remain *sub rosa* despite our close work as co-writers of the first draft of this work. Robert took his secrets straight into the grave.

As a victim of Marfan Syndrome for which no cure exists, Robert suffered from unstoppable skeletal growth, or giantism. With long limbs and long fingers and in his sixties when we wrote our first draft stood over seven and a half feet, still growing, and had to lower his head walking through my doorway. In the end he could no longer walk and sat largely speechless in a long lounge chair with his legs and feet stretched far out, and at last lost his mind as well and lay bedridden.

I tell all this about him because the great character in this novel, a Bihusi wolf-man seven and half feet high and a financial genius of inhuman skill, might be seen as in some way an image of Robert with his deep-buried international secrets and breath-catching grip on financial world greed. True, these stories had to come from somewhere, often herein with companies' real names in their colossal shifts in ownership. But let's be frank and call our novel *The Wolf Who Swallowed the Sun* the fiction it is. Rest easy, Robert, your secrets lie sucked into the collective unconscious where only Carl Jung might find them—and he lies under a five-foot family gravestone in the Protestant Graveyard at Küsnacht.

D.N.

IA TOTUL, NU DA NIMIC
Take Everything, Give Nothing
Bihusi Family Motto

I seek some child within the radiant cradle of my ribs.
Billy Baxter

I AM A BIHUSI WOLF. Although I look as human as you, my power of scent gives me seven million times the strength of yours. I think in scent, not only with my mind but with scent-cells rippling my skin. My skin and my body think.

I love a Swiss-Chinese Jungian analyst I've never met who has written a book about my religion and sent me a letter. She lives in Zürich. I live in Montana. From butyric acid her fingers left on her typewritten letter, I scent her around the planet. Unimaginable? I am of the Bihusi species. With our power of scent we can smell and at times even taste scent from the airless crust of the Moon—an odor of spent gunpowder that stings and swells the cones in our nose cartilage. It can leave a very unpleasant metallic hardness to the middle part of our tongues. Yet we don't avoid Moonlight. Far from it. Our jaws crackle and souls gulp with lust for the Moon.

Even as your blood beats with life from the Sun ours pounds in the tidal pull of the Moon. Where you become clear-eyed and purposeful by day I brim with the Moon as my each bone springs to my purpose. Our Bihusi spiritual homeland leaves us strongest at dawn and dusk. We call the Moon our Queen of Life and Death and the fiery dew she lights for us hangs heavy with messages from our Bihusi forebears. My nose feeds on dew scented with wolf-memory from the dead to the living. Our deep past goes beyond grief and grieving for lost offspring or failed parent. I grieve over what I never did but might have done had I at that time had the heart for it. Nor will my Dad's Bihusi eyes again shine amber and he dash with the pack through Moonlit forests as his shadow leaps and flows over fallen limbs and dead trunks—his bright eye biting at shadows. Bear with me; I have a story to tell, one you humans can't take in at first swipe.

Tracking her scent I board a plane bound for Zürich. I am ill and have written to two top Jungians in Zürich, Dr. Sidney Chang and his wife Dr.

Gong Li-Chang. Her books stir my deepest being—as do her jacket photos with bust abounding. When her answer arrives the scent of her fingers on each sheet leaves me dazed with hunger, though I am of a different species. At no small price the two doctors set aside one day's regular practice for a consult. In exchange I offer to fund Doctor Gong Li-Chang's pet project for bringing the language of archetypes into early-grade Swiss classrooms, along with the drawing and spelling out of archetypes of the unconscious. Start early at some limited mastery of the unconscious, she urges. It's never too soon to wake a child to the bedrock under his or her dreams and so to draw wisdom from fancies and home movies that flow out of the unconscious. Let your fears and daydreams flood forth! Give them form, make models of them. For the true structure of wisdom lies in the almonds of the amygdalae, those midbrain nuclei recording our fears and deepest self-discoveries, the true history that forms the fabled journey into self each being must face and allow him or herself to follow if unity of self is to be found. Sew up your scattered mind and be born anew, Dr. Gong Li-Chang lectures, and good Swiss school kids sit sworn to self-understanding. Her great beauty does lend urgency to the flag she waves.

Sidney Chang and I sit at a patio table whose bright china-blue sunshade pulses onto flagstone underfoot. Great chestnut branches bower the Chang garden—it fronts Lake of Zürich. Behind us hillside villas rise in terraces. Honeysuckle and lilac wash the air. I watch scarlet cardinals dart from limb to limb and attack the lawn bird-feeder. Great chunks of heaven brighten my amygdalae. I'm half-faint with the stillness, then my ears prick up. My skin ripples. Ah yes, I scent her coming.

Dr. Gong Li-Chang—shod in smoky crimson slippers and suited in black satin blouse and pants—bears a tray our way down a graveled walk that goes on a short way to the lakeshore. She serves Darjeeling and sits with us. Wise cheekbones lift under crow-black hair wound into a psyche knot and pierced by a long-toothed red comb. Her still youthful beauty glows with such strength that I but glance at her bare unpainted face. She too glances but sidelong at me, perhaps fearful I will fade along with her plan to speed up the emotional intelligence of children by plunging the Swiss classroom into scans of the archetypes that underlie Red Ridinghood, the Big Bad Wolf, and the basic Swiss income that should strengthen Grandmother's House. I scent nervous curiosity on her skin and hear the deep thud of her heart. Her crimson slippers and bare sanded toenails steal my breath. This intellectual Chinese goddess—whom I can't bear to look at—wants to know about me down to my inmost being.

Hi, she says. I want to thank you again for funding my project.

Oh, I'm eager to help, I say. Children need to make sense of their dreams.

Without classical training, she says, their personalities will dance off the table like pearls.

I believe you. Thank you for seeing me on such short notice.

Her fragrant fingers hand me a slim orange saucer with a bone cup, its tea steaming with the high Himalayas where these leaves first grew and now sting memory with my Dad and I out mountain climbing among wild tea bushes as others might recall childhood from a maple taste or ripe pear or see lost lawns and alleys, a porch or chimney bricks—a passageway in Paris or canal in Venice. My power of scent not only thinks for me but slips me into others' feelings and thoughts with a force these two doctors know nothing of and would call clairvoyance—which it is not. I read Beingness—with her the very weight and language of her body, her limbs and beating organs. For beside these two physicians of the mind I am a god, of sorts, visiting in disguise.

Your books, doctor! I tell her. I find *Metabiology and Compassion* quite stirring—in fact, mind-bending. I agree, it's an empty hope that reason at last will resolve our existential contradictions. As you say, our ancestral genes already lift fine shoots into our futures: "We face a sky we know nothing of but will grow into." That's very well-put.

I can write nonsense with the best of them. She smiles.

Even so, you're very courageous to step out of descriptive Jungian artifacts of the unconscious into higher genetics. And I'm not being sarcastic.

Oh, I enjoy sarcasm, she says. She studies my dark horn rims. It tells me things.

Sidney Chang says, Sarcasm is a kind of cattle prod. Jung himself could be withering about analytic psychology. So what draws you here, Mister Baxter?

Madam Gong's latest book! I say. *The Spear of Ahuramazda: The Will-to-Spirit versus the Anti-Will.* I have something to contribute to her argument. Something you don't touch on, Doctor.

Don't keep it a mystery, she says. What do you know?

My throat catches.

I know about greed—hatred—*and rapacity*—on an animistic scale and as a crushing spiritual urge that far outweighs anything science knows—and about love as a primal motive force among many animal forms—none of which I'd say you've touched on. In a way your book is about the soul of my family. The Spear of Ahuramazda That Sees Everything has been our most treasured family heirloom since my grandfather bought it in Malta. It gives off a blue aura not unlike this sunshade's. You might say it lifts symbols from the very face of the waters. We know The Spear as the Holy Grail of the Bihusi, my family.

Doctor Li-Chang has stiffened and now grips her husband's hand.

You have it—but how? The Spear is a priceless relic! Hasn't it been lost for over a century?

Stolen—but not lost, I say. I begin to lose my voice. A Bihusi member of the Knights of Malta thought it belonged back with *his* order—I might even say his species—and stole it from Wagner's chalet during the premiere of *Parsifal*. He thought it belonged with the Bihusi—and not languishing unused. I turn my face from her. You know more about my family's spear than any human alive. I'm so happy. So honored to meet you. Oh my God, forgive me, I say as tears spring.

I cover my dark glasses and hide from her unearthly beauty. I hear voices. Spirits dance about me—spirits I've called up for this long day with the doctors. I fight for breath as ancestral passions join a sea of losses within me. How can I tell these doctors that all day long—every day!—my whole body boils with feelings and spirits I control only by threadlike wisps—and that my superhuman powers of smell should be focused on higher goals than playing the children's games I do play among humans?

What's more, I've brought The Spear with me to show you. It's in my room at the Dolder.

My God! she says as deep almond eyes bear down on me. You've brought The Spear itself?

I scent her body hair, all of it in one heady sweep. Her taste spreads over my lips, the elegant golden nuttiness of extra virgin olive oil. Within me lift kiss upon future kiss.

Yes! It'll be delivered when I phone for it.

I breathe deep, my soul unloosed. Swans pair and nest in sedge at the shore. Three newly hatched cygnets glide and bob about them. I read their flesh and bones and feathers and sniff the lake weeds of their fine big family nest.

Beautiful swans, I say. You're on an inlet here? They like that. In Schubert the swan is desire for death. The *Schwanengesang*, you know. In Jung, I believe, the swan denotes the Sun and the conquest of death. He sees the long male neck and silky feminine body as the mystic center—the union of opposites. Well, that's just what you'd expect from Jung. Was he right?

Who knows! She hands me my napkin. Take your time, Mister Baxter. You seem—well—disoriented? You said you were ill. Coming apart!

I will—I am—I'm sorry. I'm under terrible strain—as I wrote. My father's more or less dead.

More or less? Doctor Chang says.

He's only the ghost of himself. Very much so. And meeting someone who—who knows something about—who really has a grasp of the family spear—well—I'm overwhelmed. You know, The Spear of Ahuramazda That Sees Everything really does turn the world to glass—and shows you so much more than you want to know.

Sidney Chang lights up, saying, I too am eager to see this spear. Can it turn the world to glass and foresee events *for me?*

I hear his greed, however masked, and sense deep bruises in his wife's spirit. She, after all, has written both *Metabiology and Compassion* and the book of The Spear as well as devised her course in archetypes for the collective unconscious of Swiss schoolchildren. She smiles and does not smile and I see in her strong features a hunger for even deeper understanding than Sidney or Jung himself may yield. Although The Spear…

My dear, she says, for you the world is already made of glass. What would you want to foresee?

Quite a lot! Who will lay the oil pipelines out of Baku? My patient, Sheikh Sidi bin-Bahram, might like some inside dope about that. Ha, would he!

She turns aside, silent at such boorishness. I am struck by *déjà vu* and looking out at the hills across Lake of Zürich feel I am here still again—have been before—and that all I am comes from a karma that balances accident with design to place me just where I am. Yes, a miracle has drawn me almost electromagnetically to this lawn chair by this cold Chinese and by this innocent scholar of The Spear with her large shapely ears and mouth forever half-open with soft bursts of hurt. Am I hopeful—or just carried away?

Sheikh Bahram is your patient? I say. That's not good. We may have a conflict.

Doctor Li-Chang presses her heart. Oh, no! What do you mean?

I attribute my family's business failures, or many of them, to Sidi bin-Bahram.

We will have to discuss that, says Sidney Chang. But I don't think there can be a conflict of interest about Gong's plan of mental health for school-children.

In any event, she says, the sheikh is not *my* patient. And if he were, I'd drop him in a snap to see you and hold The Spear of Ahuramazda.

She really would! Sidney says—and shrugs.

Thank you, Madam Li-Chang. Thank you. I could not withhold The Spear from you for any reason. Her eyes draw me in with such warmth my legs melt. I so much want to be your friend. I turn to her husband. And yours, doctor. But I must tell you, The Spear does not foresee events, sir. It acts only as a pivot *for* events.

Well, thank you, he says, and disappointment shallows his breath and rings in his heartbeat. But I have to warn you, Mister Baxter. I am not the same believer that Gong is in metabiology or in this "miraculous" spear.

I understand. And let me admit that this heirloom is a burdensome possession. It has devastated my life.

Doctor Li-Chang drops her soft hand on mine. I can see that in your face.

Yes, her husband says. You look beaten. In fact, quite distraught.

I am haunted! And miraculously here in one piece.

I see, he says. Now you're *not* going to tell us this spear is cursed?

Sidney, *please!* Gong warns. But you do look distressed, Mister Baxter. Do you really need these dark glasses?

You would find my eyes distracting.

Perhaps, Sidney Chang says. But you need help.

Oh, yes, I do. May I call you by your first names? I might feel less dis-tant.

She smiles. We will trade you first names for your glasses.

I take off my shades. Looking into their eyes becomes doubly hard and I find myself at best looking at their hands or ears or hair.

I need whatever comfort you have to give. The night is my comfort—and yet I sleep badly. I'm haunted by family horrors. Call it genetic turmoil. I know I can respect your confidence—dear friends—when I tell you ... I am not ... not altogether ... uh, human. I am Bihusi. I have a lupine mind and senses. I am from the nightfolk and the Moon is our mother. I'm not being fanciful. My fingers lock. I fall silent, then add, The stars are our tears. They steal our defenses and leave us open to grief.

Sidney hardens as he rifles through archetypes of the night. Why the stars? he asks.

Lust, lust! We smell the heavens but can own only Earth. From here they all look much the same. But no two have the same make. Up close no two could be alike in their atomic mix. As children we think they're all batting the same light about. True, they all burst and burst while gravity restrains their destruction. I'm talking of stars, not planets—if the planets gave off light as well as the stars, think of what a heavy rug of light the night sky would be. Makes you wonder, what is the supreme meaning of all this stony or bubbling inorganic matter? Is there one? Must we restrain meaning to life forms on Earth alone?

Gong asks, Have you told anyone else about this, uh, lust?

Very few. Just my wife. Who knew long before I admitted to it.

I point at a far, far speck on Lake of Zürich.

You see the blonde woman on that sailboat? I can smell her face cream. Sandalwood from Crabtree & Evelyn—a rival of Baxter Toiletries. We have the largest outlay of second-grade toiletries in the world. I'd never adulterate my odor with any of them. You, Gong, have only attar of roses on your skin. We nocturnals must see our way through the dark as much with our noses as with these amber eyes. The Bihusi have scent-sense and scent-memories so far-reaching that—hard as this will be to grasp—all we can do is worship our *greed for life*. Worship it. Our only relief from this greed is when we pour ourselves out to the Moon. But let me be indiscreet, Sidney. You and I share the good fortune of being married to great beauties who write.

You're too kind, Gong says.

Such artistic landscaping, I tell her and look about at the walled orchard and kitchen garden where sunflowers mass. I scent clover invading the lawn itself. *Le jardin est très joli.*

Merci, beaucoup, Gong says. I have green fingers.

Really? But this is largely an herbal garden—echinacea, gingko, sage, oregano, mint, thyme, cilantro...

There are some flowers. She nods toward a lane of lilies and an oval bed of tulips—startling, varicolored tulips—blue, red, yellow and white. But you know your herbs, Mr. Baxter.

You have no idea. I can show you how to get the clover out of your lawn. You're an herbalist?

What could be better than fresh herbs? Especially for mind and spirit.

I prefer tinctures, Sidney says and dismisses the garden. Standardized, then you know what you're getting.

I see in lush hydrangeas and feverish roses the children she has missed having.

Gong follows my eyes. Tell us about your wife, she says.

Dandelion seeds feather the spring air—drift over the goldfish pond with its gurgling pipe and glassy shimmer. Archetypes swim in a mirror and dance on their own likeness. I nose the goldfish gulping as I think of my wife and smell Copenhagen roughly seven hundred miles off.

Titania Tintagel—a Danish writer. Her gothic fairy tales have a following.

Oh, I much admire them, Gong says. But even more I enjoyed her memoir *Half-Moon Winter.*

Yes, a very interesting memoir, Sidney says. Read it myself. But isn't that her pen name?

It is. She was Baroness Karen von Vixen before we married. It's clear we were fated to marry.

Gong says, And now you're here. But not for marriage counseling.

You have, I take it from your letter, Sidney says, created a phantom limb—that floats! This is a symbol.

More than a symbol, doctor.

I have a dossier on the Changs worked up before coming here. These two Asian doctors—who came to Zürich in tandem though still unmarried—strike me as having chosen each other less as mates than as inspired sparring partners. Sidney's lordly brilliance gives off no warmth at all—nor does his round-headed shrimplike body, much shorter than Gong's. How could this cold commissar attract her womanly warmth? What spiritual pleasure did he offer her? His honors back in Beijing—where Freud and Jung have no standing and the whole field of Western psychology does not exist and schizophrenics are lectured to by nurses reading from the notebooks of Chairman Mao and even psychotic patients must give daily heart-to-heart exhortations to each other to get well—there his honors are few.

The myths that underpin Western art and thought are seen as nonsense and fairy tales and fresh-faced young social engineers ridicule Sidney Chang himself. But with his plunge deep into Chinese art and symbols and their uses in the structure and dynamics of the Eastern psyche he has lofty standing among Jungian institutes in the West and has gained high honors for his ground-breaking *Genius and Intuition in Eastern Analytic Psychology*—a field he has founded but work laughed at in Beijing. Its ingenuity limns emblem by emblem the odd magnetic attraction among Chinese archetypes that erupts as Eastern genius. Yet Sidney's brilliant but burdensome work walls off all common human feeling. Without doubt he's some kind of catch for a wide-eyed young female analyst troubled by chaotic currents that choke off the Western mind in her Asian homeland. Did she hunger for warmth of understanding here in Zürich? She looks ten years younger than Sidney, her lone fellow in this field—yet now she has more work in print in the West than he and despite her youth shines with a fruitful well-being quite distant from his focus on conferences and skilled ladder-climbing in Zürich. Although I am here to see Doctor Gong Li-Chang, the adversarial tie I sense between the Changs appeals to me and from the play instinct between her creativity and his edgy all-knowingness I hope to find more relief from the two together than either alone. Still, I face this human couple with some faint discomfort and with my natural spiky lupine dislike for looking humans straight in the eye—dark glasses or no dark glasses.

Now, this is very important, Sidney says. Does this arm seem to have weight?

Weight, doctor?

Can you scratch it? I mean any of these limbs. Are they simply imaginary or might they have a neurological basis? Or be the result of a mild brain injury? Do we need a scan? Or do we look for a psychic injury?

This is real-world stuff, doctor. With lots of guilt.

Ah, a moral injury pressing on you? Sidney asks.

Gong Li says, This is family guilt. He's told us as much.

You're a mind reader! Yes, my forebears are my problem. I am bound body and soul to my ancestral stock. It is my God—and a living one at that.

But, Sidney says, your dissociation springs from this god who has failed you? Tell us how that took place.

We're Rumanian Americans. My father, Breedwolfe Alexander Baxter Jr.—he was born Bihusi, not Baxter—has loomed over me since birth. Or even before. The Bihusi have unusual pregnancies I'll come to. It can be said without overstatement that at one time Dad owned the Earth. I was to be his prince—his inheritor. As the world knows, he's still alive. But between us I'll tell you that his mind has dimmed. And even though I'm the once and future king, he's still the figurehead.

Dad doesn't think much of humans, I'm sorry—but especially not of Hungarians. He finds them fiendishly warped past understanding, although he has some thin regard for their gypsies' gift for thievery. Back in 1904 the far-sighted Hungarian gypsies in Budapest set up the world's first auto theft ring. Never buy a car in Budapest—especially from a gypsy. It will soon be stolen and resold in Rumania, probably in Bucharest. So these gypsies have their wagons in a half-empty lot in the peasant quarter—but they have no garage for hiding stolen vehicles. Cars must be herded swiftly to Rumania. Meanwhile, my grandfather, Breedwolfe Senior, devises an idea for setting up the first Bihusi Blood Bank in Budapest—and the blood bank sits next to the half-empty lot stuffed with stolen cars. Cars chug in and out as fast as peasant drivers can be trained to drive them. No gypsy in this theft factory wants to be stopped with a stolen vehicle—so he hoodwinks a mentally stunted peasant into driving to Bucharest. But even penniless peasants need to eat while being taught how to shift gears. Enter Dad. I have photographs of my father as a lithe five-year-old—bare-legged in short pants and darting about as a shill for the blood bank—his rich dark hair bushy and wild. Even at five he looks joyously shrewd and worldly. He leads peasants to Grandfather so they can pick up a free cookie and a few food pennies. My grandfather drains a pint or two of blood and pays them their pennies. My five-year-old father does not like to see a penny wasted and—after he steals bowls from a gypsy wagon as well as a big kettle and garlic and paprika and a pet Pekinese—sets up a food kitchen for peasants. The peasants pay their pennies back to him for a bowl of good hot garlic soup thick with dog meat. As weeks go by and more dogs disappear from the gypsy camp his tasty soup becomes so well known that even the gypsies at times come for a bowl. So at five Dad feels at home in the restaurant business and really never leaves it. Grandfather watches his bare-legged five-year-old take in pennies from peasants and swells with love. He rubs little Alexandru's bushy head and muzzle and later writes home to his wife that they must feel great pride in having a son who can steal a whole restaurant and go back for the customers.

Sidney stares out at boats barely rocking at anchor. Have I heard that your father—hm—has blood on his hands?

Sidney, he's drenched in blood—and completely indifferent to death. Nor does he ever forget his first rule: Never Show Gratitude to Anybody. He's hard and can walk away from any wreck. But this indifference has caught up with him. His brain has whited out. The scans show sections smooth as cream.

From alcohol? Sidney asks.

No. Inadvertently by his own hand.

So it's nothing genetic?

No! Though I have the blood-guilt *he* could never admit to. I ask Gong, Have you any idea of how many millions of people my father has caused to die?

She sighs and clenches her teeth. Why don't you tell us?

Well, he learned everything he knew from his father—my Grandfather Bihusi—from the little town of Turda in the province of Cluj in Rumania. In 1904, Grandfather made his first big killing—literally—when he set up the Bihusi Blood Bank in Budapest—the start of a chain of such banks much like today's fast food chains. It was Grandfather's inspiration to collect the blood of Jewish peasants from the Carpathians. First he'd convert them in the Christian conversion room attached to his blood bank—so that Hungarian Christians need not be infected with Jewish blood. Then he'd drain out a quart for a few pennies. Many of his peasant donors—being penniless—recycled themselves once too often and got sucked bone-dry. From this bank grew Grandfather's world of blood labs. By 1908 he had labs as far off as the Belgian Congo and even the Central and South American jungles—where his assistants set up portable labs and bought natives' blood. He devastated the Jivaro Indians. Headmen would designate donors. Grandfather's greedy hirelings pretended they didn't mean to kill natives but most donors died—drained to the last drop. These chiefs would sell their own people. Almost a half-century later, Dad, my father—who by then had caught the gold fever of plasma collecting—found an almost limitless supply with Idi Amin in Uganda. Idi wanted to expel all the Asians in Uganda and he did it, you might say, intravenously. Idi also built up his blood trade by kidnapping thousands of donors from neighboring countries. Of course, Idi thought they were out to get him anyway—so what did it matter to him? That may suggest a certain view of my father. Idi was a vampire who murdered his people. Dad murdered countries.

Sidney asks, What did your father and grandfather do with this blood?

Well, as time passed my ingenious father learned how to reduce blood to plasma—the universal donor. That made it human gold.

So your grandfather murdered countries as did your father?

Without a second thought. But they lost their first chain through unwise investments in Russia and didn't start up the Baxter Blood Banks again until they'd moved to the States and recouped their fortunes with razor blades.

Are *you* now responsible as well? Gong asks.

Doctor, you're asking am I a murderer? Yes and no. Bihusi believe that growth comes only through continuous tension with and lasting struggle against humans. I have been born and raised to follow certain Bihusi lusts and appetites.

At the turn of the century—many years before we came to America—Thomas Alva Edison, who needed a place to hide money in Europe and knew that the financial confidentiality of Austria was far superior to Switzerland's, came to Grandfather Bihusi in Salzburg, where he then had a small manufacturers' rep. Edison cried on his shoulder, saying, I've got one hundred thousand Caruso and Palm Court records going to dust in my Turkish warehouses because I haven't sold enough phonographs. I've switched from making my old phonograph that played cylinders to a new one that plays flat disks I call records which I give away to push sales for my new machines. My North American Phonograph Company has done fairly well in the States but we're dead in Europe. Now the new Victor Talking Machine threatens to put us out of business with *its* Caruso records. You may not know that Enrico Caruso—the world's greatest recording attraction—is under contract to Victor. Alexandru, how can I get rid of all this overstock? Can you help me? Grandfather smiles and nods. He cleans up his still sturdy old handcart from Budapest—fills it with Edison phonographs and Victor records—trudges the back streets of the Warsaw ghetto and drops his wares off with potential cultured customers. Slyly, he "forgets" to leave the cranks for winding the machines. Families spend the day reading record labels and vainly looking at the phonograph. At day's end Grandfather returns—grinds his hands in apology—and gives them the crank at last. After two or three golden minutes of "Vesti la Giubba" and "O Sole Mio," they buy the whole package and extra records. Edison watches

Grandfather's technique, buys it, and takes it back to the States.

When John D. Rockefeller hears about Edison's sales success in Europe he calls him and pays for access to Grandfather. Grandfather and Rockefeller meet. I want to be the first billionaire ever, John D. tells Grandfather. This goes straight into Grandfather Bihusi's heart. He sees himself as the first trillionaire. I can help, he tells John D. John says, I have all this low quality kerosene stored up—too crude to use in automobiles. Every time I crack a barrel of crude a certain amount of kerosene is produced. How can I make some money with this? John D. sobs on Grandfather's shoulder. Grandfather smiles and nods. John, you are going to sell oil for the lamps of China! Breaking out his fleet of homey handcarts still again, Grandfather takes off for Peking, hires shills to roam freely and give away thousands upon thousands, then millions upon millions, of beautifully shaped brass Aladdin lamps and car lamps and railroad lamps and especially household lamps. Lamps that burned kerosene. China is burning up kerosene to the awe of Standard shareholders. Stock goes through the roof and upward.

It is part of Bihusi lore that every high Bihusi—every prince—must kill the king just as my father—in his own crass way—killed my grandfather—which I'll tell you about. My father has titans of finance as errand boys. They arrange his bribes and his acquisitions—and they bury the bodies. Altogether an invalid since his accident, he now stays in his Jungfrau chalet where Grandfather died. But before Dad's mind failed, he did build the eighth wonder of the world, Baxter's Buster, the huge steel deck on Lake Bolshoi from which his derricks tap into the ocean of oil beneath the lake. Aside from that monumental construction, he had another dream—one kept secret but even larger and more costly.

What could that be? Sidney asks.

That was for a space disc program that would circle the planet with lasers that draw energy from the Sun and beam it below to receptors on Earth. He owned the Earth—had a grip on the Moon—and wanted to swallow the Sun as well.

Can I describe him differently from the press—who paint him black? Certainly his deeds cannot be hidden. He dwarfs all other hustlers. But who am I to judge him? I see myself as—well, I'm an accountant. Until he decided to take me in hand Dad saw me as his perfect English butler. None too imaginative, very good at figures. But not as swift as he. He is King of Bihusi—one of two semi-human wolf tribes now dwindling out of existence. The other tribe is the Giurgiu. Dad has great pride in his logic and in being a former Rumanian aristocrat whose bounce and vigor feed on fleet use of deadly force. Earlier Bihusi were strongly tied to the Huns and the Mongols. So our sense of forceful cunning comes naturally. I am six-foot-six but Dad hovers over me. And is even more slim and like me has a wide skull and high-arched long nose—a nose a tenor might call a vault for heady tones—although Dad's throat when engorged and swollen is his great organ for song. His large majestic nostrils gape at will. These wide nostrils are unpleasant when he summons up a quite unnerving smile—so pitying and deadly as his long canines offer a low puppyish whine and his head lolls side to side. *Mmm!* he takes you in and weighs you—you curious thing. It's so unpleasant, even to me. My back chills to think of it—neck hairs stand on end. He too covers up—well—an inhuman amount of body hair, all of it now silver, sad to say—though it still bushes up when called for. Otherwise, he's the bon vivant, with a debonair slim silver pencil mustache.

With ever-lowered head and amber eyes—always half-lidded—he seems too shy to look you straight in the eye—but more likely he's *scenting* what's in your pocket or even your last few meals. Humans don't grasp that looking you straight in the eye means war to a Bihusi or Giurgiu and that you are being weighed for slaughter. This is genetic. Dad *thinks* in scent. He sees better with his nose than with his eyes—though he has super-vision. You read with eyes—but Dad reads with scent. He can scent from miles off the head of a pin you have touched. *Miles!* What it means to think in scent—to have a brain that responds to smell and thinks more richly in scent than in vision—well, describe color to the blind. He has encyclopedic power—in scent. His nose never rests—even in sleep. It breathes intelligence. But I would say you see more of his character in his mouth—his long loose lips such dark red they look black. Even at rest they look greedy and swell with gluttony when he scents a victim. Most of all they tell of his sheer innate hatred of humans—whom he sees as foolish, stupid cowards—jackals with memories short-changed—if not embalmed! Even so, he still uses them as his jackals who do legal drudgery and other work beneath his dignity. Among Bihusi the olfactory nerve-ends are forty thousand times denser than with humans, which as I have said improves our strength of scent over yours to the seven-millionth power. Dad's scent-memory intuits at proto-genius level—since it grows without limit and never rests. His cellular memory tunes into scent-memories of the Wreath of Bihusi Past much as a radio-telescope reads the heavens. Just standing here, he would know more about you, your habits, your health, your past, your mental state, your digestion and the status of your urine than you do. When he walks into a men's room, however cramped it might be, he's in a huge library. He is a mystical pragmatist who can scent the numinous ocean bottom of any pattern or sample and a profound student of rot—humus—dead things—and the language of shit—of new spirit that arises from last leavings. We envision that someday we nocturnals shall shake loose from the Moon and all its heartbreak and bound over field and fence into the Sun and dance as creatures of Sunlight. My dad bears the spiritual vision of Bihusi and of the Last Days when leap we shall as Ahuramazda's great heart calls us back to the golden plasma from which we sprang. Every wolf knows this. We Bihusi carry our family in our nose the way you carry pictures in your wallet—only ours go back to the First Days and Original Light. Bihusi, my friends, have long memories—long as crime, long as sin.

Gong says, Dad must be very old.

He's still alive—after a fashion. His *joie de vivre* grows dim as does mine. We Bihusi pride ourselves on our rapacity for life. We come from a Rumanian background but are not Christians. We feel that most religions place their rewards too far off—with far too little live food in the here and now—not even a mouse to nibble on. It's tragic. All your beliefs—Buddhism, Judaism, Shintoism, Islam and Christianity—are about service and sadness. They don't dance do they? Religions don't meet life on its own bloody terms and gobble it down—as do Bihusi. As I say, our highest value is rapacity and the creation of debtors—great banks and lands that owe us their existence. But Dad no longer sheds blood. Yes, he's killed all his partners over the years. Joe Kennedy was one of us—but of the Giurgiu clan. Dad would say, "I have no partners." He did not run with fools or even Giurgiu. And anyone who joined him was a fool.

Gong Li brushes crumbs from the table and gives me a puzzled look.

So you believe in terrorism, and walking on corpses?

Oh, now please. It's like this. When my grandfather revived the Bihusi line, murder and terror were necessary tools. You may not know it, but in 1908, when the transfer of power in the Belgian Congo went from King Leopold—who was one of us—to the Belgian government, Grandfather Bihusi brokered that deal. He jump-started his first fortune by joining his earnings from Edison and Standard Oil to helping Leopold. He took his commission from Leopold in the king's slaves who had harvested elephants for ivory and rubber trees—and reduced those slaves to a lake of blood. Eight to ten million Congolese died of famine, disease, and exhaustion. As Leopold knew, after you harvest the goods you kill the workers and then you have no social problems. You know about that, Doctor Chang. Chairman Mao—who was one of us—did away with a fifth of the population of China after World War Two—the diseased, the aged and infirm, the opium addicts, the incorrigibles. Zap them! Start fresh! Not to mention the Tibetan massacres. Did all this happen—or was it just a bad dream of *Time* magazine?

I don't criticize Chairman Mao, Mister Baxter.

Hey, you needed a new country! Just like Grandfather. Grandfather looked to see where blood was running and knew gold would follow. But too bad for him—he made a massive Russian investment and financed Lenin and that cost him everything. Getting his money back from the Communists—even after similar arms deals with the *Bolsheviki*, the *Mensheviki* and the czarists—turned out badly. The Reds killed Granddad's Russian agent in Mexico City with a climbing ax—Comrade Trotsky—to make the point that they weren't going to pay Granddad back. He and Father never forgot his huge losses in Russia. So Granddad wound up in the US and sold razor blades. He could smell blood getting ready to spill in the States and waited for his lucky chance. As did Mao after the fall of Japan when crushing the Kuomintang and cleaning up China called for a bigger bloodletting than both Sino-Japanese wars put together. Or didn't you know that?

Please, Mister Baxter, Sidney says. We do not discuss People's Republic. My land of birth has blood on its hands. I agree. Now shall we go on?

I ask Gong, Your father? Is he dead?

My father died treating Asian flu victims in Manchuria.

Ah, Manchuria! Well then, we have something in common? But perhaps not to the same degree,

Gong shakes her head. My father was sent to Manchuria as an alternative to execution after students named him a capitalist-roader and took over his obstetrics clinic. In any event, blood-guilt is without degree.

But transferable? Aren't the sins of the fathers passed on to the children? Isn't guilt genetic? Isn't that the first tenet of your profession?

No, Gong says,

Sidney says, We wander, Mister Baxter.

Hell, I don't think so. Your wonderful wife here, she's your reward from the People's Republic? Sorry to be brash. And please don't think I have anything against Chairman Mao. He is a hero of the Giurgiu clan, as I say the largest wolf clan following our own. His picture hangs in all our homes. That smile, so benign! Those twinkling eyes.

Sidney tells his wife, Here is transference and we are not even Freudians.

Gong sighs. I don't think we should be talking about this. We are here for you, Mister Baxter, not to take us to task. We understand that you attack us for national sins to show that the sins of Bihusi are no different. Point taken. Shall we go on?

Thank you. How can I trust you if you don't admit your own sins? I'm going to tell you some pretty rotten things. You may think heavy guilt is why we Bihusi rarely look anyone in the eye, even God. By whom I mean Ahuramazda.

You want *quid pro quo?* she says. We understand that! Normally, I will not give in to a patient. What if a patient tells me, I can't discuss my adulteries unless you tell me about yours—otherwise I can't trust you? Obviously, I would stop treatment. But in this instance, I will make an unburdening, Mister Baxter. I would not be a doctor and here treating you—nor my father have been an obstetrician and brought many babies into this world—if People's Republic had not arisen. That good springs from evil may be the central duality of my life and why I wrote *The Spear of Ahuramazda.* Any good I might do in my life rests upon governmentally enforced optimism which you see as a great evil. My work is a flower once fed by corpses. I can see that, sir. But remember, my blood-guilt is buried under two generations of recovery from a dehumanizing evil first visited upon my people by the Japanese. Had they not raped Nanking and set the example, who knows whether terror and murder decked out as social conscience would have become tools for postwar leaders?

You're so right! I say. But the bad example wasn't set by the Japanese. It was set by the Russian monsters that Mao imitated. You have a distance from your evil that I don't have? You can't palm your guilt off on the Japanese. The Chinese have terror and murder locked into their genes by the carload.

Do they? she says. I don't know about that. But if for the sake of argument I say you're right, you are still fighting hungry ghosts in your family. But *I* don't fight my family ghosts the way you do.

Well put, Sidney says.

Oh, doctor, I say, you have no idea what I know about the People's Republic and its ghosts—buried and unburied. I mean hordes of ghosts and gold unimaginable.

Stop! Sidney says. You know what you know but it's too far afield for now. Why come to Zürich to see a Jungian if you really want a priest?

Gong says, Do you think we are alchemists who can turn your guilt into gold?

I have enough gold. Speaking of alchemy, and *not* as a pseudoscience, do you think there is a spirit that rules the depths of everything? My scientific mind resists the thought. But I now find myself stoned by it. It strikes me that understanding can come only by *dimming* logic and marrying my mind to something illogical, mad, and equal to the idea of spirit in the depths of matter quite equal to the atomic lava bubbling in the stars. And this spirit I must presume bubbles also at the birth of consciousness such as ours—well, especially mine. A new logic arises beyond normal understanding, a speechless logic past all our ability to make sense of it. This is a terrible event for me, my surrender to the unexplainable. My father would whip me for these thoughts. But the truth is I need a fresh path beyond logic toward the supreme meaning my dreams demand. I need a new planet to walk on. I've been robbed and Earth stolen from under me. Nietzsche tells me God is dead. But that is only one God, the phantasm men swear by. I am searching behind the stars as we know them. I've lost entirely the joy of greed, although aside from the Giurgiu I pretty much own the Earth—which I need not prove to you. But to own the Earth and find it lacking, that's how I find myself today as I seek a supreme meaning that will restore my spirit. A sign I can see, though I'm not looking for any teaching or instruction from you. We each need to go our own way. We three stand apart in our search for supreme meaning, though we are each half-blind, half-deaf, and afloat on chaos. I hope you don't hear all this as prattle. You see, I have achieved everything possible according to my nature and yet have nothing—which points to the shortcomings of my nature. My Bihusi desires have fled and I see illnesses and horrors so strong your ears would wither to hear them.

[And then for a moment I fall into involuntary gasping as I see fully what I cannot speak. They sit shocked as my jaw freezes wide. My breastbone at last allows me to fill my lungs. My soul returns, blind. Who are these Asians?]

Ohh! Oh, yes, sorry. I get these attacks and forget where I am. At times my visions seem to crack my breastbone and break all my ribs. It's weird. I put away all my science and look for the divine—and then get punched in the chest as payment.

I see I sit here as if you two priests of analytic psychology might offer me a new religion. It's something like that. But I need an Earth transformed past our present understanding. Of course we have but one life—but in a way the dead speak to us and we too will someday speak to the living from our dust. But something has led me to you to have my horrors tempered and purified. I've had a strange journey to this garden. Could it be these Alps, that draw all three of us here—the atomic lava at the axis thrusting the stone spirit of the Earth heavenward? That's an image I find viable for my search—and an image is half the journey toward an answer as the mind pictures the way ahead. Can these Alps free us from science and lead us upward into the unfathomable? Do our three souls hunger for the judgment of others or do we lust for something beyond books and prizes? For revelation!—however brief its glow. Is my soul the unacknowledged feminine side of myself? What do you have, Madam, which I seek for myself and halfway around the globe scent from your fingers on your typewritten letter to me? Having read and now meeting you I can well believe you have some answer to my losses. That you hold something that will not just repair but replace the dead system I hold within me. Or is this visit my desperate endeavor to return to science and *human* knowledge? If you were my soul—sitting right here!—could I tell you apart from this garden or these swans and their lake brimming with heaven? Whatever you possess, Gong-Li, whatever hovers in your soul is but half of what I need. For even as Sidney I must possess the world as well. My half-human wolf-soul feels poor and in owning the world owns nothing. Is it my wolf-soul or, as Dad would tell me, my humanity that poisons me? There is no question that you have a wealthy soul and much to offer me. That's clear from your book and the light and wisdom you find in Ahuramazda.

Thank you—and what does my husband offer you?

Oh, he and I are more alike than it may look. Where we differ is that I already own the goal he seeks for himself.

What goal is that? she asks.

Of world conqueror. If I say I already own the planet, believe me. But I also own its horrors, its wars, armies, political sinkholes and all its plagues body and soul.

Sidney asks, What is a plague of the soul?

Well, for one, the plague against womankind in the Middle East.

I don't have a plague like that.

No, yours is right in your own home and springs from greed. Greed is a plague of which I have the deepest knowledge possible. You are just approaching a change of life I have already passed through. You are still young and eager in your late thirties and hope to conquer a world of Changian analysis of the psyche and, with the death of Dr. Jung, hope to lead the way into greater depths than he achieved, even as he left Freud behind as at last meaningless to him and, as he said, man cannot stand a meaningless life. So off he went into the collective unconscious. Quite an adventure! You have no idea of the dragon you feed within you. In another thirty years you may have another change and all greed for fame lift from your soul. A fresh wisdom *should* arise and help you set your greed aside. Will you turn away from it or with bottomless ferocity just plunge into it—and challenge your fate? You will have a choice—to have your soul return to you, with all your ambitions achieved—or you will look on these ambitions as dead systems and worldly acclaim not worth the sacrifice of your soul. I say none of this to judge or teach you. I say only that you will spend and exhaust much of your instinctual energies along the way and will return to this very garden and lake, these hills and married swans with their cygnets, for your soul's refreshment. Ambition will draw back and with luck you will find in nature and Gong the libido you have in great part wasted on the world. You can earn great wealth, Sidney, and with your wealth and fame in hand arrive at poverty. Perhaps only then will your instinctual energies lead you into a wisdom that lifts you above the world and its greed. In my case today, all that now returns from the blood I have spent is not enough to feed my soul. I am barren.

Sidney listens to my silence. He sips tea—stares at clouds. So why have you come here?

I choke up, still silent. Pluck a dandelion seed from the air—crush it with my thumb.

I look for a fresh image outside myself, an image of what I must search for, an image that'll take me half-way to my goal. Or do all such thoughts only mock me? I'm not blind and deaf to myself. My life has held and still holds much evil, although only in human terms, not Bihusi. My wolf-soul is not evil. But I hear my depths speak and unite sense with nonsense to create a fresh grip on my actions—and on my heart. I need something to live for and must question myself: Where in my soul is my true axis, the being that gives me gravity and holds my mind and body together? My sense of science tells me that reason alone should guide me. But reason falls short and I need to go to unreason for full guidance. I hate to discard reason, and yet my soul is now a child and answers to something else than reason. Please bear with me, I find something fresh in repeating myself. I need an image of myself as a leader with ripe thoughts, and that image will get me half-way to the marriage I seek within myself. You see, I must become the servant of the child and this child can only be the image of a God I have no faith in. I would much rather take a woman as my God, although I never sense *myself* as a woman. I live onward and, hopefully through you, will engender and give birth to the spirit of the depths. I seek some child within the radiant cradle of my ribs. Believe me, I laugh at these thoughts—but they come and now achieve a torment that demands I listen. Yes, they divide and bedevil me, make me scorn myself—they whisper poison in my ear.

Something at the absolute center of me, a sky pulsing the azure of recovery, wants to find a voice, and a deep springtime before my final days. Not this chaos in which long life spreads before me as passionless babble. I should laugh at myself for saying such stuff—but I can't. Is this damned nightmare necessary—a step before greater learning, greater life? Going by my father, now in such vacancy, I'd say no. Any long fulfilment will be evasive indeed. I carry around something dead within me.

Gong smiles. And aside from all this disenchantment you're in perfect health?

Thank you. I know I've been—*ha!*—crying wolf. Forgive me if I sound full of false alarms—I'll get back to business. I look over my holdings and find that my future will not be a plate of grapes, just one juicy day after another. No, I've been taking inventory of the Antarctic and my new oil fields under the stars of the Southern Cross. I enjoy visiting those fields, even in the long night. The Southern Cross led my father to the Antarctic and studying it. The fact that there is land under the lower ice cap led him to develop drilling there as well as to offshore drilling in the rest of the world, mainly Lake Bolshoi—which became an incredible contribution to his wealth. And mine. I have my oil fields in Baku—where I even enjoy the gray wastes of the Azerbaijan peninsula—and especially the sight of my derricks pumping away and my gas wells burning under the midnight Sun. I now have my *offshore* drillings in Venezuela and Scotland. Did you know that the sweetest crude on the planet comes from the province of Kabinda in Angola? I own that and lease it to Gulf. I have my coffee plantations in Kenya—and sweeping tea plantations in Sri Lanka. My Darjeeling plantations! I own business towers in Manhattan, London, Buenos Aires—even an ugly gray but very impressive cluster of office buildings in Moscow—built by Stalin but which I now love and treasure. It's Moscow's tallest building and you can see the whole city from the roof. I speak only of my buildings around the globe I've had a chance to *visit.* My homes—my hideaways on Nantucket and in Monte Carlo and the Congo—Dad's chalet on the Jungfrau, and so on. Dad and I together own fifteen percent of Earth's land surface—which I assure you is a controlling interest—because seventy percent of the planetary surface is water—remember? I also lease most of the Siberian oil fields from Moscow. The richest—which I am now tapping—lies under Lake Bolshoi in the West Siberian Plain. I'll tell you more about that—and my deals with Sidi bin-Bahram—and my old partnership with the KGB. In all, I own more land than I can see in my lifetime—even the cream of it is too vast for me to visit or half understand. In some ways, it's too big to manage—or for one mind to encompass—even a mind of Bihusi Genius. And yet the time came when Dad and I set out on a technological project—our space program—so vast that even we can't fund it. We needed twenty percent of Earth's wealth for our greatest deed. But it didn't pan out and, what's worse—thanks to Sidi bin-Bahram—we couldn't get our money back. I want you to know, this loss was tragic beyond belief. The whole world suffers today because of it. Though your little poet sheikh probably doesn't mention that.

You mean the space disc program? Sidney says. He may have mentioned it in passing. But I can't say. Is that failure why you dream about coming apart?

Without a doubt. I'll get to that... And to my art treasures. All of these— my favored treasures, even my unfinished last novel by James Joyce—are uncatalogued and unknown works.

What last novel by Joyce?

He began it after publishing *Finnegans Wake.* It's handwritten despite his bad eyesight—about the sea. The sea struck him as a worthy subject following the dream novel. I love it. It's his best writing ever. Liquid light! Clear English again!

This manuscript has never been catalogued?

I have the only copy. I bought it from a British collector. He came to me complaining about the way my waiters treated him in one of my Paris restaurants. The one with the circular staircase—what's the name of it? It'll come to me. It was the best restaurant in Paris and so probably the best in the world. You want to know the manuscript's provenance?

No, no. I believe you. Do you go to the Joyce Society meetings here?

No, I'd be too embarrassed. I've contributed SFr 1, 000, 000 to the James Joyce Foundation. Otherwise, I keep the manuscript beside my bed. That's enough. Would you like to see it sometime?

I am not a Joycean. Doctor Jung poked around in Joyce. But I find him unsophisticated. Nowhere in Joyce do I sense a real grasp of the archetypes. But let it go. Now, how can I believe all this outrageous stuff you tell me?

I'll demonstrate! Let me have a telephone and privacy for fifteen minutes and we'll adjust the sterling to Swiss franc exchange rate. That will show a little clout, right?

That's really not necessary. You were telling me about your holdings and your art treasures. They mean a lot to you, of course?

But not for their market value.

What works are we talking about here?

Well, there's a Michelangelo *Seated Aphrodite*—his only statue of a woman who looks like a real woman. It's uncatalogued, of course.

The Madonna mourning in the *Pietà* doesn't look like a real woman? Gong asks.

I stand corrected.

You weren't just testing us? Sidney asks.

Oh no.

Where do you keep your *Seated Aphrodite?*

I keep it safe in a climate-controlled salt mine outside Memphis. I have a lot of stuff stored there. My father bought boxcars of art treasures—sight unseen—that the Soviets grabbed from Himmler and Goering and were transmitting to the Hermitage. The treasures never got here—they wound up in Benelux—before the B-29s that Uncle Sam loaned Dad brought them to Memphis for storing in our salt mine. The man who masters air freight masters the world. And B-29s are seldom used for air freight. Today I have pieces I love—but my grasp of art is quite superficial. I just dabble.

Don't you own an airline? Sidney asks.

I own a couple of airlines today.

Why didn't you use C-47s?

We had to move fast and Uncle's bombers were right there. Well, I leased a Swissair 747 to come here to Zürich. Why? I don't own Swissair yet. And Switzerland produces the best white wines in the world and exports none of them. Not a drop! If you want Swiss white, you have to come here. But it's also served by Swissair, so I lease from them.

So, as I said, Grandfather and Dad went broke financing both sides of the Russian Revolution. That's why Dad felt especially keen about underwriting the Berlin airlift when the Wall went up. But let me explain something. You can't understand my father, or even me without understanding Grandfather Bihusi—Breedwolfe Alexandru Bihusi, Senior. His name received one of those Ellis Island shifts of spelling and came out Baxter. After his terrific failure with the Communists, he started all over. In the teens the first German safety razor was introduced to the American public by Breit of Berlin—a razor with a guard that kept the blade from cutting deeply—and Grandfather Bihusi went into business in the mid-Atlantic states selling blades and the new razor from a handcart—a cart pulled by my nearly full-grown twenty-year-old father, who was now taller than his father. Many shavers would not give up their much admired straight razors and the new safety blade did not catch on right away. In Virginia Dad happened to knock on the kitchen door of Secretary of State Bainbridge Colby on the very day the draft bill for war against Germany was passed in Congress. When the Secretary saw the new razor being offered at his kitchen door by this boyish giant, it struck him as the perfect blade for a soldier's pack. He fell into a chat first with Dad, then with Grandfather waiting with his handcart out front. Grandfather, who had the entire mid-Atlantic stock of Breit's Blades in his handcart, offered to deliver as many razors and blades as the Secretary thought the Army might need. Soon Grandfather was selling hundreds of thousands of razors and millions of blades a year. And the Bihusi/Baxter fortune revived. Now what really showed Grandfather's mettle is that the Breit razor was first patented in Germany by a Swedish inventor, Nels Borg. That German patent didn't hold water in the States and Grandfather patented the Breit blade and safety razor as his own. He never paid off the Swedish inventor, and after the Armistice he went worldwide with the Baxter Safety Razor and Baxter Blades. More to the point, he never expressed gratitude to Secretary Colby, nor acknowledged the Breit company. As Grandfather told Dad, this deal shone with Bihusi spirit: Admit Nothing and Don't Look Back.

When Grandfather got the contract from the military services, he needed capital to expand with factories. A study of shaving soaps showed him that what really gives a razor a smooth ride through the beard is a heavy load of fatty acid in the soap. He devised his own creamy glycerin soap formula and set about offering cheap free shaving brushes and mugs with a cylinder of his soap inside along with Baxter's Safety Razors and Blades. The fatty glycerin sold the razor—though buyers mistakenly believed that superior blades had almost licked the beard off their face. Next he sold his soap formula to Thomas Toiletries—who knew a good thing when they saw it and underwrote the first Baxter factory for safety razors. We later took over Thomas Toiletries.

Helga, the Changs' young Swedish maid—with eyes swimming—rushes into the garden with a written message for Doctor Chang. *Bitte, bitte!* she says, and hands him the note.

Doctor Chang goes white. A Swissair has gone down off Halifax, he says, killing all aboard. My compatriot—Dr. Richardson Waite—went down with it.

Gong cries, My God, my God! Was it *terrorists?*

Nobody knows! Sidney says.

This wasn't terrorists, I say. Nobody hates Switzerland—it's where they all have their money. There's no terrorist allotment for Switzerland. But if it were terrorists, I know just the bastard who did it. He was after me and a day late. I'm sorry for your loss, Sidney. Do you want to put our meeting off for a day or so?

No, one day of this black history of the world's money handlers by you is all I can handle. We both know that Sidi bin-Bahram is no angel either. We go on. My dear, remind me to phone our condolences.

Gong turns to Helga. Excuse me, Mister Baxter.

Billy, please.

Very kind, thank you, she says, and in Swedish tells Helga to bring a pot of green tea, their bone tea service—and some biscuits. She turns to me. Some fresh gunpowder tea will brace us up after such bad news.

Won't it! I say. If it was terrorists, Sidney, there'll have to be an exchange. We always know which terrorists. There are no secrets.

Exchange? he asks.

Do you remember the Iranian 747 the US shot down outside of Lebanon? The exchange was the US airliner dropped off San Francisco a year later. That was ascribed to empty oxygen containers igniting. It was, in fact, a SAM.

A missile! A terrorist missile launched from the United States?

Yes, but offshore Marin County. That's all part of it. It's just money. Blacked-out history, as you say. You don't believe me? The world is full of targets, Sidney. In Russia, from the mid-nineteenth century to the fall of Communism, poets were targets and could be hauled off and shot. *Poets!* Poets are targets back in Beijing. People are murdered left and right for the slightest reason. Angola! Before the Cubans left, the diamonds on the ground in Angola lay so thick that starving natives would steal into the fields at night to harvest them secretly. The Cubans, who policed Angola using Soviet choppers, would fly over, pick them out with floodlights and shoot them with Gatlings. Machine-guns! For a price, you could go on human safari and pop poachers from the air. Unbelievable? Not in Africa. Idi would line up a string of victims back to front, give each man a rock and have him smash the head of the man in front of him while waiting to have his own head smashed in by the man behind him. Nor have your countrymen in Tibet been angels. But even in Beijing you have seemingly indiscriminate mass crackdowns on kids merely reading books. I don't know. Maybe you believe in big government and absolute mind-control. I find that goal unbelievable and no worse than indifferent Cubans murdering foodless Angolan diamond thieves. Mankind is monstrous wherever you look. I ask her, Am I right or wrong?

I don't like to think this, Gong says. Her big almond eyes beat back her feelings but well with tears anyway. People's Republic is not without fault. I was raised in a communal democracy, not a democracy based on individual rights. She wipes her cheeks, saying, All citizens understood this and agreed to it. We had a sewing machine, a radio, books, a few sweets on Sundays, and felt spoiled. I often had to read in near darkness—but the revolution was worth the darkness and the faint power supply to my village. All shortcomings were worth the communal gain. Did everyone eat? Yes, they did, at the communal canteen. Good noodles and dumplings, with plenty of sauce. Oh yes, some sacrifices, however necessary, could chill your back. She caresses her arms, and says softly, Even so, I want human beings to act humanly.

Something within her screams for life. I scent the hair on the arms she caresses—her breath, her last meal sweet as sorghum in her pores. *I want, I want.*

But these terrorists are beasts, she says. They're not human! Why would it be you they are after?

Oh, my father and I are often targeted. Sometimes by accident or for things we don't even remember. One night in the fifties my father dined at Toots Shor's, a famous midtown Manhattan restaurant, and Dad bet Toots he could find a swankier dinner jacket than Toots could find. Dad ordered a fancy jacket cut, sewn and shipped to him from his tailor in Japan. As it happens, Toots knew Dad's tailor, wired him his measurements, and had an exact copy of Dad's jacket cut for himself and shipped. When it arrived he stashed it in his office and waited for Dad's next visit. One night Dad shows up wearing his pale, tomato-red dinner jacket with salmon cummerbund and looking like a trillion dollars. Sonofagun, if Toots doesn't appear a minute later in the same tomato and salmon outfit. Just then four Yugoslav diners get into a shouting match and Toots throws them out. But before they leave, one of them nails Dad as the very bastard who'd ripped off his family's fur business in Belgrade and left them hanging in the wind. The Yugoslav lurks outside, waiting for Dad. When Dad steps through the doorway, the Yugoslav plunges a knife into Dad's upper chest and runs off. Dad gets really pissed. Pressing his fingers around the blade in his chest, he chases the assassin. In his bloody new suit he chases him through crowds two whole blocks downtown until he catches the guy in front of a camera store on Forty-Ninth Street. He picks him up, throws him through the store window. Then he crawls through the window, grabs a piece of glass, cuts the man's throat, drags the bleeding hulk back out, and sits on him, the knife still in his chest, until the ambulance comes. The Yugoslav dies and my Dad's back at Toots's with a new bet within the month. By the way, if you ever get stabbed—leave the knife in until help comes.

We've both been attacked a number of times. I was personally slated for death by the Palestinians—a Mossad commander informed me. In my defense, let me draw a slight veil over this. I, uh, sent a sniper to the Palestine terrorist camp in the Bekaa Valley in Libya and had him wipe out ninety-three terrorists over a period of months. Then I made sure that Mossad informed the Palestinians that Mossad was not responsible for these deaths—that I was irked at having been targeted by the Arabs—that I had limitless guerrilla capacities for retaliating, as I was demonstrating. The heavy .50-caliber round which blew each victim's heart out his back was the sniper's signature, and these absolutely unexpected and frightening deaths by daylight or utter darkness spread pure terror among those in their midst used to dealing out terror. Their knees shook whenever they came out of their barracks. Day or night you could be walking down the road and someone's chest or back in front of you might explode. Night was no cover, since my sniper had a nightscope which turned darkness to daylight. The only moments anyone felt safe were during a heavy rain, and in the Libyan desert that doesn't happen very often. At last I was told that, for their sake, I'd been struck off the list. I think this is all quite regrettable. I mourned each man's death, believe me. But until I knew I was off their list and that the allotment for murdering me closed, I had to press on. That was, by the way, only one sniper who did all that nasty stuff for me. For reasons I'll get to, I feel I'm more valuable alive than dead, and so I experience no sense of guilt for this mode of defending myself.

Ninety-three men! Gong says, and covers her mouth. Sidney sits back, speechless. I see them wondering. Do they sit with a mass murderer who might himself be shot to death before their eyes? Sidney glances about for snipers. Her face clouded, Gong turns from me and stares at blue vines on her tea service. Under a palm, her breathing leaps. She's never more rich and feminine and attractive than when looking aside, her thoughts veiled. I want to rush into that heaving chest and plunder not just her heart but her ribs and undergarments.

All right, Sidney says. I think we have a grip on your father and grandfather. Shall we get back to you and your feelings of inferiority?

Your disenchantment, Gong says.

You don't hide your guns, do you? I fall silent. Giving you my family history actually gives me relief and I feel free to bring up the somewhat metaphysical stuff I'm sucked into. My unconscious seems to spill out into the metaphysical. Our search for a supreme meaning to our existence is so laughable that the future will see us as Stone Agers. But at the moment I stagger under just such impulses. And there I go, overstating with what my father despises as wasted effort—such high-flown stuff you and I can talk about only in metaphors about paths and gates and bridges and words like salvation which mean nothing to me and leave me groping for a language that might reveal the water hole I seek. I need a new language and can't bear this metaphoric slop I think in. Funny!—I loved Omar Khayyam and at twelve memorized the entire Rubaiyat with its big laugh at religion and philosophy, and now I'm twelve again, still a child but bearing a world of horror along with my child's innocence. And it's a world of horrors I must in part answer for. That world's only half-real, despite the crushed peoples and bloodshed on my hands. So I say I need a good solid image to strive for, and perhaps redeem myself and the Bihusi heart I bear. If I rattle on like this I may even find something. I came here poor and empty to beg something from you—but *what* I don't know. How can my clever wolf-soul stoop to this? Each century thinks itself cleverer than the earlier one and now I find myself too clever to believe anything.

Gong says, If you seek an image with which to transform yourself, only you can find that image. It's not one that we can hand you.

No, you can't. But I need someone I can bear to have listen to me, and in *The Spear* I felt I'd found the ideal listener to help me dig that image out of myself.

Well, you are educating us as well, Sidney says.

Gong Li nods, reaches out, pats my hand. We want to help! But you are the most dumbfounding patient I've ever had. Please go on.

I should think you find me your sickest patient—someone looking for a divine madness amid reality's bottomless shortcomings.

Each man needs his own answer, Sidney says.

I shrug. And each wolf-soul? I ask.

I can give you no easy answer.

Or image to guide you, Gong says.

When I speak of mass deaths and plagues, it's personal. I am responsible. Or have inherited the responsibility from my tribe. To free me from such guilt do I need some kind of blood sacrifice? My level of guilt would seem to call for it. But sacrifice to whom or what? I'm too clever to experience such a sacrifice at depth, and gather its rewards, though I must say that speaking to you offers me some sort of confession and relief. I am, of course, the only one inflicting this suffering on myself.

Still, Gong says, one could see in what you seek some kind of heroic virtue on your part.

Thank you, but I clearly don't see any such virtue. For one thing, my quest is absolutely selfish and not meant to be a path for others. My familial evil is too old and deep and unforgivable in human terms while thrilling to my wolf-soul. What can I say? Am I only looking for a goat to sacrifice and stand in my place for the shedding of blood? How can I not feel that the highest truth lies in the absurd and that my search is nonsense and that its goal should I reach it is an overwhelming fantasy that drinks me to its depths. And there I would be as I embrace the supreme meaning I seek— this all-absolving fantasy, my new wisdom. Well . . .

Now as for my dreams. When I wake from dreams of my limbs floating off, I began to think of my treasures. I could feel my unfinished Joyce manuscript under my fingers and smell Joyce himself lingering on the pages as one of us. I could feel the contours of *Seated Aphrodite*, all of her. I could see my lakes of sweet crude in Kabinda. I felt them leaving me—being sucked right out of me. Then I felt Manhattan move from under me and slip from the edge of the earth. I felt everything my life stood on fall this way and that. I lost the very ground beneath me. But even more, I saw all my treasures in the salt mine survive me and being sold off at a world rummage sale. I'd lost everything. I'd lost my oil fields. I'd lost my wife and children. I'd lost my Joyce, my Rembrandts. And why not—who was I? I'd spent my life getting much of this stuff together and now it would all just go into the furnace—like Kane's Rosebud. Christ, I *still* feel this dream. I'm half-dead. Just parchment, cash and stocks ready for the torch. And the heartbreak? Devastating. I could not detach from my possessions. Or my family guilt.

You really admit family guilt? Gong asks.

As in the House of Atreus, I say.

Sidney says, So, you come to us about heartbreak and blood-guilt?

I'm in pain, Sidney. I've avoided some of my family flaws—but I've taken on more than enough of them.

Well, he asks, which flaws have you avoided?

Since childhood I've known that, as a Giurgiu, my mother is Dad's distant half-sister and that their sex borders on miscegenation. Or even qualifies as? Let me put it this way. You may agree that Asians or Orientals have sharper minds than other races. Well, the Giurgiu are not as bright as Bihusi. Yet there are far more females among Giurgiu than among Bihusi. For genetic reasons I'll get to, Bihusi must reproduce with Giurgiu to carry on the Bihusi. There are not enough Bihusi she-wolves, and those there are don't carry the wolf gene. Only the Giurgiu carries it.

Gong asks, But he dominates your mother?

Oh God, no. She'd take his head off at the neck if he tried that stuff.

Anyway, I hope to do some good for the planet—and make up for all my misdeeds done with Dad. They weren't misdeeds when I did them. But I've changed and now he's slipped off the planet. He's still here. But the planet's slipped from him. More or less. Well, for the moment Sidi bin-Bahram has a good grip on it. My problem in part is that—much against my family's wishes—I've married a human—a woman with no wolf genes. By abandoning the Bihusi, I've lost the world. I cannot reproduce the Bihusi line without a Giurgiu mate.

You've given up the world for love? Gong asks.

Not really. I never wanted the world. I've lost something else—maybe my sanity. But let me ask you. Does all this Christian mumbo jumbo of alchemy have any real meaning to you? I mean as a spiritual slip horn into the afterlife? Or is it just a tool for analysis?

We are not priests, she says. But the reality of the metaphysical should not be doubted—after all you own the Sword. I can tell you what I think about what you've told us so far. All the complexities of your unconscious have compacted themselves into a central hermetic guide—a compass for living, a guiding inner balance we must call your spiritual compass. It's lost true north, however, and you can't reset it, although I must say you are making an admirable effort. You depend on a vision of yourself that can only be called metaphysical—the word moral does not encompass enough. You have a psychic system that flows upward into conscious action. But this system in which you envision your being—as Billy Baxter—has somehow mingled with a Eurasian wolf species and forms its own sub-species. Otherwise you wouldn't believe in your own existence. With you instinct is reality and without your instinct for possession you would not have the energy to exist. Apparently you lack a full complement of human genes to master or at least drive down this wolf-soul. No question, binding your lineage to Ahuramazda creates a metaphysical sink pit—a true marvel—but not altogether divorced from normal human reasoning. At heart you ask us to find and help bring some healing aspect of this semi-human mass psyche up to consciousness. We are born into a pattern in the genes. You hope to master something primitive and archaic in you and help yourself heal some pain you have not yet made altogether clear to us in your vision of yourself falling apart. I can tell that your present state has emerged from a greater history than you or your father knows, despite this vast sense-library you say you Bihusi carry. You are, in fact, at this moment, Billy, walking out of a mist into daylight fresher than you have ever known. Look forward to a great adventure.

Yes! I will! Oh my God, that was almost—I'm ready to faint. And yes—I know I first came on with you as overly self-regarding, aggrandizing—puffed up with possessions—I *do* head the Bihusi Empire. And that's just not enough. Am I right that Jungians do help people accommodate themselves with the next world?

The next world? she says.

I don't want to own it, Gong.

Sidney says, If *you* believe in the afterworld, then *we* wear the mask of Hermes and lead you through as best we can. We know the guideposts—as much as a man can know them. You would be a very interesting case to help through these adjustments of spirit. Since you wish to talk analytically, I see in you a man full of aggression and animus who seeks his anima. You've lost your religion—your family. You're coming apart in your dreams and need to be made whole again. This is like Osiris being pieced back together by Isis. As you put it, your God has failed you. You are the child and grandchild of what you describe as two psychotics. If I were you, I'd be worried too. But what I don't get is why your family guilt doesn't seem to be as strong as your heartbreak over someday losing your possessions. I'm confused. If you feel drenched in the blood of millions, why isn't that more painful now than losing your possessions on some distant day?

Sounds like I am psychotic, doctor, and I know you don't treat psychotics. How can my possessions be that important to me? Is it genetic? It's taken me decades simply to get over saying, Oh, I have that, or I have two of those, or I have this or that—always one up! It's compulsive. Say it's a plane. Someone says Lear Jet, I say Gulfstream. It's tiresome to hear myself talk like that. Of course I have more this and that than they do! I have more of everything! People don't like to be reminded of this to their faces.

Well, tell us more about your broken heart, Gong says.

I catch my breath—and burst out:

My father sits around in living death! My mother has gone off the deep end with occult philosophy. I'm disturbed by bad dreams that stem from a massive business loss. Thanks to Sidi and my own faint-heartedness, I may well lose everything my father brought together. My sex life is nil. I keep all my fears bottled up from my wife and three sons. I can't breathe!—Agh, I'm sorry, I'm sorry.—Oh God, I didn't mean to get weepy. Second time today,

Billy! This is very unlike me, believe me. Wolves weep not.

Gong says, Take your time, Billy.

I jam on my shades—then shuck them.

If I could just get my heart together, get my breath back!—the rest might follow.

I fall silent as Helga brings the fresh tea service.

Don't you *enjoy* being rich? Gong asks.

Rich? Rich? It's demanding—you have to watch your back. Between us my father and I were the two richest men on Earth. Then he fell sick and I failed to watch our backs and we dropped to second place. Tell Sidi to enjoy himself while he can, Sidney. But do I enjoy being rich? Maybe I haven't been clear. I was born much richer than you could possibly know—and by that I do mean my genes. Set beside most men, I'm superhuman. Although, uh, when I don't look you in the eye, it's not bad manners or shiftiness. It's genetic.

Gong says, Tell us more about that.

At heart I'm timid. I'm not at all aggressive. I really have no urge to fight Sidi—although I must. When I'm not thinking about recovering what we've lost to Sidi, everything goes dim. I cloud over—I'm unhappy.

Vengeance perks you up? Sidney asks.

Redressing an injury to my family? That's only part of it.

What's the rest? Gong asks.

I really don't think it's fair that I should die unfulfilled. I have a large deed I must perform to pay back the planet for my inhuman misdeeds. Until then I fear I'll stay fixated on terrible images. For example, everyone I see has a corpse-light about him. I forever am facing the skeleton beneath the skin. Oddly enough for someone with the incredible aural powers I have, I'm upset by human ears. I see humans as they really are—I mean despiritualized by having these beastly, almost marsupial ears. *You* live caught up in the human illusion but I see an upright beast with strange, depersonalizing appendages winged on each side of his head. The wolf illusion differs at depth from the human illusion. Humans walk about in a dream. The power of scent among Bihusi, however, layers us into an organic and mineral sense-reality far denser than you can imagine. We mold our purposes with a foresight far beyond the human. Even as I speak with you now I can smell Sidi's downfall only months away—the way *you* can hear Niagara Falls a mile off. The seasons seep through us with a force stronger than philosophy or religion or those other abstractions with which you bury your fears and dress up your lives. Sometimes I want to kill my human grandchildren to save them from living the beastly lives before them. More likely, they'll keep the human illusion for many years—perhaps even until they die. But once lost, it's gone. With me, only works of art reinforce and help me rise above this breath-stopping loss of self. Great music and great players becomes pure feeling and lengthens the seeming brevity of life—.the Mahler *Adagietto* in his Fifth Symphony, or the new course his life takes in his Tenth—how I envy his grip on the courage to change. When I think how Michelangelo knew that the beastly ears he shaped with his fingers—the mortals he fashioned—the spines and noses and muscles and bones that he'd idealize into superhuman forms—then I'm boggled by his heart and courage. He knew the wolf spirit. That's why he gave Moses a wolf's eyes and gave all that massive bone and hair and muscle a wolf's heart. He knew something he could say only in Carrara marble.

With his chisel, Gong says. But go on.

To Moses these beasts were dreams made flesh by the hand of God. My Rembrandt late self-portraits—particularly *The Laughing Rembrandt,* with the painter laughing through tears at all the tragedy he's suffered—and my two Vermeers with wives like human angels walled up in Dutch interiors as morning light falls over them from leaded windows—and the dainty fingers of *The Lacemaker*—these rise above beastliness and are works I can't bear to leave behind. I can't bear to abandon the musical narcosis of Joyce's sea-manuscript. Just on a human level, when I think of murder as an act of kindness toward my family, I find I can't bear to lose the joyful intelligence of my wife's eyes—or the wit entangled in my three sons at Harvard—all that human innocence glows at me. I may die at any moment and enter the Wreath of Bihusi and keep all my wolf ties but lose all my human ties. I don't like that either.

Who does? Sidney says.

But you do believe in an afterlife then? Gong says.

My dead are still alive and speaking to me. But the thought that I may leave my great deed undone saps all my energy. I have so much to offer!

Why do you think you may die at any moment? she asks.

That's always an immediate possibility with world leaders. Look at the Kennedys. I get terribly short-winded in the Middle East.

It's a heart ailment? she asks.

I veil my worst thoughts and tell her, It's a physical mosaic. Let's not go into it. But occasionally I dislocate my lenses. I'm advised not to fire a long gun often, which I find disheartening because I'm a Meisterschutze—a master sniper. I've designed a special rifle built for me by Colt with a double trigger set so that I can hit a pie plate at two thousand meters. The rifle however is so delicate that I must slow my heart rate to forty-two beats a minute and then fire between the beats, or else my body vibration will affect the accuracy. My rifle fires .50 caliber machine-gun rounds—and the recoil from that could break your collar bone. So I had to design it in such a way that the recoil slips past me. The scope is on the side of the barrel and the stock goes into your shoulder and you rest your jaw against the cheek piece. Your eye is at the scope on the side of the rifle and the barrel recoils past your head and over your shoulder. You're able to get up to about 3,000 feet a second, which is the speed at which the bullet travels and so for over a mile has almost no drop. It's so fast it gets a flat trajectory.

But won't this dislocate a lens? Sidney asks.

How true! That's why I had to stop.

I'm very interested in your mechanical skills. But perhaps we can come back to them. You have some physical ills?

Forget my perfect health. The most dangerous piece of my inner mosaic is cardiac impact. One day I'll be walking around and suddenly a big black rubber stamp will come down and mark me PAID. I'll be in the Wreath but my skills will go to waste unless I can pass them on.

Gong says, So you do fear death?

No. What I fear is not finishing things.

Things you haven't told us? Sidney says.

That's why I'm here, doctor. Not just for depression or whatever you want to call it. Why do I feel less passionate about family guilt than about losing my treasures? That's because I *am* working on my family guilt but am failing at it. I am drowning in futility. Am I trying to do too much? Not a bit. But whatever I do, I must do fast. By midnight I might not be here.

Billy, she says, get to the heart of the matter. We can bear it.

Thank you, I say and take a deep breath. To start with, my father's a mass murderer. And when I think of the late Idi Amin slaughtering his own people, I see our plasma labs and the women and children dead at my father's feet. Amin, though, was a very tiny puppet in my father's business family. Can you imagine inheriting—as I have—a family business whose derricks pump blood? Talk about depersonalization! Yes, we all pass through disillusion. But my father has spent his life depersonalizing mankind. And who trained him into being this monster? *Grandfather!* I once asked Father about this, in a circuitous way, and Dad's answer? *History.* Mass slaughter, he said, is only the creation of statistics. The dead? Mere numbers. Humans are cheap light bulbs while *we* Bihusi live in Ahuramazda. I tried to argue, but his Genius overwhelms anyone. He would have been the world's top chess champion almost since infancy—if he thought there was any money in it. You can't argue with him. He can justify anything, and make you feel stupid for questioning him. You folks—products of Chairman Mao's *The Little Red Book*—you know what monstrous intelligence can do. My dad is only one monster among many. Unlike political geniuses, he didn't have to support armies and navies. He only built and sold ships—armaments—air forces. He designed force and sold *power.* My father did not come into the world to make men better but rather to make their weaknesses useful to Bihusi. He is a scourge and a sacker with a love of absolute greed. He would drag the whole world into his pocket or else destroy it. If it resists him? Take it down in flames.

Let no mere man *or* wolf—let no one at all—look to have more than the King of Bihusi or think to sit in triumph over him. Not even Sidi, whom Dad rather admires. Dad sees himself as an unparalleled idealist. His tutelary divinity is his own father, but also the great and revered memory of earlier Bihusi—his thousands of forebears. Of all Bihusi past and present, he is by far the leading figure and gifted with a blissful Genius none can match—a titan of finance who revels in power. *Power without guilt.* It is a privilege, even for me, to watch him work. Knead an industry—bilk a fellow bandit. Does such a being ever look for a magnificence of living to equal his limitless joy of money? No. He has no need to display his wealth, no political goals—he is, rather, a barbarian. Far above the rules of mankind. And with great gusto everything not nailed down gets gobbled up. He is an original and rooted in a wolf nature pumped up by rapacity. He achieves financial effects not by the skillful use of common tools but by sleight-of-hand. A dollar earned is beneath him—a dollar stolen divine. He paints the world as he wants it to be, then from the most distant corners of the universe assembles it from fanciful materials—from places you and I would never associate with the world he plans for himself. When I see how his financial plots work out, absolute pleasure suffuses me—the uniqueness!

the originality!—moves I'd never dreamed possible, not in my lifetime. As you will see, his innovative faculty is so fertile that his versatility in exercising it—of inventing credit out of thin air and turning corporations around on a shaved percentage point—is child's play, with a thousand variations and alternative avenues that swim with the very wantonness of novelty.

But in the end, Dad's eye is not on the money, it's on the controlling interest. He imitates no one, especially no human. He brings all his Genius into the world with him—a sudden surge in the current of Bihusi—a power refined by his father down to the smallest tenth of a decimal. For the Sun-power plan we're working on he has measured the exact amount of radiant energy his thumb and forefinger can collect from the Sun with our receptor dishes. For relaxation he works math formulae and diddles about with cosmology. When I was ten I asked him, Dad, what's out there? Why do you want to know? he said. Are you going somewhere? I just want to know, I said. All right, he says, but it hardly bears thinking about. You start from a fixed point or nothing means anything and no sensible measure possible. Let's start from you, Sunny Jim. At first appearance, from you outward, the universe is light, matter, X-rays and cosmic rays and thermal radiation— just a big magnetic soup. That's fine. But let's get back to you, little Bihusi. The Bihusi line lies in time like a very long gene going in its present form from prehistory back to the Sun in our earliest existence in the big soup. All memory is made of radiance and printed on light. All memory is magnetic matter. So is the universe. The universe is a big magnetic memory of itself in which coexist before, during and after. If you see a spark dancing, that spark has no dimensions—no past or future—it is all in the present no matter whence it comes or where it goes. Its existence is always right now. The universe is a big dancing spark. It's illusory to ask about its size or where it came from or where it's going. With you as the fixed point of reference, it exists only in the present. And that's where you have the controlling interest. With a mind like yours, you can make the whole damned thing dance on the head of a pin— just as I do. Does that answer you? Think about it. We are sitting inside a big spark.

After the razor blade coup, no one could hold Dad back, not even Grandfather. In fact, going by Bihusi tradition, Dad had to kill the king— Grandfather—who indeed spurs him on—an act I as well must someday do to ensure purity of greed and rapacity in the clan. It's no tragedy. For even in death Bihusi never leave each other. At any moment I can see Grandfather before me as clearly as I see you. In him and his son nature has worked out a strong and peculiar feeling—a harsh and unpleasant ravenousness that forces its way out past all stopping it, and that you will find at this intensity nowhere else—except in our Bihusi forebears Attila the Hun and Genghis Khan. They are beyond imitation. Today my father bunkers on the Jungfrau. He's gone to fat and doesn't care for his teeth—his incisors, large and discolored by tar, are thin as hangnails. And he's swallowed so many navies and gulped down so many armies that his brain can't contain them all—and couldn't even before it was pulped. Today he's a pale rock that can still radiate fear at will. Don't get too close to him. He bites. He has blank candleflame eyes—a look out of hell that burns your skin off. It says you haven't a clue as to what the world is about. Today he's a psychic cannibal. And I but hint at the man he was: an ax murderer with a cell phone who lopped off heads by a number punched.

His favorite dish? A hand pickled in garlic. He sucks the soft flesh off like pig's knuckles. He was turned on in the Congo when Idi sent him a gallon jar of hands, along with headcheese made of body parts—including eyes. Dad didn't know I was watching him through his bead curtain. As for the hand, Idi had left a wedding ring on the third finger. Dad kept it as a lucky token. But luck?—he has it by the ton. He's six inches taller than I and at that height it's a thumping miracle he outlasted his assassins. Well, most of them. They can't get him now.

Why not? Gong asks.

He's a ghost. He lives in dreams.

And one of his dreams is vengeance on Sidi bin-Bahram? Sidney asks.

He doesn't say. Despite everything, Dad might've been less beastly if he'd only known how. At times, he depressed himself. This is not well known, but I'd watch him sit for months paralyzed with mourning. There simply was no remedy for his ghastly nature. Any full Moon he'd be out running naked through the woods. The Bihusi male is heavily endowed with hair and one could not call Dad in any way human when running about naked. Or at any other time, if you saw the wolf within. If I'd cut his throat during one of his black periods, he'd have praised me for being a good Bihusi. Like me, he too failed to kill his father, at least not directly—a dishonor that weakened the code of Bihusi. After Grandfather suicided, Dad often told me his brightest hope was for an early death. But death eluded him, despite every illness—although he's more or less dead now, as I've said. How often he'd cry himself insensible. I tell you these things so you can weigh my background. At his very worst moments, when spurned by Mother, he'd whimper with pain. Her very shouts would dislocate his lenses and leave him with diminished sight. Half-blind, he'd howl to Ahuramazda for his full power again. But there really was no ointment for his wounds, neither physical nor spiritual. He was bred to royalty with the heart of a wolf, but his whole being felt sealed into an agonizing membrane. He'd snap at his own arm and chew it bloody trying to gnaw himself loose from the trap he'd been born into. And yet, despite these lapses, he was a wolf of good cheer. I have to rest a moment.

I usually give the leftover bread to the swans, Gong says rising.

Let me sit here and think, Sidney says.

I rise to join her.

We stand at the sedge and break bread into pieces and throw it far out. Two swans and their three cygnets give up feeding off bottom moss and glide like electrons toward floating bread. The yellow beaks and spiny tongues of the cygnets snap at the bread as the mother shakes her great downy wings urging them on. The large marshy male swims between us and his family and stands guard, beady-eyed and ready to hiss and attack.

What family spirit, I say. Do you have children?

No. I have conferences.

You make children sound like a transgression. Trembling, I look her straight in the eye. You deserve children.

Well, I'm not shot down yet.

I lean down. You *deserve* them. And when The Spear arrives, perhaps you'll discover what the Sun has in store for you.

Her heart throbs, which I hear. Breezes ruffle her coiled black hair. Stunned, she nods and reads my face, her whole being intent on heaven's message. As greed to believe fills her, a wolf-charge rises in me and I will her my ravenousness. She yields to a dream born in her womb and rising in blood through her flesh. Her face flushes and a red shimmer fills her eyes. Heat flows about her. Her frame trembles with such strength that I pick up the shout along her nerves and beam back a calming glance. Dry hungering lips fall open as her breasts rise and fall. I struggle not to embrace the pang ringing through her. I lose all restraint and close my eyes. I am random bodiless flame and close her hands in my flame. An etheric glow binds us body to body. I step back. Her eyes hope, unquenchable.

Thank you, she whispers.

So now, how can I go on telling you about my ridiculous life? About my father and our despicable business affairs?

You may tell me anything, Gong says. This day is under a spell. All words are permitted. Now we go back—I need tea.

Ah, I invaded your privacy.

I liked it.

As we return I resist touching her. I lust to kiss the back of her neck. Ashes slip down my heart and lungs. I need water.

Sidney looks up from his notes as we sit.

How does your father explain himself? What does he see when all these deaths—well, you tell me.

I often ask myself this. How could a seemingly blind force of Nature like Dad achieve such fabulous intelligence? It's a terrible question. I'm baffled. Is he the despiritualization of divine power into an equal and opposite rage for organized chaos? A carnivore who walks upright on his hind feet, a *Corporation tyrannosaurus* fattening his paunch on butchery and business? These are moral questions and I can't give a moral answer. I can only say what I see, images of Dad burned into me from what might be called his great spiritual wars, both high and low. First you must understand the low war in prehistory between Bihusi and mankind, a battle in which Bihusi, slaughtered without qualm by men, lost their freedom and were driven into darkness where only the night welcomed them. In regards to the higher war, he *has* leaped out of that earliest darkness before the Logos gave order, and become the great Combatant who will bring mankind to its knees. He was never a reasonable being. Something in him, a yellow fire in his eyes, remains forever beyond reason. He is now a lunar animal and supremely dangerous even when well-fed with fresh companies. Let his supersensitive muzzle catch wind of a starving company with its ribs showing and my father licks his chops and gets ready to suck out its marrow. In an instant, he gobbles it up and it's gone before knowing it's been attacked. A chief executive officer barely glimpses Dad sniffing at the window before he's dead, drained dry, and Dad's prowling around his office, eager for new messes, a fresh massacre.

Though much like mine, his voice is difficult to describe. Very high-pitched, it needs the merest whistle or urging of air or grunt to turn you to stone. You hear an energy you don't want to touch for any reason, psychotic musings that feed on chaos, the sheer joy of a wolf in the hen house, sending blood everywhere, slavering in ecstasy, an inhuman, a destructive abstract energy in your own unconscious, but a muscular force that forms a material evil, an anti-Creation. He's the very opposite of heroic. Stupendous fear is his main weapon. You feel night falling around you when he smiles. Even that shifty little porcupine Sidi bin-Bahram cringes when Dad selects Sidi's high-bridged nose to study. I won't mention his perversions. His sex drive is both extreme and has its difficulties. Once locked into a copulatory tie with a she-wolf or a woman and having ejaculated, he needs nearly fifteen minutes for his volcanic inflated penis to disgorge enough blood to be pulled free. This is a greater social problem than it may seem, since often enough he's not charmed by his companion's mind and so must limit himself to his cell phone when going back to work. And yet I'm hopeless, I love him. No, as with any pitiless monster, I pity him. He carried our line to its greatest height when it had all but died out and in a world that had long ago rejected us, and then fell wounded on the verge of his greatest victory. That it would have been the greatest accomplishment in world history, though carried out for what to mankind would be the wrong reason, must be weighed in as well. For him it was the right reason. He solved a number of incredible problems for the wrong reason, a solution to world hunger, problems in offshore drilling, and even was about to give us perpetual power from the Sun. But perhaps supreme Genius divorced from a passion for truth and goodness simply can't be loved.

He had his longings, and on a summer night delighted in a crescent Moon, a star hanging from its tip, when he romped through some wooded paradise with an alpha female. Even tyrants need queens. Though not human, he saw himself as a valorous guardian who destroyed the shackles constraining customary human behavior, for he is the slave of freedom. And now he's in eternal twilight and I oversee his world and its horrors. I must take upon myself his plan for a power undreamed of, his last plan, the blueprint for a ring of space discs to harvest the energies of the Sun. He was out to conquer the Sun's energies as the prime source of our planetary power, placing mankind itself beyond oil and stock prices, a triumph never before achieved by any leader, not even a Bihusi. He would chain the Sun to Earth's purposes.

So I have in my hands a Bihusi blueprint for the new cosmic order. The Fourth Reich? *Peanuts.* The Communist globe? *Small potatoes.* The information giants, Bill Gates? Rupert Murdoch? *Still in their playpens.* Sidi bin-Bahram? *In diapers.* I have been given the opportunity to revamp for good the pattern of evil that my father built out of darkness. To give back to Earth infinite energy for household and factory. To stitch up all wounds with Sunlight, you might say. That is the plan I must fulfill and am in despair that I will go mad before I can accomplish it. I will die trying, if I must, to build an energy pathway to Earth from the Sun. But my dreams tell me I'm running out of gas. And what if some psychopath like Sidi takes over the plan and turns it to his own purposes?

The Changs silently study each other. One or the other must say something.

This is a wild story growing ever wilder, Sidney says.

Well, let me say something. I am perhaps looking for my daughter.

Do you have a daughter? Gong asks.

No, only males, whom I must train as my father trained me. Poor things.

And now you want a daughter?

Yes, a human daughter whom I would not raise as a Bihusi.

Really? How could you do that?

It's only a dream that haunts me, though haunts is not the right word. But I'd give my heart to raise a daughter who would be for humans all that I have never been. I'd raise her as a goddess for humans. As I say it's only a dream I can't dismiss. The problem of keeping the Bihusi strain out of her being would overwhelm us both. Our evil aspect, how could this innocent forgive it? It would be her lifelong burden. I may want to do something noble in raising a goddess, but I would in fact raise a double-hearted monster of inherited evil striving for perfection, and failing, even as I am failing to find the image I need for my redemption—if it can be called redemption. I don't know what to call this image I need to restore me, although I think of it as a daughter. Restore me, hmm. Is this the wrong word, when I've never been other than as now. Where this weird hunger for her image comes from I don't know. It's very oppressive. Perhaps my daughter could be my companion as well and with her own vision lead me out of hell. And what would I then do as her father-companion as she sets about repairing the family evil? I dread my own riddles. How could such a daughter ever love such a father when she got to know me through and through? Who murdered the hero? The hero!—blowing his own horn. And all I say now is wary forethought before I really think and set forth on what may land me chained to a rock with a vulture like Sidi eating out my liver daily. It's this: If the image I seek is a daughter as the right hand of God doing good deeds, I am myself only cast into deeper darkness, self-humiliated and groping over stones. No certainty, all my nameless goals more distant, more chaotic. But this is just where I belong if I want a clean slate and her unblemished image before me, although I bear the very weight of the Earth my tribe has sucked dry. And in the end will my daughter want my head on a platter to save the world? It's possible that her only way forward will be to destroy all I've done and me along with it. And this *is* the daughter I would venerate more than life itself, while my death would sanctify her as a woman who gave up her father's love to save mankind. I see my daughter wringing her hands in full foreknowledge of all these decisions and actions on her part. Can all this be taken seriously?

Gong rests a hand on mine, saying, But we do take *you* seriously.

If not the ideas, Sidney says. You describe what Jung calls enantiodromia, an inversion of evil into good as good inverts into evil, like a pair of spirals passing through each other. This is the eternal inversion of duality, all things turning into their opposites and back again. In your case, the force of your fears drives you into rebirth. You become your own daughter. Rebirth! Well, I'm the one who started talking about great spiritual wars.

So, Sidney, what do you think? Is the birth of Sun energy from our disks a good or bad act for me?

Normally I wouldn't tell you. But since we meet for only one session, I'll say a few words. As I see it, you are trying to break free from your Bihusi unconscious at its deepest, or to revise your present one—which from everything you've said I doubt is possible, any more than the leopard can change its spots. Your wolf-soul is with you forever.

I agree, Gong says. But it's admirable that you want to surrender to your feminine side and assume a deeper human persona—although your wolf-soul is locked permanently into your Bihusi psyche. All this you know already, though perhaps you had hopes that the daughter imago you want to raise from your unconscious can lift your tribal guilt. But then you also find yourself at the deepest possible odds with this imago should she arise to help you swallow the Sun with these disks. I think we need to know more—although your daughter simply as a woman will have knowledge of things for which you have no eyes.

For which I have no eyes?

Well, you hope she'll inspire you. How could she if she sees only what you see? She will also have intuitions that outstrip yours but can give you warnings.

Warnings about what?

You already have a hard vision about what you want done. She will have more personal feelings about which you don't approve.

That's possible.

Oh, it's very likely, Sidney says.

More than likely, Gong says. It's clear that you are very fixed in ways she won't like. Or do you just want her to respond to your orders and that's it? You are trying to change the world—the Bihusi world at least.

I should change my nature?

You do have a feminine side from which she has appeared. Just now you account it a virtue to suppress your feminine traits. But it is these alone that will allow your daughter to join you in your search for—well, for wherever she's taking you. And where do you want to go? You haven't told us yet, although it sounds as though you want to win back your soul.

Give us a little more background, Sidney says. In my opinion, however, you look for an anima figure who must be obeyed even by you—to find a structure to your soul, a woman to renovate your unconscious and change you at depths you can't foresee nor will be able to resist. You want to surrender to your feminine side.

I agree, Gong says. Please go on, Billy.

Gong pours me a fresh cup of green tea. The gunpowder flavor drugs me as I sip.

Ah, I say, a hint of firecracker smoke in this gunpowder. Something of a warning?

It's a bit smoky, Gong says. It's called gunpowder because the leaves are rolled into tiny pearls to hold their flavor. So, you are not a mass murderer like your father?

If I were I wouldn't be here.

Of course you wouldn't, she says. And when you tell me that, it helps you.

But understand, I am my father's son. Many hold me in low esteem and see me as the same butcher he was. This hurts. They think I'm Dad's pimp and walk with a pimp roll down Wall Street. And then I did blow my *first* real chance to make good with the space discs. I'm no hero. But while I'm alive, I still want to bring a message from the Sun.

These discs, Billy, Gong says. What's all the difficulty? Tell us about them.

I'm having a holovision promo made showing the idea in 3D, but it's not finished yet. They're up in space, or will be. Lasers. We're creating All-Earth wireless power. It's like the invention of the wheel or how to handle fire—a step upward for intelligent life. I almost had the money—for a moment—and now I need even more to put up enough discs for the job needed. This project dwarfs building a trans-Atlantic tunnel. And I'm not Superman; I can't just lift these discs up there myself. I need limitless financial energy to get this off the ground. The fact is, the money *is* there. It's buried in Siberia. You might say the Sun is buried in Siberia.

Hm! Sidney says. Explain that.

Trapped under Lake Bolshoi on the West Siberian Plain is hundreds of millions of years of solar energy in the form of oil—from the dinosaurs and the vegetation. It's actually under a much larger space than Lake Bolshoi, but Bolshoi offers an easy way down into it—a hole into the barrel. I have to suck the Sun up out of Siberia. But problems abound. There are families in Siberia that are linear descendants of Cro-Magnons—people never fitted into the old Soviet Union—or the new one. The only major upgrading of their lives lies in their weaponry. They have traded the spear for the Kalashnikov. They once speared saber-tooth tigers. Now they spray them with semiautomatic fire.

Sidney's jaw drops. There are still saber tooths!

Yes. And incredibly large, bigger than polar bears. These tigers could take down mammoths—when there were mammoths.

Gong's gaze cools me. But what will happen to the Cro-Magnon descendants in your new scheme?

Probably nothing. They've survived everything else. They've never fought in a Russian war. The Russians can't deal with them. But I must. They have to learn. Or die. This has happened before, with the Chechen in 1943, when the male Chechen were all away fighting on Russia's German front, Stalin relocated the state's population of women and children to the Urals, which is where Lake Bolshoi is. As cattle cars full of refugee Chechen moved slowly north, they were accompanied by earthmovers, or tractors. A train would stop. They'd offload the dead from each cattle car. Bury them in common graves with the earthmovers. And go on. Today's Chechen are the ones who came back from the war and now give Russia hemorrhoids. Nobody can deal with the Siberians, not even Dad. This is the same problem the Fahd family, the royals of Arabia, have with the Bedouin. The Fahds want a more sophisticated society and want to get the Bedouin off the desert. So they've built magnificent apartment complexes for the Bedouin. But the Bedouin will not move. Their culture says stay in the desert. The same holds true with the Siberians. Their culture says stay in the hills, stay in the woods. You have to give up with people like this. Stalin killed them by the millions and couldn't get them to move.

The disc project depends on the oil. But we can't get the oil if there are people living on top of it—even if they are hunter-gatherers—and in this case sturgeon fishermen as well, since Lake Bolshoi is the world's largest inland supplier of sturgeon and caviar. But these people are in the way! All of Siberia is only a thin crust on an ocean of oil. After Dad solved the big Siberian drilling problems, he planned to use that money to finance his disc program and tap the Sun. For years we could not beat the problem of the Siberian spring. Each spring the tundra thaws and shifts. The earth's crust shifts. Sometimes for miles. Again and again, it destroyed the shafts drilled to get at the oil. Pipes bent and burst in the thaw, derricks fell, and we'd start all over on areas devastated by oil spills. Year after year after year. The disc project was Dad's downfall and I inherited its recovery. But I also inherited the guilt he never experienced, and now am plagued by a need to repair his misdeeds. It's not that I want any goddamn glory I'd steal from the Sun. I want to give the Sun to mankind. But I'm failing.

We'd poured generations of lives into this project, always convinced that the answer was just one winter away. If we could only come up with the right idea that broke the thaw problem. Finally Dad's Genius found the answer—I'll tell you about it in a moment. But now I'm running out of time. My depression drowns any chemical aid. Nothing can brighten this black lake I sink into daily. The hope I still bear is to revive the Russian economy, pay back everything my father has stolen from that people—and from the world—by handing them an infinite pool of energy inside their own borders. This would rescue the ruble forever. But our fees for this would have doubled Dad's googols and underwritten the space discs.

Googols? Sidney says.

Money in zeroes beyond comprehension.

You can double zeroes beyond comprehension? Gong asks, and shrugs. I'm interested in your depression. You said your sex life was nil.

It's not what it should be.

You have erectile dysfunction? Take sex pills?

No, I take the herb yohimbe. I know that without regular and frequent ejaculation I'm a sitting duck for cancer and prostate problems.

Then you haven't come to us about your libido?

Not really.

That's hard to believe, Gong says. Quite often everything really does come down to sexual dysfunction. What do you think of when you think of sex?

That's a strange question. I've never thought of it quite as you suggest. You're asking what archetypal image stands for sex in my mind, aren't you?

She nods, smiling at my grasp of her interest.

Well, you won't believe this, but I'll tell you, I say. When I think of sex I see a pregnant womb with a pineapple in it and big leaves flowering out of the crown.

Oh, that is fabulous, she says. Does that image mean anything to you?

I think of the womb as a Sun or ripening place and the pineapple as a hermaphroditic fruit. As you may know, the pineapple is both male and female. Self-reproducing. How do you see my pineapple?

Gong looks away, clearing her throat. I would say it shows painful yearning in the pine cone and desire for the female fruit.

This is all quite fascinating, Sidney says. But let's get back to Earth.

Fine, I say, though with a binding glint at Gong.

I am haunted by sexual horror as well as my father's bloodletting. My father has given mankind global syphilis, not to mention millions of AIDS deaths. I'll explain that, but it makes seemingly impossible any sense of spiritual relief for me while millions are dead or dying or will die because of him.

You want to *dismantle* your father's empire? Sidney asks.

Oh God, no. I can't. I need it. Have you any idea how it feels to have *almost* solved the problem of Russia's economy, and failed? *Almost* to have brought limitless power and light to Earth, and failed? I need all the uplift I can gather to get back in the saddle.

Sidney asks, Then you just haven't pulled it off yet?

I don't know. Dad's empire goes everywhere and shifts like the Siberian mantle. I know what. Let me tell you about Hollywood.

Surprise fills Gong. You want to save Hollywood! Like Siberia?

No, it has to do with sewing up Japan. You've got to get a grip on how Dad works. Financially, Hollywood and Japan are in marriage—by miscegenation at the moment. And my father cleaned their clock in Beverly Hills.

Sidney says, Cleaned their clock?

Stripped them of *billions*. And had me blamed for it. Not only blamed but drowned in obloquy. I am not welcome in many financial centers. Before Dad invented the Bihusi Bed—which the whole world has heard of—this was the greatest scam in history.

Skinning Japan? Hah! I wouldn't want to miss this, Sidney tells Gong.

She asks, How did it work, Billy?

I close my eyes and jump in.

My father's Genius is on its last legs as we fly to Tokyo. His coalblack mane now has a wide streak of pure silver. His eyes pulse and glow and dim down like cigarette embers in a dark room. He sits fixated by a glimmering, cherry-shaped girasol on his finger, a fire opal the size of a testicle. Seemingly asleep, he's deep into plans. You take your life in your hands to speak to him. When he's in this planning state, you do not want to be near him for any reason. Not even I, and I have to sit beside him, listening to his broken snores and soft grunts, watch his hands plan and twitch in his sleep and cover ground like paws, our whole double seat bathed in his shaving spices. Baxter Blades has led him into toiletries and grabbing half of the four-billion-dollar annual scent market. He often tries out the men's newer fragrances, the drearier deodorants, chemical aftershaves, and cheap metallic colognes that are our best-sellers. We've been warned by the Swedes that the aluminum in Ice, our underarm deodorant, is quite likely a cause of cancer.

That's quite true, Sidney says. Aluminum absorption kills.

Dad only smiles at the warning. We've not changed the mix, the formula. We make over a hundred chips a year on the Ice line and its varieties, Arctic Wind, Maylaysian Lime, Clove, and Poppy Smoke.

Gong says, Chips?

Millions. A chip is a million. So Dad wants to sell Hollywood to the Japanese. This is like selling them the Brooklyn Bridge. It involves an old-fashioned but very complicated scam on my father's part which he does not warn me about. I think we are just out to lease America to Tokyo, starting with the West Coast. We'll sell them a sumptuously valuable movie studio as a starter, a top-drawer studio with a great inventory and lots of face, oh, a sweet deal, all cream. But in fact this studio trembles on bankruptcy. We own a controlling interest and Dad wants to dump it. You've heard, Don't be a jackass? My father'd tell me, Don't be a jackal. To Dad all humans are stupid jackals ready to be robbed. And to him the Japanese are jackals, and, as it happens, so am I. I am long married to a human. Dad intends to give me a hard slap for that peccadillo and force a doctorate in trading on me as well. Now Dad, you understand, has no *personal* animus toward me. He simply wants me to know that my worst enemy is my own foolish sense of *trust*. Trust in a human wife rather than a Giurgiu she-wolf is bad enough, but trust in trading is sudden death. You'll see. As we fly over Japan the temperature and smell of the coast awaken him and he flips through his catalogue of Hiroshige and Hokusai first printings being traded in the underground art market. The earliest known impressions struck from original woodblocks are softer in tone than those using the later coarse European dyes. These works normally never leave Japan, unless replaced, of course, by perfect forgeries. You might think that knowledge of and a seeming obsession with priceless Japanese prints, and with Chinese artifacts such as Ming vases and tenth-century scrolls—scrolls altogether richer and more spiritually adventurous than even the freshest Hiroshige monkeys and birds and most of Hokusai, aside from *The Great Wave*—scrolls much, much less decorative—but even the Chinese porcelains are better—well, anyway, you'd *think* all this art-awareness points to a certain humanity in my father. Such is not the case. He wants these works, and especially some superb Japanese pornography from the Purple Phallus school of Edo Whorehouses, to go with his Tantric Hindu temple sculpture from Orissa, all that lingam worship, with horny Shivas and big-busted Parvatis creating the world—he wants them as spicy baits for his Hollywood studio scam, baits that might shimmer and blind the Beverly Hills vulgarians who think themselves connoisseurs of Orientalia and Hindu art. He has already salted away the freshest and most delicate impressions of Hiroshige's *Fifty-three Stations of the Tokaido* and Hokusai's *Thirty-six Views of Fuji*, including *The Great Wave*. All our forgers, by the way, are Japanese, artists of unsurpassed skill at imitation. Well, you two know the Japanese. It's only that Dad is an unadulterated psychopath and himself a Genius at imitation. And he loves his raunchy pictures of big pricks rising to a man's belly button—loves his bestiality, which I won't describe. That's him, Dad at his most human. And he's out to fill their Sundials with Moonlight.

Another idiom? Sidney asks.

Charm them blind. And lead them to grandmother's house, where he lies abed in granny's nightcap and a sheepskin jacket.

Gong sits back. May I suggest that you *don't* love your father?

I've forgiven him his horrors. Which is no easy task. What's more, I've seen him return from the dead more than once, and who knows what he'll do now? Ten years ago, standing in his living room, he suffered a fatal heart attack or aneurysm, or what seemed to be fatal. He fell to the rug. His heart stopped. Before Doctor Zeitgeist, his cardiosurgeon, who is nearly stitched to my father's side because of Dad's fear of a heart blowout, before the doctor could squirt some digitalis into it, my father's heart started up again. He'd been playing possum to test the doctor, and, *peripherally*, lying their dead, watching the good doctor.

Quite remarkable, Sidney says. Your father can stop his own heartbeat?

And start it again.

Gong says, We are in Hollywood?

No, Japan. So we are met at the airport by the board of directors of Mitsui and escorted to the Emperor's Palace where we inspect the royal gardens and golden carp, which attract and eat up all the evil spirits around the palace, before we get down to business at Mitsui headquarters. The Emperor, whom Dad greets with a *Hi, fella!*, is a marine biologist and, among other fish, keeps a pool of piranhas. Delighted, Dad gets on his knees, pulls up a sleeve and, before anyone can stop him, playfully plunges an arm into the Emperor's piranhas and, just as they pile up to his elbow as if gobbling a loaf of bread, he jumps back before even one bites him. The board members are shocked by his fun with the fish, but they really turn red when Dad blithely slips from his breast a slim silver pocket case inscribed to the Emperor that holds Baxter Toiletries' latest product, a set of multicolored monogrammed condoms ridged with hard, rough little raised feathers and pimples and slick with aromatic menthol and coconut oil. You will find this better than yohimbe! he tells the Emperor, who thanks him deeply, and then all take off for the business meeting, leaving the Emperor with his new clothes.

Meanwhile, the Japanese try to get past Dad's strange odors. These men would never be smelt dead with Baxter Toiletries' cheap scents. What's more, a gagging undercurrent comes from him, because Dad has an odor specific to psychotics. I don't know if it's called psychotics' odor, but it's musk something like evergreen jojoba oil mixed with heavy sex juices, quite addictive to women—his bed sheets and laundry basket overwhelm you. And Malaysian Lime can't quite paint it over. As far as I know, I don't have it as strongly—much to my wife's disappointment. She adores Dad's odor. She tells me, It's like he's always in season. And never think he's dead. He may still have a last shout in him.

I should mention our blood type. It's devastatingly rare. Every two months I give a pint and have it stored against emergencies, should either of us or my children need a transfusion. And with the family's occasional heart problems, I may need that blood, though Dad is past all that. By now I have three hundred pints stored around the world, wherever we might become ill or have an accident. Our blood cells have a surplus of adenosinetriphosphate in the mitochondria, too much juice from the power plant, you might say. This cellular supersaturation of metabolizing power-grains in the cytoplasm may account for a modest form of telepathy in our blood line, an electrolytic sensitivity to danger that lights up the whole family tree when any one of us goes into overload. This is not telepathy of words or images, but of the life-current binding the Wreath of Bihusi into one family, much like that shock when you spray one branch of poison ivy and kill the whole plant right down to its roots. As far as I know, it's generic to us. Maybe it's something like the homing instinct or any number of other group instincts that certain species share. Suddenly, in the middle of the night or at dinner or at work, my heart catches and begins pumping hard and somehow we all know which one of us is experiencing hypothalamic shutdown or some psychic violence. And it takes your breath away. Do you have a religion, Sidney? Ancestor worship? Socialist realism? Jung?

What? Oh, please. Maybe you joke?

No, I'm interested.

But I'd rather not say. An answer will only color your responses, whether you want it to or not. Why? Are you religious?

Oh, very much so, in our fashion. I have faith in power, Sidney. I trust power. Power from my family most of all, and power from Ahuramazda, the Sun. I feel its heat rise through me like hot steam. And power from oil derricks, stock exchanges, banks, power from music, from art. I get spiritual and woozy when I tie one power cell to another, painting by painting, bank by bank, derrick by derrick, company by company. Also, I get power from grief. I know that my grief is a dry cell whose electrolytes will recharge and turn losses into a restorative energy, and give more light than before, more power. I have never lost anything that did not bring me back more power than before. Being open to pain and loss is a form of prayer. That's the surface of my religion. It goes deeper, down layer under layer, although it turns inside out what most humans call religion.

I got off on this because with us religion is both cellular and instinctual. Bihusi are born religious. Just as a turtle comes out of its egg with an instinct that tells it where water is, we are born with a scent for reality that binds us into a Wreath of divine remembrances built up in our cells over tens of thousands of millennia. You, perhaps, dream of heaven in the afterlife. We are already in that dream. You meditate to achieve the Now. We scent layer upon layer of the Now every waking moment. Where you have an abstract sense of time passing, I smell it cooking in the oven and feel its flow over my skin. This is a gift from the Sun. Well, there's much more to Ahuramazda—but back to Hollywood and Japan.

Think about money as a device, a tool. Don't think about it as having its own character or identity. At Harvard Business School they say if you come away with this one idea your Harvard education is complete: *the opportunity value of money.* Money is not only a means to a single end you may have in mind, it should be weighed as well for what it can do for you elsewhere. That's the opportunity value of money. If you put a million dollars into a fishing reel company, might you have used the money better elsewhere? What is your money's highest possible use? Big hitters, like Dad, weigh that thought instinctively while sweeping up the lesser investments we test.

The background on our Japan deal is this. At the end of World War Two my father put together the Marshall Plan in Germany and the MacArthur Plan in Japan. Each kept the Soviets out while he got tax breaks and took a commission from organizing each reconstruction project. And he got involved up to his ears in both economies. His big opportunity came when the Japanese thought they could stand alone and then orchestrated what would have been the biggest short sale in history.

I'm lost, Gong tells Sidney. I don't know what short sale is.

Tell her, Sidney says.

Okay. As simply as possible.

But I am not a Swiss, Gong says. I am a poor psychoanalyst. I know nothing about stock exchanges, especially in America. I'm already in over my head.

I'll be clear. There are three stock markets in New York and one in Chicago. They are exactly what they're called: Markets where buyers meet sellers through a go-between. It started way back when a group of men met under a tree on Wall Street to buy and sell interests in each other's companies. That's just what happens today, except its deals are bigger. The go-between takes a percentage of the sale and the markets record the action. Over time these go-betweens have gotten a lot smarter. A few hundred years ago the British common law created the idea of a *future interest*. In other words, you could do a trade today that actually takes place in the future. Say you make candy. You want to guarantee your wholesale customers a price for their purchases next year. You've got to know what next year's costs will be. So you and I make a deal. I agree to sell you your sugar next year at today's price. If by next year the cost of sugar goes up, I make less money when I deliver it to you. If the price of sugar goes down, I make more money, because your payment to me for the sugar delivery next year was set today. Some twists have come in, but that's how it works. That's called *futures*, the right to buy or sell an interest in the future at a price set today. In a short sale, the seller bets that the cost will go down and he'll deliver at a profit to himself. Short selling has a shady history and has added a good deal to the Kennedy wealth. When Dad reenergized Japan through MacArthur, Japan in turn was supposed to behave and follow Dad's lead. The Japanese were not unaware of Dad as a player in their recovery. Instead, they became bold, proud, and insulting, and chose to take a run at the American economy— and Dad. They went after the biggest short sale in history.

Now here's why Japan moves like an infantry squad, every body in lock step—with a rare sport now and then, the screwball who commits public seppuku.

Seppuku? Gong says. Suicide? Yes? Yes.

Gray clouds pile up under the Sun like Balkan banks and glide toward scatterage and loss.

You see the leaves on your lilies? I ask Gong, pointing.

Yes?

Each cubic centimeter of green leaf takes in two calories of heat from the Sun. Dad has measured it. If Sidi gets the Sun before I do, he'll charge you for those two calories. Dad and I plan to give all that heat away free. We'll charge only for power from our receptors.

Disbelief fills her. How can Sidi possibly charge for Sunlight?

Tell her, I tell Sidney. Tell her about the dew and the Moonlight.

Sidney sighs. Sidi has already leased the Moon from Allah, he tells her, and is charging,

Ah-ah! I say, that's enough. Don't tell her anymore. We'll get to that. Much of Japan's government and politics exist on myth. Japan is completely owned by a double handful of trading companies, run by nine men. Everything, from the global banks and auto makers, to the little osoba wagons selling hot spiced noodle soup to laborers, all wealth, all debt, is owned by the trading companies. The companies work both sides of the national balance sheet. The occidental has not yet learned to prosper on the debit or negative side of the global balance sheet as the Japanese have. Simply put, the Japanese make money from debt. This means that when they do something right, they are marvelously leveraged, they borrow a buck, they borrow eighty cents on the buck, they borrow sixty cents on the eighty cents, and so on. When it's going for them, they win big. But if it ever goes against them, they're finished. First the nine men directed all of Japan's banks to rewrite the national credit rules. You could get a hundred-year mortgage on your house. You could hock the land under your factory for more than the value of the factory. In short, credit was unlimited. Companies used this credit to buy shares of American businesses. They bought everything, as much as they could get, in every industry. Block after block of shares. Then, at a signal, all these holdings were dumped. This would drive down the prices of all the stock issues and scare the shit out of other investors who in their panic would unload their shares, drive the prices down further, and give the Japanese the opportunity to buy back everything at a fire sale. That, folks, is the opportunity value of money! Doesn't Sidi ever talk to you about this? Try to guide your investments?

I probably should not answer that question, Sidney says. So I won't.

Well, then I won't give you any advice either. One October night in 1987 Tokyo orchestrates a major dump. Americans and Europeans awake to find their blue-chip stocks under horrendous selling pressure. Investors panic and sell. The market drops by over twenty-five percent in one day. Had this been allowed to go on for two or three weeks, American industry would have dropped in value by eighty percent. Think of it. A Japanese sells a US share for a buck. Other investors see it go down and get out. When the value gets to twenty cents, the Japanese buys it back. The Japanese has just quadrupled his shares. Let's be clear: There's no slack in the earnings of these companies the shares represent. The companies are fine, strong firms. And now the Japanese buys back at twenty percent of the original price after scaring nearly everyone else out. The mighty Samurai sword of fear beheads the lily-livered Americans.

Gong blinks deep in thought at Sidney. Somehow, she says, I don't put this past them. Remember Pearl Harbor?

Sidney smiles. Yes, I do.

Well, I'm only *suggesting!* she says and eyes me to see if I've picked up Sidney's veiled tone.

Shall I go on? I ask. So Dad looks at this brouhaha, sees the game, and chooses to teach the Japanese better manners when using his money to stab their neighbor in the back a second time this century. As the market plunges, Dad buys. Buys more and more. He gets the greatest bargains since 1929. Bit by bit, he sucks up the shares that the panicky are selling and turns the market around. This means that the Japanese have to deliver their futures, their promised shares, at a price higher than what they sold them for. Say a Japanese buys at a buck, begins selling for ninety cents, keeps selling down to forty cents, Dad starts buying at about sixty cents, rides it down as the Japanese go on selling. Since Dad is buying it up, the price rises. The Japanese now have to buy back at eighty cents stock that they sold at forty cents or not meet their future obligations. They go broke.

Ah ha! Gong says. Good show, Dad.

But for several years, Gong, these bandits hide their losses. Keep giving more and more credit in hopes of somehow repairing things. They can't repair. Dad now owns all the shares the Japanese bought—*ta ta ta!*—but at far less than the Japanese paid. He takes in all of Japan's US holdings. Now they have to deliver! They come to Dad to buy shares for their buyers. But the law of supply and demand plugs in and the Japanese have to deliver stock at a higher price than they can realize from their buyers. They've bought a *lot* of stock. They've promised to deliver the stock to their buyers at a price fixed today. They bet that they could drop the price through the cellar, so that on the date of delivery the price would be lower than the price the buyer agreed to pay, and that they would keep the difference. Such stupid pride! Thinking they could do an end run around Dad. They got caught on the wrong side of the short sale. After Dad runs the price back up, they have to deliver shares to *him*, their intended victim, shares that cost them more than he'd paid. Well, that's what happened some time ago, but it's short sales today, folks, that are bankrupting Japan as I speak. Did you follow all that? Oversimplified, but you get it.

Oh, I think money talk is thrilling, Gong says.

Sidney says, Sidi bin-Bahram is seldom this interesting.

Ah, but there's that Nobel Prize for his verse drama about economics. It's not bad. *A dollar on the wind, beloved.* Seriously, I should think he'd be a knockout to talk with in private. That little thief is an untrustworthy bastard after my own heart. Dad and I both went to his wife's funeral.

That was ten years ago, Sidney says. Your relations have deteriorated since then?

Yes. But I hope you'll explain to him that I still respect his business sense. I know he's still a terror. But I'm sure that building that incredible mausoleum for his wife has mellowed him.

I'll tell him you hold no grudge. Please go on.

As a cherry on top of his profits, Dad decides to sell Mitsui his nearly defunct movie studio, a sale that will drive a psychic stake into Tokyo's heart. He does this to add insult to injury and truly humiliate them. He sells them a studio that they think has a major film inventory. But all those films have already been sold to television and the cupboard the Japanese buy is bare. But he does sell them a string of contracts for a stable of crazy managers and actors which costs them heavily to this day.

Wouldn't you think this was revenge enough? But Dad's not done sticking it to the Japanese. He owns a woman named Dolores Rand, from the Transvaal, whose great passion is South African currency. She loves to lay naked all covered with Krugerrands, big fat beautiful one-ounce gold Krugerrands. Her benchmark greed matches Dad's. She even thinks she can outsmart Dad though she works for him as his beard, or front woman. Sinuously, she comes to Dad as if for advice. Daddy Breedwolfe, she whispers, her eyes fluttering, the federal government wants to issue a secret investment. Oh? Dad says, speak up, my girl. Well, Dolores says, it's to finance global AIDS research in a way that avoids any self-righteous backlash. But, my friends, this secret investment, the pivotal fraud at the heart of her scam, does not exist. Dolores spells it out. Uncle Sam, she says, will offer to a limited number of wealthy elite players a superb investment opportunity. In five-million-dollar increments, these people are allowed to buy and sell a supersecret government bond. You have to buy *and* sell this bond every month and you receive a two-percent return when you buy and when you sell. When you buy, the government gives you two percent of five million, which is a hundred thousand dollars. When you sell, the government gives you two percent. You are guaranteed the two percent when you buy, when you sell, when you rebuy, when you resell, month after month! Now at four percent a month, that is forty-eight percent a year. However, you have to give half of your profits to the AIDS research group, giving you really a return of twenty-four percent a year. The golden hook is the assurance that you can't lose any money because you don't put up any cash. You go to your bank, buy a five-million-dollar Certificate of Deposit, and show that to the person who let you into the deal as proof of your wealth. You keep the CD, so your five million is never at risk. Your money never leaves your hands! What temptation!

Gong says, I smell a skunk.

Well, as a matter of fact, you should keep a cat. The smell of mouse urine under your porch is intense. I can smell it from here.

You can! Gong says.

Sorry.

We'll take that under advisement, Sidney says. So what happened with Dolores?

Too bad for Dolores! I laugh. Dad has seen this scam before and has worked it himself in Europe in the fifties when it was meant to "save" starving black Catholic orphans in Africa. Now Dolores smiles and reminds Dad of Ben Franklin's maxim, Money makes money and the money that money makes makes more money. The sweet thing puts the sugar in front of him and explains, as if to a child, her very seductive investment algorithm. The algorithm is that when you divide your compound interest rate into seventy-two, Daddy, the answer is the number of years it will take your principal to double. And under the investment which these people are buying, which earns them 24% a year, their five million becomes ten million in three years. Did you follow that, honey? Have I described it correctly? I think it's a very desirable investment, Breedwolfe, she murmurs, a forefinger pressed to her lips thoughtfully. Well, my friends, Dad hears The Roller coming. This scam is called The Roller because the heart of the illusion is the monthly rolling in and out. One puts the mark to sleep with the confidence that at no time is his money at risk. He holds his money in the form of a five-million-dollar CD still in his own hands. Once the mark is in place, he gets a monthly statement delivered by Dolores or her friends, an authentic-looking computer printout showing monthly profits. After two or three months, with income clearly building and the big CD still in the mark's hands, comes the sting.

Dolores leads Dad into this marvelous investment opportunity while asking for counsel and advice. Should *she*, little crinkle-eyed Dolores, get into this program? Perhaps *he* might like to get in. *Hm?* Dad lets her pet and pet him like her pile of Krugerrands. He actually likes Dolores, her blue eyes have a Dutch porcelain sparkle and her skin is made of money. Dolores lets Dad help her come up with fifty or so investors just from Beverly Hills and the movie business, then another one-hundred-fifty from all over Europe, the Middle East, and Asia Pacific. All told Dolores and her friends have about two hundred players. Now recall, these two hundred people have total trust and confidence that there's no risk. They hold their money in both hands. Don't they own and possess the Five-Million-Dollar CDs, with income already rolling in? Dolores's main business buddies are Robert Bakely, a Beverly Hills dentist, and Glenn McReynolds, a Beverly Hills plastic surgeon. Now here's the game. The doctors come in terror to the players. Somebody senior in the US Treasury Department has leaked the secret of the superinvestment to Chase, the global American bank, and Chase demands to be let in or paid off. If we let them in, the word will get out to every other big bank in the US probably within days. The best thing?—quietly pay off Chase to shut up and stay out. The plastic surgeon has already begun bargaining with Chase, and Chase, well, *will go away* for the Lehman Formula. The Lehman Formula is a commission schedule of five percent on the first million, four on the second, three on the third, two on the fourth to infinity. From the first million that the group of two hundred has invested Chase takes, let me repeat, five percent on the first million, four percent on the second million, three percent of the third, two percent of the fourth million to infinity, which means that they take one percent of every million after four. What's so sweet is that this is such a modest, even demure amount, while Chase stands there like a teenydeb twisting innocently. Pocket money! So you see, the magic is that the sucker watches and is reassured by his Five-Million-Dollar CD, while Dolores and her crew take their two percent of everything, with a hundred-fifty-thousand-dollar kicker on the first five million. But that presupposes that all they have are minimum investors who have put up only five million each. The reality is that it generates about a few hundred million, quick and easy.

That's what they'll get away with.

Now is this worth Dad's attention? Not as set up. So he improves it for her. But first he smiles to his back teeth and says, *Darlingk, darlingk, where have I seen this before?* Oh! in fact, I have run it myself for starving black Catholic orphans in Africa, poor things. Well, Dolly, you've shown me yours, now I'll show you mine. But mine is bigger! This is a great way to discipline Dolores, train her, and later bring her in as one of his runners. So Dad chooses to keep Dolores clean.

He shows her his spin on the sting. In her version, she, the dentist and the plastic surgeon come to the investors in a fake panic, telling them that word of this secret investment has leaked out to Chase, and Chase's silence *has to be bought!* That's going to cost two percent per mark. This under Dolores's program is the money that they plan to steal. Dad yawns as she tells him this and sighs, *Boring, boring.* He'll show Dolores how to grab the principal itself, the minimum five mill per mark. That's Dad's big improvement. This also shows how Dad operates: there are hundreds of billionaires around the world, but only one trillionaire. Only one player who reads his income in "googols." Well, with Sidi, now there are two. Here's how he grabs the principal. When the marks have been lulled by the sweet returns on their authentic-looking printouts, and are ready to be harvested, Dad persuades them to move their money from a CD to a bearer bond. Signals should go off in their heads, but as W.C. Fields said, You can't cheat an honest man but you can always swindle a crook. They ain't gonna get it back, their bearer bonds. His pitch is, Loan me the bearer bonds for 48 hours, I'll show them to the Secretary of the US Treasury, convince him that we are real, and he will short-stop Chase's run at us. But once Dad has his hands on them, the bearer bonds are gone. Bearer bonds are rich people's cash, like a ten-dollar bill but for five million, and it's cash with no name on it, no owner, no memory. Beautiful, beautiful cash. Dolores's game is that you steal a percentage of the principal. Dad's variation is that you steal the principal.

Look! I say. See that mouse under the left porch post? A good mouser would get that morsel in a minute.

Yes, yes, yes, Sidney says. Please go on.

This is how I become bagman, collect all the bearer bonds from two hundred donors, and hie myself to Vienna. Why Vienna? Because Dad and I know that *real* secrecy for offshore banking lies in Vienna.

Sidney cries, That can't be so!

Swiss banking secrecy is bullshit, doctor. So is Cayman's, and Panama's. For top secrecy surrounding black money, try Austria. Austria just doesn't advertise. When the movie people see they've been had, Dolores complains that she's been taken too. Now they need a fall guy. The dentist and doctor present themselves as gulled investors. And I, who have been the European runner for this mom-and-pop business, am painted as the architect. But knowing that I've run somewhere with the money, and proving it, are two different things. Still, my name's shit in the movie business. Meanwhile, Dad gets away with the total rakeoff by showing Dolores, the doctor and the dentist the doors to the federal prison in Atlanta, where major bad guys go. Dad's hands, of course, really are clean, though he offers me up to the victims to keep Dolores clean and show his concern for her well-being. Dolores has been the hook, who attracted the mark. All cons work in this fashion. A hook pulls in the mark, the dip takes the money, passes it to the cannon who fires it to a runner who takes it away. This is as formal as a jewel heist with a professor who does the layout, a safecracker, a wheelman, a fence and so on. This is the model and this is how Dolores did it. And I was the tailgunner who got blown away. Since then Dolores has been Dad's man in the picture business while the dentist has given Dad a free set of molar implants and the plastic surgeon keeps his jaw line firm. Also, Dad cottons to Dolores's Dutch-blue eyes and her fun rolling around bareassed on a million dollars in gold coins on her king-sized bed, and doing other things, all of which Dad attests to.

How about a snack? Gong asks.

Wonderful, I say. I think I'll use the room. Excuse me, Sidney.

I drop back a moment to let her get ahead, then follow crimson slippers and pleasing hips and psyche knot into the house. She guides me to a bathroom off the kitchen. I see a dining room and living room splashed with scarlet mallow-flowers and the pointed Chinese petals of large and showy but delicately rosy-red hibiscus. Vases of cool, fleshy tulips in mixed colors, blue, red, yellow, and white, stare at me with beautiful eyes. I scent from the walls jasmine and gardenias from an earlier day. The house smells hugely fresh with the kiss of life everywhere. Lucky Sidney! The bathroom has flouncy shower curtains with entwined red herons and a cram of toiletries and lavender scent that leave me feeling I've invaded my hostess's senses, if not her body.

I wash and take out my cell phone and call the owner/maitre d' at Les Armoires, a tiny hotel chain restaurant in Geneva and Zürich that has about twelve rooms and the best food in Switzerland.

Henri? This is Billy. You know the barrel of extra virgin Spanish olive oil in the cellar? Do me a favor, mon ami, and have a half-gallon of it delivered to Dr. Gong-Chang.

With great pleasure, Herr Baxter, Henri says. At what address? Eduardo will drive right out.

I join her in the kitchen as she pulls a prepared tray from the refrigerator.

Let me carry this, I say.

All right, since Helga's off shopping. She lifts a pitcher of cider. I'll bring this.

As we approach the lawn table I tell Sidney, I hope I'm not exhausting you two. My wife can't bear all this business talk. Taxes, politics, oil prices.

Have no fear, Sidney says. We are not bored.

Gong serves cider as a nutty, faint sourness rises from the tray's smoked salmon, dried beef shavings, aged Gouda, Swedish ambrosia, Appenzell Rass, Gruyère, pickled onions, and small saucers of yellow olive oil with slices of peasant bread. A second dish holds slices of coconut orange cake with white icing and slivers of orange rind in the cake. A tray to ravish.

Hard cheeses no good for you, Sidney says. I stick to fish.

Sheer delight, I say. I may faint from the smells alone. Did you make the cake?

I did. Don't eat it if you are dieting. It's not very healthy. But once in a while we forget the calories. The Gouda is *really* old.

Oh, I can tell. I collect cheeses. Uh, by scent. Identifying world cheeses is a hobby.

You don't collect the cheeses themselves? she asks.

No need to. Let a small sip of this fresh apple cider wash out the tastes between cheeses and I'll remember each one. My favorite is a simple cottage cheese made from unpasteurized milk of West African water buffalo. That is a cheese with Africa on its mind. At breakfast it refreshes you like a mountain spring. I'll be happy to send you a gallon.

Unpasteurized? Sidney says and waves the offer aside, but Gong says, No, no, Sidney! That would be very kind of you. A cheese with soul? Irresistible!

I recall scenting olive oil on Gong's lips earlier this morning. Dipping a piece of bread into the nutty oil becomes a dream come true.

I know you probably think poorly of Dad, but he's mellowed. Mightily! One summer day—this is not about the language of money—when I was eight or nine we took a trip to the Carpathians and to Mother's home town of Turda in the Rumanian province of Cluj. On an earlier visit home, father married my mother, who is now Angela Magdalena Giurgiu Bihusi (she refused the name Baxter) but then was thirteen, and he brought the whole Giurgiu clan to Paris as his personal retinue. I was born shortly thereafter. Soon we were moving about the globe to father's homes, though, of course, being father's child, I am a US citizen.

As I say, we went home when I was eight or nine and were spending a day in the woods, Dad and Magda and I. Dad told me to go off and catch crabs in the stream and turn a few hours to profit by selling the crabs in Turda, which was now undergoing a famine. Later, as is well known, my father became a beloved associate of President Nikolae Ceausescu, kept the paranoid megalomaniac on his payroll, and he'd suggest ever more riotous plans to feed the President's mania for gaudy architectural fantasies and his demand that "my people" help raise all the great pillars and lintels he needed, while Dad supplied materials at a cost that bled the nation and brought famine without end. But Dad and Ceausescu did finish the supremely grandiose Palace of the People, the totally useless but longest building ever built, too big to be heated. Dad made sure that Ceausescu paid off every penny of the national debt, since the debt *was* to Dad. You may have seen films of orphanages Dad helped fill with diseased, starved, often brain-dead babies and fly-covered shrunken children caged into cribs, many of them sucked dry by his plasma labs, which delighted the eyeteeth of Elena Ceausescu, who detested seeing a drop of blood wasted and going unsold.

However, this great day in my life I speak of is before Dad had Ceausescu take over the country. We are in the woods and I am crabbing and finally tire of the stream and go running about. Suddenly through flashes of Sunlight I come upon my father stretched naked on a picnic table, lying on his hairy spine, and my small but dazzlingly beautiful young mother bullying him for his endless talk about gain. *Money, money, money, Alexandru! Always money! Oh my God, my heart cries out, where are the years of my youth? You sonofabitch!* And then, my God, he jumps up on the picnic table, clears his throat warningly and strides about nude, a colossal, naked Adam, his seven-foot frame staring down from far above at the small barefoot she-wolf below him, breathing deeply and rolling his great, overlapping biceps and flexing his forearms and fingers, and from the table he leaps upward to a tree limb, lands on it sitting, away from Magda while she climbs onto the table and strides about, hectoring him from below. I stand thunderstruck by his great, naked leap, the sight of his long body stretching upward, his pale, hairy breast and stomach, and legs snapping up to his chest as he lands on the limb, and by the drama of mother calling him back. But he looks away from her and gazes above at a squirrel running from him. All right, she says at last, and walks about the picnic table stripping off her clothes. Small but muscular, she stands below him, naked as Eve, her loosened black hair waist length and her crotch shockingly thatched with black hair bushier than any ever seen on a human. *Catch me, bastard!* she cries and leaps upward, surprising him. But his arm grips her waist and draws her to him. His smile spreads, godlike. She waits, intent, her heart slowly unveiling its bond to him. A whimper rises through her. Softly, he nips her neck and the two of them begin sniffing each other's muzzle and hair and genitals, yipping and softly barking, while his wolf prick shoots out of its sheath, wiggling red and wet, far smaller in girth than a human's but richly over endowed with quivering nerve ends. At last she lays him backward on the limb, climbs over and straddles him, then lowers herself, her voice now charged with pleas, *Come, my love, I suck you up into me, my arms long for you, I caress you, I kiss you, you are my life's dream! I shall care for you to the end of my days!* And as they couple in Eden she rocks and rocks on him while he drools and moans on the heavenly bow, fondling her girlish breasts and, struggling, ecstatic under her slender hips, lamenting his surrender to the power and darkness of her black, black eyes.

His soul blisters with love for her. For their first ten years they howl with rapture, he barks and growls and whimpers at her feet, licks her ankles, mocks at gruffness, plays the crazy Transylvanian wolf to her cowering Red Ridinghood. But at twenty-three, her own psychosis kicks in and all hope of joy in marriage turns to mud. Magda begins mysterious pursuits Dad cannot fathom. She runs about the Jungfrau chalet in a flurry, hides meat bones everywhere, hurls the kitchen pots like a poltergeist, and shrinks onto her bones, her black hair matted and sprouting like yarn. Dad loves this dismal madwoman more than ever, ordering up dresses and bringing in couturiers and milliners for her, but unless laughing and murmuring to herself while tugging lifelessly at an elbow, she remains mute, her doll-sized black pupils a blank Raggedy Anne's.

Tour d'Argent, that's the fabled Paris restaurant, the one where, after Callas's *Tosca* debut, Madga disrobes in the restroom and descends the grand circular staircase wearing a Chinese scarf floating about her waist and shimmering with candlelight upon breasts bare as the flawless Bihusi Rose. An aura of gold clings to her, and Dad and Sunny Jim (that's me) sit dazzled by her Fairyland. Childish delight lifts him from the table but as he comes toward her she raises her long nails with a warning hiss and gives him a sleek, knowing smile. He seats her and slips his tomato-pale dinner jacket over his childbride's dainty shoulder blades, hides her breasts behind the massive and tasseled menu, then sits in cummerbund, ruby studs and tie, shooting his shirt sleeves with a proud sweep as he lifts his menu. I'm shocked, not having seen my mother's breasts since the woods. Soon the maitre d' arrives, a pleading quiver in his brow, but Dad's joy disarms him. Brilliantly alive, Dad orders himself a double snifter of cognac topped with Dom Perignon, (all from grapes! he cries to the sommelier), and for Magda, slivovitz, the mild plum brandy that takes her back home to Turda. Such a wild thing, she sits there ruling the roost and under the tablecloth thrusts her hand up his leg as he smashes the crust on his *crème brulée*. Spoon to mouth and crunching crusty custard, Dad feels a rush crash through his joints. His eyes flutter as he whispers to me, This is a complete dining experience!

We sit nibbling cheeses and crunching pickled onions.

Just as this tray you have set for us is a complete dining experience, I tell Gong.

Almost, Sidney says.

Gong Li laughs nervously and breathes in the bright morning freshness.

I dip a pinch of bread into oil. The aroma fills my mouth. I taste her oily lips on mine.

No, I say. It's complete.

Replenishment floods me. I go on.

I doubt that I've told you this, but Dad owns much of the Fifth Arrondissement and later sold its own parcel to the restaurant when he tired of the chef's tuna with raspberry sauce.

The day comes when my beleaguered dad turns to Dr. Simon Paracelsus, perhaps you've heard of him? the Singing Shaman of London?—to cure Angela Magdalena's condition, though he knows that she'll mutter monstrous secrets about Bihusi males and their sheathed and hairy penises.

Oh, we've heard Paracelsus on tape, Gong says. Singing to the British Psychoanalytic Association. Frankly, he sounds like a rabbi. What did he recommend?

He treats her as the downy angel she still seems, though she's turned thirty. Don't forget that Dad is genetically driven as a devastator of any flock of investors weaker than himself, and that leaves no one out. So a loony all-powerfulness blooms in his blood. But when Magda finds herself falling in love with the Singing Shaman, eating and sleeping on Doctor Paracelsus's Viennese couch, the colossus of the Bihusi feels paralyzed, powerless, disemboweled, and castrated before the song of the psychic troubadour. The tabloids ask: Is this Splitsville for the Baxters? Dad retires in a beclouded twilight to London's Kennel Club and by day under a mound of boardroom meetings crushes his great torment—that open wound he licks nightly until driven into dreams his heart sleeps for an hour or two. Will Magda's latest madness ever pass? As you both know, the canine heart fills the whole body and becomes a bolt of love on four legs. Yet lupine love is even more powerful and disorienting, far more so than half-hearted human efforts to bind to another. If anything can be called eternal love it is my father's for Magda. His heartbreak swallows the Moon. Serving her wholly, he has surrendered to Magda the dominant role in their marriage and when that snaps he becomes wild by day, slaughtering companies, chewing the inner organs out of chief executives. His stress twists upward and carries along with it burst cartels and savaged countries. Through spies, he keeps unwavering vigil at the shaman's door. Exhaustion harries him. One day he turns to me and sobs, *My name is Ozymandias, king of kings, look upon my works ye mighty and despair!* That is my introduction to the English romantics. But when all feels hopeless and his heart lacks words he has a uniquely flexible intelligence. Strangely, he comes to look a bit like Mother. His muzzle molds itself to her soul. A certain fugitive furrowing of her eyebrows becomes his. Tics in her smile. Gnawing his thumbnail as she does. A yearning darkness fills his glance, as it fills hers, the world's well lost and no longer worth the game.

Does he seek out my child-mother to slake an unknown, an unadmitted hunger to be human by having someone on Earth to serve? You may think him hungry to be fully, well, semi-human at least. Maybe he's seen too many movies. I'll tell you, when he runs about naked on a full Moon, the sheer joy or melancholy of his far-carrying howls thrills my spine. No urge to be human can match this. Didn't *she* bring excitement, a paprika into his life he'd never know merely from owning Earth? He must own at least one heart as well. When I come along, I do not truly enter his heart, though he mockingly calls me Sunny Jim. I am, such as I am, to be trained as his inheritor and to handle his businesses with icy smile. But I lack a certain weaselish, wolverine urge to bite off balls. Meanwhile, Dad bugs the shaman's office and hears song by song the singing shrink pluck out her heart and caress it in his palm, *I wonder who's kissing her now* and *The purple dust of twilight time steals across the meadows of my heart.* So Dad starts writing her love letters, and one especially I can recite from memory:

I am the dog of dogs which is Magda's, let her mouth shower me with kisses and let my tongue rush over her face and lick her neck with delight. She summons me to her palace and I run after her fragrance. I yip and bark and snuggle about her knees. Her breasts are wine, they are two doves held in cashmere. She is beautiful, her eyes and hair are dark as the goatskin tents of Cluj, where she was the brush-tailed fox who raided the grapes of Turda, whose vines have tender clusters sweet as the breasts of my beloved. This is my little fox, in whom I am well-pleased, and who thrashes through the cornfield with her tail on fire. I present my backside to her and she nips at my grapes. My bride's breasts have only just budded. Her couch is strewn with blossoms. She has nipples of sweet cream and cannot rest at nightfall without my kisses. My beloved awaits me under roof beams of cedar and ceilings of fir. Among maidens she is a lily among thorns. The voice of my beloved! She comes dancing upon the mountains! She leaps the hills like a young deer, she is a hart at the water brook where I lead her to drink. No fruit has ever tasted as sweet as my beloved's lips pressed to my teeth, her kiss is spring rain that refreshes and chills not. I faint with love as her teeth close on my neck. I fall on my back and turn my whole being up to her, her left hand grips my stones and her right hand fondles me. Now I sniff at her hairy diadem. The jewel of her lotus opens to me, the bride receives me, and the voice of the dove is heard throughout all lands of the Earth. I have entered the cleft and am inside and pluck at my beloved's harp-strings. She is full of figs and sweet scents. I am a wild goat grazing on her hills. Rise up, my beloved! Your eyes are on me, and the day breaks and all shadows burn away! Your lips are a split pomegranate, your breath is cinnamon and clove. You are a garden of spices and hung with orchard fruits. Let me blow through your garden like the soft South Wind and press out your spices. Oh, I have eaten of the honeycomb and I am heavy with the dews of the night. Of all the daughters of Turda she is the most ruddy, her lips bloom with the juice of raspberries, her hair blazes black as a crow's plumage, and her belly is a heap of wheat. Return O daughter of Turda that I may gaze on you again!

My God! Gong says. He's a lyric Genius.

He thinks Sidi is better, I say. He keeps *The Profit* by his bedside. *When you earn earnestly you rise to meet in prayer those also earning at that very hour and the world becomes a dawn prayer of earning, for earning refreshes more bountifully and is more beautiful than pleasure, and too much pleasure is an offense to earning and the sweet music that comes from earning even as the bee gathers pollen for honey from the flower. For earning is wheat ripening in the noon Sun and pleasure only a faint light in the field.*

I can't read bin-Bahram or Joyce, Sidney says.

I look at Gong. A shrug and grimace say that her soul shuts down with Sidi bin-Bahram.

Did your father's letters move her? she says.

I think they raised a smile, I say. Not just a poet, he's serious, purposeful as a spear, and moves straight into Magda's heart. Where the Singing Shaman is something of a lyrical quack, Dad presents himself as studious, focused, thoughtful, and full of ideas. He tells her that the new wolf blood-cell being created by his molecular biologists at Wolfington Labs on Arpeggio Farms flattens the offerings of Paracelsus. This all-purpose new cell, based on enzyme behavior with proteins added to the adenosine triphosphate, with genetic reshuffling, may cure every known wolf disease, especially rabies, though it yet has no human use. Can it make wolves immortal? Let's not go too far. With some hopeful test results from Wolfington tucked into his database, he dances in on the Singing Shaman, an alpha wolf recovering territory he has sprayed. In all this Dad remains pure, psychotic wolf and only smiles and scrapes so that he may pass among men as freely as Mother Hubbard gowned in sheepskin and woolly nightcap as she begs for food or for Red Ridinghood's grandmother. Truth is, among men he has no natural enemies, either by race, species or the hierarchies of world economies. Welcome sweeps over him in Zaire, up the Amazon, or strolling through the Chicago stockyards. When you meet him you know he's too tall to have enemies and is at the top of the food chain and a unique specimen with its own outsized appetites and a lone sense of foraging. This giant can't be thought as a *human* enemy, whereas humanoid psychopaths like Saddam or Hassad or Idi would be eyed sidewise in any foreign country. His great personality split comes with Magda, who awakens his tail-wagging, his kissing and licking, lowered shoulders, back roll and squealing for a hard rake of her nails, all of which he does at home. Yes, Dad makes all the big decisions, but love for Magda wells upward as pure pleasure, nothing barred. Among humans he does find his innate lupine friendliness useful. Ah, you two didn't know that wolves are friendly? Not to be tamed, of course, but friendly. As I've said more than once, he never looks a human directly in the eye but always just past. With Dad that is both real and an imitative friendliness, and he will even stand off from a fallen company while humans nose about it. But I admit, you might see him smile unsuitably and even hop around while someone is suffering, their pain passing him by completely. He has a nice smile, but deadly. Has he no redeeming trait? Well, he's a *noble* psychopath. Proudly Rumanian! And with good reason carries himself like a king. He *is* king of a very lonely pack with very few members. He trusts no one, with good reason. He sees most humans as childish, fawning jackals and fights against crossbreeding or the genes of his offspring being thinned by jackals. Becoming a homebody jackal was never his plan, or even possible. Never limp in his presence.

Just then I spy a chocolate Lab, a bitch not fully grown, leap a fence on the villa terraced above the Changs' home and rush toward us. I can tell simply by her hellbent gait that she spies the swans and as a water dog feels the genetic tug to retrieve any fowl afloat.

Oh, oh, here comes Greta, Gong says.

I leap up and rush to the sedge. Drop to all fours, roll over, and wave my limbs, my bare neck inviting death or friendship. The surprised retriever hears my attractive male whines and soft howls and stops to look over this strange, clothed being with limbs pawing the air and neck bared in canine welcome. Her muzzle lowers over me. Not looking her straight in the eye, I see, peripherally, large chocolate ears, powerful, clean-cut jaws, and yellow eyes as her serious black nose sniffs my muzzle. I give off my wolf smell strongly. The confused dog barks in friendship, her tail whipping her sides so hard she almost knocks herself over. I grab Greta's neck playfully and give her a fast lap. The Lab presses cold muzzle to muzzle with me, whimpering on her paws. We both scent at once a ground squirrel and fill with eagerness as it races by fits and starts up the near chestnut and scampers over a limb. Oh, if only that peabrain rodent were in *our* territory! We whine and scent in the grass a whole grid of paths where the squirrel has passed earlier. Then we both get a whiff of the pissy field mice under the Chang's house and want to jump up and chase them down. Greta trembles, urging me to join her for a quick sniff under the Chang's porch. *Come, come!* she barks. We both feel bonded to the world with wordless intelligence of being, bonded to the sky, to the message-carrying breeze, with the electric grass the ground bass of existence as an utter absence of mystery radiates from us to infinitude. Such sensations, overflowing with promise, are a kiss without questions. When open to it, natural beauty shocks me to the core. The fluffy young bitch, just coming into season, hopes that I have an erotic interest in her, her head flattens into the grass with intense shyness but her tail-wagging signals, *Keep asking, you want, I want, nip my tail, let's run off together! I like you!*

I hear Sidney's head thinking as he comes toward us, a kind of branch cracking slowly afar or voice ringing in a sewer pipe. Sidney's fingers lock under Greta's collar.

We'd better get her back home, I say. Or she'll empty the lake of all its birds.

This has happened before, Sidney says.

Yes, Gong says. Greta is beautiful but dangerous to wildlife. Let her herd sheep.

I will take her back, Sidney says, and give Otmar and Lisa a good Swiss thrashing for letting her loose. We don't want blood tracked all over our lawn.

Oh, she wouldn't draw blood, I say. She's a retriever.

Greta looks back at me, heartbroken and whining. *Aren't we friends? Can't we play? Bring me your sexy scent again!*

I squat, watching, adding my look of mourning to her tail-dragging.

Well, it might be nice, lying side by side with Greta in the firelight. Chasing a few mice and spiders. Snacking out.

I sit with Gong as Sidney hustles the bitch uphill.

She says, You shocked the hell out of me, jumping up like that and falling down. Greta's really a very mild, even-tempered dog. But all spirit!

Tell Sidney, I say.

She leans toward me. That probably wouldn't help.

I'm sorry I'm here only for one day.

Who knows? You may need to return.

I say quietly, That would be wonderful.

I am so eager, Gong says, to see The Spear. When I was twelve I was given a 300-power Swiss microscope that peered into the smallest things. I took up insect-collecting and thought of becoming an entomologist. But at sixteen I read Jung's *Two Essays on Analytical Psychology* and found myself peering into the collective unconscious and seeing the archetypes emerge. So much more interesting than bugs, putting the microscope to the psyche. What will I see when I hold The Spear?

I shrug. Who can say?

How will I know it's true?

How do you know the collective unconscious exists? I ask. You don't. You only have a corroborative fantasy shared by Jungians.

So will you share any fantasy The Spear brings?

How can I tell her that I already *am* sharing a fantasy The Spear has brought me?

You will have no doubt, I tell her, that I share your fantasy.

She smiles, then turns forlorn. But what *is* fantasy?

I think it produces very tangible things, I say. Brooklyn Bridge, the pyramids, Beethoven's piano sonatas. Fantasy breathes and becomes a dream that rises out of a block of marble. The Sun itself was once a fantasy when some kind of incredible yearning within the condensed darkness of space sent out the fire-dream of Ahuramazda and gave it the power to create creatures through which Ahuramazda can watch herself and double her own existence, just as a mirror doubles the light from a bulb or a window.

She looks at me as if waking from a long sleep. You have brought up an archetype!

Ahh! I shook your tree, huh?

I have not heard that idiom.

When you love someone's peaches, you shake her tree.

I see. She reddens, and turns to Sidney, clearing her throat as he sits.

Did you thrash Otmar and Lisa?

He shakes his finger. I smiled, he says. I was the soul of patience. I waved my anima before them. That sent an even stronger message than anger.

Very keen of you, Sidney, I say, knowing he has failed to train his neighbors with the sharp looks and withdrawal of affection they need.

Gong and Sidney fall silent, waiting for me to go on.

Dad deals around the world, it matters little where he's at. While in London he keeps pawing over companies and marking industries with a squirt of piss. He knows that if you own fifteen percent of an industry, you really own as well fifteen percent of any company in that industry. Working like this from the top down, you control companies you don't yet own, or even need to own if you have a lock on the industry. Does Dad want or need Allegheny Airlines? He does not, since he already sets rates worldwide. This is the way he works.

His double agents, celebrated analysts whose public responsibilities are to evaluate companies and markets but who work privately for him, filter throughout the financial exchanges. One woman, Glynda Gold, a stock analyst on TV, works wonders for Dad. Glynda'll choose a market, say the airline industry, and then singles out for fine study the most powerful, profitable airline. For the public she'll judge the balance sheets, profit and loss statements, which are a snapshot of how the company is doing, and so on, and for Dad she looks into the executives. What do they own? What do they owe? How bright are they? How critical to the success of their current organizations? Glynda brings Dad a dossier on the firm under study that is far more complete than anything IRS, NSA, CIA, KGB or competitors have on this company. Nothing's denied her, nothing's kept secret, because the principals of her target companies believe she's there to help boost their stock. She and Dad know she's really there to kill. Once she has singled out for him the key men, or women, Dad picks up a controlling interest in a smaller, less profitable, almost competitive airline. Once Dad controls the weaker outfit, he pursues the names given him by Glynda. Traveling executives will get phone calls late at night in their hotel rooms around the world and offers will arise out of the shadows. A confidential meeting is set up, perhaps in a private dining room in Basel. The target receives first-class airline tickets, hotel reservations, and lots of cash strapped in a rubber band. Just to meet, only to meet. Deals are done, arrangements made, employment contracts signed. All secretly. After Dad, with Glynda's help, gathers his executive team, pilfered from the strongest company, one of his runners throws an elegant luncheon, maybe at Harry's, for all the airline analysts. The announcement of the new, proven golden management group is made. They're led in. And the analysts all go back to their offices and tout Dad's airline. I mean, look at the team he has playing for him. When his stock takes a happy ride, Dad pulls out his investment dollars, keeps the appreciated dollars in the form of stock in his portfolio, and he now has a sizable investment that as a practicality has cost him nothing. See, he buys control at five bucks a share. By the time the cart and pony show is over, the shares are at least at fifteen dollars. Punch line: *He* now controls the airline that has the population of superexecutives, since he looks at the *man*, not the *money*.

This is simple, but we should know that in addition to Glynda, who is one of the world's great thieves, Dad's lawyers and accountants are all over this process like bugs. Glynda, meanwhile, destroys a company and rises as a sacred monster seen regularly on television, simpering through what secretly is a commercial for what will be her own company. She's had a lot of surgery and looks like innocence itself. Figures drip off her tongue like molasses. Dad often did one of these ploys once a week or so. As I speak, Dad and I also have a large, famous accounting firm that in reality is very much like our golden Glynda. The public purpose of our CPAs is supposedly to give accounting services for clients. Their real purpose is to take a first cut at all deals being proposed to Dad by Glynda and her pals. Before Glynda can even get in to see Dad, she has to run her idea past the CPA firm. The payoff for the CPA firm is that in the end all of Dad's companies become their clients. You need short cuts to make trillions—mere buying and selling will never do it. A little game we run secretly in conjunction with the IRS and the Courts, which is too dangerous for me to spell out, gives Dad the handiness to increase his money geometrically. Now he gets enough to take a run at his greatest project ever: the Sun.

Well, dangerous secret or not, I'm not despairing, Gong says. I shouldn't say this. But that's just *business*. These games are just games. It's not like the plasma labs.

Oh, people get hurt, Sidney says, looking at me.

Yes. Many widows, I say.

Are the plasma labs still going? Gong asks.

Oh, yes. They perform a service in Third World countries.

You aren't killing people any more? she asks.

I can't say. We lost Baxter Blood Banks to Sidi bin-Bahram. Somehow I feel that Sidi has not upgraded Dad's old practices. Ask him about it, Sidney.

Sidney says nothing.

Please do, Gong says.

Well, that's how it is, I say. Everyone tries to hit on Dad. He has ties in Corsica, Palermo, and Osaka, as well as in the Teamsters Council in the States. Let's go back. In the thirties Japan was after steel from the Third Avenue elevated they needed to build their battleships. Dad owned the shipping company that would transport the steel to Japan. Now there are no good guys in this business, Sidney, let's be clear. There are only bad guys and tougher bad guys. The Japanese crime cartel, the Yakuza, have the Japanese dock workers in their pocket and want to dip into Dad's pot for themselves. Dad takes me to Tokyo to show me the "tea houses" he controls in the Edo district. We arrive in the early evening and check into the Imperial. The Yakuza have already got a message to Dad: he plays their game or the steel won't be unloaded. Our bags are handled by the doorman and we go off to Maxim's for dinner and then to see the Kabuki dancers. When we return, Dad picks up our keys at the desk and we go up to our corner penthouse. Dad opens the door and as we step in we see that a door to the adjoining penthouse is open. A naked Japanese woman sits on a bed, a silk kimono around her waist. I'm shocked. Dad grunts, giving a small smile, and pushes me aside. He goes straight through the open door and closes it behind him. That's when I hear bodies colliding, and then a horrid tearing and rending arise, and snarls and snapping such as I've never heard and then something hits the door. I sit in a Louis Quatorze, stiff, listening. Then Dad slips back into our rooms, saying, Let's get some sleep. He's unmarked, unruffled. And so to bed. As I lie awake, Moonlight turns the room green and I remember this strange snarling at some earlier time in my life. Was it from my mother's bedroom? No, it was from the maid's.

Gong asks, Who is this woman?

The Yakuza hope to get tight with Dad through a whore. But I heard him on the phone tell someone, This is not the way to do business with me. I'm not interested in your games. If you want to play, I have my own muscle. By the way, I expect you to liquidate whoever planned this little fiasco. I am not to be mugged and I can't work with people this stupid. Now let's meet tomorrow and settle this. You can come here. I won't bite.

You see, Dad does not catch his prey by lying in ambush, like a cat, or stealing up close to it, and making a sudden spring. Not at all. He runs it down in open chase. Everyone sees the trading on the boards. Once a leading company sees Dad buy a controlling share of a weaker competitor, it knows that blood will fly, since he is fast, ferocious, gluttonous, and has an iron will with immense financial endurance for the battle. He does not have partners, but he does need helpers, gofers, spies and so on that form a pack whose sheer will can take down the largest insurance elk or automotive bison. Not only full-grown companies fall to him. Quite young companies that can barely count up to five are favorite dishes. He may look tame while out dining. Or merely dreaming in a lounge chair at the Kennel Club. But never touch him when his eyes are closed. He snaps. And will eat anything. Strangers should not trust him.

He disappears and reappears by magic. You may think he's *not* here, but that's an illusion. He creates a sense of absence at will. Where's Breedwolfe? He was right here, then pops up in Liechtenstein or Geneva, then is sighted here in Zürich driving down the Bahnhoffstrasse. You know that the one qualification for sainthood in the Catholic Church, one that does not need investigation, is bilocation, the ability to be in two places at the same time? Without fail, Dad's victims feel disturbed, panicky, even hallucinatory—is he stalking them? He keeps them sleepless and fatigued. His stealth is uncanny, he blends into Earth. *Your* grip on reality turns to grease and sweat. You want to fall on your back, bare your neck to him, beg for pity. You have no idea how foreign the mere idea of pity is to him. Between courses at the Dolder, he can drop you into a decade of major melancholia. You will not be susceptible to treatment because he shares your bed and his long tongue nightly seeks you out and licks your nerves raw. You can't eat, you lose weight, you shake and tremble. Feel dull, listless, worthless, guilt-ridden, tearful, brooding, and irritable, can't think or stay focused, obsess on suicide and burial. Health fades, you're easily startled. Delusions of child abuse arise, since you now have power only over children. You dream of great tidal waves and earthquakes, and the end of the planet. You feel penniless whatever you earn, whatever you own. You grieve over love, your dimming sexual attractiveness, your lack of heart to keep up friendships. You feel infected with rabies. You have the Breedwolfe Blues.

I jump up and walk about the flagstones, forefinger flicking my hair back.

My God, I say, I feel it just talking about him. I need to gather myself. Every time I think about his mind games I get weird.

I sit, my brow in my palm.

I'm all part of this. Gofer, errand boy, worse—I had to learn the ropes before he took me upstairs with him.

Would you like something? Sidney asks. A Swiss white?

No, no. No alcohol, thank you. All right, I'm better.

Gong rubs my hand. You'll feel better getting rid of all this.

Maybe so. Well, I can't be in Dad's mind, thank God!, but as the first California fields of thousands of windmills begin to store energy from the wind, Dad begins building his big plan, bringing ideas together for his push on the Sun. Already he'd urged Kennedy more deeply into the space program. His idea: if wind, why not the Sun? First, Wolfington Labs must perfect a blue, short wavelength laser beam for compressed transmission of power. His secret council, the Boardroom of the Sun, does plan-and-layout for Bihusi Sunbeams, Dad's personal space program. But this push demands even more wealth than Dad has. He sets out with a vengeance to gather for Bihusi Sunbeams every penny, every erg of financial power he can from the world's money markets. He'll own Earth with cash, credit, and oil, but hopes to own and move it into the near future with Sun-power. So he buckles down to sweep up absolutely everything already at his fingertips that he doesn't yet own.

I ask Gong, Is Dad at last becoming an altruist? Is he doing this for Magda? These are not mean goals in his eyes. Sun-power *is* altruism of sorts, though concern for others usually doesn't cross his mind. Is his new ploy to try a little tenderness?

I doubt it, Gong says. Why is he doing it?

I think he wants to rise above life and death, and face rebirth in the Wreath of Bihusi with Promethean grit and power. Doesn't all organic life come from the Sun? Perhaps the secret of organic life can be learned along with mastery of the wolf blood-cell. Dad at heart doesn't believe in any God the world knows, although he has two, the second being Ahuramazda, or the Sun. His first sense of God is family. Even as Bihusi are a psychic Christmas tree that lights up when danger threatens, Dad and I have as well a soul-memory of our race. We can see faces in our bloodline back through countless generations to pre-human times, before man infected Earth with low cunning and stupidity. Our family is a higher race of Genius. Yes, we have our gains and losses as a race, but our intelligence is the cream of Earth's essence, and we are now the new Prometheans who will steal power from the Sun. Our destiny, Dad thinks. He actually has a spiritual program in mind, a rival program to that held by the jackals' religions. Though he does admire the Mormons, sort of, he far more admires the Zoroastrians, though their Sun-worship does not go far enough. He admires them enough to steal some of their images for the Boardroom of the Sun and even place Zoroastrians, who were called Persians when he recruited them and now are Iranians, as well as certain Parsees of India, in the highest seats of his council.

In a way, Dad has nowhere else to turn but to the Sun, since he disdains the Great Jackal Gods who enthrall mankind. There can be no lasting serenity for him without a higher purpose. After his second trillion, something in him stopped growing. He needs a higher power. He does at times feel like the walking dead and great hunger overcomes him. *Give me more, give me more! I have a life but I don't know what to do with it!* One day, he watches the Sun rise from the Sahara and thinks of himself as the parched desert and Sun as pure energy, and a billowing surge of spirit burns through him. It's a spiritual rebirth, a recharging that will last him the rest of his life. His sense of personal power redoubles. He feels worth four trillion. He chooses to believe in the Sun. But he's no Buddhist who prays for the happiness of all living beings. Never think that. He's all spirit, but not as the world knows it.

He had a transfiguring experience on the Sahara? Sidney asks.

Yes! Gong says. So, how is he spiritual?

He's happy! Happy as a pup with power over the world. With few lapses, he's almost always happy. Bright-eyed, bushy-tailed. He tried to teach me, lead me down his spiritual path. And despite the river of blood his great gains cost, I find myself loving my father with joy, not simply as my parent. He's gobbling down the world like an apple pie and yet the old wolf seeks a higher power. Amazing! Three times daily, rain or brightness, he falls to his knees on a rug of woven gold and speaks silently with the Sun. Do I think him false as tin in his new spiritual program? Oh yes. Companies left and right lie beheaded, with the Head of Dad screwed on in place of bloodied chief execs. So how can I fight this rising power of love my bandit dad draws from me? You have to remember a disarming shyness or timidity in the way he carries his head or his amber eyes sneak up for a peek that won't upset you and that show something innocent or even angelic under his skin. All his evil actions spring from his outlaw status since birth. We distrust gypsies whose heavy garlic smell and social need to steal offend us. They're born horsethieves. But after a thousand years as outlaws it's their conditioning, their nature. Thievery's their blood, their souls dance to it. And if you're born a wolf, you're not a housebroken little Pekinese.

But, Gong says, you said earlier that he had dark moments.

Oh yes. He's not always cavorting in his lusts. Darkness eclipses him for months at a crack. And then it comes to him, *Let go, Bihusi, and ride the Sun!* In tears he falls to his knees on woven gold and prays, *Ahuramazda who art in heaven, hallowed be thy name. Thy Sunbeams come! Thy will be done! My labors are all for you!* And so on. Something Herculean or Christ-like shines in him, in the immense work he has taken upon himself in bringing Ahuramazda down to the globe at any cost. And cost him it has. He has his own theogony. As with the Zoroastrians, he also draws breath from Sun-worshipping Aztecs and Incans, followers of human sacrifice not known for their gracious hearts. Ikhnaton also meets his approval, as do his hymns to the Sun, and as does the Sun God Amenhotep III whose majestic statue of himself and his wife Queen Tiy sits in the Valley of the Kings. To Dad the sky is female but fiery and sword-wielding, and the male Earth in thrall to the pale and delicate Passions of the Moon. I'm mangling his thoughts but they are something like this. To wolfen, the Moon fragments and disappears into Earth for three days each month, while the invincible Sun rises burning and aglow, conquers the heavens, then rests under Earth until her heroic rebirth from Earth's phallus. Nothing fragments or dissolves the Sun. Death and resurrection hold no fears for the Sun. This accounts for Dad's ancestor worship and hailing of our bloodline as the sign of a Genius beyond the merely mortal. For wolves never die. We carry our ancestors with us day and night and visible to our inner eye. Their eternal Wisdom saves and protects us. Just as the breath of Yahweh blows through the Old Testament and, bringing up warm and waving wheat from Earth, revives the Jews, so the living breath of our ancestors fills and heats all Bihusi and Giurgiu. Great thoughts, balanced judgment, and powerful wills are our heritage as we seek the Supreme spawns in all the bodies of the universe—like so many frog's eggs over which she spreads her milt. In all this, Dad sees Ahuramazda as a belief-spirit risen from his own unconscious. That all his thoughts are objectively untrue means nothing, just as the cosmic systems of Christians, Jews, Muslims, the Hindus, Nordic warriors, the Egyptians, the Eskimos, and tribes of the Congo and the Amazon rain forest are beliefs divorced from objective reality but which energize their followers, salve their fears and guilts, and give them heart. If you think there's a Valhalla, a Muslim Paradise, a Hindu Nirvana, a Heaven, a solar boat to carry you to the land of death, fine. I don't, but that doesn't matter. The point of a religion is to bind its followers to a common purpose, and with Dad the purpose is to convert wave forms from the Sun into Earthly power, with the Boardroom of the Sun and Bihusi Sunbeams as his Vatican and Mecca. Dad's followers are largely Persians, as I've said, and not a very scientific crew, aside from their stargazing, mathematics and inventing the concept of zero. But all this is no matter. Not beside Ahura.

Sidney asks, Why offer us this hodgepodge if it doesn't mean anything?

Sidney, my father chooses to believe it as a blueprint for Bihusi Sunbeams. That it doesn't mean anything is unimportant. The Greeks lived by gods in the heavens and named the stars and mazda, the hermaphroditic cosmogenetrix and his ovarian reproductive system planets after them, names we still use. For three hundred years the Moors, the Muslims, and the Saracens occupied Sicily, Italy and the Spanish peninsula in the name of Allah. There is no Allah. But Allah ruled a pretty large part of Earth for a very long time and focused the energies of tens of millions of those sworn to his name and his will. Few today believe in the Greek gods but the power of their fantasy still lives. You've doubtless heard of the Trilateral Commission, the Bilderbergers, the Club of Rome? These world leaders, who meet in secret and are often whispered to be masters of world economies, know among themselves that they are loons and that ninety percent of what they do they do incompetently and that economies stay on track by the remaining ten percent of luck, chance, and accident. Dad sees himself as superhumanly gifted and above the petite-bourgeoisie manipulations of these small players who run companies and countries. He sees himself working in world energies, powers vaster than currencies and credit, and he and his Zoroastrians have a wheeling imagination unbound by Earthly concerns or the common moral restraints of elected leaders. Dad cut his teeth on Nietzsche, who was one of us, and then grew fangs.

Does he have a conscience? Does he sleep badly? No. He's not human. Just as a wolf has no memory or feeling for the rabbit it killed yesterday, to him the dead are just a meal. The idea of conscience is as unthinkable as his falling in love with his victims. His conscience, such as it is, attaches itself to solar purposes no telescope will fathom. Know thyself, to Dad, means sensorial satisfactions: has he got what he deserves, is he well-fed, has he cared for his prostate with proper sex? A *sensorial* conscience, doctor. It's not that he doesn't know about your conscience. He hears ahead just about anything you're going to say before you say it. When he's going to strike, there's no sign or signal. Just a piercing sweetness in the yellow depths of his eyes as his hands thicken, and suddenly you're dead, only a shadow, icy with wonder, while a very tall man hops about like a happy wolf. After Dad, the whole knot of your life loosens and you lie there. Now that you're dead, he can breathe again, for a moment, his throat thrillingly flaccid, relaxed and open, before his next victim gives a brief surge to his life. He needs a conscience?

You see, time gone by is gone by. Aside from what he learned from Grandfather and from his ties with Magda, he has no social pressures other than as King of Bihusi and ruling with the imperiousness taught him by his mother, which Magda reveres. He's not just the alpha male of the pack; he's the alpha male of the universe. With his clan, in the clash of battle, he is a wolf among wolves, subduing blacks in Johannesburg, Cro-Magnons in Siberia, but he has no partners and feels no need for allegiances. He is not a business romantic. The only good partner is a dead partner.

Which brings me to the Bihusi Medicine Man and the Medal of Honor. The Bihusi Medicine Man, Dad's spiritual adviser and the monstrous guardian of Bihusi mythology, who is shut up in the bowels of the Transylvanian Alps where he awaits the annihilation of the planet in the maw of Ahuramazda, stirs his bones once a year, shakes himself, and glides by darkness from his cave to Dad's Jungfrau chalet to collect several ounces of Dad's lustrous silver sperm which the Bihusi Medicine Man pours quickly into a die-press where the sperm hardens into a medal the size of a silver dollar with milled edges and gets stamped on one side with a raised image of The Spear of Ahuramazda That Sees Everything and on the other with a Bihusi wolf head and the motto IN DAD WE TRUST. Dad's slant eye watches over every step to ensure that no drop goes to waste. A fresh medal is then strapped for three days to the head of The Spear where it drinks in a touch of the energy of The Spear to gaze into futurity. This Bihusi Medal of Honor is awarded to wolves who have slipped into financial quicksand and taken the fall for Dad. Even dead Bihusi weep when this award is made. Their ghosts peer down on Attica, Atlanta, Sing Sing and all state and federal prisons where Dad's saints twist past body builders and the criminally insane. Dad always delivers the Bihusi Medal of Honor himself, speaks to his fellow wolf through clear plastic in the visitors room, and holds up the bright silver medal for the other to see. The message is clear. The inmate thanks him, holding his heart and bowing, but turns down the medal since, almost without question, he will be killed for it by fellow inmates. And he may be killed for not taking it, since the very sight of Dad bearing the medal into the crucible of Atlanta or Sing Sing, fearless as Hannibal the Conqueror, makes the inmate catch his breath loudly, look away and out the window, his heart thrumming as he sees the last day of his life hanging in the vivid air, nothing left, winter hanging black and white, nothing left now that Dad's here, nothing left, only this lighted chickenwire window, winter black and white, all lost this very day, as the inmate's folded hands rise, sealing his lips for all time with a prayer to Dad. *I won't give you up, Dad.* Dad rises to leave and, *Ciao!* sparkling on his lips, raps farewell on the plastic window. The inmate wobbles on his chair, a kicked dog, speechless in overload. As Dad tells me in the car, burnishing his Medal of Honor and pinning it back into its purple case, *That shuts him up.* It is, of course, the only a Rumanian coin made in China.

Sidney leans back, hands clasped behind his head and weighs Dad's medal of honor.

The warmth of Gong's sudden smile chokes me. Ah, she knows something about me Sidney doesn't. I like this, playing one off the other. But then I catch myself up and tell Sidney, I'm here because I think I'm in a darkness that is so dark that things become clear, as if I'm standing in starlight with no Moon. It's the three-day night, the phase where the Moon disappears. Maybe this darkness is necessary for self-understanding, but it's also disheartening. There are things I can see only in the shadowless purity of starlight when no Moon obscures with shadow, and buried or hidden things rise up. Things normally passive and held down by the Moon break loose from the deepest darkness and float up, as if I'm standing beside a dark river in whose depths I see the stars, something Moonlight would otherwise wash out. Everything you take for granted sheds its outer being, its shell, and shows its germ, the heartlight at the core of things. You see into matter itself and find an ultraviolet world so incandescent that you are beyond logic and reason and stand on a bed of pure matter as it squeezes up from no zone known to common intelligence but which is the utter intelligence that binds all things into the field of being.

Oh, heavens! Gong says. You should write that down.

I do write these things down. But later I ask myself, Should I write or shoot my brains out?

I trust you won't do that, Billy, Gong says.

I'm almost fearful to talk about this stuff. But it does help me understand Dad and his vision of Ahuramazda. These thoughts come over me, symphonic bass notes as waves lift upward through my nerves. *I'm alive, I'm alive.* My mind stretches through Dad's great shipwreck. I feel feeble as a child in tears. I gather heart and go on.

Dad grows ever more short-tempered as he moves toward Bihusi Sunbeams. He sublimates nothing, ever. He acts on impulse and is swift to rage if he does not get his own, which is everything, and get it fast. He rests only with movies by Anthony Hopkins, a master of human masks, but fears that the story of man-eating Hannibal Lecter may foretell his own imprisonment and crucifixion by the jackals. Planet Earth? It's all his. I want, I want, I want, and without censorship, conscience, or any sense of unworthiness stemming from his actions. After a day's work he likes a shower and a nap, something munchable. Raw calves livers go down like oysters. His Genius, power and financial alertness let him abide in a different reality from yours, a reality so distant, way out on the edge of things, that often even I have trouble following him. He swims in a different fluid, not air, not water. Methane gas, perhaps. He has perfected a mask of virtue and shy friendliness that is a highwatermark of wolfcraft. Otherwise he could not save so many starving black Catholic orphans in Africa, Gong, or devote himself so selflessly and successfully to fostering AIDS research with Dolores Rand. But even Dolores has no idea who Dad is or knows the depth of his insensitivity to anyone but Magda. Or where this self-serene, sweet-smiling lack of anxiety comes from. Whatever the cost to others, he bites off what he wants, and has ring within ring of devilish underlings grabbing the cookies and companies to feed him. He's bitter about and resents mortality, but Wolfington Labs is at work about that and Dad avoids any addictions that might undermine his powers. Alcohol, tobacco, drugs. He truly likes a clear mind. His leap of intuition over all twaddle and bullshit is addiction enough for him. At rare moments his utter logic dances him about on his hind legs. You two must think him mentally ill or morally beyond the pale. Believe me, he's past all therapy, and was born that way. His heart learned to swim in his big-headed mother's blood, and she could leave you with brow torn and a skin flap hung over your eye. Grandfather adored this demiurge, as did Dad. Dad would hop and dance when her howl called him to gorge, chunks of venison convulsing from her belly and into his long teeth. She's his sweetest memory from cubhood.

He's also *your* father, Sidney says. You seem to have dropped out of your family's moral system or grown away from it.

Pretty much, not completely.

How do you think this has come about? Gong asks.

I married a human, Gong. One who loves wolves. Now she wants to be even more wolf than I am, while I see things differently. I'm still my father's son and chasing Bihusi Sunbeams, but I'm also detaching from Dad's blood thirst. Right now I need a few minutes rest.

Fine, Gong says. But let me ask, if Dad doesn't really believe in Ahuramazda, why does he pray three times a day? And on a rug of woven gold?

Why not? I say. All religion is myth that spiritually energizes us, as Jung tells us. If you want to read a poet or hear music three times a day for rest and recharging, do it. Dad takes great stock in the Wreath of Bihusi and praying gives him time to concentrate and consult our ancestral voices. As for the rug, it's a Babylonian Sun-shape once owned by Nebuchadnezzar. An exquisite work. If you owned it *you'd* want to pray three times a day. It really lifts you.

I stare at the dock and a rowboat tied to it. How about a little row? I say.

If you like, Gong says. It's only a half-mile down to Bollingen tower.

I want to write up my notes, Sidney says. You two go. But be back for lunch.

In an hour, Gong says.

I lock the oars in and pull away from the dock. Gong faces me in the bow, her knees to one side. The breeze carries a fresh scent from her.

You've changed to Missoni, I say.

Very lightly. How can you tell?

We had a controlling interest. Now it's Sidi's. Tell me something about yourself. Any siblings?

I had a younger sister, Poppy. She died in childbirth of puerperal fever and peritonitis. The doctors couldn't stop an infection. She was only eighteen.

I'm sorry. Did the baby live?

Yes. But it was a girl and her husband gave it up for adoption.

I see. I didn't think adopting girls was a popular idea in People's Republic.

It isn't. She looks away. The child no longer knows her own birthday. Nobody cares.

Did you want to adopt her?

Yes, I did. Sidney said no. If we ever return we would not be allowed to have another child under the one-child system. Sidney would never have a son.

That he doesn't want anyway, right? Sorry again. Don't mean to butt in.

Keep near the shore. The tower is just around that outcropping.

We look down into the lake where Sunlight scums brown rocks and greengold moss. We break into reeds.

I don't want to return anyway, she says. I have my village memories. But I also remember hopeless poverty and famine and corrupt leaders. If we went back we'd soon be in the thick of a lot of rivalries. Psychoanalysis has no scholarly standing back home. Jung rates zero and Freud's not much better. When all scholarship is for communal ends, then Western research fails to meet certain standards of validity. And even if we were allowed to practice, it would be quite boring dealing everyday with some neurosis or lack of purpose in living that arises from despair with communal belief systems. It would be like dealing with the grocer, all day, every day, six days a week, and attending conferences about dealing with the grocer. A demanding prospect. That we can't practice back there with any degree of respect while countless countrymen reel about in need of our services, is heartbreaking. And my heart is not easily broken after the Great Famine of the sixties. Back home I might not even want to be a mother.

You're a mother already, I tell her. Even if you don't have children.

She stares, trying to fathom me. How do you mean?

I stop rowing. You're a divinity of nature.

I don't feel divine.

Of course you do. I see it in everything about you. Everything.

Everything?

Absolutely. Do you want an inventory?

Do I?

Right now you feel a breeze on your back. That breeze brings news. It comes from an unoccupied hinterland you are moving toward and where your children await you. You are passing through a wall into a feeling of fullness. Everything in you rises and presses toward a life you've never known before. Your spirit is taking in these sparks and jets on the water and is unlocking a light within you, a glare in the future you can't quite see through. You sense a flame filling you, your deepest self coming to birth. You are these rocks and moss. You are the water. You are a swan feeding on the moss. You are these reeds. You are the sky, big as it is. Your memory goes back to before your birth. You see your home village a hundred years ago. You see hard dirt and pebbles everywhere, and huts and stables the same as the huts and stables of your childhood. The same horses are in them that were there over a century ago. They're being fed the same hay. Life hasn't changed! In a million years has the landscape on Mars changed? Barely a rock has shifted. Has the landscape of China changed in a million years? Some villages, mining, lumbering. But it's the same dirt and pebbles. Has Lake of Zürich changed? Maybe a few new springs feed it, or the volume of water has grown. All this is eternal. You're here. You're awake and breathing, in all your loveliness. This is no dream. You're this divine being. Don't deny it. Do you think eternity comes only after you die? This is it. You're sitting in it. And you are divine. Trust a Bihusi to recognize this in you. Here we are. This is Jung's tower?

What? Oh, yes.

I row in through reeds to a shore heavy with small rocks.

Are we allowed to walk around?

I chair the board of the institute, she says.

The handbuilt rock tower is four towers of differing height that form a small chalet at water's edge.

Don't get out, I say as she starts to rise.

I slip off my loafers and step barefoot into water up to my ankles and pull the boat ashore and take her hand and waist and help her onto small white rocks and pebbles. I leave my loafers.

You know what you were saying, Billy?

I say nothing.

About eternity? she says.

Mmhm.

When you are in analytic psychology, sometimes it backs up on you. Under layers and layers of beautiful pathology, you find the futility of words.

I'm sure.

What I liked about your words was that I could see through them like water. I felt everything you said. Except that I'm not a mother already.

Yes, you are. It's just unmined. The yearning is there but the gold lies asleep within you. And it *will* be mined. I know it will. I really know it.

I lay a finger against my nose.

I can smell these things ahead, I say. Ripeness is all.

How about over ripeness? she says, then starts to slip on a rock.

Ah ah! I grab her. Take my arm.

We walk about studying figures Jung carved on his stone walls and slabs and...

Ah, Dad! I cry and run my fingers over Jung's wall-carving of The Trickster.

It doesn't look like him, I say. But I know who this is.

We go through a small court to the door, leaving my damp footprints on flagstones. Gong looks about, then lifts up a flagstone and finds a key.

Voila! she says, unlocking the Romanesque wooden door and we go in.

So, I say, I hear this is where he came to get away from his wife and play hanky-panky with his mistress.

A whole wall of firewood stands neatly packed just as Jung left it.

Well, he got away from Emma, yes, Gong says. But really, this was for dreaming and concentrating. No phone, no electricity. Water pumped by hand.

I'll put it another way. It all rests on your scale of observation. If you were the moss on that rock you would say the universe is water, rock, Sunlight, and Moonlight, and you would have no sense of duration. If you were one of your swans, you'd have a different sense of what the universe is, including a bundle of quite different instincts, and a limited sense of time passing. As a human you have your present senses. But let's say you have an even larger sense of your existence and that you are a biospirit urging life into all organic matter. Long before this you were inorganic. Then the soup is stirred and you come bubbling up. The one thing we all agree upon about organic life is its urge to reproduce itself. It's not too much to say that all organic matter is this demiurge, this biospirit, forever healing its hurts and broken parts and making itself anew. Now from the scale of observation of this demiurge you are only one cell urgent to reproduce itself. But let's say the demiurge is not merely a mess of chemicals in conflict but actually a great memory of itself and carrying that self forward on protein memory chips below, or even above, our level of observation. Is everything I'm suggesting utterly improbable? Or is it more improbable that everything's just a soup of energies with no purpose? Despite the fact that molecular memory clearly exists and accounts for patterns being carried forward in time? Is it too wonderful to think that this great memory is in fact a consciousness both in and above organic matter, even as human thought is in and above living beings? There's no proof, only analogy acting as proof. This is to this as this is to this. I enjoy this kind of thinking and carry on with myself at great length. What I'm getting at is that just as all levels of purposeful awareness, from the amoebae to man, rise and join into a commonality among species, so the great memory itself takes awareness from all living things and although it is growing herbs in this part of its garden and flowers over there and birds here and men there, and these living things feel species-specific in their awareness, the great memory has a larger view, and a greater urgency, as it takes its most basic food from the Sun and heats the big soup down here. This leads on to other questions about the Sun, but locally it prompts us to ask, Where do we come from? Why are we here? Where are we going?

And the answer is. . . Gong says.

The answer is that the great memory springs full-blown from the womb and is printed on our chromosomes, just as I bear the Wreath of Bihusi. We are all part of a great breath blowing through organic matter. Does that breath have awareness and purpose? Someday we'll read our own bones and find something we've overlooked or not had the brains to see earlier. I hope you discovered with your 300-power microscope that monocellular beings are quite complicated physiologically and have gone through astounding anatomical changes over the last six hundred million years while still remaining monocellular, as their fossils show. The great memory has used those old monocellular forms and cast them off for sturdier and yet more rarefied forms of organic memory. These cells bear a history of internal structures I'll skip over, other than to say that the great memory has its million second thoughts, its million third thoughts, and just like us is addicted to chance and luck. Up, up, here we are. I'll carry on about this another day, if you aren't bored stiff. Maybe it's hard to take in when you're hungry.

No, I'll be interested to see where your biological pantheism carries you.

Thank you. Sidney. *Sidney,* we're starved to the bone! Let's eat!

I think we probably have some fried squid, Sidney says.

Gong tells me, That was a joke.

I follow Sidney's stunningly blood-colored cordovans up the garden path to the wide porch with its hammock and wicker. My sight hazes over as we leave the Sunlight. Brilliant varicolored tulips glow on the dining room table where we lunch. Noon pours in and lights up framed classical Chinese landscapes around the room.

Nice scrolls, I say.

They're of little value, Sidney says.

Oh, don't say that, Gong says.

Don't say it? Sidney smiles. All right, I take it back. These are immensely valuable paintings, Herr Baxter. Very old. Beyond price. Ahh, smell the fish? We eat our big meal at noon, so you're lucky.

Actually, Sidney could give you a lecture on these scrolls, Gong says. He's very knowledgeable about Chinese art.

Am I? Perhaps I am, Sidney says. But I have deplorable taste. I prefer the fresh ink of reproductions to faded originals. Also, all of these repros are slightly undersize, which gives everything in them a heightened reticulation. Lines look more firmly controlled and everything's slightly less relaxed and more intense. If I had the originals, of course, I might grow to like their pallidness. But who wants a washed out reproduction when the original's color was once brilliant? I mean, hundreds of years ago—or a thousand!

Helga brings steaming Mandarin pancakes wrapped around pieces of Peking duck and Mu Shu pork. Our places are set with Western silver.

I'd like chopsticks, I say.

Why not? Family style! Gong says and brings us three fresh sets from a drawer behind her. We all begin eating from the same platters and bowls.

Helga lays out a plump carp sautéed with scallions in ginger-orange sauce and stir-fried walnuts with two kinds of mushrooms. Surprising me, the Mandarin pancakes turn out to be maple-flavored.

Hm. These pancakes remind of the one time I saw Dad get outfoxed— that's before his illness, when Sidi got to him.

We'd just taken over the Tabasco and red hot pepper industry down in New Iberia, Louisiana, I tell the Changs, and while passing through the airport Dad bought some large maple sugar leaves at a sweets shop. On the back of each leaf was pressed the motto AN HONEST LIVING. Dad's so taken by the flavor, and the motto, he asks where these leaves come from. From the Nearing farm in southern Vermont, he's told. Dad diverts our plane to Vermont and we head for Nearing's. Dad now has his eye on the maple sugar industry. As evening falls we drive up to the farmhouse. Behind it lays a barn, a woodshed, two sugar sheds, and sixty-five acres of maple trees. The house itself has a strange God-given glow. At the door stands Scott Nearing, a philosopher farmer and his wife Helen, who whips us up a big dinner in only ten minutes. We eat at the kitchen plank table. Dad sees low-cost implements everywhere. Well, it's a sweet farm.

Simple food for the good life, Helen tells us. I don't believe in time lost to cooking.

Time is money, Dad agrees. So let's get down to business.

If it were, I'd be Croesus, says Scott Nearing, who is himself one-hun-dred-and-five years old. What can I do for you?

My name is Baxter.

Heard of you.

I'm moving into the general food industries and am interested in buy-ing your farm.

Want to tap trees, do you?

Not personally.

Then you'd miss the whole point.

Scott absently picks up his spoon and pours some syrup into it and sucks it clean. Sunlit honesty pours from his eyes, and ridges his long, wrin-kled cheeks with deep furrows and his jaw with square edges. His weath-ered face has a God-given maple glow.

Well, why in God's name would you want to get into sugaring, Mister Baxter? You can barely make an honest living at it.

Just barely, Helen says, heaping our plates with horse chow, a mix of old-fashioned raw oats, raisins, lemon juice and sea salt, moistened with olive oil. She serves it in a large wooden bowl and we all get a wooden spoon. We're like the Chinese here, she says. We chow down from one family bowl. Jump in.

I have a sweet tooth for companies, Dad says, digging in. This chow is delicious! It reminds me of some peasant meals in the Austrian Tyrol.

Dya like ta get up early in the morning? Scott asks. I mean, very early.

I rise early at times, yes. Looking for the worm, ha ha.

I'm saying ya got to chop a lot of wood to keep your sugar fire at top heat to get out the best flavor. Low fire ruins the flavor.

I see.

That means early to the woodpile to split the day's fuel. Tell ya, Mister

Baxter. You would not be buying my farm, you'd be buying my soul. And my wife's.

I hadn't planned on going that far, Dad says. But I could work it in.

What Scott means, Helen says—serving a second course of eye-glazing mouthwatering butter-fried winter turnips with chopped parsley, also in a wooden bowl,—is that when the first thaw comes in late winter we go nearly crazy. Your heart starts squeezing you like nothing you've ever felt, with the trees calling to be tapped. It's a heartbreaker, listening to those maples sing like frogs mating in a spring pond. You melt inside and your tongue turns sort of light amber.

I like a solvent enterprise, Scott says.

Ahh! Dad agrees.

We put three hundred dollars into this land. My God, sir, the times we've been through, it was three dollars an acre when we bought it! Then all this lavish building of sheds. New maple shingles for the house. The expense, sir, was enormous. Even today, with all the modern miracles in pots and tubes, I'm not sure it's something you'd want to get into. The burdens, Baxter, are backbreaking. But it's a sweet life.

Well, Nearing, Dad says, you look like an honest man.

Nossir, I don't.

He means he *is* an honest man, Helen says.

Through and through, Nearing says, downing a second spoonful of syrup and sucking his spoon clean of every maple molecule. By Christopher, that was a good year, he tells Helen, his fierce big fingers rounding on the syrup pitcher.

Let go of that pitcher, Scott Nearing, before you eat us out of house and home.

She fills a spoon for herself.

But you're right, she says, that was a sweet year. You see before you, gentlemen, a house that sugar built. We sell sugar and syrup for cash income, but everything else we grow is for neighbors and visitors. We have a comfy maplewood guesthouse for whoever comes, including you folks. We believe in workable, simple living and each for all and all for each. Glad ta have ya.

Dad's stomach turns at such simpleminded neighborliness. His dinner asks to be tossed but he packs the horse chow back down. He gags at the smell of health from these two. I hear teeth grind behind his torn smile.

Built it all by hand, Nearing says. The whole works. We pay no interest on loans and no fees to architects, contractors or lawyers. I'll tell you, this year our sugar sales greatly exceed our syrup sale, which allows a margin for capital improvements. We may very well put two-hundred-and-forty-two dollars into an additional sugarhouse. With fireproofing it should last thirty or forty years. Does that kind of money frighten you, Baxter?

Dad sinks, throwing up his hands. Sir, I think I'm getting in over my head.

Thought that might be the case, Nearing says. Fact is, for a big fella, I mean a full-grown youngster, you're sort of a greenhorn at bargaining or you'd know you can't make a dollar at this for your first five or six years. I better than break even because I know what I'm doing, having been cured by industry. You know what I mean by cured by industry?

No, I don't think I do, Dad says.

Getting hardened by extra work, big fella. You think there's only so much work you can do in twenty-four hours, but it happens that there's another six or eight hours of full, rewarding labor hidden away in there if you put your mind to it. It's like trying to boil sap with green wood. Good sugar wood should be dry, it goes one-third further than green wood, since a third of the energy in green wood goes into drying the moist wood and not into boiling the sap. That misdirected third part of the energy makes the difference between breaking even and going under. I know you haven't thought of that.

No. Not at all.

Cured by industry means learning short cuts through heavy trials and lots of misfortune. Well, errors. I couldn't take advantage of you, Baxter. It's true, I'm getting on. I can't chop as much firewood before breakfast as I used to in my nineties, not any more, sir. I'd hate to see a city man like you out there wielding an ax in the pitch dark before first light. You could give yourself a terrible injury.

Nearing sighs heavily.

I just can't dump all this on you, Baxter.

Helen's not quite sure though and tells Dad, But if your heart's set on it, sir, it's an honest living.

Dad twists about in deep thought. Then his slant eyes take in the two humans.

I don't think I'm up to it, he says. Let me apologize for the time I've cost you.

Ah, well, don't worry, sir, Nearing says. I've got another ten years in me if I keep my flesh good and dry.

Helen slaps the table. You burn me up when you talk like that.

I sure hope so, darling. Ain't she sweet, fellas?

After toasting our own maple-flavored marshmallows for dessert, Dad and I drive off, waving and smiling, having bought a box of maple sugar leaves and gallon of grade A light amber—dark amber being less flavorful.

Dad's face drains into deep silence. Suddenly he kicks off his shoes, rips apart the box of sugar leaves and grinds them to dust, raging, Jesus Christ! Christ Christ Christ! There's no goddamn way in, Billy! All that nature-loving simplicity is a brick wall. That is the worst stinking human being I have ever met, all those slimy, God-given honest wrinkles—and that wife is no better. It's like looking the greatest human monster ever born straight in the face and there's nothing there. Just. . . *honesty!* We'll never cheat that sonofabitch!

We pass over a small country bridge. The syrup drops like a dead baby.

Gong sits with her mouth covered, her eyes ringed with tears.

Oh, so you think it's funny? I ask her.

I can't help it!

Well, I used to eat out on that story quite often, I tell her. Sidney, may I give you some advice? This is from Dad. Let me suggest something. Say you have patients who pay tardily, and I'm sure you do, although your patients are largely middle-aged and well-to-do. Am I correct?

Yes?

Our suggestion is this. Give your receivables clerk one percent of every franc collected in less than thirty days. You have my word that within two months your receivable aging will be cut in half. My bandit dentist adds twenty-four percent interest for late payments and over three years I would be paying one-hundred-fifty percent of the original bill. My prompt payment costs him dearly. Do analysts charge interest?

None that I know, Sidney says. At least not Jungians.

Good. I think interest on medical services is usurious. Legal theft.

Sidney shifts the talk. I think you've been hard on the Japanese today.

But they deserve it, Gong says, her sticks picking at white carp meat with its spicy ginger-orange sauce and quickly going back for a scallion bulb. Bones show already on her side of the fish. Both she and Sidney lift rice bowls to their lips and shovel and loudly suck in white rice to clean their mouths between the duck and pork pancakes.

Oh, I could be even more hard, I say. Not long ago Dad wanted to obligate a Senator Ryan Seinfeld, the Irish-Jewish US Senator from New York. The senator wanted to join a country club in Fairfield County owned by and restricted to Japanese. He calls Dad for a favor. Dad phones a Yakuza guy in Osaka and says, I want Seinfeld in that club. So the club even waives the million-dollar entry fee for Dad's new friend, the traditional way that keeps Gai-jin, the round eyes, out of Japanese-owned US golf clubs.

So we never sucker the Nearings, though later we do have Wolfington Labs buy a pint of Scott's blood for research—it turns out to be some photosynthetic compound, simple Sunbeams and glucose. The one man on Earth beyond our reach chops firewood and taps a sugarbush up in Vermont, his face a force of nature bearing truth and beauty to God's doorstep. Sickening.

You're being ironic? Sidney asks.

Not entirely. Having failed to cheat an honest man, Dad decides it's time for me to be apprenticed—to learn the art of the deal. The only way to do that is do a *big* one. Big? Here is big:

All our Presidents are advised by three primary intelligence groups, aside from "independent contractors," or killers who leave no footprints. Tops are the high-profile CIA, the middle-profile National Security Agency, and the lesser-known spooks of the military services. As everyone knows, these spooks often work at cross-purposes. Why? Well, because conflicts stem from budgets, loyalties, and the kind of normal confusion with mega sized organization. Dad has me join him in exploiting the unfocused intelligence services, and shows me how to pick up power and money from their bumbling. The Chinese ideogram for crisis is two words: problem and opportunity. In every crisis, Dad always takes the higher ground and seizes opportunity.

I know that ideogram, Sidney says. But what's it mean to your father?

Tricksters tricking tricksters, Gong says, will themselves be tricked by *The* Trickster.

Right! I say. And this is the picture as Dad shows it to me. The White House wants to buy the President of Lebanon. He's going to cost at least two billion dollars. The NSA agrees with this program. The Pentagon thinks it's dangerous, and the CIA hopes for a failure, which will give them more leverage with Israel. So the NSA lays out the plot for the White House. It's simple stuff. Two oil companies will litigate. Finding a corrupt court is no hardship. Texas will have all the dirty players that the White House needs. Elected Texas judges always need campaign cash, so they solicit gifts and many steal with both hands. What's going to happen is this. Oil Company A sues oil company B. Well, it's Okla-Oil and Bowie Petroleum. A ten-billion-dollar judgment will be made, it's a boat race.

Boat race? Sidney asks.

It's fixed.

But I find it hard to believe, Gong says, that Texas courts are corrupt. We do not have corrupt courts in Switzerland.

I see. And in Beijing? I ask. You can tell me, I'm not wired.

Please don't disappoint me like that, Gong says. Yes, People's Republic has corruption—

—and exposure brings execution, Sidney says.

Well, the US has a manure pile of corrupt courts. Those in Plaquemine County in Louisiana and those in Suffolk County in Boston are notorious. The Texas judge involved in the payoff to the President of Lebanon is a cousin of the President of Lebanon. A cousin! The Texas lawyer who is plaintiff's counsel has a brother in the Bekaa Valley outside Beirut who is a warlord running a private Maronite Christian army. When the judgment is paid, the plaintiff's lawyer will take a forty-percent fee, or four billion dollars. Now I'll say this slowly. What the US president intends to do is to give the Texas lawyer a special IRS dispensation and let the lawyer keep his four billion tax-free. There will be no IRS examination of the lawyer's *income* this year. The lawyer will transfer two billion dollars, half of his fee, to his cousin, the warlord, who will pass it on, minus his cut, to the President of Lebanon. The oil company that *apparently* suffers the loss will be compensated by another tax decision granting it a special temporary increased depletion allowance until it has its ten billion back. They'll make it back in three months and this is how it's going to be done. But, *we* find out about it. We find out from a Saudi prince, who is buying options on the defendant oil company's stock. He has come to Dad for money to get more options. The prince is so naive. He's convinced that when the public discovers the Middle East web reaching into Texas for these billions, the judge will be recused, the suit dismissed, and the stock of the defending company will take a jump. Spike! Go up sharply. You see, friends, the Saudi prince and his buddies think that the US government will stop this corrupt move. They don't realize that the Executive Branch is behind it! Dad shows me where *we* come in. His contacts at CIA, who want the thing to fail, and at the more neutral Pentagon, lay out the plot for him. Dad asks me, Billy, my boy, what's in this for us? I say, Well, there are probably a few things we can get out of this. We take the story public and, like our friend the Saudi prince, we take big option positions in the defendant's stock and when the suit is dismissed the stock rises. We profit. Or we let the public in and use somebody like *60 Minutes* to spell out the scheme and the players. This is another way to force the US president to kill the suit.

The big Arab money believes that this scheme has been put together by a Texas judge and a Texas lawyer who are tied to Beirut to rip ten billion dollars out of a global oil company. The judge and the lawyer will split the fee. That, of course, is not the real situation. Dad listens to me and my thoughts, and says to me, Okay, you have a pretty good picture, but you're not thinking big enough. You're still in small change. We are going to do this right, wind up with both oil companies, control of the Lebanese president, and the juice to blackmail the White House. *Power.* So Dad tells me to design this one. Then the judgment comes down for seven billion, not ten, still a huge amount of money. The Texas lawyer gets forty percent. Two point eight billion. He trundles about a billion and a half over to his cousin, the warlord, and the warlord to the Lebanese president, who would now be in the White House pocket. The White House is happy, the President of Lebanon is rich, the NSA is smug, and the CIA wants to torpedo this whole schmear. When that happens, Dad and I will step in and take it all away.

We fly over Okla-Oil on the Great Plains.

Now, Sunny Jim, Dad tells me, we'll give the White House the paint job it deserves.

And his slant eyes glisten as he opens his portfolio and shows me the Okla-Oil and Bowie annual reports prettied up with fields of derricks sweeping over the Great Plains and under a bayou Sunrise. He glows and slips them back into his portfolio, looking deeply enlivened, eager and pleased.

He beats my knee as the breath shoots out of him. My cub, can there be anything more beautiful than an oil field? Just the smell of fresh crude lifts my heart. I've got to admit, it brings out the idealist in me. I watch money pumping up out of the big teat, and I am simply humbled. A terrible decency and sense of noble purpose rise up. I get stuffy and teary-eyed. Know why?

A derrick is a real thing, real business. It's not just credit and finance. You can touch it! That's why your grandfather used to love owning the gas companies and street-railways all across this country. You could actually turn on a stove and see your money in a crown of blue flames, or look out the window and see your stock rolling along every street and dripping sparks. By God, money used to mean something. I loved the Union Loop in Chicago and the New York elevated lines, before I sold 'em to Japan. Of course, I made money on the other end too. But high finance is a bitch. So abstract. Like a woman, you can only buy her things but never understand her. You wait for her to give you something, give you something, *if* she feels like it. All you can do is *beg*. It's not logical, high finance—at heart it's all luck and accident and begging the stars. Or like getting down on your knees to a blonde. Why do poets and writers make us financiers out to be such bullies and monsters, so second-class? We folk who move the world, Billy, we're treated insufferably. Believe you me, Bihusi are first-class, we are the top Rumanians, we are not peasants. Take us or leave us, we command from the heights. Can we help it if our wolf nature is inhuman? Do you wonder *why* we are wolves? It's because we're necessary to nature's purpose. To Ahuramazda. To the Sun. Must we cheat like gypsies? Do we need to snatch and chew like some Australian crocodile swallowing up television stations and newspapers? You might as well ask if we need to eat. We have over-brimming hope and bottomless hunger. We live perpetually in an upbeat mood. We jump at every rabbit, big or small. You see how the Sun provides for us? We eat our cake and have it too. There's always another bunny in the grass. I'm no villain, my son. My heart hurts like anyone else's. I just never slow down to feel much. I can't rest. Even to me I'm fantastic. Well, they say you can't have everything. *HAH!* We'll show them. They'll know who has everything. They'll know when I stroke their necks what a genial sonofabitch I am. These humans, with their cheap little religions and mysteries, their psychology, their weak artworks that pass for sublimity—they have no idea how meaningless their lives are. What floss blowing in the wind! What do they know of the *Überwolf!* I will lead them into a despair they've never dreamed of. And be perfectly composed when I do it.

Dad, you're a poet. You should let people know you have this poetry in you. They'll follow you into hell when you speak like this.

I hadn't thought of that. Maybe I should loaf a bit. Wander about the Louvre. Write verses, like Sheikh Sidi bin-Bahram. That Kuwaiti camel-thief is a master of melancholy: *My hanging gardens are gone, but still too much with me. . .* I wish it were trash, but I rather like it. Pathetic of me, huh? How many copies has *The Profit* sold? *A dollar on the wind, beloved, and then no more of thee and me.* Fifty million worldwide in hardcover alone, mankind's all-time best-seller, aside from the Bible? That's a pretty penny, it adds up. It's like printing money! I have a touch of the poet myself, along with an artful touch of larceny, but out-writing Sidi would be no honeymoon. Where would I start? *My heart leaps up when I behold a gusher fill the sky.* A prosperous beginning, Breedwolfe? That could be it! *The Prosperous.* Like it? Or *The Investors' Bible.* People love to read about money. They suckle financial news like milk from a virgin. Did you know that eleven percent of all newspaper readers read the sport pages daily while nineteen percent follow the market? Why do Baxter's Personal Empowerment Seminars do so well? The clucks flock in, we pump 'em up, and an hour after they float on out and the gas goes out of them, they're dazed and turn to our handbooks and tapes, and then stand about like hypnotized chickens waiting for corn from heaven, not knowing the ax fell when they paid their entrance fee. Then the greediest airheads come back for the Master Class. But I don't know, with the world's greatest best-seller Sidi's cornered the market. Maybe you should read my letters to your mother. *This is my little fox in whom I am well-pleased, and who thrashes through the cornfield with her tail on fire. I present my backside to her and she nips at my grapes. My bride's breasts have only just budded. Her couch is strewn with blossoms. She has nipples of silver and cannot rest at nightfall without my kisses.* Hm! A little volume of verse? Thank you, Billy. So you think there's some money in it?

I'm sure there is. Somewhere.

Dad stares at Earth below. His great heart leaps. He laughs and sings. *Oh, what a beautiful oil field! Oh what a beautiful day!*

He claps my knee again. I got a beautiful feeling, lad.

Everything's going your way, Dad.

We sing out together, *Oklahoma! Where the Sun DA DA DA DA DA DA!*

Then he studies me seriously, and asks, Would I really want to be remembered for some little ten-cents-a-word four-line verse? Wouldn't I rather have it said of me, *He chased blondes.*

His bright smile flags. If only I understood them, Billy. The stupid beautiful things. . . and what storms they have, what scenes, what tears! They terrify me but I can't stop my hands from drawing them in, like *doves.*—Like doves. . .

He sighs. Remember when we controlled the Diamond Match Company? I loved those little blue boxes. Fifty matches in each. What were they, two cents a box? But you could hold it right in your palm and strike off one-twenty-fifth of a penny and watch it burn, and know that people all around the globe were striking your matches and piling up your earnings for you. Then we traded it to Planters for peanuts. Peanuts came out of Earth, what could be cheaper? You didn't even need to chop down a tree. Tell me frankly, do you think we should send a *message* up to Vermont? I like the feel of those little maple-sugar leaves. What are the big ones, a dollar a leaf? That bastard has struck gold. People everywhere eating up money for you, pouring it on pancakes, and wanting more, more. *Syrup, Billy, syrup!* You could not lose a penny, you just couldn't. And yet, that farmer, that square-jawed hick with the God-given eyes, swizzled me out of it. Well, I'll tell you, that sharpens my edge for the next sonofabitch.

Pass judgment on Dad? Tell him, *I know thee not, old man, fall to thy prayers.* How can I?

Hah! *Falstaff,* Sidney says. Another greedy thief.

He is pragmatist like the whole Gang of Four at once, Gong says. But go on about Okla-Oil and Bowie Petroleum.

The CIA has no charter to operate inside the States. So often they use Marine reserve officers to front what they want to run. Undercover stuff, secret ops. We have our eye on two Marine officers, both black, a major and a first lieutenant, working in New York. Publicly, Lafayette Oil, another big Texas company, sponsors these two guys who run a team of scientists trying to relieve Third World famine with anchovies.

Anchovies! Gong cries.

Oh yes, the most available source of protein on Earth. These scientists want to farm and harvest anchovies, then somehow convert them into a protein that doesn't carry the anchovy flavor. For years they've tried drying and mixing anchovies and krill into grains and feeding them to the scrawny, meatless chickens found in Nicaragua and West Africa. But the Third World objects culturally to eating anchovies or anything anchovy-flavored. It turns out that anchovies and krill fed to chickens turn chicken meat to anchovy. If we can slip anchovies and krill into the food chain in a way that doesn't bring their taste along, we'll solve Third World hunger overnight. Now we know that these two African-American Marines, whatever their ties to the Company—

Which company? Gong asks. I think I'm lost.

The CIA, Sidney says.

The Company is what spy groupies call the CIA, I say. People with the CIA call it the Agency. These two Marine fronts, Major Fred Steele and Lieutenant Nelson Truesmith, are truly noble men, both black as I say— they *really* want to run with the anchovies and feed the starving millions. The CIA and the government trust them because they're Marines, and under the guise of helping Lafayette Oil scientists feed the Third World with anchovies, and wearing their full military trappings as they carry US humanitarian aid to the underfed, they go about the world without suspicion while actually working on Uncle's secret projects. I think only Dad and I grasp that they've become Believers in the Anchovy. And even though CIA has set up the anchovy/protein research with Lafayette Oil as a front, these two guys have their own ideas. The CIA can go whistle. Get this: a solution exists. There is a lack of food on land and excess food in the ocean. The anchovy/protein conversion project itself is not a CIA scam, it's a genuine private enterprise funded by Lafayette, just used by the CIA as a means of getting these two guys anywhere in the world, no questions asked. Emotionally, though, they're co-opted. They think this thing really do-able. They're such believers that they don't drink or smoke, and I really love these guys when I meet 'em. Their faces hold the history of the Corps: the Halls of Montezuma, Tripoli, Belleau Wood, Wake Island, Guadalcanal, Saipan, Iwo Jima, the Chosen Reservoir, you name it. Steele and Truesmith have glory locked into their eyeballs and are ready to cry *Semper fi* and die. I mean, their essential decency tells them to take a hit on the spookshit, roll with it, and feed the world. Nice Marines, good guys. Dad likes them so much he pins a Bihusi Medal of Honor on each. They're the only two US Marines ever to receive not just a Rumanian medal but *the* Rumanian Medal of Honor stamped with the Bihusi Wolf-head and IN DAD WE TRUST.

We have a meet with them at Arlington National Cemetery and they come fully bedecked in dress blues and fruit salad, ribbons for valor and recognition of some of their more silent services for Uncle. Dad just whacks them straight out and says, I know about your CIA spookarama, I know what you're supposed to be when you go to Angola as saviors, and I know what you *want* to do. Steele and Truesmith have taken out some very big arms dealers and buried a number of bad guys deep in the sand. But Dad is blunt. He tells 'em, I have an offer. I know where you can get the money to do your anchovy deal so it works. I have trunks full of Angolan currency sitting in Zürich, Lisbon and the Portuguese Antilles. This currency has two values. Every week the *Journal* tells the world that the exchange rate is three escudos to the dollar. Having been to Angola, *you* know that the unofficial street rate ranges around thirty escudos to the dollar. The governments involved, the US, the UK, Portugal, Angola, and Brazil, maintain the three-to-one fiction. I'm accumulating at the unofficial rate. Because of my mark up, I can give you enough Angolan cash to put a fix on your afterlife, if that's what you want, *or* to buy the entire sweet crude production of Angola's Kabinda Province out from under Mobil and Gulf. If you want, you can bring Angolan crude out to Europe, the US, and Japan, using Lafayette supertankers. The sweet part, gentlemen, is that you are not going to have to give up your affiliation with CIA. The CIA, in fact, is going to greet you with love and kisses, because with this Angolan oil my son and I are going to kill a certain Lebanese deal the Company wants scuttled. At that, Dad shuts up, leans on them eyeball to eyeball, and bets on their deep pride and proven fearlessness. But Dad and I know that the Company wants to kill the Lebanon deal along with the Lebanon president's approval of Israel getting into Lebanon. The NSA wants Lebanon to let the Israelis in. To a less obsessive level, so does the Pentagon. The Company wants to keep this opportunity away from Israel because the more threatened Israel is the more it's a manageable CIA client. That's why the Company doesn't want the President of Lebanon in the White House's pocket. If you understand this, Gong, you would have made a valuable spy.

As well as beautiful, I add.

How do you know I'm not a spy? she asks.

Ah, Sidney! I say. She has clients from Credit Suisse or Banc Suisse who interest the leaders back home?

Her client list is a dark secret we never discuss, Sidney says.

Really? Gong says.

Go on, he tells me.

Next, Dad donates three hundred million dollars for a string of Hubble Observatories around the planet to study feasible placing of his space discs for Bihusi Sunbeams. His credit and assets now achieve rock-solid authenticity and unlimited grasp. The marks rush to hug his knees.

Meanwhile, we strongly suggest that the Lafayette scientists perform new tasks Dad thinks up one night while driving his beloved yellow Deusenberg down the Big Sur coastal highway and listening to Sibelius's *Fifth*. He's trying to define the molecular structure of bacteria in anchovy enzymes. As you might guess, when problems arise, he has the lightning-bolt mind and red-blooded ferocity of an attack dog, a lust for difficulties. He wants the folks at Lafayette Molecular Systems in Alameda, who were lost in tawdry solipsistic debauches going nowhere, to determine genetically what gives anchovy granules that herring taste, then to knock out the flavor molecules either by radiation or by a polymerase chain reaction and mutation in the nucleotides, and then to see if the flavor molecules from the Spanish peanut can't be substituted for an added strong nutty flavor that overcomes any residual fish taste. Secondly, he wants their agronomists to try feeding a mix of granules and cooked and crushed Spanish peanuts directly to the chickens. This method does not get rid of the fish flavor, it only covers it up. Thirdly, he wants fresh garlic rather than peanuts added to the granules, to see if a garlic/anchovy granule might not beat the taste factor. He is actually looking, though, for the cheapest way to change the molecular structure of anchovies raised on vast fish farms. Is the flavor in the fatty acids, the lipids, the phosphates, or the protein? Or is it a microorganism? Isolating the source of the taste is a simple question. Basically, we are out to change the fabric of life. Well, the fabric of a fish. Will we betray nature's purpose in the innocent anchovy by reinventing this fish? I think not. But I get ahead of myself. This problem very nearly kills me.

Sidney's finger rises. This reminds me very much of—

Doctor Frankenstein and Doctor Moreau, Gong says. Take your pick.

No, no. We're reconstructing only a small fish, not a monster. Frivolous human engineering never enters our minds. Dad has no interest in human destiny. He looks toward the rebirth of an almost extinct race of Genius, the Bihusi. I mean lots of tall people, doctor, who look out over the heads of the, uh, shortchanged.

I see. Well, does he think his wife, your mother, who was not born a Bihusi, has been shortchanged? He overlooks her early passage of mutism?

Of course not. He sees it merely as a case of arrested puberty. Mother was unusually tall at thirteen, nearly six feet, with her full growth still before her. And before I forget it, I should tell you that mother's analysis with the Singing Shaman was not an entire loss. He diagnosed her mutism as a symptom of hysterical anxieties stemming from the trauma of much too early invagination. The time came, Doctor Paracelsus said, when burying the repulsive and repeated shock of submitting to a Bihusi's unique genital and its period of extraordinary inflation during the copulatory tie shorted her out and left a scream frozen in her throat. She identifies her mouth and vocal chords with the vagina and orgasm. According to Doctor Paracelsus, there is some similarity between the head and hair and mouth and cheeks and the bottom cheeks, the vaginal mouth and pubic hair. His treatment consisted of singing to her frigid vagina which, sadly, led to an attempted seduction of his patient, and other malpractices. I don't want you to think Dad hasn't been a bulldog in seeking a cure for her.

Sidney says, Shall we go back outdoors?

On the porch I scent and look up to see a vee of mallards turn in the big blooming blue noon and glide down to near sedge for rest and a feeding. I scent the birds on the water. I scent Gong. I scent and I scent her. I scent the whole prickling kingdom of her. Must I stop? Unbearable. I catch the big brown butterfly wings of her eyes watching me. She's aware of my thoughts? She looks down and self-assesses her crimson slippers.

As I go on my voice deepens as though I've smoked three or four nine-inch Monte Cristos. We sit at the table on the flagstones. What if I slapped the table hard and bared my teeth at Sidney? Would he jump up and run away? I pity him if he'd try that. He'd find out what fear freezing his back felt like. Can you outrun the great bell ringing your death knell? I catch myself and shut down these wild thoughts, though clearly I'd like to make soothing noises to Gong.

When Mother left the couch of Paracelsus for our mansion in Mayfair, I say, she remained mute, although Dad's letters had clearly moved her. Dad is an excellent pan pipist and can make his Rumanian pipes howl chillingly and weep hopelessly. He has perfect pitch and on foggy autumn afternoons amid the fallen leaves in our greenhouse he'd spoon her marrow cream with oxtail marmalade and *foie gras* toast and play his pipes and sing to her, so mournfully, and hold her hand through long rainy London evenings, waves running down the glass roof and walls, her face wavering with water-shadow, as he whispers for her return. *J'attendrai, Magda, j'attendrai. Dis! Quand reviendras-tu? Les fuilles mortes, Magda! Un jour, tu verras. Non, je ne regrette rien. La vie en rose, Magda, la vie en rose!*

Pardon me, I'm sorry, I'm sorry,

Take your time, Billy, Gong says.

You see, Mother cannot be allowed pets. They do not survive. Even newborn puppies run from her odor. Nearly all animals avoid us. We stay far from traffic horses.

Sidney asks, She has this so-called psychotic odor?

Dad's odor you might ascribe to the unusually heavy pelt you glimpse at his very thick neckline and sticking out at his wrists. Mother's, well, she'd begun to change. Physically. Her aureoles blackened darkly and her nipples became ripe, milky pale dugs. When I was born I had a twin brother, who died. He had certain anomalies neither Magda nor Dad would ever describe to me, so perhaps Bobby and I weren't from the same egg. But I always knew that he was my elder brother and preferred by Dad as steward of his fortune. Though Bobby died almost in the womb, Dad still sees him as clearly as in a photograph, or even more clearly, since Bobby's death set off ringing danger signals throughout the Bihusi Wreath of the dead. Dad only hints at Mother's other changes, but these include a second set of dugs as if expecting a much larger litter. It's always veiled over but as you might have guessed by now, Magda really is in the Bihusi line as well as the Giurgiu and is both Dad's niece and half-sister. We Bihusi have such rich fantasy lives that we think ourselves above the more feared genetic mishaps. So Dad swept aside all monstrous possibilities and married Angela Magdalena Giurgiu. Anyway, as he's told me, the first time he saw her in her puberty he had to swallow his drool time and again. He knew destiny had picked her out for him. Like Dad, I too am given to excessive drooling during the act. We really get into it. But I'll say no more.

All right, Billy, Sidney says.

Gong says, It could be a revealing area. Incest, an anomalous twin. . . Do you have sexual fantasies about your mother?

Sidney looks askance at this question.

Well, Gong says, why wouldn't he? Is he abnormal?

Well, I'm sure semi-conscious responses were implicit during adolescence when Mother was in season. Estrogrens are estrogens. But Dad is the Bihusi alpha male and, short of his death, maternal incest is out of the question.

Didn't you say killing the father is traditional among Bihusi? she says.

I see where you're going, I say. But I really think I've slain that dragon.

But, she says, you've suggested that over the millennia patricide has been imprinted on your genes. Doesn't the alpha female then attach herself to you as pack leader?

Yes. But her estrogen levels have changed and younger females are just far more attractive. What's more, I'm married and have my own offspring.

When I say this, however, galvanic waves ripple my skin, which Gong sees.

Your mother is no longer sexually attractive? she asks.

I'm sure she is. Power attracts, even among females.

Yes. However, you've shown explicit aggression toward your father all morning, not just love. And you present your mother quite erotically at the Tour d' Argent and on that swaying bough.

Sidney rises and walks to the far side of the flagstones. Come over here, he tells Gong.

Excuse me, she tells me and crosses to her husband. Though I turn my head from them as they whisper and natter, I hear every word. For that matter I hear Helga far-off talking quite low on the kitchen phone.

Sidney whispers, Where are you taking this?

Well, it's too far to go in one day, she says. If his androgens originally produced cathexis on the mother's genital area, that's a very durable imprint. Billy may want us to ratify killing his father. Apparently his mother as well wants him to stand up to his father and do him in.

Then he doesn't need *our* justifications.

I think we should be careful, Gong says.

This could backfire?

Quite severely, she says. We could become legally culpable. *My doctors told me to do it.*

Or even *They didn't stop me. . .* Well, let's not be so obvious.

Sorry.

When they return, Sidney says, Sorry. Where did we leave off?

Well, back to the Marines, I say. So Dad tells me the best way to learn the art of the deal is to do a big deal. There are only so many business variations, like there are only seven main plots to storytelling. What makes Bihusi unique is degree, the size of our ventures, not the method. I have to put together a way to pick up these two oil companies and get some serious control of the US presidency and do it inside the family motto: TAKE EVERYTHING, GIVE NOTHING. First, I tell Dad, we're going to do the Basel Variation. And we'll merge it with the Sears Conversion. Okay, I say, let's walk through them. First the Basel Variation. Why do we own so many retail shopping malls? Did we buy them? No, we don't buy things, we take them. And here's how we take a mall, doctors:

A *contractor* puts together most of the pieces he needs to build a shopping center. He's got a zoning permit, he's optioned the land, and he's got the drawings. Like all contractors, he does *not* have the money. For this, he needs a bank. So he goes looking for cash. He presents his package to the money fellas, probably us. We thumb through it and ask, Where's your Anchor? Who's your key tenant? Where is that single, big, financially strong long-term lease, at least twenty years, and advantageously placed at one end or the other of your mall, that locks in a sizable part of your revenue stream over the life of the debt? When the contractor has an Anchor, he gets our money, builds the center, takes his money and runs. Jackpot!

Like most human endeavors, financing normally is routine. But not with us. Dad knows, my friends, that if we control the Anchors, we control the life or death of the malls. We own something necessary to contractors all over the world who want to do their own little deals. By controlling the Anchors, we have something of value. And anytime you have something of value, you get paid for it. At times the little guys forget this. We never forget. The contractors come to our big retail networks, our banks, our real estate companies, our insurance firms, and suggest that we sign leases in their forthcoming mall. Then they do a sell-job on us: they tell us why we should stick one of our banks onto the best corner of their mix, a corner slot that will harbor the first shop or a bank nearest the parking lot.

This entrepreneur naively trusts his own salesmanship. He comes to us, say, about a mall in Kali, Colombia, where people walk around with shopping bags full of hundred-dollar bills and where a mini-industry is building warehouses that are temperature- and-humidity-controlled, and rat-proof, as places to store and protect tons of cash, and usually he believes that he's going to persuade us to become tenants by spelling out the constellation of benefits that will accrue to our corner shop or bank if it's built in his shopping center.

Comes reality. We tell him that he's going to pay us to join him. So this local player sits there stunned with his eyeballs rolling as we explain, often three or four times, that we know he has financing if we come in, he has nothing if we stay out. Isn't that beautiful? So we draw up *two* agreements. The first he takes to his money guy and it says he's got our shop or bank committed to his big corner for at least twenty years, at an expected rent that makes sense for the location and the space. The lender sees this and puts up the bread. We, of course, have a second agreement, where we are compensated because we have made everything possible for this venture. Other people have over the years learned this technique and the aroma of chocolate hangs over many malls in a choking cloud of sweetness.

Hm, Gong says. I'm not sure what that means.

They've brought in Swiss investors, Sidney says.

No, I say, it's our own chocolate. Swiss is overpriced. But the Swiss are our baby brothers in the mall sweepup. For centuries the Swiss paid little notice as to whether or not their out-of-country operations made money. They focused on cash flow, because given the laws and circumstances of Switzerland they could make so much money with cash flow that they didn't need profits from their overseas ventures. Before *we* became their partners, the Swiss yawned about their money abroad. Nestlé, for example, almost never showed a US profit. But this means nothing: when the dollars come into Switzerland they multiply beyond any profits they'd get from tight or competent management of their US resources. In other words, bring Geneva the money and forget the origin. Twenty-five years ago Dad and I partnered up with Switzerland. In our first meeting we made it clear that there was no sensible reason not to make money everywhere. Dad didn't care whether or not the *Swiss* needed the additional profit. If it's there, *he* wants it. He once told me he'd kill *me* for two hundred dollars, and he was only half-smiling. Thanks to our partnership, the Swiss now make money everywhere. Each step in this sweet-smelling process throws off earnings. Most of the malls in the world now have us in some fashion on a corner. Baxter toiletries, Italian shoe shops, knock-off dress shops, low-rate banks, and as chocolatiers to the world even sweets shops, all linking up in global chains. It's quite wonderful. Our deals enable contractors to get financing and are structured so that the mall's payoff back to us for our presence usually gives us title to the whole mall after twenty years. Our under-the-table compound return is in the form of equity. Every mall is a huge candy store for us and, as I say, the smell of money hangs like Baxter's chocolate over the malls of the world. Dad has a sweet tooth for malls, all those pretty little shops and high prices. Is this clear? It's a major game and not many know how to play it.

Sidney asks, What if they get their financing and then refuse you the kickback?

Oh, I'm so happy you asked! Remember who *we* are. Everybody Pays Us.

So the Basel Variation is the first half of our program to pick up the oil companies and control the White House. Now comes part two, the Sears Conversion, and conversion is the old English legal term for theft. Earlier I asked if you understood that our big retailers own most or all of their key vendors. I asked if you thought we had bought the vendors. And I told you that we hadn't. This is how we pick up a key vendor and it's the second step in Dad's training course for me. I get dippy about the Sears Conversion.

First identify a key vendor. Next, see what that vendor's total production capacity is. This year buy half his capacity. Next year buy his total capacity. The goal is to acquire the vendor for nothing, so if you wind up with an oversupply of his widgets, no problem, they'll go back into inventory when you own him. The third year you buy all his capacity again. The fourth year you order two hundred percent of everything he can make and you promise to buy at that rate for the next ten years. Now, if he wants this, he has to get financing to double his production capacity. As soon as he's locked in and built for the additional capacity, we *Cancel*. Completely. We stop buying. Hey, he's desperate, terrified, hysterical. By now he's not only making widgets to Our Specs, but he's stopped marketing and sales elsewhere since we're his only customer. Now he sends lawyers and we remind his lawyers that Baxter Industries is *always* in litigation. This is what drives the shoe clerks out from under our feet. We're serious players, and always hungry. In short, sue me! They know we'll keep them in court past Widget going bankrupt and penniless. So, nice guys, we offer them stock options and decent contracts to hold off penury. They *must* take the offer and we wind up not only with the company but with management as well, and they now work for us. This sing-along-or-we'll-break-your-neck works wonders for us. Just ask our employees running the World Trade Centers in Manhattan, Amsterdam, London, Boston and other cities. It's so comforting to draw all those buildings into one big hug.

Whoo, Gong says. This chicanery is all quite dazzling, Billy.

It's in our genes, I say. To Dad the Genius of the wolf submits less to evolutionary chance, luck and accident than to the family's guiding, purposeful Oversoul. We have no Neanderthals, Cro-Magnons or missing links. Genius is above evolution, above mere tool-making and burying the dead. It comes from another source. Our Genius partakes of a purpose as magnificent to itself as it is hidden from human eyes, just as Jung's collective unconscious remains forever untouched by the conscious mind and is truly,

truly *unconscious* and lighted only by archetypal bits and images rising from it. Dad sees Ahuramazda as a plasmal cosmogenetrix, which accounts for the revirginizing of Giurgiu mothers—demiurges born straight from the Sun. We look upon all Giurgiu she-wolves, even those giving milk or with several litters, as Perpetual Virgins. This differs little from most religions, which revere virgins even among matriarchs. Bihusi know that a Giurgiu has given birth to the Son of Ahuramazda. But I reserve spelling out how Ahuramazda has descended to this planet by way of a Giurgiu virgin. Simply put, Ahuramazda is fulfilling her own birth-cycles through Dad.

Gong asks softly, But not through you?

Perhaps not.

Well, we'll get to that, Sidney says. But are you and your father setting up a new religion? Zoroastrianism for all? All bow to Ahuramazda!

Sidney, my father no longer hopes for anything. Nor has he ever shown the slightest interest in human nature. He is a mass murderer, doctor! He has no insight into mankind's religions, whose grappling with the afterlife he sees as flies buzzing against a windowpane or worship of upside down dead flies on the sill. The Transfiguration in the Desert awakened Dad's muzzle and sent him sniffing out fresh victims to help him harness the Sun-God for all wolfen. He would no more offer Ahuramazda to mankind than preach to lice. Men corrupt, like scabies and ringworm. To him, mankind is a misbirth in the universe, mere scrawny jackals and coyotes. Dad teaches that humans exist only for our gain and to have their last drop of blood wrung from them for Ahuramazda's purposes. Even so, and strange as it sounds, I've both lost my love for him even as I renewed it.

Now, I understand that at times you both need a rest from my tutorial. I'm eager to get on, but may I ask you a few questions that have quite naturally arisen in my mind?

Sidney throws his hands up. Oh my dear chap, please do!

Were there consequences back home when you and Gong left to study in Zürich?

Naturally. But we reconciled ourselves to them. Study here seemed worth it.

Worth it to you, but *not* to the People's Republic?

Sidney leans back in thought and weighs Gong awaiting his answer.

The only way to change the world, he says, is not by fiat but one man at a time, starting with you. You can't cure a whole madhouse at once, and altering the communal mentality back home is not anything we would attempt. Spreading Jungian analysis in the People's Republic would be pointless. Unless we translated it into simple humanist terms, there'd be nobody there to receive it. Jungian concepts would have no force at all and we'd be called dupes. We'd have to restrict ourselves to proletarian psychology and functional illnesses quite difficult to treat analytically. When the government itself is often the main malefactor in causing mental illness, how can we treat deeply repressed fears if such neuroses or whatever result from assiduously following state-sponsored programs that hide discomforting truths about the state itself? Could we treat neuroses stemming from an inability to adjust to entanglements with the socialist legal system, entanglements and misadventures which often carry the threat of death? Could we preach a healing detachment? We'd soon be jailed. Jung would tell us, Lead them back into their state religion, socialism, since it offers some kind of affective framework to support them. Spiritually, we'd rebuild our patients' spines by enjoining rote behavior on them. Life, frankly, is less lockstep and more rewarding for us here in Switzerland.

Gong says, Here we have positive feelings and are sad and gloomy only half the time.

Yes, Sidney says. There is more to love than to dismiss in China but shrimp will whistle before Jung has stature in Beijing. It's not hopeless, of course. Why did Buddhism die in India and move East while being replaced or overwhelmed by so many gods and divinities? Because like the Chinese before the Revolution the Indians wanted fierce, dogmatic gods to empower them, not passive figures like Buddha. They wanted a blinkered, narrow path they could swear to and follow, not Siddhartha's calm surrender to events that smiles equally upon life and death. As with Islam, which Jung rated as spiritually above Hinduism, they wanted allegiances to die for. Ours is not a society given to patty cakes and playing in the spiritual sandbox. On the other hand, there is a great hunger for ideas and fresh exploration of the mind. That this hunger must overcome the inertia of the system is clear. Jung's day in China will come and the collective unconscious will suddenly open under the People's Republic and a great symbolic poem using local imagery will arise from the darkness. Unless some other all-consuming idea strikes mankind, it must happen that the Chinese will tire of life without energies from the unconscious, and see through the blinkers of socialism, and discover an empowering new universe of Jungianism that's been walled off from their view. So for now we stay here.

And you have Western cars and Western movies, I say. Western books, a beautiful villa, and professional recognition. Why give all that up?

It's not as easy as you think, Sidney says. We have many fond memories and ties to our homeland.

But many damaging memories as well, Gong says.

In Beijing you were trained as psychotherapists?

Precisely, Sidney says. We worked with functional disorders.

Sidney was a prodigy! Gong says. He went to Beijing Polytechnical at ten.

Later, Sidney says, Gong herself was a star pupil and entered at twelve.

Gong says, I met Sidney and became his student and he led me into psychotherapy.

But, Sidney says, there was something missing in strict psychotherapy. We wanted an intellectual substructure that wasn't simply sensation raised to illness. Gong began reading Jung and arguing with me about his methods. She couldn't stop talking. I must say I was disgracefully dismissive of her ideas.

Oh, no, no, Gong says. You were just devil's advocate.

In any event, the institute here decided to try to make inroads into the Oriental idiom. After all, China has many dragons that deeply engage Jungians and might reveal creative new avenues of growth and self-realization.

Not all dragons are devils, Gong says. Jung sees the dragon as a repressed mother-image showing hatred of incest. The self cannot be fully realized without slaying sexual attraction to the mother in the unconscious.

The mother is the dragon? I say. I have to think about that.

Yes, she says. Billy's ideas are quite different.

How so? Sidney asks me.

Let Gong tell you.

Billy is a pantheist who believes that we a carry a chromosomal great memory registered on us by the biosphere and we are all message-bearers of a larger-than-human intelligence arising from the life force in all organic matter and that this somehow joins us to the Sun. Did I get it right?

Yes, pretty much. Though we've left out a lot.

It is metaphysics of biology, Sidney, she says. I was always good at theoretical physics, but theoretical biology was never offered at any school I attended. I would imagine that study of this field would be forbidden in

Beijing.

Sidney guffaws. You are so right!

You see! Gong says. Sidney is a very witty guy back home where the pressure is great. You let him roam free as a dog in Zürich and he gets gloomy. He needs a sword hanging over his head to feel happy.

Or more likely a gun pointed at it, Sidney says.

His problem is that he is a perfectionist, Gong says, and Jungian analysis is a far from perfect science. Then I matured too rapidly and part of him never grew up. That's the part he has to cover up or the institute won't think he's serious.

I admit it, Sidney says. I'm a solemn ass.

Or a barrel of monkeys in disguise? I suggest.

Keep it under your hat, Sidney says. If you're rested, let's get back to you.

Fine! Remember, I started out making clear to you about how we took these two big oil companies? Okla-Oil and Bowie Petroleum of Texas? We wolves think in first principles, Sidney, and the first principle of oil is: *Oil must be kept moving.* Like the shark, it moves or drowns. If you stop oil anywhere in the production chain, it congeals. It's very unlikely that you'll get it moving again. I'll be clear. If it's not moving it's sitting in storage. As you make more oil you fill all your tanks and at last have no place left to store fresh oil. No more storage forces you to shut down your refiinery. And a refinery that stops turns to gum. A refinery is as delicate as a good watch. If you make the mistake of putting heavy crude through a refinery made for sweet crude, that's the end of your refinery. Our Canadian cousins found that out the hard way in Hudson's Bay. They put some heavy crude into the world's finest and most advanced refinery. The refinery had been designed for sweet or thinner crude. Within twenty-four hours the Canadians saw their multibillion-dollar machinery strangle on its own blood. This happens if you pour syrup into your gas tank. It happens when you put heavy crude into a system designed for sweet. You've got to keep your refinery running and keep it running with the designated crude. If the refinery stops cracking, it gums up just like an auto engine and as the Canadians found out it costs more to clean and restart it than to build anew. So, stop refining and your refinery dies. Your tankers and your pipe lines are also limited in capacity. You stop pumping through the pipe lines, and they gum up. If you don't have a place to offload your tankers, you have to shut down your well heads. And they gum up. And cost a fortune to restart. You want to kill an oil company? Stop its flow. That's the *effect* we had to produce to make the two oil companies kneel.

Oh ho! Sidney cries. You're going to undersell the two companies with Angolan oil! And with some of your other oil.

No. You might use sweet crude to run a racing car or Rolls-Royce or to oil a watch spring, things with ultrafine tolerances, but not to run your common automobile or to heat a house or big plant. Sweet crude is simply too good and too much gun for simple energy production. The world can't use much sweet crude, it's too thin, but what they need we've got. You don't use cut diamonds for industrial abrasives either. Anyway, Angolan is only one of our oil fields.

We choose instead to bring the two oil companies' distribution system to the *edge* of interruption, with the threat of stopping altogether. We won't go over the line, of course. If we go over the line, the oil companies gum up and are worth nothing, to us or anyone else. They're valueless. But if we don't come close enough to stopping them, Okla-Oil and Bowie Petroleum will think we're running a bluff and ignore us.

At this point the Australian magazine *Sterling* wants to publish its yearly list of the world's wealthiest people, including Dad and the owners of Okla-Oil and Bowie Petroleum. Dad makes a phone call. He wants to be sure he's not on the list. It'd be simpler to buy the magazine but then somebody else would just start up another and give your name to every thief and terrorist and kidnapper in the world. While *Sterling*'s list, or anybody else's, usually totes up four or five hundred of the world's wealthiest, there are actually some two hundred more global thieves who are *really* wealthy and not on the list. Their PR firms' sole job is to keep them out of the public eye. Thus they don't need armed guards for their kids, razor wire on their electric fences, or Rottweilers growling on their bellies. These folks can walk the street without fear of being kidnapped. Meanwhile, the heads of Bowie Petroleum and Okla-Oil are on the list. They're not as bright as Dad. But then who is? Maybe you can't hide an oil company, but you can hide the owner. Thousands of people in the US out earn top movie stars and magnates, but when they go out to dinner nobody pesters them. You can't stop anybody from being shot. But you can stop just about everything else, such as bodysnatching, assault, and so on.

Meanwhile, Major Steele and Lieutenant Truesmith take charge of the

Angola project, with their eye on the anchovy and the chicken. All these things weave together.

Dad asks me, Which company will you take first?

Okla-Oil, I say.

You see, as the craving to grow turns crazed, the drive for bigness creates a soft spot in any business. The B School tells us that.

B School? Gong says.

The Harvard Business School. When a man has been to Harvard, Gong, or a woman divorced, they let you know in the first two minutes of chat. B School research shows that growing too fast causes most business failures. If you want to attack a company, the soft spot has the yellowgreen glow of leprosy. Hit it where it glows. Does growth need capital? Of course it does. And no matter how big the company grows, no matter how solvent, debt is ever-present. The place is in hock. It always owes money to someone. And that someone wants his money and his return. That will be the source of pressure, as will the threat of *Distributus interruptus.* Stopping the flow. We face Okla-Oil with a shutdown of cash flow *and* oil flow that just about kills. Then we snatch it from its owners at just the last breath.

If a half-educated hacker can get into the Pentagon's pants, then our snoops can bring us the details of Okla's customers. That's where we attack. The cliché is that there are three things to offer a customer. Speed, price, and quality—that covers the world of trade, but you can only have two of these. If you have speed and quality, you lose price. If you have price and quality, you lose speed. If you have speed and price, you lose quality. So we approach Okla's *customers* and offer them all three, plus we say we'll indemnify them for any legal fallout that comes from breaking their Advantageous Contractual Relationship with Okla. We steal the fucking customers—it's so beautiful! And when Okla gets pissed, we say *Sue me!* Our new customers are Economic Men, a genus that acts in its own interest at all times. It's a given that they'll switch. I often wonder why Skinner the behaviorist didn't use the business world as a proof of his basic theorem that *All human behavior is determined by perceived consequences.* In our case, we point the customer's head in one direction and say, See The Money, The Money, The Money. That summarizes Skinner. Do whatever you do for what you think is in it for you. This one thought sends out business ripples past infinity. It makes clear all human action. It's what you *think* is going to happen that sets your course. The Money, The Money, The Money. Dad's instincts are lupine, not human. As the Arabs say, My brother and I against my cousin, my cousin and I against the world. Dad sets our course, makes weighty plans simple, and goes after the globe by giving his marks, in this case Okla's customers, just what they want: a hugely more rewarding deal than that with Okla-Oil. We remove the customers, close the pipeline. The oil backs up. The tanks swell to the brim. When they're topped off, the refinery must stop cracking. There's no place to put the stuff. The supertankers anchor offshore, the debt service goes up and up. Up and up and up and up. The well heads must soon be closed. The owners look into their graves, plan their headstones. And we're about to rescue them in the nick of time. The wonderful Baxters will rescue them the same way the retailer rescues his vendor. They give us the company. As with the shopping malls, we give them options, and management contracts. The shareholders, of course, get clipped. But if Ahuramazda didn't want them shorn She would not have made them shareholders. How did we do this? We made it impossible for Okla-Oil to market its product. And, Christ, *we* don't want it. But if they want to give us their company, rather than go under, what the hell, Sunny Jim, let's take it. And reward them for shafting their shareholders. If we need any extra leverage, we get it by closing off the balance of the world market along the way. That's the Sears Conversion. We won't let any other companies buy oil from Okla. At the same time, we grind up Bowie Petroleum and swallow that too. Dad approves of me. I have taken both companies down, elegantly, with no blood on the floor, and no noise except for the whimper in passing of a widow or orphan, the investors, that is. Wall Street fogies and moldy figs always cry about widows and orphans. Those farts don't know what widows and orphans are. Dad's ghastly army of broken widows and skeletal orphans crawls like a private Bangladesh through *my* bedroom.

Now recall that Dad had told me not just to take down the two oil companies. I still had to gouge the White House and set it up for some heavy foozling.

Sidney says, You mean blackmail?

Only if you're not wired, Sidney. The CIA, as I told you, blessed this process from start to finish. They waited for the tab. I presented it to them. And they paid it. They gave us a detailed report, with photographs, of the Secretary of the Treasury, the President's most trusted confidant in the Cabinet, in *flagrante delicto* with the top Cuban with his presidente erect. You didn't know he liked guys? Now you do.

So now the Marine officers call. They want us to meet with them and their Lafayette scientists about the anchovies and chickens. Dad's happy, and he has a second job for them, something new in Siberia. We meet in Kansas City, Missouri, where the real action is barbecued ribs at a black-owned restaurant—Steele and Truesmith are blacks and know it's the best rib joint in the world. I come from a land, Dad tells them, where a man's uniform and medals are his proudest possession. He inspects the white-gloved and hard-jawed Steele and Truesmith as they harden in their stiff white service hats and brilliant dress-blue blouses with red piping, red-striped blue pants, gold globe-and-anchor Marine brass on their high blue collars, gold buttons down breast and sleeve, wide white canvas belts, bright fruit salad of medals and decorations, and colorful red-and-yellow overseas hashmarks stacked on their blue sleeves—all told a sight to dazzle the heart. He weighs their medals thoughtfully, including the matched Bihusi Medals of Honor. Gentlemen, be seated. Ribs and bibs! he tells the waiter. Although he does not thank the Marines for work well done, their anchovy/chicken dream still floats. You will be paid, he says. Now, I've something for you to think about. You like to solve problems and I have one. I need two managers I can trust. This is a matrix of problems and I will spell them out.

They watch Dad's molars crack a dripping rib and his long tongue dig out the marrow and lick his cheeks. A wise move this diner's bib.

You must go to Lake Bolshoi on the West Siberian Plain as my support group. I have leased Siberian oil fields under Lake Bolshoi from Moscow. Soundings show that the greatest body of oil on Earth lies under and around Lake Bolshoi. Mistakenly, we began drilling on land. All attempts to set up permanent derricks have failed each year. When Earth thaws and the mantle shifts, derricks crack and fall and all the pipe we've drilled into the mantle splits all to shit. I am trying an entirely new approach. My offshore drilling in Venezuela and Scotland leads me to think that Lake Bolshoi itself can be the center of my production. I plan to build a nearly four-mile-square floating steel platform that will support my new derricks and be kept exactly in place at all times by gyrocompasses instructed by computer-controlled lasers in orbit. This platform will float like the Imperial Hotel in Tokyo, designed by Frank Lloyd Wright to float on pontoons on a swamp and be earthquake- and thaw-proof with the swamp as its natural shock absorber. Our platform must be utterly stable, and be warmed throughout for snow-fall to run off through vents and for heat baffles sending out currents of warm water on all sides to keep ice from forming. Lake Bolshoi, as frigid as any body of water known to man, gets Sunlight for only two months a year, just long enough for the surrounding land mass to thaw. It is also among the deepest lakes on Earth. Its basin sinks well over three miles, which alone gives our offshore rigs a great advantage over drilling by land. We are going to get that Siberian oil if we have to kill every sturgeon in that lake. Rock dredges and deep earth sampling have shown Earth's mantle is at its thinnest under Lake Bolshoi and keeps us from our oil by only a few kilometers. We are going below the Mohorovicic discontinuity where the upper mantle meets the lower crust and the shift takes place each thaw. Where *we* will drill it never freezes, and we will warm the whole lake, if needed, to get at that oil. The Mohorovicic discontinuity usually occurs at about twenty-two to twenty-eight miles under the continental crusts around the globe, but the ocean of oil under Lake Bolshoi, quite possibly the largest bed of oil in the solar system, begins at less than a mile beneath the basin where the mantle is thinnest. This bed of oil dwarfs anyone's imagining. The being who owns this ocean owns Earth. I won't say I'm letting you in on it. I'm not. But this project will lend direct support to expanding krill and anchovy research on a scale far beyond all your food programs put together. Gentlemen, if you warriors agree to go to Lake Bolshoi, we shall yet save the Third World. More ribs?

Secondly, earlier pipes have been too weak, made of much too poor materials to resist the stresses of resonance on the drill string, or cyclic or vibratory motion transmitted over such long distances, and have snapped. They were made of shit on medieval potters wheels by Russian monks who wanted the pipe concession and used ground up clam shells that collapsed if you coughed near them. But today we are sinking triple-thick, triple-diameter titanium alloy pipes that God himself couldn't bend. Our titanium drill pipe could go from here to the Moon without buckling. I have already done secret samplings under Lake Bolshoi, while flying the Greenpeace pennant, and Bolshoi sediment from the late Jurassic period—about one-hundred-fifty million years ago—shows concretely that we are on the right track. I've already locked in my main designs. The next big job is keeping the drilling rigs centered over the drill holes at such great depths. But our space gyros, orbiting computers, and laser beacons will handle that and give us dynamic positioning. We will have less than a three-quarter-inch drift at all times, probably much less, with our laser-guided propellers and massive thrusters on all four sides that will keep us absolutely above drill holes miles below in the basin. We call our platform Baxter's Buster, because we are going to bust into that big black tit of Mother Earth. We must plunge ahead and create our instruments as we go, and we must assault and erase our earlier errors. The tried and true will not work here. We must dare. Who dares wins. We must gear up for a hard push to reshape the planet. Otherwise we remain little blips who eventually flatlined. We have a thrilling project here that will chew up heroes like herring, but we cannot hide in the past. Think you can handle it?

My kinda . . . job, Major Steele says slowly. Very slowly, a stop in his voice.

Piece of cake, Lieutenant Truesmith agrees, fearless but thoughtful. Gosh, I th-thought this was gonna be a hard one. But we still gotta lick the anchovy, Pops. I could never face my mother again if I gave up on the chickens.

Major Steele sighs. He's a little screwy. He calls his mother daily, wherever he is.

Dad takes a Bihusi cellular from his pocket and gives it to Truesmith. Use this, he says. It works anywhere. Call your mother whenever you wish. And you can call me directly any time you need help. Charge Baxter Titanium, and don't worry about it. I hope you two feel the glory in this challenge. We must break through fogbound methods and ideas that have stultified offshore drilling. Technology must clothe itself anew. *We dream big.* And if anyone can take this new beachhead in oil production, it's US Marines.

Major Steele reads Dad. I think you'll only need the two of us, sir.

Gentlemen, Dad says, as we say in Transylvania, we must bleed a fresh goose, and by that I mean the Russians.

Major Steele nods, looking up at Dad, who towers over me even seated. Do what you can get away with, sir, but always protect your flank.

The flank, yes, Dad says. Good thinking. I always keep a couple of very solvent, cash-rich, high-credit-rating companies for extra armament.

Armament, sir?

They're useful for targeting competitors getting too big, or to wound some pissants sticking their heads up, who want to buy what I want to buy. This is an ongoing strategy. I'm always in negotiation to buy. But understand: sometimes I'm seriously interested in buying, sometimes only in killing. A flanking company protects you but also can attack and then you go in over the top and wreck the bastards. You two may be interested in how it's done! *More ribs!* Did you know that these soak in a marinade of mustard, brown sugar, Worcestershire and ketchup for twenty-four hours before they're cooked? Well, of course you did. The point is, this little attack to prolong negotiations only *seems* bloodless. We try never to let the blood show. We really don't like to have it noticed when we bleed a company to death. You get into negotiations with an upstart and, as a feint, you offer to buy it. Buying it is complicated. Takes time. And really takes time if you intend never to buy it, at least, not at its current worth. The only time limit in this parrying is that point at which the company is truly crippled by having waited for the deal to go through, a deal that I never intend to do. Now, I've sworn the senior people in the target company to silence. They think they'll come out smiling like sheikhs, and can't talk about what we're doing, and since *we're* the ones pleading for confidentiality, don't tell any-one, swear it!—most often they don't see that we're the ones leaking out all this shaky news. These leaks scare the hell out of management in the target company. Sooner or later the best people get so anxious that they look for other jobs. We create deep indecisiveness, a feeling of on again, off again bargaining. On Monday they're going to be bought, Tuesday they're not, Friday they may be, and next Monday they will be again. Like Skinner says: you put a rat in front of two buttons and you teach him to push a button. When he pushes the button on the left, a peanut comes out. When he pushes the right button, he gets shocked. After a period, you reverse the buttons. The rat will very quickly learn to push the new peanut button. Then you switch it again. Again the rat will learn the new peanut button. Then you put the buttons on random. Within minutes, the rat will sit quivering, push nothing, and starve to death.

Jesus, God in heaven, Major Steele says. You belong on the Joint Chiefs.

Those chimpanzees! Sorry, I know you mean that as a compliment. So we disorient or even wipe out top management and perhaps the whole com-pany. That's why we're always bargaining. If we get the company, fine. If we don't, what's left is of no use to anybody. I expect you to apply these princi-ples in our new Siberian endeavor. If you need help, I'll be nearby. Even as I do my job, you must protect your flank from the media. Remember, *I* con-trol. I will not be understood, I will not be analyzed, I will not be explained. The media is there for me to *use.* I allow it no life of its own. Know this about word in the media: when it comes to you, it's the obverse of their vaunted objectives.

Whose objectives? asks Lieutenant Truesmith.

The media's, Dad says. After all, this platform will be the eighth wonder of the world, like King Kong, and attract men's eyes. The media will say, when reporting about us, that they want to be accurate, timely, and complete. But I have a business axiom based on speed, price, and quality, which I have had printed up on this card, please read it. It warns that most companies never expect to deliver all three, that is speed, price and quality. The media parasites promise to be quick, complete, and accurate, but actually they give us nothing: they're always late, incomplete, and wrong. Keep that in mind when *Izvestia, Pravda* and the networks come after you. Their reporters will overblow anything about us to ensure a byline and their own livelihoods. I tell you this because when they're watching you in Siberia, and you must assume that by the time their information gets spoken by the TV newsreader it will be a smudged copy of a smudge of a smudge—they will not get it right. *You must make sure they get it wrong your way.* The media? Listen. You know that today there is deep anxiety throughout the US about economic problems in the Far East. The anxiety is real but the problem is not. That anxiety is media-produced. Just realize that Indonesia's total GNP—

Gross national product, Major Steele tells the lieutenant.

—amounts to less than one percent of the US GNP. Looking at it from another angle, Merrill Lynch all by itself manages more money than you'd raise if you put the whole of Indonesia on the auction block. The media people lie like hell about the impact of Indonesia on the US GNP. Sadly enough, in recreating their lie again and again they create a self-fulfilling prophecy. If you get enough people to think they're in trouble financially, they *are* in trouble financially. And that's what's going on right now. Perception becomes reality. Now, if you add Japan and China to the mix with Indonesia, their total GNP has less than a three-percent impact on our GNP. Aiding the media is the fact that the Japanese like to think of themselves as scary samurai rather than salarymen. Look at their movies. They never have a cool villain. The bad guy is always jumping up and down, screaming, snarling, and chewing scenery like a Kabuki lion. The silent Western hero walks out and shoots the villain on the main street. Emotionally, the Japanese are in bed with the media, delivering the Chicken Little message that their problems have global impact. In fact, their problems just don't. Even in the seventies, at the peak of their supposed buying spree when we were told they were buying America, their US investment didn't amount to a hill of beans. They own less than one-third of what the Brits own here. The Brits in the US out-own the Japanese by threefold! The media warn us, Beware the yellow peril, and there is no yellow peril.

A final caution, warns Dad. Draw any heavy weapons you may need. I don't expect you gentlemen to handle industrial aspects of this project. But there will be bad guys on this beachhead. Russian Mafia types who want to muscle in on our show. These uncouth people, who have no idea that our whole Siberian venture is a kind of charity ball for the Third World, must be taken out when they rise up, and then never again be seen. We should help them cement their ties with Lake Bolshoi's sturgeon. Need I say more?

We wipe our chins and for the moment leave Steele and Truesmith raising anchovies and krill and chasing chickens.

But have I pocketed the White House? With my Cuban backgrounder on the Secretary of the Treasury's bedtime sins, I would say so.

Now I've shown the old man that I know how to deal. But, I ask myself, how do we get the last big stack of chips to do the Siberian trick? For openers, we're ready to liquidate everything, put it all on the table, and bet the bank. But we also need one last colossal shot-in-the-arm of cash to float Siberia. Put everything at risk. Our suspense is not small, since we use Siberia to launch Bihusi Sunbeams, harvest the Sun, and let Ahuramazda shine on armies of Bihusi soon to be bred from the dark folds of Dad's DNA.

Dad never was human. But he told me once that even a wolf has devils. Some parts of his deepest darkness still hide from me, and yet I sense them in the family genealogy, fears passed down through wolf generations without number. Genius is a vapor, a mere mist on the mind, as the fleetingness of mathematical genius shows among humans, and can dry up in an instant, at any age, any second. Dad never feared death. He feared loss of his lupine nature, just as humans fear loss of humanity. Well, I don't want to strain in trying to draw his dark side. If spiritual darkness has degrees, Dad's is darker than any I'll ever know or grasp.

I look up, scenting a young Indian woman in a lavender sari as with tiny steps she glides from the house. I'd been wondering when she would come out. A gold net under a head scarf holds her dark hair, parted in the middle, behind her. A black dot on her brow matches a gold droplet piercing her nostril while short but finely worked latticed gold earrings swing from her lobes.

I saw a big spider in my bedroom, she says, but I let it live.

Rani, this is Billy Baxter, Sidney says. He's visiting us for the day. Billy, Dr. Rani Gupta, a postgraduate student of mine at the institute. She's from Pakistan.

We exchange greetings.

Rani also has some patients, Gong says. She stays with us.

You're from the northwest? I ask. Somewhere around Peshawar?

Yes! How did you know?

Oh, lucky guess, I say. I've done some drilling up there.

And? she prompts.

And I can smell asafetida on your fingers.

That's true, she says. You have a good nose.

What is asafetida? Gong asks.

Rani tells her, It's a medicinal spice widely used in the north.

You call it *hing*, I say, or food of the gods.

Yes, hing, she says. That was a lucky guess. Sometimes it's food of the gods and sometimes, Mister Baxter, this evil-smelling stuff is called devil's dung.

I didn't know that, I say.

Nice to meet you, Rani says. I'm going to rest before I go back to Zürich, Sidney.

You have another patient today? Gong asks.

Sheik Sidi bin-Bahram, she says. He was quite upset by Sidney putting him off for a day and needs some hand-holding. He's taking me to Les Armoires. I understand it's some place known as the Gun Factory.

Well! Sidney says. You're in luck.

He's never taken us there, Gong says, and tells me, This hotel and restaurant is the finest in Zürich but a great secret. Very elegant.

Oh, I know of it. You've heard of their olive oil? I ask Gong. Supposedly the best in the world. They have one large vat of it in their cellar and are the sole purchasers of a limited production.

You seem to know a lot about this restaurant, Rani says.

My father's a partner with Henri Scammelle, the owner and maitre d'.

I must wash the asafetida off my fingers, Rani says.

That devil Sidi will never notice, I say.

You know him as well? Rani asks.

We've been, uh, trusted business partners for many years. Give him my regards. Tell him I'm sorry I stole his hour today.

No, no, don't tell him that, Sidney says. Mr. Baxter's visit is confidential.

If you say so, Sidney, I say.

Gong says in a low voice, Watch out for him.

Oh? Rani says.

Keep the table between you, Gong says. He's quite old and sometimes his hands forget their manners.

Sidney warns her quite seriously, If he tells you he's looking for a new wife, and he may very well do that, be warned. He already has a number of wives and tribes of concubines.

And each has her own house and staff of servants, I tell her.

Mmm! Dark-eyed Rani glitters and smiles gaily. This should be quite interesting.

Sidney, maybe you should go, not Rani, Gong says.

Oh, it's too late for that, Sidney says.

It certainly is, Rani says. I wouldn't miss Les Armoires.

I nod at Gong and tell Sidney, It's all right with me. I really came to see my family historian today.

Rani asks Gong, You are the Baxter family historian?

In a way, Gong says. Billy's family owns The Spear of Ahuramazda.

That Sees Everything, I say.

No! Rani says. Wow. I'm stunned.

And he's brought it along to Zürich, Gong says.

I tell Rani, Be back later and you'll see it.

With your permission, then, Billy, Sidney says, I will absent myself for a few hours, with great regret. I had no idea that old man would make a play for my protégée.

Sidney, this isn't necessary, Rani says. He said he'd be quite happy to settle for lunch with me.

I'm sure he would. Jealousy creeps behind Sidney's mask. But I'm coming along. I will not abandon you to this sexual predator. Call me when you're rested and I'll drive you to town.

Yes, daddy, Rani says, gliding back to the house. But I look good in money. *Ta ta.*

Her bottom swings and switches rather immodestly as she goes in.

Gong looks about at some suicidal dark crime on the flagstones, then says to me, Let's get down to the heart of things. Where do your father's ideas come from?

My skin ripples faintly at her sudden harsh focus on the source of my problems. I scent a slight blood flush in Sidney and blood drain in Gong, oddly enough both temperature shifts springing from anger.

Will you believe me if I say Ping Pong? I say. Dad is a Ping Pong master—I've never beaten him even once—and with his great height—I'm six-foot-six and he hangs over me—his smash is unreturnable. When he plays his eyes detach, he scans the air peripherally and doesn't seem even to see the table. Ping Pong is a meditative experience for him. He becomes dreamy, a poet, waiting for a voice from above to enter and guide him, wash him clean, heal the seams of his wounds, whisper to his soul and point the way. We have Ping Pong tables in every house and office. He racks up more billions during playtime than while working. The only player who gives him any kind of a run for his money is that melancholy old paranoid, Sidi, who is not one of us, as you know, but who has a strangely meditative, very low-net serve that sends the ball over like a mouse fleeing on its belly, and also a baseline trick of standing still and barely moving his paddle, as if guiding the ball telepathically by his eyes alone, things that get Dad whipping about and leaning all over his end of the table. Their play has dreadful intensity, like a wordless slanging match between two poets of the Ping Pong ball. Their rallies often last three or four minutes on each point. Dad has a Homeric grasp of his end of the table. Sidi is more reserved and composes verses while he plays. You can't quite hear what he's saying but it's sort of, *A ping and a pong and ping pong ping, a ping, a pong, and a pingeddy pongeddy ping pong ping! Ping pong, ping pong, ping pong ping! A pingeddy pongeddy pingeddy pongeddy ping pong ping!*

Our score is seventeen-to-two on the Gulfstream when he says to me: Now we have to steal everything.

SMASH!

Eighteen-to-two.

Everything between the ice caps, he means, and as it turns out we must steal the Moon as well. Unlike the Star Wars program we'd snookered the White House into, our Bihusi Sunbeam space discs are real, and make the Star Wars laser weapons a joke.

SMASH!

Nineteen-to-two.

And I want to rape Sidi when I do it, Dad says.

Our stomachs growl to haul the Chinese, Russian and US space programs into Bihusi Sunbeams. We glare at Switzerland and hunger to swallow it whole. We slaver over the land masses of China and Russia, and feel thin and underfed. Our plans will not work without at least a twenty percent growth of our wealth. We must gobble up nearly all of the planet's land surface and absolutely all of its money. This is global slaughter. Company after company go down. I grab them by the hind quarters, those shareholders shaken by our news leaks, and Dad clamps his teeth into the tender noses of tempting CEOs, his massive jaws whipping and thrashing them side to side until the skin pops down to the bone. They lunge about but buckle as we tear into their bowels, and steam rises from warm inner organs. We eat everything down to the marrow, every dollar, every penny, and lick the blood off the grass.

Wherever Dad travels he leaves markings that say, This is mine. Do not come near my border. And he travels like crazy. He can smell a mom and pop company across the Atlantic, and its spoor stuffs up his chest with longing, breathless longing, as he looks at me, his haunted eyes asking, How can we have missed that? Distance means nothing. He trots for days at a time, keeping downwind, fierce desire building, until frenzied, crawling forward on his belly and beholding an abundance of game in a single company, he cannot hold back. His blood rises in a tide, and staring in joy at a mere fawn, he sees Ahuramazda hand him dinner on a silver platter, and he yips and hops. Even hooves and hide look tasty. He relishes a company through and through. Why? Because he sees our current plight financing Bihusi Sunbeams as hard times that demand genetic endurance. All financial valleys must be explored and every penny lent reclaimed. Moose or mouse, his sudden cubby leap of pleasure, and his victim-paralyzing soft puppy whine of joy, scare them stiff. Even little corner-grocery grasshoppers aren't safe.

But Dad's savagery remains incidental to his brain, which truly serves and keeps him on the high ground at all times, his eyes wide and blank, alert for victims. Remember, he's out there solving the Third World food problem, he's building drills and titanium pipes to suck at the ocean of crude in Siberia. He dreams up and designs our Bihusi Sunbeam orbiting space disc program. He conceives and designs almost all of our complex business practices, the Basel Variation, the Sears Conversion, and all of the hidden and blacked-out techniques that big players like Sidi later imitate and slip into common use, oh ho, just check with Nestlé about that. He changes the investment world from transactions to fees and accumulation. His wolf-smarts and the blood on his lips make him unbearably attractive to people who really want something out of life. And he does get it himself, as you'll see. His watchful imitators learn that you can get laid more often with gray cells than with muscles. Of course, Dad doesn't always lay with human jackals (well, blondes), and when younger he did find silverhaired wolf bitches more attractive. Dad feels he's monogamous by only living with one wife, Magda, although he's duty bound to spread his seed among other Giurgiu and Bihusi. Yes, some jackal dancers and actresses offer a rich twinkle that piques his fancy, he's not dumb to human beauty, or being locked up in sturdy leg bones, and all know that as a dashing young wolf he enjoyed the foxy favors of Rita Hayworth, while she was married to wealthy playboy Ali Khan, and that Dad led his brightest blonde paramour into the Lincoln bedroom to distract Kennedy from Baxter money-laundering in Cuba—tragically, she died besotted with this womanizer. But he sniffed out less well-known playthings, Park Avenue debs in plain dress, not always dolled up in diamonds, choice ingenues in small-town Little Theaters, and tender widows with appealing eyes and still some juice in them. Dad's outward looking left eye makes the tie, and the inward looking right eye pulls the prey in. That's how it works when you're a charismatic and sport a genealogy of rapacity going back to prehuman times before wolf became partly human. When we nightfolk invaded humankind in its sleep, the wolf gene crossed with human chromosomes, a synergistic burst that created today's outsized Bihusi. See him! See this figure, now looming over everyone? At sight of him, humans faint with envy. Who is it? Some tall movie actor? No, no. It's Dad, waiting in lobby or Duesenberg, cutting a world-class silhouette that kills.

Well, Sidney says, let's return to The Money, The Money. Doesn't Dad have enough yet to put Bihusi Sunbeams in orbit?

Ah, but we need more. More, more yet, and still more. Whatever levels of wealth people have, sooner or later they want more. This happens with Dad, but bigger, faster. At first he thinks the path to the Siberian venture lies in money handling. Arbitrage. Buying and selling the same commodity in varied locations at varied prices. Fortunes have been made in arbitrage.

And it's easier now, because of the Cray supercomputer, which allows you instantly to see the play of prices around the world. In Tokyo at six a.m., yen is fifty to the dollar. At the same time, adjusting for zones, yen is fifty-two to the dollar in Johannesburg. You pick up two yen, or four percent, at once. This takes time, figures, and thought. Dad knows that in our case too small takes too long. So we go faster and bigger. We're going to sell shares in an ocean of Siberian gold. Black gold. He figures out the master ploy. Dad and I are the only ones who know that when we harness the Sun, oil sales will fade to a trickle. Oil stops being energy, is good only for oiling hinges. The nations that buy our oil shares will learn that the hard way.

Here's how we sell our ocean. Through the UN we learn every country's energy needs and how much money they've got. When necessary we let the World Bank give us alms in the name of Mexico or Bulgaria. We work it like the diamond cartel. *We* decide how much the investor can buy. Let me show you two innocents how the diamond business really works, since that became the method of our new scam. South and west central Africa, Siberia, and some parts of the Andes produce the world's raw diamonds. This supply is cut up by fiat among cartels and nations. Their agreement includes limiting how many carats are allowed onto the market. The dealers around the world offer to buy. The masterminds weigh the offers and decide how much each dealer gets. That number is influenced by how much was bought by any dealer last year, how obeying, how willing, even how polite the dealers are. It's a tradition that the dealers get fewer carats than they ask for, and bow and bless and scrape and crawl out the door backwards. Never show the King your ass. Now the diamonds are brought to the clubs. The clubs are hidden around the world in suites in buildings that often look like apartments. Except that the door is solid steel, so are the walls and all hallways are studded with cameras. When you get inside the club, you can almost always buy a decent breakfast. The rooms have small tables scattered around, four chairs to a table. Seated at each table will be one primary dealer, distributing his purchase to two or three wholesalers who will be allowed to buy less than they want. Once the wholesaler has his cut or uncut stones tissue-wrapped he moves to a long central table where he does the great diamond magic act. The wholesalers sell the diamonds back and forth across the table to each other. Creating instant provenance, so that the retailer will see in the wrapping a history of transactions adding layers of profit from a string of owners. The diamonds usually increase in value by a few hundred percent in ten minutes at the long table. I have sat at the table. The uncut stones still have a shiny-pebble look. And the cut stones lay like stars on the slippery surface of very thin butcher paper. All the diamonds are wrapped in this paper, and folded into little paper packages. They then go by routine first-class mail or are hand-delivered to the jewelry makers. When you realize that it's all sleight-of-hand, you understand the diamond industry and all the bowing and scraping as the cockroaches scuttle backwards out of the room.

We're going to make energy cheap and plentiful. There really won't *be* any Third World after this! So, friends, here is the model for raising our last bag of money. Each playing country will bid for a share of the ocean of oil under Lake Bolshoi. They'll get less than they want. The rulers will trade their shares back and forth to drive the price up as shares move around the globe. In the oil crisis that we made up in the eighties, one tankerful of oil was sold four times en route from the Middle East to Long Island Sound and three more times as it lay at anchor. We assume the boys'll do the same thing again with our oil. But on the positive side, eventually the world's going to know that for the next few centuries petroleum-based energy will seemingly be limitless. So they think and we don't care. We want cash for the Sun trick.

Suddenly my eyes water and I turn from Sidney and Gong. I catch my breath, stand and walk about the flagstones for a moment. I sit again, sighing, sighing.

This is when I begin to feel a deepening estrangement from Dad, I say. Everything is *changing*. Dad has taken a turn that at best will leave the Third World or any other part of the world starved to the bone. The oil will be matched by an ocean of blood. I have to take a very deep breath, weighing this. Will the good coming from the Sun discs be worth the bad visited upon the jackals? I never torture without purpose. Day by day, I am less my father's son. If I see this in myself, does my father also see it in me? I begin to think about the oil grift and feel queasy and hungry at once. The hunger I understand. The queasiness is new. Of course, we'll always need oil for lubricants and to make plastics, explosives, and petrochemical derivatives, I tell myself. But we'll never need it again for energy.

Now, the world is dangerous enough, don't you think, and this century more dangerous than ever, with the trading of pathogens about the planet as never before, and whole species being wiped out, and all of us facing viruses we've no resistance to. These interweaving waves of bio invasion lead harmful insects into new lands and destroy forests and sea-life. And I have to think twice about turning the oil industry into a gigantic Galapagos tortoise stranded on its back. Am I helping or killing the planet?

Anyway, once we understand the diamond industry is all smoke, mirrors, and mere baubles, it's child's play to take over. Even so, a well-cut big stone will always be a thing of beauty that we judge by the four C's: cut, clarity, color, and carat.

Tell me, Sidney says half-shyly, what is carat really? I've always wondered.

Weight, Sidney. But color really makes the difference. Until Mother revealed and began wearing her stone, The Bihusi Rose, a diamond with one tiny brilliant arterial red drop in it that now ranks first in the world in all four C's, everyone thought the Windsors had the world's greatest diamond. But they haven't. And The Bihusi Rose with its mystic center is Magda's favorite prop. She sees its blood drop as the moral and intellectual center of our clan's rapacity. My father sees in its hue his warlike Genius and calls its blood drop his dark Myrmidon. The world sees it as the perfect gem and my mother's breast its perfect setting. I've asked Dad about its provenance but he says only that Ahuramazda gave it to him. It's the only piece of jewelry she wears, aside from the Bihusi Tiara, a gown of turquoise beads, a few globs of amber, and a rainbow of Fortunys that only Ahuramazda could price. When they married, Dad gave her the Rose, knowing that when at last he'd fully drunk in his tall child-bride, he'd dissolve into her, they'd be one being, and the Rose would remain as their eternal union.

Oh-h boy, but my queasiness grows when Dad arranges the assassination of a snotty diamond wholesaler, a Monsieur Feydeau, who runs a little independent shop and buys diamonds straight from smugglers. As I said, smugglers go into the diamond fields at night and pick up stones. From his popcorn stand as an independent, Feydeau has had one of Dad's foreign sellers killed, unaware that the seller was on Dad's payroll. In celebration, Feydeau, a very wealthy Parisian, holds a Champagne brunch in his flat overlooking the Seine. Midbrunch, his butler brings him a phone. Feydeau takes it. *Bon jour*, he says. Dad says *Bon voyage!* An eighth-ounce of Semtex triggered in the earpiece blows a flea into Monsieur Feydeau's ear and shatters his skull.

Moments like this serve Dad equally as well as bonuses, and keep everyone in line. Positive reinforcement is an effective management tool, but occasional punishment also goes a long way. I begin to have attacks of phantom colitis. My guts bubble and gas will not stop gushing from me. It's ugly, doctors. I have surgery though my bowels are perfect. The trouble seemingly lodged in my gut is all in my head.

It's just at this time that Dad has the Lafayette scientists test an airborne nerve gas for Saddam. The Lafayette folks laugh at Saddam's gas, so mild it's barely harmful, though Saddam prides himself on earlier tests in Kurdish villages and thinks it wonderful. The scientists revamp the gas into a true killer whose faintest molecule sucks out life in a finger snap. The vastly improved formula so brightens Saddam that it inspires his overgenerous payment to Dad for this small act of fellowship. Well, we need the money, don't we?

I pause. An anguished *My God* escapes me.

So Saddam tests the new gas in another Kurdish village, whose lurid harvest prompts the spread of his deathclouds from one village to another in a bloodfest. Dad commissions me to inspect the killing fields. I'm sickened by endless blocks of bodies throughout the villages; their smell belches from my stomach and floods from my skin for weeks. I can't wash it away. I see the dead jackals massacred by Hussein's hyenas not as poachers, their flesh torn by large wolf packs vengefully saving their feeding ground, but as victims of an act monstrous beyond measure. I strive to rise above the thousands dead in doorways and kitchens. Babes on the breast, their faces and little limbs stiffened in the hot Sun like dried-up clam flesh. Yes! Dad *is* a mass murderer! Saddam's deeds only sharpen Dad's smile. But steel blades pierce my Bihusi heart.

When I report to Chalet Bihusi on the Jungfrau, Dad's failure to speak well of my survey and his characteristic lack of thanks I nonetheless see as warning signs. We step out on the deck, above a blue-glowing sideslip of ice and snow, and eye a fattening long black line of thundersqualls riding toward us. Lightning prickles far darkness. Dad reads my eyes, then speaks more softly than usual.

You can't take all this seriously, Bobby. It's not personal. Someday they'll all be gone, the jackals as we know them today. They'll be replaced.

He calls me by my dead twin's name, who by a few minutes would have been rightful heir and future King of Bihusi. I do not correct him.

Then who shall we have for slaves? I ask.

We'll simply destroy all male chromosomes with lysins and electrolysis, reverse the ions to positive-positive, something along that line, and genetically reproduce a slave state of women only. It'll be much more peaceful, believe me. Reproduction could be, hmm, quite demanding.

His charmed teeth sparkle.

But women aren't strong enough for some work.

Oh, we'll fix that. Bigger women! A new species, I look forward to it.

But won't they miss men?

They'll get along. I'm happy not to be a she-wolf, but there is some payback for being the life-bearers. Suckling is quite pleasant, from all reports, and limitless orgasm among human females in all seasons, you can't laugh at that. Our bitches have no orgasm, only a terrible itch followed by a pleasant rubbing, and a very short season, and after that you can get your grapes bit off for trying. I'd like to replace the whole population with well-developed women. Look at it from the high ground, Bobby. I'm sorry, Billy. Human males are laughable. Shortchanged! They can barely recall two generations back. We'll aim for brighter minds all round, and make 'em happy to be monosexual. First we weed out all icons, memories, pictures of that missing link, man. Teach 'em our line, that their new endowments are the next step up in evolution—I don't believe in evolution but *they* will, that's all the farther their minds can see. But all belief, even ours, is a purely sentimental choice. So they'll be enjoying the voluptuous utopia all women have longed for since Lysistrata. Think of it. No weaponry, no armaments, no battleships. *The savings, my boy, the savings!* His pupils tighten to points and his lids close to razor-edged slits. Did you see that mouse? There! past the crevasse, down in Interlaken, in the shadow under the ski-lift. He licks his lips, irked to see even one mouse not being put to good use. Without armaments we'll save centuries of labor. Time being money, I know I'm right. Men must go.

My yachting cap flies off down the crevasse. The sky glows green and yellow as a squall hits. Deck boards lattice our shadows in the lightning. French window panes turn lurid and Dad's face casts a bloodless white aura. Under such towering Alpine blasts, how can I deny my far-sighted father's hunger for a slave state of human females?

Rani steps out of the house. Let's go, darling!

Gong trades glances with Sidney.

Billy, I'll see you in a few hours, Sidney says.

Enjoy, enjoy.

A deliveryman left a package for you, Gong, Rani calls.

Thank you, Rani.

Hmm, I say. You should go see what that package is.

Why?

What if it's something important? Aren't you curious?

Not especially.

Sidney walks back out with a wrapped package and sets it on the table. It's from Les Armoire! he says. There's a note.

She opens the note, then looks at me. *Gift of Billy Baxter!* What's this?

Just something for the kitchen, I say.

She strips open the taped bag and finds a two-litre clear wine bottle of golden deepgreen olive oil.

Is this what I think it is? she asks.

Yes, it is.

It's that limited-supply rare olive oil, she tells Sidney.

From a little Spanish hillside, I say.

Sidney smiles. Thank you very much, Billy.

Yes, indeed, Gong says. I'm overwhelmed. She traps my arm. Now you'll have to stay for supper.

My pleasure. Use it sparingly, just for salads. Once you taste it you'll want to use it in everything. But this is like Kabinda sweet crude, only for fine-tuning.

We're off, Sidney says.

Thank Henri Scammelle when you see him, I say.

Rani's sheer silk lavender sari and scarf blow faintly as she waits, afloat on the breeze, and takes Sidney's arm. He glides her around the house to his Lexus.

I can't wait, Gong says and uncorks the wine bottle and smells the oil. *Ooooh!* she sighs and wets her finger for a taste. She jumps back, startled at the flavor.

Oh, that is fruity! I can't believe this, she says. It's essence of olive oil.

Extra extra virgin. Best on Earth.

Thank you again. This is a treasure. So where did we leave off?

We're about to do the Siberian show by forcing the diamond card into our clients' hands. The Boardroom of the Sun meets—our inner circle that Dad uses, at the Ritz in Madrid. The sweeping penthouse looks down on the city and its gypsies suckling their young by doorways of ultrafashionable shops. Aside from Sidi, who is a Kuwaiti, ours are not tough guys but Zoroastrians of high intelligence and big teeth, merely wolf pretenders. Their job: follow up on the deals we strike, collect for shares bought by the nations, and keep the nations half-asleep. First they must convert these corporate and political world titans into lambs. Dad's orders to the board: bring the lambs to the slaughter, chewing their cuds, obedient and ready for the knife. You don't *shear* lambs, you kill them. We figure out each lamb's net worth. Indonesia, six trillion. UK, twenty-three trillion. Brazil, three trillion accessible, eleven trillion possible. And so on. Each member gets a shopping list: Go forth and collect. The lambs know that they are buying the hope of eternal energy. The Ultimate Fund backed by Bihusi Sunbeams, which holds our wealth, secures their wealth, that's their guarantee. They can't lose. We underwrite any loss. Should the unthinkable happen and Siberia fail, our shareholders liquidate us and their every dollar returns. And that's how we put a pirate to sleep.

If possible, we look for twenty percent of each entity's value. This, plus our own holdings, funds the Siberian Venture. Don't worry about your money; it's secured by our money until we tap the ocean under Lake Bolshoi, the classic con. The mark watches the guarantee and we take the real money. The board knows that when we bring in the oil we take back our guarantee, and while the lambs watch their oil we suck out its value, building up Bihusi Sunbeams' Siberian riches. When an industry steps forward, nobody ever catches up, as with the earliest automobiles which had whip sockets on their dashboards. There'd always been a whip socket on carriages, so there was still a whip socket on the horseless carriage. But oil would never be a whip again.

Just like the diamond cartel, before Siberian shares are offered to the public, our board members and Dad and I trade them back and forth over the Boardroom table, creating provenance and value. We set up the shares for the shearing.

Each board member gets a portable high definition TV. When they meet with each client titan, they show them the Bihusi Sunbeams' Siberian Magic Show: the ocean of oil, and the technology to get it, a show we've written and had filmed by Industrial Light and Magic. The show goes like this: Satellite view of Siberia. High resolution optics bring the view down to Lake Bolshoi and Baxter's Buster. A computer-generated penetration, three miles down into the lake, arrives at the basin and the first drilling platform. We show the new titanium alloy pipes, the drilling through the mantle, our drillheads sinking into the crude, then the capping off of derricks on Baxter's Buster, and the piping of crude to supertankers on the Kara Sea. If there's anything a mark can do, it's follow a visual, especially in widescreen high-definition brightness and color. They feel the West Siberian winds in their hair.

Much to Dad's annoyance, some years ago I married a human wife and founded a human family. Going by Dad, who should know, this leads to my loss of the ring of recurrence in the eternal feminine for, as I've said, our wolf gene is passed along only by the Giurgiu she-wolf. Neither I nor Dad has the essential wolf gene, nor do any Bihusi males. In short, I may be giving up eternity and, in doing so, limit Dad's energy in eternity. There will be fewer wolves to carry forward and keep alive his memory in the Bihusi Wreath, his only path to eternal life, an eternity first won by a leap of seizure at physical death and kept bright by the power of rapacity in one's cubs. Eternal life is less physical than philokinetic. Dad will not be reborn; he will leap to the angelic orders and seize the Wreath. How do we know? We know because all Bihusi have the Wreath during their lifetime, just as humans have radios, phones and television. But the Bihusi Wreath is wire-less, powered only by greed, by gorging and digesting and by riding the thunderbolt of the Wolf Force in organic matter. We are the life force, and it is not a sentimental energy.

Now, Dad himself has jackal children he thinks little about but whom he cares for and supports. Who knows, a lupine female sport might simply appear among his human children. Sports are sports! My birth and that of my dead twin brother, we weighed thirteen pounds apiece, robbed Magda of her cub-bearing. I must now, sadly, tell of my three older sisters, Ruth, Sibby, and Ramola. All three have borne Dad cubs. But Bihusi inbreeding goes on with such intensity that he can never be certain that deformities will not arise, two-headed wolves, or mental defectives, among these cubs who are also his grandcubs. None of them, in fact, shows any grasp of busi-ness or greedy sense of the Wolf Force anywhere like Dad's or even my own. What's more, Ruth, Sibby and Ramola's lupine instincts are watered down by Dad's wealth, by the ease of human contacts for richly cared for she-wolves, and by being drawn toward common human pleasures and artistic expression. They pass like octoroons and high-yellows. Ruth runs a high-fashion Paris dress shop for Paloma Picasso, Sibby still dances in the New York Ballet and has seduced other dancers into the high-slit, bare-hipped leotard that makes her pelvic bone hypnotic, and Ramola works the celebrity circuit and scribbles novels under the pen name Rainbow Ransom. All are estranged from Dad, but incestuous ties with him have driven Sibby through two mental hospitals. I, contrariwise, had been handed heaven. My heart sang when I thought of my human wife. My home was a golden honeycomb.

Gong says, You become quite lyrical about her.

Titania, my wife, doesn't demand all my time. When I'm off with Dad, she's patience itself. Understand, she knows what I am and that I have not passed on my lupine nature to our offspring, since I don't have the gene. But I can hardly hide my surplus body hair when undressed, or my coated genital sheath. She says she's been touched by fairies. What's more, she's very taken by wolf lore. So much so that the more I curtail my wolf nature the more she says that she's married a prince who's turning into a frog. Nor can I hide my anxieties from her, since she insists that our three sons become Bihusi. Well, they're all at Harvard Business School. I've fallen into the human abyss, Gong, and through human children found a love in my veins stronger than the greed and hatred my father fed me. In fact, a time came when Dad was so shaken by my marriage that he told me he'd have disinherited me if I weren't his only living son by Magda. He really meant it. I'd put him in a bad place. I'd become the weak member of the pack whom the leader might have to kill—for the good of our collective Genius. But I'll get to that. Today I have only my wife and sons to bear me up, and they're all immensely disappointed in the way Sunny Jim has turned out.

And your mother?

Hard to say. She and my father plan to dissolve into a single being in the Wreath and mingle the Bihusi and Giurgiu blood into one angelic empire. So you see. . .

Tell me about your wife. Would you mind?

Not at all. I met her when I was twenty-eight. In my twenties . . . I'm bitter, unbearably bitter. My stomach can't digest and food acids rise up my throat. I'm dying on my feet. I desire, I need someone to give me peace in body and mind. All things, great or small, look bizarre to me. The Taj Mahal?, a monstrosity. The leglift of the Radio City Rockettes?, no thrill at all. I become voluminously expert on the last works of artists. My rich olfactory sensitivity obsesses on turds—I read the end of life on Earth in white dog turds like old gravestones. My mind is a lupine encyclopedia of turds. Death drives me. I long to sniff out, categorize all forms of organic excrescence from the dung beetle to the whale. Urine is a living newspaper in which I read endless layers of history. I can't fathom my existence. Sunlight depresses me, I shun the outdoors, I grow pale and gray as my mind darkens. I delight in rain, death, blood, dusk, shadow. Stars frighten me.

Stars frighten you?

Don't they you? I ask. They should! I see Father's religion of Ahuramazda as a purely local belief, something within our solar system with no tie to the heavens, nor even to any Earthly religion. We are not Zoroastrians. We're Ahuramazdans. I see all local planetary beliefs as based on the seasons, on life and death, and on reinforcing communal laws and morality. Just a human guilt-trip and Yahweh the big guilt-maker ties the tribe together with his impossible demands. Don't you agree that Jung's great poem about analytic psychology and the collective unconscious is a local tribal belief or Pentateuch for Jungians corroborating each other's big mind game? None of these religions have anything to do with life on the infinite number of alien worlds where some other form of communal life might exist. Do the various races on Planet X in the Constellation Virgo have archetypes—and a collective unconscious?

That's possible, Gong says. Jung finds the archetypes distributed equally among all intelligent beings. It's hardly to be questioned. Called or uncalled, God is present.

I question that! Some call him endlessly and He doesn't come. Seemingly.

Gong, the universal likeness among totems around the globe only shows us making the unknown less fearful and friendlier. I'll tell you, the planets frighten me. They're so stony and impersonal. All the stars we see, aside from our local planets, are burning, so there's no life on them either, at least not as we know life. Not one bright light we see up there has life, not one star. What's more, each star exists at some different point in time past. The whole night sky is an illusion of time present. Sunstarts on a stream. Though some scientists say the odds have increased for alien life—quite likely it's a trillion to one—that most of the far planets, which we can't see anyway, are as barren as the Moon or Mars. Just rock, ice, or gas! If you think of all the planets everywhere, the most distant and the nearest, joined into one planet, they would add up to a seemingly infinite deathplace of rock, forever and ever, not a scratch of life anywhere, just infinite rock. And here we stand on this one lone grassy atom. It frightens me. I feel lonely. I go crazy. Even my wolf genealogy is too limited and doesn't help. I'm here on bright Earth but emotionally I'm on Mars. Luckily, I've a dark angel looking out for me at my gloomiest.

So, at this black moment I meet my bride-to-be, and am hooked at first sight by utterly mystical Titania Tintagel, from Denmark.

Tin-*taj*-ul? Gong says.

Yes. As in Castle Tintagel in the Arthurian tales. She's a storyteller of great intelligence, who'd married a Chinese aristocrat who ran a string of laundries and lived in a fancy flat on Half-Moon Street in Limehouse, though she'd first been in love with his twin brother, a voracious womanizer. Well, even her husband had been off seducing shirtgirls before he married her. All the twins' dallying and their tie with Titania are quite confusing and something I could never clear up. Her first lover was the dominant twin and he couldn't give her up. She married his brother as second best choice between the twins. She and her husband leave London to run an African coffee plantation west of Nairobi, at the foot of the Ngong Hills. She's quite successful but his womanizing leads to divorce. After ten years the world price of coffee falls so steeply that her farm and her Kenyan beans go under. She sells everything, packs up, and goes home, where she begins publishing her memoirs and Gothic fairy stories.

I'm on business in Copenhagen and later take a long turn through the country to study the wolf packs, and meet her at Stargarden, her country estate, to which she'd returned from Africa quite homesick. I wait on the big lawn and look about when she rises from behind a great rock and floats toward me over the grass like the Primavera. The dazzle of her Botticellian blue eyes drills me with the power of womanhood, and I know that as this gleaming creature glides my way on the lawn I am being granted—as one finds in dream the joy of flight by mindleap alone—a gift I can never repay. She invites me to dinner and, since I've read none of her work, I ask first about the local wolf packs and then about her storytelling and over coffee and a tart lime pie she asks for an opening sentence and then, Scheherazade herself!, out of pure candlelight teases an endless golden dream across the linen and silver, an enthralling tale that runs on for hours, about fairies and elves who live with wolves, and that ends with the queen of the fairies roaming the Earth with a malignity in her blood, returning home to die or recover and finds the heart to live when she spies a handsome wolf while sitting behind a great rock and netting fireflies to pull her carriage through the starlight. I tell myself, Someone up there wants me to hear this. It's a fairy story full of dark yearning and black heartbreak and its flow of fantastic detail stuns me. When I look into her eyes as she tells it, suddenly I know I want no other female on Earth to be my bride. To live out my life with her becomes the chief desire of my soul, above wealth and power. I want to live with this singing creature forever. After a brief courtship, we marry in Copenhagen and my solemnity, at least in part, lifts.

On our wedding aboard the *Köenig Frederik* cruising in the Gulf of Bothnia, I am timid and put off our bedtime. You might expect that someone who pets fairies might be broadminded about wolves. Though our passion has deepened, we're not intimate beyond kissing. I have a rage for her, yet a shyness that unmans me. I fear showing myself to her even in darkness, where her fingers surely will tell her as much as her eyes. But I fear even more my physical invasion of her honeycomb. It's like invading a fairy's web, Gong, a creature of masks and tissue and fantastical stories who may never have known bodily lovemaking or known it only on Half-Moon Street in Limehouse with a semifictional Chinese and his even more fictive twin brother. You know my wife's imagination.

They don't sound fictional to me, Gong says. I'm quite familiar with their type.

Being Chinese yourself?

Being a woman!

Ah, of course.

How old is Titania?

We're the same age.

She's gone through menopause?

That's not over.

It's never over, Gong says. Please go on.

I can no longer remember it exactly as it was.

Why not?

Well, she's written it up in her memoir, *Half-Moon Winter*, and I've read it so many times that reality is replaced by poetry.

Oh, yes! Gong cries. I remember that passage! I thought all this sounded familiar. Well, you tell me how you remember it.

I sit in Moonlight as she drops her peignoir and bares to me the whitened shapes and shadows of her body through a sheer nightgown hung in webs from her shoulders. I drink her in, moans stir me with shuddering lust for the dark silken patch before me, I'm afraid I'm quoting her, and the twin blessings that sway above. My hand shakes on my knee as I begin my confession but she calms my trembling.

Don't you think I know about you?

I raise my startled gaze to her.

Really! she says. I don't think you have so many secrets from me. Her lashes flutter. I don't from you, you know. What secrets could I still have from such a fierce Bihusi as you?

None, none. . .

She raises my palm and traces my lifeline with deep interest, then stares into my Moonstruck face, saying, I know your dad isn't human.

The heart falls out of me.

I whisper, How do you know that?

From everything you've told me. He's a wolf. A very tall wolf. Look me in the eye and say he's not.

I can't. Yes, he is, I say softly. All wolf, and very tall.

Darling, I've had some business with wolves. She strokes my cheek and runs fingers through my shag. At Stargarden I was raised with packs of wolves living round us. So I'm not afraid, my pet. They're quite harmless. Friendly, in fact. We'd never feed them, of course. If they lose their fear of humans, they can't tell the difference between a dog, a cat and a baby. Actually, they have no taste for livestock or for human flesh. On a winter night a starving wolf might come down out of the hills and steal a chicken. But what's one bird, my dearest love? She smoothes the hair around my ears. Mmm, there'd be a big noisy fuss and one bird would be gone, with blood on the snow. Wolves don't frighten me. I've lived with them all my life and from my bedroom window seen their eyes in the forest since childhood. I'd see them far, far off, their eyes flashing Moonlight in the dark woods. Some nights I'd sneak outdoors to see them and walk into a field dancing with fireflies as big as fairies. The wolves wouldn't hurt me. You might say, I had a pact with them. They'd flow around me in streams of fur and beg and whine. I gave off no smell of fear. Perhaps they thought I wasn't real, a fairy queen? Those nights haunt me still! Many mornings I wake up smelling the coffee on the stove below and think of wolf. Do you have any idea what it means for a grown woman to long for a wolf lover? Each night in dreams to feel him slip about you, rub his big, big head on your thighs and nose about you, and with his long black lips beg to be petted? A wolf whose hunger can be satisfied only with your fingers and hugs! His *greed.* Do you know how I have waited for such a being? Can you imagine how my heart raced on the verandah when you asked about the wolves in our woods, and your frank, handsome eyes turned to me, minted with Moonlight?

Relief floods me. How absolutely wonderful, I say. Well, for the wolf. But how did you know?

Your eyes! Even in here, Billy Baxter's are amber and have been since the first night I met you and we walked on the porch. It was a short seven-hour day, remember, Billy? Dark before supper, and we went out while the table was set. Your eyes were such hungry blanks of Moonlight. And then you kept asking about the local wolves. How could Titania not know that you wanted to save and protect her? Oh, my big, greedy guardian, my love! Do you want to lie at my side and keep off my devils? Have you not heard of the Nordic wolf Fenris, shut up in the bowels of the Earth, who at last breaks his chains and leaps up to devour the Sun? I want to lie down with Fenris! She reads my soul to the backbone. Would you like to call me Titty for short? she asks. When we're alone?

I think not, I say as she strokes my cheeks. Our first night together, I say, you told me about the queen of the fairies and her wolf lover. I'd never heard anyone tell a story as you did. Just make it up! Where does that come from? I'd ask myself. You were so bright with invention that I dried up entirely. Too awed to speak.

Well-l, she says throatily, for such a sexy guest I put a little icing on the cake.

I love you, Titania.

Poor wretch! I know you do. Titania sits on my lap and pulls my muzzle to her breast. But, my little romantic, I warn you, I don't live on dew drops and pixie dust, as you seem to think.

I'll bet you don't.

She pulls back, grinning. I like cognac! Very old. Back to Napoleon, my prince!

I'll get you a cask for your birthday.

A cask! *Rr-really?* It'd cost a fortune. She pushes my nose in with a finger. If I drink only one thimbleful a day, it will last until I'm very, very old, won't it? Are you sure you can afford it?

Whatever Titania wants she shall have, I solemnly promise.

You're a rich wolf then?

Very. My fortune is inferior only to my father's.

He's very rich? How rich?

You won't believe it.

Why wouldn't I?

You just won't.

Try me!

He controls fifteen percent of the Earth's land surface.

That sounds impressive. Is it?

Nobody's wealth matches it.

I'll have to chew on this.

Get back to me in the morning.

She digs a knuckle into me. I'll get back to you! But I just can't see a pile of kroner that big. It would fill all Schleswig-Holstein! That's part of Germany now. Well, there's no money in Denmark anyway, but I sense you know that. You're not a bank thief or like that? No, of course not. Isn't your family's money a kind of money curse? That's what I've always heard. I'd like that! You do, don't you, bear some family curse? Or are you in with the Illuminati? And the Rosicrucians? The White Brotherhood? Ah yes, I can see it. You have some awful madness that comes over you at the full Moon. You do, don't you? Tell me. I won't hold it against you. I'll just love you all the more. I'll help you, hang on with you when dark feelings come up. I want to be there, fight for you, keep the Moon from blanching your soul. I want to take you into my deepest part, and hide you there. *Then* you'll know what you've been missing all your life! You'll feel me holding you, saving you from icy night, burning you with my heat. Watch out, I scorch. I'll pulse about you like a thousand fireflies. *You'll love me then.* You only think you love me now. I haven't shown you anything yet. I'm going to save you with kisses you've never dreamed of.

I think you might. Yes, that money may be cursed. I mean it.

Oh, how wonderful! She strokes my cheek. We're in our heyday, Billy. She glows. Shall we make hay while the Moon shines, huh?

Make me immortal, I murmur, fondling her luminescence.

Oh, things die, Billy. Even fairies. We don't live forever. Fireflies just live for a day.

Her eyes flash with sadness. She pouts with thoughts of death. Suddenly she turns about. Do you like this gown?

Are you wearing a gown?

See how sheer it is!

What's it made of?

Dear heart, you cannot ask that question.

Oh? Why not? I do like it. It glows like St. Elmo's fire or maybe some kind of yellow swamp gas. This material has phosphor in it?

You might say that. Or you might say, it will disappear at midnight.

Disappear at midnight! How wonderful! Does it tingle?

Oh, more than tingle. It's temperature-controlled.

A temperature-controlled gown! What will nature think of next? And will the *Kåenig Frederik* turn into a pumpkin?

Well, don't believe me. But she whispers, When I wear it I tingle all over and my wolf is rubbing his pelt against me. My blood heats right up. But I have to tell you, this present gown will not last past midnight. I can't wear it but for very short periods.

It takes time to recharge? I ask.

She laughs. But it does release musk. Titania holds an arm to my muzzle. Can you smell it?

I sniff blonde prickle and by her love-smells know at once that she's richly in season.

So I'll say no more, you big bad beast. But you must swear never to speak of this nightdress again. Such questions are not good for my health. And now, let's get back to the business at hand. Stop that. Now be serious.

What big eyes you have, Titania.

She growls. The better to see you with, my fieldmouse.

And what bright teeth you have, Titania.

The better to nip you, my dear.

And she nips my nose.

Is it midnight yet? she asks.

It must be. Look at the Moon.

Then I have something for you, she says and closes her eyes.

The gown melts into thin air, leaving only the blue veins of her breasts in the Moonlight.

Eyes closed, she asks, Can you see my heart in there?

Yes. It has my name on it.

And can you hear it?

Yes I can.

You have very good ears. That comes from listening to numbers pile up in you bank account?

I admit nothing.

Now I wonder, she says, her eyes still closed. When you break into a bank, do you come up through the floor or down through the roof? Oh, don't tell me. I'm just making jokes because I feel too much! But let me tell you something, my cat burglar or master criminal or whatever you are. When your years really pile up and your heart wears out, like some old fan belt or toaster, and it will, then you can have mine. Because mine will go on beating for you long after I'm gone. I will live in you until the whole planet falls into the Sun.

What can I say to that? Open your eyes.

No. I can see you better with my ears. Stop that. Didn't I tell you not to get nosy about my gown?

Mmm.

You've been very good. Now it's time for your reward.

You've hung up your aura for the night?

Oh, so you really do know about my gown?

I have a knack for puzzles and mysteries.

That's all very good. But just what do you think you know?

That you glow in the dark? You do, don't you?

When I wish. After all, I'm queen of the fireflies as well as the fairies. But you are a terrible snoop. How did you guess?

I have a long nose. Why didn't you want me to know?

Oh, who wants a woman shining in bed all night?

I do.

But not a weak bulb like me, going off and on.

My queen, you glow more when you're off than most women do when they're on.

But all this pillow talk is very painful, Dr. Li—her foresight on our wedding night that she must die earlier than I. Painful! Because I'm going to live a very long time, my mitochondria decree it, although I do dream of coming apart. And have come apart, which is why I'm here. I was born after the Second World War and have lived a fair number of years already but I will live much longer than you can imagine.

I'm not so sure, Gong says. I mean, about your wife. Danes are long-lived and for all you know, if she's what she says she is, she could outlive you.

Gong, Titania is not the queen of the fairies. Queen of the fireflies, maybe. I think she was carried away by reading Shakespeare and *A Midsummer Night's Dream* as a child. And maybe too much Isak Dinesen.

She doesn't glow in the dark?

She surely does and I've had her blood worked up at Wolfington Labs. Bioluminescence in humans is completely organic, the enzymatic result of luciferin combining with adenosine triphosphate and converting luciferase into a somewhat yellow glow. It's nothing occult. Even some mushrooms give off a steady glow all night long, and some algae and plankton, and there are worms and fish who control their own glow—and even the rare human can give off a mild yellow light.

But, Gong asks, you said the wolf gene is stored in adenosine triphosphate?

I said it was in a surplus of it stored in the mitochondria, the power plants.

Doesn't that sound like your wife might have the wolf gene?

Only if wishing made it so. She just has a similar enzymatic reaction to certain proteins.

I don't like to belabor this, Gong says. But you did say she turns this glow off and on.

Oh, yes, it's a voluntary blood flush. Her blood has high luciferin content. She can actually create a soft yellow glow by bringing her luciferin to the surface and converting chemical energy into light energy. And more people would glow if they wanted to as badly as she does! But she can't make people or palaces appear out of thin air. I think she's stuck with a child's spirit in an adult's body, and works an adult's power and energy into a child's sense of magic. Like Dad, she's one of those sacred monsters who can blow you out of the room when she gets worked up. Her eyes turn superhumanly blue and her anger rings like a Rhine maiden's. If she'd never been named Titania, she might have grown up, but been a lesser mortal. On our wedding night, we lay naked, next to the truth about each other and so carried away that we only held hands with our eyes closed into the dawn. I speak of complete spiritual rapture.

Gong sits back, resting.

You have quite a literary turn at times, she says.

No, actually my wife does. She wrote up our wedding night as part of her novel *Wolfwind*. I have a photographic memory. I was reading aloud.

How did you feel about her revealing such intimate stuff?

She writes beautifully.

But did she catch your true feelings?

I guess that's what they were at the time.

Gong says nothing. At last she asks, So what aren't you telling me?

Well, we came together, had three sons, and now have grown apart. She's glamorized by my father and I'm disaffected by my sons. She thinks she'd have been better off marrying him, or as his mistress, though I know differently from the way he treats all bearers of his human offspring. I've failed her. She wants to be a she-wolf. She takes endless cues from my mother, copies her gestures, grimaces, and tone of voice and Magda has taught her to withhold sexual favors until she gets her way.

I should think that's not in her best interests, Gong says.

It's not. But she's passed through her climacteric and wants rebirth as a she-wolf. What can I do about that?

What does she think a she-wolf is? Gong asks.

A creature who lives a very long life filled with greed and devoid of sentiment. I'm her choice victim on whom she's sharpening her new fangs. She imitates Dad's detached killer smile perfectly. It sends a chill up my back. If I raise my hackles I play into her hands and become more like Dad. *Oh, you do have some balls, Billy?* I tell her, You can't know how such statements affect me. She's hopeful I might want to kill her. At which point she would throw herself down and open her throat and legs to me. A little rapacity on my part and she'd feel her retraining of me was nicely underway. She writes about this in a number of her stories, and quite beautifully. She trained our three sons almost completely out of their humanity and now they are cheerfully greedy mock wolves imitating Dad and snarl at each other for dominance.

I thought you were being humanized by your sons? Gong says.

I am. They're each slightly unbalanced. It's heartbreaking. I have to detach from their illness but it's still heartbreaking to watch. They pretty much detest me. I'm the sick pack member who should be killed. Bihusi training, remember? Which of the three of them will kill the king?

Kill *you?*

Whatever Titania wants Titania gets.

That's terrible! Gong says. That's *sick!*

That's my wife.

Gong is silent, sifting thoughts, then asks, What do you plan to do?

I plan to see a doctor. And here I am. I really don't want to see my sons out selling nerve gas to the Middle East.

Billy, you are in deep trouble. I don't see how a daughter could help.

Yes, I am.

She grips my hand and holds it.

I'm so sorry for you. And a daughter as the right hand of God, serving as your transforming agent? You want not just the world but heaven too.

Thank you! I whisper, holding back a sob. This is why I'm coming apart.

She embraces my shoulder, patting me. Suddenly, in a fit of rhapsodic risk, I can withhold nothing, clutch her and fall into sobs against her breast. Gong murmurs, There, there, that's all right. Let it out.

I can't help myself!

Of course you can't.

Can you help me?

I'll do my best.

I wail, I feel that I'm going to my children's funeral after they've all been k-k-killed in a plane crash!

It must be terrible, Gong says.

Oh thank you, thank you. I sob, my muzzle deep in her bosom. This is the best day of my life, I tell her.

How can that be?

I've never cried on a woman's breast before! Never, not once. Even as a cub. It feels so human!

Well, I suppose it is.

As she reaches for a box of tissues on the table, my sobs grow and I hug her harder. My tears wet her bosom. She stares at my neck strangely swollen for mating, then at my crazy timid eyes as I look up for help. Brain cells sparkle in bright dark eyes. Sanded eyelids charm the bridge of her nose with corner folds. Sensitive brows and lashes frame intense curiosity about my facial signs. Jesus, I'm speechless. She's even more achingly beautiful than her jacket photos. As she reads my grief her reserve melts. She groans, a downy flush mounting her cheeks. Her heart pounds. Her eyes resolve as if dying, going still and not moving stare into me from another world. I sense surrender. Without thought I find myself bolted to her face and lapping her mouth, begging her to disgorge chunks of love for Sunny Jim, her cheeks, her nose, and the sudden dark joy of her eyes as they close under my tongue. My pent up heart bursts as I lap on and on and dig at each ear. I feel her blood shudder and churn, her breath choke with pleasure. Her well-kept fingers and plain nails sift and grip my hair. I've reached into a deep grief of hers and she answers me, grief to grief, a reckless sweetness sweeping us into a rapids. I cup her breasts. A thrill washes over her, from head to foot the trembling release of a fearful joy. Her lips pulse under mine.

These are meant for lactation! I cry.

She draws back in surprise. Her eyes ask, What kind of an affair are you suggesting?

Oh my God, what am I doing? I cry. *I'm sorry, Doctor Li-Chang!* This all happened before I knew it. Lapping just springs up among Bihusi and Giurgiu when they're sad or overjoyed.

Still in shock, she stares at my own wet face.

I so want to be human, Gong. Will you help me?

Of course I will, she says as she tissues her face and catches her breath at last. What do you think we should do?

I don't know. Look, I *am* sorry. That was absolutely spontaneous. May I tell you something you won't believe, although it's true? Among Giurgiu females, if a mother must leave her cubs in the company of a virgin yearling for long periods, that yearling will develop lactation as a substitute mother without ever having been pregnant. What's more, if the mother dies, the yearling is stimulated to full lactation and takes over all the mother's duties. This is true among wild wolves as well. When I say you're already a mother, I really mean that. It's built in. Have you ever been pregnant?

No, I haven't.

But when your sister Poppy died in childbirth, do you remember if you felt the first stirrings of lactation?

I don't know. I may have felt something like that. But affective lactation would have been too bizarre for me to recognize.

I can understand that. Well, thank God we're alone down here. Shall I go on? My hands shake at my lapse of manners. What do you think?

I think we haven't got to the heart of things yet, Gong says. But we've come a surprisingly long way for one meeting. Why don't we go on?

Where should I start? I ask, sitting back.

Where you left off.

Abruptly she finds herself hiccoughing.

I, I, I, shouldn't—get so excited—after eating!

I stand and pat her on the back. This does no good. So I let a Bihusi roar ring over the lake, stifling all birdsong. She jumps back, her jaw fallen.

Ah, did that do it? I ask.

What?

Your hiccups?

Great.

I breathe deeply, looking at the lake.

Thank you, she says.

I'm so jealous of those swans, I say. Do you think they know love?

No, Gong says. Companionship. Family feeling of sorts. Alertness to danger. Any playfulness is limited to mating ritual.

You're right, it's a completely different world, I say. I should know. I've been there. All right, I'll go on. We married. And so last Thanksgiving, at our family compound in Montana, the largest wolf packs in the world gather in our hills, with Magda and Titania and our sons, my sisters and nephews and nieces all seated about the roast boar and sating themselves. Dad takes me aside for a walk in the birches. The air stills, intense, clear, and each tree stands out and looks closer than it is. I feel trees march in upon me. Distances sometimes do trap me, despite my farsightedness. This time my mindreading Dad gives me a sterner lecture than usual.

I see the flux, the turbidity you are going through, Billy. Saddam has no sense of right and wrong. He's pure appetite and hunger, which we should *respect*. He's one of us. He needs to get even.

With whom?

With everybody! He's impatient. He's oversensitive. He gets upset! Remember, he even butchered one of his sons on a whim. Poor fellow.

What *whim?*

Who knows? Some passing irritation.

And here I read Dad's mind, as he watches Saddam search through his stupid remaining son Udai's mind and, despite Udai's brother's death, still find yearning for power, apostasy, desertion, and overthrow. The usual Bihusi duty.

Sons must be sons, Dad says. Saddam told me, Scores of people plot to assassinate me. But I am far cleverer than they are. I *know* they're conspiring to kill me even before they actually start planning to do it. I take them out before they have the faintest chance of striking.

Shock charges me. I see my own grave in Dad's pupils, my body under the birches.

Wordlessly, Dad waves my thoughts away. Looking aside he says, Pooh pooh.

Gong waves a halting hand.

But, Billy, you say you will live much longer than I can imagine. Do you mean physically or in the collective lupine memory?

Both, both, dear heart. I partake of an intelligence no human can grasp. Not even my wife. And her intuition hits at top level. She will at times try to fit into my mind and look down my ancestral path, but it's hopeless. It's a great gift to have what I have, a genealogy alive in infinite detail, an ever-available cellular history, Gong, based largely on scent, not on intellect or imagery. Scents of ancient cities, the villas of overfed old rulers and senators, the mating stink of cats at midnight when the Coliseum was new, of long long-lost farms and forests and mossy paths, the smell of every creature known and unknown to man, voles, mink, crow, mammoth, clams deep in Adriatic mud ten thousand years ago, and yet what human can imagine a Genius based on scent? I don't say much about it since its scentabulary has a breadth I can only hint at. What's more, aside from our widespread murder by humans, ours is an infectiously joyful history. You don't see it in me today but a great strain of gaiety yips away in us. My inheritance keeps me forever a pup. I usually have a cheerful sense of absolute purpose, superintense curiosity, compassion for my clans. I don't say we don't have a black mournfulness that even the Moon can't brighten, but all these varied qualities mirror the spirit of the fallen angel who fathered us. Fathered by an angel? Believe me, more humans than not have similar beliefs about mankind and its origins. But Bihusi and Giurgiu are bound into one proud Wreath of memory by the indescribable fearlessness and rapacity of their dark angel. You saw me break down, yes. For the first time in my life. But I would never show a Bihusi my weakness, Gong. It could mean my life.

Look, you're a thorough-going realist, Billy, Gong says. When you say dark angel, what do you mean?

I'll do my best to tell you, I say. But the dark angel lives in a language beyond human senses. I'll go slowly. To my power of scent, you are a lighthouse shining at midnight. The organic world is alive with messenger-substances based on scent. Some are hormonal. I can smell a well-washed cockroach or other insect as strongly as you can smell a strong cheese. A single molecule of pheromone from any creature triggers in Bihusi a sense of distance and direction, and joins all Bihusi into a higher unit. Though usually we are separate we nonetheless respond to sense stimuli as a pack, like a school of fish or flight of birds all turning at once. We have a common sensibility and are always in touch with each other on a social level that combines instinct and intellect. Millions of scent nuances pour over us at once, carrying scent-images that excite or attract us or which we dismiss without conscious thought, though thought is the wrong word here. We are a super organism, versatile, ingenious, open to great fury, and hungry as army ants. These smells or excitants and attractants register on one great memory, a structure of need that blueprints all of our behavior. What I'm telling you is barely a skim of what I'm getting at. At the heart of our sensibilities is a third eye for the supernormal, a togetherness that leads memory back to a queen from whom we all sprang, a demiurge of greed who still exists glandularly in our mass memory, and is our mass memory, or dark angel. I can't describe this memory to you very well, only to say that like clashing winds it creates whirlwinds in its own being and these corkscrew winds get greedy beyond belief and suck up human energies with an intensity that devastates whole peoples and leaves millions upon millions dead and rotting.

Gong chokes, looks aside and back. She asks, Why does it do this?

Why not? Its hunger reaches a critical mass, then bursts forth in a pestilence of one kind or another until it's full and has something to digest.

Gong stands and walks about the flagstones digesting what I've told her. At last she says, This calls forth more questions than it answers.

I shrug. I warned you.

I feel very conflicted about continuing, she says. I mean, your personal problems are one thing. But your being at the mercy of . . . of . . . some supernatural angel, that's more than I can deal with.

No, I'm a sport. I've dropped out.

I understand that, Gong says. But the only way I can work with you is to shrink everything you've told me down to a level of analysis that, frankly, must deny the validity of this fantasy-construct you live in. I mean, we are in different worlds.

And different languages, I agree.

If I ever wrote this up, with proper safeguards for your identity, I'd be the laughing stock of my profession. Not that I mean to write it up. But you did come to me as an analyst familiar with at least part of your family history. The Spear. For that matter, how does your dark angel tie in with Ahuramazda?

Do you really want to know? I ask.

I'm not so sure I do, Gong says.

There you go. Why does the Sun consume itself and make more energy? You tell me.

Because it must. The hunger to exist demands energy.

All right, Billy. Let's get back to Earth. For awhile, at least, so I can get grounded. Okay? So your father foresees your defection and is threatening you. What's next?

Dad calls a news conference of all the major television anchors and launches the Baxter Human Rights Crusade for the Third World. It's a public service, he says, with his usual easy grace with the press and even a flash of humor. Let's lift Albania and Slovakia out of the trash and give them liquidity. Let's get rid of the old pickup truck on the back roads of Nigeria and go for a great new Dodge Caravan. Doesn't that sound good? Hell, yes. And while we're at it, let's help boost all of the Third World debtor nations up by their bootstraps with heartfelt infusions of good old American cash. I'm for creating new customers. I know we all are. Right? New customers to beat the debt crisis once and for all? Get with the program, folks. Here's a chance to do well by doing good. It's your country, get behind it, and enrich yourself. Eat up. The pantry is open.

But, Dad tells the media, let me move on to gathering Siberian venture capital and Bihusi Sunbeams selling shares in the ocean of sweet crude under Lake Bolshoi. Russia gets a commission per barrel, and as well supplies her own energy needs forever. These extra dollars help build a third trans-Siberian railway so more people can go back and forth easily and we can attract more workers into this desolate country. Today a Russian can get rich quick by owning a truck and carrying produce to the city markets. Otherwise the food rots in the fields and workers in the cities starve. *We're gonna give Russia a truck!* he says. Where the Arabs have failed to bring the Bedouin out of the fourth century, Russia will succeed with the Kulak.

I tell Gong, The powerful message we hand to our market is: This is a unique opportunity. Grab it. We're selling the world a new world. On a scale never before known, one that dwarfs world recovery after World War Two. We will make rich the dirt you walk on. Buy every acre you can, the planetary supply is limited. Why is Russia such an opportunity? Because it has always failed. And now Bihusi Sunbeams brings success. But these stupid, sick Russian drunks will miss sucking on their depression and want to go back to it.

So we gather Steele and Truesmith into our 747 and fly to Pakistan to test our plump new peanut-flavored krill-and-anchovy chicken on starving Muslims.

Krill? Krill? Gong says. What is krill?

When I say anchovy, I imply also krill. Krill, protein-rich, much like small shrimp and in infinite supply. You know why the Northern hemisphere and the Southern hemisphere grow grain, wheat, which grows meat, livestock? I ask Gong.

Why? Gong asks.

Because they have winters. Winters make Earth ready for grain. No equatorial winter, no equatorial grain, no equatorial livestock. No chicken, no beef, no pork. So even before we do the Siberian Venture, we charge like Red Cross Knights into the dragon of world hunger. Great PR for Bihusi Sunbeams. We look like angels. We raise our global psychic credit rating to a spiritual level. People pray to be allowed to trade in our shares and give us credit. Dad and I love the anchovy almost as much as we love Mexico's corruption and its gifts to Bihusi Sunbeams.

As we fly over mountains between Pakistan and Afghanistan, an engine gets hit by a golden beebee: the fan inside the jet cowling whines to a stop.

All right! Gong says. What is this golden beebee?

Cluster fire. During the Viet Nam wars, back when the French were involved, the Soviet advisors, who had only light weapons to supply, taught the VC to fire rifles and Kalashnikovs in clusters at hostiles overhead. An antiaircraft gun does better, but if you fire a couple of hundred bullets at once, you've a good shot at bringing a plane down. The Soviets call this golden beebee fire and we'd been hit. Now Dad's wise demand for four engines pays off. The airplane yaws slightly, the pilot trims the other three engines and we fly on. How comforting that a 747 can fly on one engine. But a second golden beebee blows out a second engine. Rifle and AK fire drill the fuselage and wings with twenty or thirty holes. Rips burst upward in the deck. A flight attendant drops to her knees between two rows of seats, shaking, shouting and mumbling. First Lieutenant Truesmith unbuckles his seatbelt, stands up and goes to her. He helps her to her feet, sits back down and holds her in his lap, soothing and calming her. She doesn't get up until we land. Dad watches Truesmith's act and tells me, That kid has the guts of a wolf. When we unload the chickens from the cargo bay, many of the birds lay dead or wounded amid spent rounds rolling about. Dad is aroused by all this danger and takes the trembling stewardess to his private berth and soothes her.

Looking back at our caper, Gong, I see Dad at cross-purposes in Pakistan. Even among starving Pakistanis he lures to his food trials, he looks for candidates to keep his sexual organs toned up and ensure good prostate health. While Steele and Truesmith set up free food kitchens, Dad picks and chooses his mates from among huddled, wide-eyed skeletons, the nearer death the better, and sprinkles them freely with Malaysian Lime. He thrives on a height above pity, and stares with cold eye on this human rubbish. Failures of the life force goad him to vengefulness. Even the most beautifully befeathered high-born women, he sees only as rabble and gilded sluts. They have bad breath and fishy scents, he often tells me, or stink of lavender bathwater. I go on about this not to blacken Dad but to show the instincts born in him, to underscore the usual lumpen human stupidity his Wolf Force daily deplores. Things fit together better for Dad than for anyone I know, or they did. He has boundless finger skills with knife, paintbrush, or even molding statuettes of wolves at bay, heroes snarling and risen on their hind legs, or with throats massively broadened for hailing each other from hilltop to hilltop. I have heard his melancholy, long-drawn howls choiring heartbreak up and down black valleys, while his noble statuettes far outclass Remington's lone Indian rider or bucking broncos in bronze. Of Dad's pieces one must say here truly is the Wolf Force. The power in his fingers leaves me avid to hold and ravish each figure's slant-eyed rages.

You hear the very song in their throats.

This is eternal art.

Nor does peace come easily to him. Wrath and grief flood him as mankind usurps the wolf Genius and keeps our species wild and poor, while humans live on flesh and sugar in heated rooms. He will sometimes meet a woman with pure breath his sensitivities can bear, and be struck dumb, unable to abstain from the pleasure of her cries when he puts his mind and long silken tongue to rousing her. He's no butcher when it comes to female flesh; he handles it with warmth, and drools ecstatically while meeting his partner's surges. I know, because when he's beside himself inside a woman and his mind widens its iris and his body opens its floodgate, a radiance washes over us all, wherever we might be, driving or eating or sleeping, and at whatever time of night or day. Once daily at least I receive this giddy, golden telegram with its addictive boost that catches me up and makes me snort and suck hard at its scent. True, nearly all women lack the eternal feminine he seeks, but their little human joys can burn away his devils for a moment and lighten the darkness, most powerfully at the sudden rush and struggle of their release. I permit myself all things, he tells me. He plunges into the coldest woman, married or single, overthrows her boundaries and, without a second thought for the woman's danger, leaves his hungry wolf-spunk. He makes even frigid women, those who have never known high joy, rise from the dead and thank heaven for shockwaves and bird cries God himself has released from them. They miss him when he's gone and stagger about their homes and offices and dance stages only half there, minds locked into a midair flight of love among the eagles. Or rather, on dreams of finding themselves cast into a den of wolves, and loving it.

Meanwhile, I join Steele and Truesmith and feed the masses. For weeks I stir bubbling pots and fry thighs and breasts on great ranges. Everywhere about me tight-skulled little children sit with bare fingers chewing on chicken. The dancing eyes of the two Marines infect me with their flow of joy and humanity. A gold stream of fellowfeeling burns my blood and flesh like a curse. The eyes brightening about me in the small Pakistani heads read me with engulfing curiosity about my size and the magic food I bring them from that Fairyland my wife makes spells out of. I scent their human enchantment with the glowing frycook. I cannot fight off the love upwelling in them and that will follow them the rest of their lives as they call forth memories of the amber-eyed giant, Baxter, who brought them such savory, sweet, soul-saving chutney chicken.

Well, you might ask, do Dad's affairs never lift his wrath and vengefulness? Is he completely untouched by the food kitchens? And do his human lovers in no way soothe him? He may love them as his teeth grip their necks and still them so he can enter. As I said before, affairs with jackals don't count, and the Wreath demands he lay with his own daughters. For that matter, all Giurgiu and Bihusi females know it a privilege and only right that the Seigneur lead them into the wolf world when their first season comes.

Obsession rips him each time that scent arises and the power of Giurgiu and Bihusi musk overwhelms him. He hates himself, Gong, for every seed cast into human flesh, and for every anchovy wasted. Each ejaculation only underscores a shrinking of the Wolf Force and Genius man steals from him daily. For this theft, he will slay the Earth down to the last man, and skin that man alive and then set him free to wander.

Gong chokes. Surely you can't call this love?

I don't know what you'd call it. Especially when my mother knows about it each time a young bitch fills with alarm and lust. Should a bitch long to stay under his eye, he at last drives her out to find another mate. Sibby has mental problems and with her sisters comes home for family festivals only to see how Dad has aged or his Genius thinned. By now the girls seem half-jackal to him, and he hates himself for liking what he sees in them, their jackal switch and vigor.

But back to the Sun. As we bolster Bihusi Sunbeams and gather toward our goal, Dad moves without stop. I often hear him through the bathroom door, panting on the stool. His only rest comes when an unavoidable dead evening or so arises and he flies home to Magda at the chalet and sits around the kitchen with her while she rolls and slaps together his favorite nutty-tasting, seven-grain Rumanian bread and bakes it in her open hearth oven. Not very queenly, but it takes her back to Turda, and he enjoys toasting for her a few of Scott Nearing's addictive maple marshmallows while the loaves rise. He falls asleep in his smoking jacket in the library. Nobody wears smoking jackets any more but Dad loves his half-length blue-silk robe and a Sunny Honduran cigar to carry him off.

About seven years ago Dad began dictating his memoirs and hired a private typist, the beautiful redhead Billie McLachlan from Aberdeen, a top grad of the B School, to go about the world with him on our 747, Bihusi One. His memoirs are a dryasdust flow-chart of Bihusi business deals since Baxter Blades. For this memoir he composed a glottal wolf-whiny lingo only he and Billie understand, which he thinks of as a Rosetta Stone for our descendants to decipher when following his business practices. To spark his interest in this ongoing project, he keeps his vastly overqualified typist gowned in a loosely strung red bead dress through which her nipples poke. She's a nice place to rest his eyes when playing his Pan pipes. He toys bodily with Billie when no one else is at hand, but his first interest lies in grooming her business skills, since she is in the top hundredth percentile of human intelligence and has adopted from Dad some of the shifty moves of the wolf. She keeps all seven main areas of his business interests afloat in her mind at once, and could probably keep twenty-four more. With Dad she's like the king's daughter and her sashay down the cabin aisle in the swaying red bead dress, and her mental shapeshift into she-wolf, have kept Steele and Truesmith spellbound.

Earlier, one of Dad's human great-grandchildren had been hit by a car and needed an immediate transfusion of fairly rare Type O blood. Since that is Billie's type, she volunteered to give, was tested and used. Tragically, the child came down with AIDS and the virus was traced to Billie, who was herself unaware of her infection with a particularly virulent strain of the disease. A virgin at graduation when she hired on with Dad, clearly she'd got AIDS from him. He'd picked it up years ago in Nairobi, passing it off as a light cough. Although a carrier, he is, in fact, species-resistant to the disease, and after a while it dawned on Dad, during a long lull while dictating, that he'd infected thousands of women and sent them to their deaths. Billie'd never suggested this to him and it hadn't popped up earlier because he's never ill and rises above infections that would fell the strongest human. I, of course, have nothing physical to do with Billie, who is Dad's all-purpose, adored confidante. He keeps her sprinkled with Malaysian Lime and relishes her globes and beads, her bright lips of dewy copper, her powerhouse mind in the body of a champion mare. Why not have the best? he asks me. I too admire Billie, think her strikingly beautiful, sexy, and a mental marvel. He expresses no regret for having shortened her life but does keep her supplied with the latest drugs for fighting the disease. She's still alive, works for Bihusi Sunbeams, and looks great, although she's never married, and a glint of tears sometimes cools her blue eye. After all, what human lover could ever bring this tough Scot to the heights her demon lover affords? She's spoiled. In many ways, he treats her much better than any of his human daughters.

She's had two girls by him and both still hang on. She rarely sees them, though both daughters have spent time aboard Bihusi One. Does she secretly hate Dad? Well, she doesn't see him as having cloven feet, but that hatred is a sweet, sharp business tool to Dad hasn't escaped her. She may weep in private but she holds her tongue and allows no frost to show. She collects paintings of lilies by Georgia O'Keeffe, the Impressionists, Fantin-Latour and others and keeps them hung in her bedrooms and living and dining rooms at Sorrowgrass, her Aberdeen home, so that wherever she walks in her house, holding her daughters' hands, she's strolling through the hills of heaven and soothed by lovely mountains of funereal lilies. Although she and Dad laugh about his crazy lingo as she takes dictation, there is no question of happiness as she awaits the first sarcoma that will begin tearing apart the fibres of her spirit. I bring her up only to show you how disease-resistant Dad himself is and why he lived through the accident that at last stole his Genius and left him much like a wet-brained jackal.

Skeletal Pakistanis mob Steele and Truesmith's food kitchen, pleasing Dad and wearing the two Marines limp. Try some! Nelson Truesmith cries to Dad, holding aloft an A-1 Sauce bottle to go with the alluring recipe for Baxter's Chutney Chicken. A-1 Sauce on chutney does the trick. But like his favorite wolf rhapsodist, Jack London, Dad savors his duck or chicken boiled for only three minutes and half-raw. He tells chefs, You can't fool me with your sauces, a bird is only a bird. But he's still more demanding with anchovy chicken, and if the slightest fish taste, even under sauce, alerts the Pakistanis, Dad will junk the whole project and at once ship Steele and Truesmith off to the Siberian Venture where they belong, though Baxter's World Fisheries, Baxter's Chicken Feed and Baxter's Chickens now take in an Everest of cash. Since my palate is closest to his, and so that his sensitive nose won't be poisoned and drive him into a rage, he appoints me food taster. We have whole trainloads of cash riding on anchovies, and his luck holds. Neither I nor a single Pakistani tastes the brave little anchovy that has swum through the guts of a chicken. We unload our peanut-reflavored chicken feed granules on the staggering Pakistani nation, as Nelson and Truesmith turn an eye to the deeply underfed worldwide.

Truesmith's mother is very happy, Major Steele says.

You gotta try her peanut chicken with biscuits and gravy, Nelson tells Dad.

We must hand these chickens over to Billy for a while, Dad says. We have another bird to pluck.

We turn like Mongols to Baxter's Buster and our raid on Siberia. The Bolshoi basin is a great dumping ground for land worn away from the dark, rocky face of the Urals rimming the lake. We have plain Earth to dismantle, then unknown types of mud to move, red clays, iron ore, hardened lava flow, coal, quartz and softer matter, and lastly, a mere afterthought, we must drill through the crust below the mantle. High temperatures under Lake

Bolshoi are not foreseen, but how hot will the crude be? We can't tell, and great heat can be ruinous. Will high heat soften our drill bits? Will the electrical insulation on our cables become inelastic? Will it simply melt? Can the drill string hold together at depth? And how deep can we effectively drive cement? This is Armageddon, Dad says, a war for eternal energy to save the planet. Or that's how he sells the oil scam and the disc show to the Boardroom, though not every aspect of drilling enheartens us, *and* we must also begin laying the massive groundwork for space disc launching pads on cheap land in Albania, Slovakia, and the Balkans, and for the making of tens of thousands of small-bore rockets to carry the Sun discs aloft. We are moving.

Steele and Truesmith oversee laying the first giant pontoons for floating Buster. Test drillings at Buster's chosen center release heat into the Bolshoi basin and several dead sturgeon wash ashore. Soon Greenpeace has a hard look at our work and the sight of dead sturgeon moves their green little hearts against us and we find Greenpeace ships raiding our sites and trying to sink our pontoons. We mount a fight against Greenpeace, led by Steele and Truesmith. I'm giving you the short story on all this, Gong, since our engineering adventures don't tie in with what we're talking about. Despite waves of environmentalists, we get our platform built and derricks standing tall, as the world knows, and the sight of the pink October dawn shot with Northern lights rising over the steel lid at the lake's center and of dozens of derricks pricking the wintry morning scud is as well-known as the pyramids. It is the greatest engineering wonder of the modern world, and yet, as few know, it's size will soon seem stunted by the Saturnian ring of space discs rounding the planet.

We pump oil from under the crust by the millions of barrels when Magda's chopper lands silent as a snowflake, its roar lost in the hoarse lift and fall of derrick pumps grounded on steel, whose colossal uproar bursts horrendously as if a Titan pounds the great steel drum on Bolshoi, and Mother, in a tall, black baby-lamb astrakhan hat and wrapped in a magnificent black lamb cape-and-coat gleaming with waves and curls, steps down onto the steel deck, grasping The Spear of Ahuramazda That Sees Everything. I am shocked with happiness to see this weapon once held by beloved Nebuchadnezzar, king of Old Babylon and one of us, who destroyed Jerusalem and built the splendid hanging gardens, The Spear that then by misadventure fell into the hands of Joshua whose great shout felled the walls of Jericho, and later passed to Herod the Great, Rome-appointed tetrarch of the Jews, also one of us, who massacred all the first-born babes in Judea in hopes of killing the forespoken King of the Jews at birth, executed John the Baptist, married his own niece, and handed The Spear to the Roman centurion Gaius Cassius, later known as Longinus The Spearman, whom he entrusted with killing Christ before the Sabbath ended. On horseback, Gaius Cassius carefully ran the blade between Christ's fourth and fifth ribs rather than break all his limbs as was then customary to ensure death. Herod, then secretly the highest-born member of my mother's Giurgiu clan, had a nail from Christ's cross bound by gold, silver and copper threads to the two halves of The Spearhead. It's the great spiritual heirloom of the Giurgiu and someday will fall into my care.

Above the roar I shout, Why did you bring The Spear?

What better day? she shouts, then sees Dad. *My wolf! My wolf!*

Her eyes shine at endless derricks stretching for miles about. She strides across steel under great ashen Siberian skies. Her joy boils over. *Freedom!* You have given me freedom, my wolf! I have my heart back.

Dad shouts, You have always been free, Magda!

No, no! Not like this. Never free of the jackals. She grabs Dad's arm. This is the greatest thing you have ever done.

She tears off her astrakhan and shakes her hair free. A heavy breeze spins her curls as the firstfall of fat wet moths sticks unmelted to her pelt. Fat moths fall ever faster into gray chop, families of flakes from here to faint landfall. Silent heavens drop on roaring steel as dark derricks in twilight march out of snowfall—here trek the armies of Xerxes at Thermopylae. Her blood trembles on the sublime.

I feel wild and free, Alexandru. You have made this the grrreat magnetic center of the planet.

Dad nods and smiles, pleased by her praise.

Financially, I agree. Buster *is* the very heart of world capitalism.

Figures in a dream, Siberian and Indian oil riggers dressed in headbands and heavy leather hustle everywhere testing pipes and joints while crude from miles below flows through pipes that run to nearby tankers and overwater to the mainland. The roar drives marrow through bone. Jeeps race about, skidding nightmarishly on slicks of melted snow and crude. Magda draws down a deep breath of raw, putrid, head-clearing crude and sparkles at her stinging sinuses.

Whew! This stuff's been down there a long time! she shouts. Smell the money! But how can those riggers stand it?

Dad cries, Siberians will breathe shit for the right pay. You're smelling the runoff from below the mantle. Millions of years old.

This whole lake must be full of mud and rot by now, she says. The stink, the stink! I love it!

She wipes oil-film from her cheeks, and then tastes it.

Wet and dirty! she cries. Wonderful! We're at the top of the world, Alexandru! All of our pain has paid off. She looks about. May I be happy that it all works? Boom boom boom! Otherwise, and she taps the deck with The Spear, you'll have to torch it for the insurance.

Bright-eyed, I lie belly-flat on the deck, my behind slowly wagging, as I follow the talk of my elders. At her mention of insurance, I yelp, rising up on all fours. We own all the insurance companies, Mama! That's not a good idea.

She laughs and bumps against Dad, telling me, Silly goose! I wouldn't burn all this, my son. Better it should be recycled to the Japanese. Anyway, I'm not worried. We won't starve, not when we embrace our karma. It's when we resist our karma that real pain begins. *Me?* And her voice drops into her chest. *I resist nothing.*

Untamable eyes flash. Such a beautiful she-wolf, dreaming hair snow-heavy. She pinches my nose.

Throw off your shroud, my boy! she cries. You are too solemn.

Your mother has wise bones, Dad tells me, so prick up your ears. She knows things in her bones that jackals try to read in the stars. He raps his brow. In business, she'll whip your ass any day.

Her mouth gleams, earthy and moist, as she growls, then drops to the heated deck where snow melts into oil film, and rolls about on her back, still growling at the skies, at snow lapping her cheeks, her eye-slits just born and vastly curious about the pleasures of wind and the film of crude her long pointed tongue licks from her long black lips.

It's not that she hasn't quite grown up yet, Dad shouts. She sees into every mystery, the bones of it. No veil, my boy. No veil, no fear. She unmasks everything. He points to The Spear. Sees everything! I'll tell you, he giggles, your mother was never interested in needlepoint. Always in focus with her eye on the ball, that's Magda. But don't get her angry. She gives off heat like a ceramic stove.

Frankly, Gong, I thought she looked epileptic. But she unfrogged her black lamb coat and cape and lay there radiating heat as if just having effortlessly stretched herself in a five-mile run through deep snow, bosom panting mildly, face exalted. Still a maiden. Blossoming. Her blood thrives on planetary energies and on the natural juices of her wolfheart. Can you grasp this? Your human life, Gong, is to a Bihusi or Giurgiu a dim, senseless dream. We don't know how you put up with it. You wander around drugged by business and swamped by intellectual inertia. You try to work but walk into walls. Dad says, I'd rather be dead than human. Well, even humans like my wife and sons will never have access to the Oversoul of the Bihusi, or to the glory of our genealogy, never know the transcendent energies of eternity, much as I or another Bihusi might like to grant them to you. Our idealism is an instinctual knowledge which awakens even before birth. We are born fearless! Fresh and smelly and fearless. We know that our mother will return to the lair with swinging teats and disgorge big, raw chunks for each of us when we lick her lips and trigger her loving convulsions. No famine can kill a Giurgiu or Bihusi. We dream in the womb and come forth fully alert. Within hours our eyes flash like Sunlight on ice, burn with a brilliance known only to a handful of humans at a later age, though even with these rare humans genius fades in their twenties. Gong, believe me, we live off the fat of the land, and in the darkest of circumstances sense and avoid every obstacle ahead, while yours is a wasteland of the blind and bumbling.

Gong breathes slowly. Her hand covers mine. And yet you come to me.

A crazy wolf is a disheartening sight.

You're not crazy, she says.

You've never heard crazy like a wolf?

She rubs my hand and gives it a small shake.

Let's get back to your mother, Billy.

Help me up! Magda says. I am restored. Brought back to life. You see into my very heart, Alexandru, and have given me blood from your own veins. For now we are truly one, Babayaga, beloved, and I want to creep and crawl about your every derrick, my husband, my husband. Look at what you have done, Alexandru. Think of the power! And she rubs his trousers, saying, I want to feel you standing furry and strong, your arms about me.

As Dad falls onto his knees beside Magda, I sense a flood-lamped soul hanging over Baxter's Buster, some indestructible family spirit while the black blood of the Bihusi pumps up from miles below and flakes melt about us on the steaming deck and a buttery glow lifts into the clouds.

Dad's potency fuses to her joy. What he feels I feel. Buds of pleasure prickle his arms and back. She gathers his spirit into The Spear and sets it growling, pouring her soul over and into him. A lush brilliance thrills him as she strokes his hand and head. She fertilizes him with a pregnant kiss. His excitement crests above any earlier joys. They trade their wolf beings without pain or shame and soon, softly, howl together, face to face, as thick snow falls and their eyes trade and burn with each other's spirit. The call of their instincts binds them. She stands infected by his appetite and greed, his gift to her, a wild cry from his heart that makes her a dancer naked in the snowfall. She grins with lust for her mate, aroused, sexual and inventive. Her hungry fingers dig into his ears and lock onto his ravening flow of force. She wolfs him down by gobbets after a winter famine. She must rampage through his heart and tear playfully at his bones. *Nip, nip! Nip, nip!*

Snow clouds boil above and overwhelm the horizon. Perhaps one must be a wolf to grasp this frenzy as they nip and lick and hop in circles, cackling, shaking their spirits with a bittersweet whining and whipping about that swells and doubles them as if breaking their backs as they circle each other's rump and bark, and whine and sniff and yowl. Dad snaps at burrs of snow on Magda's black lamb and licks clean each leather finger of her gloves. *Achhh! Achhh! Achhh!* she cries, wrapping her long black hair over her mouth and burning eyes.

How have you brought this about, beloved? I want to know every detail. Tell me as we walk over this vundrous structure. Every little trick, my clever hero! *How you pull de str-rings!*

I glide along in Dad's unrockably wide-set Humvee as they move about the massive deck, their voices tumbling and trembling, his great howl handing her the key to their castle of derricks.

You could steal the world without getting caught, Alexandru!

He laughs. Where would I put it?

Put it in my heart, she says. I keep it safe for you.

Oh my gypsy, I will steal even more for you.

More than what?

More than the Earth, Dad says. I will give you a candle.

A candle?

A candle for the great darkness we must live in among men. A candle that blossoms on the night and awakens our deepest being and energies. You shall be richer in spirit than any creature who has ever lived.

You make me rich, Alexandru. All by yourself. And she purrs, *Mmmm! Mmmmm!*

Darkness falls on the derricks. Magda has packed a lunch of half-cooked chickens and they sit under a floodlight in falling snow and tear into birds, crushing bones in their strong jaws. A huge flare of nightlamps explodes for miles about. These are lights struck from your chest, she tells him. She strokes his head and again speaks her secret name for him. *Babayaga, Babayaga, beloved.* Dad swoons with love for her. Her strength rises above and encloses him in her deep, wild eyes.

Mama, Mama, he says. I could not live without you.

You won't have to.

Are you mine forever?

Even longer.

His lips gape and eyes appeal to her. What are you? What *are* you?

I am preparing the way and making a bed for my lover, she says. A lair for my heart to come home to when he is done with the world.

Her mind races with the genealogy of the Giurgiu clan and entwines with his genealogy of Bihusi, forming between them a single Wreath of muzzles and brilliantly yellow slant eyes going back to the Original Light of the dark angel. The Spear of Ahuramazda That Sees Everything glows beside the lovers.

Now tell me every detail, she says. How you did all this. Spare me nothing.

But Dad still swoons and plunges his nose deep into her lap.

Speak, she whispers.

He shouts, Touch me first!

She rubs him hard on the cock.

His eyes roll up and he begins his story.

This is the story of Dad's sob ploy. Dad dwells on Grandfather's image in the Bihusi genealogy. Yes, in a way, he killed Grandfather. But Grandfather glows at him benignly from the Wreath of Bihusi and whispers into his pricked up ear, Remember the phonograph, Alexandru! Remember the oil lamps!

I remember them, Gong says.

Well, with Grandfather's great triumph selling oil for the lamps of

China in mind, and wary of Grandfather's massive losses in Russia, Dad begins dreaming about the oil-rich Middle East as an area ripe for scamming and goes out to sell the sale of a brand-new concept: a hospital bed in every Arab home, to prepare for that unpredictable but certain illness or infirmity all must face as chemotherapy illumines even the Sultan's Prostate with a blast of light, as Omar might say.

Dad keys in on Grandfather's selling skills. He has a market that consists of every family that owns a dwelling. A chicken in every pot, a car in every garage, and a hospital bed in every home. Dad goes into isolation for forty days on the Sahara, the place of his first transfiguration, and comes back lighter in weight but billowing in spirit with an irresistible sales approach: *Sympathy Sales.* He identifies a population of well-spoken sociopaths, bright enough to remember a basic pitch. He trains them in his new Sympathy Sales. Perhaps a description of his most effective sales disciple, her appearance, technique, results, would help. She's a short, plump, middle-aged lady. Her market is Boston. She will earn several million dollars a year selling beds door-to-door because she always gets *the highest price on an item that is not priced,* and Dad splits fifty-fifty with her. It works like this: the mark has answered some kind of ad, television, radio, magazine, whatever. She now has the name, address, phone number. She calls and agrees to meet them tomorrow night at seven-thirty after dinner. She goes there and rings the bell. Then she sits on the front porch steps and begins sobbing uncontrollably. The door opens. Standing in the doorway will be the homeowners. She doesn't look up. She keeps on keening, if it's an Irish home, wailing and tearing at her blouse if Jewish. In Boston she doesn't bother with blacks: no money. She's inconsolable and loud. They go to her. They try to learn what's happened. Can we help? Through her agony she somehow lets them know that no, they can't help, her life is over, it has no meaning, she wants to die and is in the wrong place to do it. She's sorry she took their time, she's going home. By this time the marks are totally puzzled and themselves on the verge of tears. Somehow she manages to let them know that she intended to be here to show them the Bihusi Bed. But she simply can't do it. And again she loses herself in pain and sorrow. They try once more to lift her spirits. They bring her inside. Offer her coffee, tea or something stronger, she accepts the tea. After several moments she becomes composed and says that she had come to offer the comfort and health-giving properties of owning a Bihusi Bed and of the concern it shows for your relatives. Oh, such love. But she can't do that now because of what just happened to her. Well, what did just happen to her? This desolate mother was contacted an hour ago by the Department of Defense, telling her that her son's remains were just identified in Vietnam. After a decade the day-to-day torture of hope is over. Everything is over. She wants to go home and face the mourning that she's buried and avoided for so many years. Believe me, Gong, they buy the bed.

So now Dad rings up Sheikh Sidi bin-Bahram in Kuwait, who has five times the wealth of the Aga Khan and claims to have leased the Moon from Allah by promising Him a world-encircling ring of great mosques not all that different from our ring of space discs, and tells him he wants a meet tomorrow night at seven. Sidi's in his fattest concubine's new palace. How did you get this number? Sidi asks, although he is a member of the Boardroom of the Sun. I bought it, Dad says, from that guy in Cleveland who for a price gets you the number of anyone in the world. But why should I see you? Sheikh Bahram asks. I'll tell you why, Dad says. How much money did you make last year? The sheikh names a wildly overblown figure, and adds that it is five times what the Aga Khan made. That pip-squeak, Dad says, I made forty times that. Look, Sidi, beggars can't be choosers. Maybe you should listen to me. I think I will, Sidi says. Tomorrow at seven. Have *you* met Sidi?

Not one-on-one, Gong says. Sidi sweeps into and out of Sidney's office like a shadow risen from an abyss and flowing back into it.

Dad jets over to Al-Kuwait and at seven in the evening has himself announced to the great rascal. To Dad, Sidi is the very highest form of jackal alive, nearly wolf, although fatally crippled by one cancerous germ of compassion and thus a perfect patsy for Sympathy Sales. The sheikh has his major domo escort Dad to a walled garden where the sheikh's favorite wife lies entombed. Flashing jasper and agate trim her sarcophagus. On its marble lid lies a warm, pinkish, smiling life-size effigy of her splendor and perfection agleam in the center of a smooth oblong pool ringed by fountains and adorned with long marble pavements and dark cypresses as white-marble minarets rise at each corner of a walled enclosure inlaid with pearls and semiprecious stones while a great white onion-bulb dome tapers upward into a spire aglow with one solid gold crescent overlooking all.

When that great poet, the spidery, wizened little Sheikh Bahram, who has shrunken cheeks and scary white eyes, comes out through high double-doors cut with flowery arabesques to meet Dad, he catches his breath in shock to find Dad having waded out to the coffin and on his knees and, by Allah, beating madly and beyond all reason on the late wife's spotlighted pink-marble bosom while howling and weeping in a grief past all comfort. Can it be, Sheikh Bahram wonders, does the good man weep for the sheikh's wife, or is he overwhelmed by Sheikh Bahram's magnificent good taste and the matchless beauty and supreme poetry of the coffin in this twilight hour as the Sun's last rays bathe the onion bulb with sharp glints of gold under the first stars hung in a turquoise sky?

Oh my good man, Sheikh Bahram's little-boy voice says, gliding out of his dark cypresses and over the water for the fly in his web, I know, I know. It's beauty too great to bear!

But Dad sobs on, wildly and unstoppably, streaming with tears and rubbing some rubies with his sleeve.

Yes, yes, yes, Sheikh Bahram sighs. And that great woman deserved every gem you see. Have you noted the dome's reflection in the pool? Isn't that fabulous?

Dad can only whisper, Architectural genius!

Wild-eyed and waving, he crawls up the coffin and stands broken and crushed.

Sheikh Bahram sighs at his late wife's stone smile. She's so alive!

But Dad wails, then throws himself headlong into the water.

No, no! Sheikh Bahram cries, while Dad crawls about blindly in water up to his elbows. Dear man, it's not deep enough to drown in.

My sobbing father beats on the water as Sheikh Bahram implores Allah for Dad and cries out, Be strong, be strong! The world is too much with us! We must fight intimations of immortality! The rainbow comes and goes!

For Sheikh Bahram *is* a star-tossed poet of Wordsworthian lyricism, as to my sorrow he later proves. Dad rises and again wraps himself over the dead wife's divine bosom as he sobs, Oh my God, come back!

Bahram's arm comforts him. But the good woman is dead, my friend. Dead!

Dad sobs, Of course she's dead.

So how can I help you, dear man?

But Dad can barely stammer. It's too much! I can't speak!

What are you saying?

My life is over!

What?

Agony courses through him. His mouth rips downward into a tragic mask that cuts his throat open. Sheikh Bahram can see deep into inhumanly huge howl-muscles where Dad's wide red throat gapes into his lungs.

My life has no meaning! I want to die! But this is the wrong place. Help me! Oh my God, show me the bed she died in. Perhaps I can find peace there.

What do you mean?

Oh you poor man, Dad sobs. She did not die in a Bihusi Bed? I'm going home. I'm so sorry I've taken up your time.

And Dad beats his brow with shame. False pearls speed from his eyes.

Sheikh Bahram beats his own breast for comfort. His shallow, reedy baby-voice gasps, But you have come all this way, Mister Baxter.

No, no. I simply can't do it. I came to show you the soon to be world-famous Bihusi Bed. But now there's nothing left of me. My heart won't allow it. I feel I may fall dead at any moment.

Would you like a drink of water?

For God's sake, no water!

How about some delicious jasmine tea, sir? It was my wife's favorite.

I don't want anything that will keep me alive. Oh my pain, my pain!

And he falls into sobs torn from his flesh itself, a sorrow beyond human reach, for now he has risen to a pitch never before heard in person by any human, the true, world-shattering Bihusi howl. Sheikh Bahram stands thrilled from scalp to backbone as bitter, grief-laden gall floods from my father's ripe red throat.

HOOOWWOOOOOO! HOOOWWOOOO! Dad's wolf eyes watch the sheikh's every terror.

The trembling sheikh begs, Oh, let me lift your spirits some way.

Dad catches himself midhowl, and struggles to say, You could help me one way.

Compose yourself, sir. Please pull yourself together.

Well, you do know, Dad says, that I'm the richest man in the world?

You own the Earth, sir!

Yes, I do what I can. And you, of course, trail in third place after my son, Billy. My dear Sheikh Bahram, I've come to offer you the comfort and health-giving properties that owning a Bihusi Bed franchise offers for you and your relatives. But here I find your wife already dead! You poor man! I am lower than a dog that I didn't get here in time. When did she die?

Ten years ago. It has taken that long to build the mausoleum. And to carve the effigy as she was when we married, a thin young thing so in need of food. You and your son came to her funeral.

Oh my God, this is that same beautiful woman? I thought this was your young new wife!

That wife is still alive, Sidi says

Then there's hope! Hope! Dad cries, clasping the upraised stone hands awaiting Sidi in Paradise.

This beauty, my dear friend, Dad says, dwarfs the Taj Mahal. Having the coffin outdoors especially, instead of inside under the dome, the dear woman open to the Sun, the Moon, her face running with friendly rain. Did you think of that or did the architect? No, don't tell me. I know you are too modest to take credit for this water mirror, the most heavenly moment in world architecture. Your love dreaming on her coffin amid the stars! She saw the plans before she passed on? You could not have kept them from her? Oh God, I'm crying again. What more could a wife on her deathbed ask for when you have given her this? What more, I ask? What but a Bihusi Bed as her solar boat to Paradise! Have I got your attention, sir? I pray I have. A man with a Bihusi Bed may give up his next appointment with his sex therapist, which is a serious consideration. More importantly, should tragedy befall a loved one, or illness, or by accident a bone be broken, a Bihusi Bed gives comfort beyond chemical support. Sleep in the palm of Allah could not be more restful. No desolation can enter the body cupped by a Bihusi Bed. As for myself, today, oh my God!, I received notice of my niece's remains being recovered in Vietnam. She'd been a Navy nurse who'd gone incountry with a Marine unit years ago and never returned. Not an hour ago the Department of Defense faxed me aboard my Gulfstream that rags and bones and a hunk of hair of Lieutenant Commander Mumtaz Mahal Bihusi—she was half-Persian, Sheikh Bahram—have been identified. The day to day torture of hope for her survival is over. She is in Paradise. I must go home and face the mourning I've fought off these many years. I haven't the heart left to tell you of the world-wide system of franchises I wanted to offer you. Everyone dies, effendi, and those who die in a Bihusi Bed die like babes in their sleep. No home, no relative should be without one. There will be no end of customers, hardly a man on Earth who cannot find deep comfort and fulfillment spending his final days with us. For the Bihusi Bed shall someday live on all men's lips as their joyous last words, *As Allah wills,*

I leave for Paradise in a Bihusi Bed!

These franchises include not only sale of the individual beds but also their manufacture, which most cheaply can be carried out in the Middle East. The franchises also require the importation of steel from the US, to give your shipyards work, the making of bedstuffs and motors for the beds, to help diversify your factories, and, with the more dear models, encrustation with pearls and precious stones and for Middle Eastern customers canopies of silk with Arabic designs and blue-silk roofs that might in fact bear richly reproduced images of this very mausoleum, with your late wife smiling down from a starry twilight not unlike this very moment, her lovely arms and bosom welcoming those being ushered into Paradise. Before this tragedy struck today, I meant to offer you world rights to the Bihusi Bed, franchises without number for the endless billions who will be your customers. I must go now. My family awaits me. But before I leave, can I put you down for at least one franchise? I tell you, straight in the eye!, billions of eager customers await your answer.

Oh, Sidi says, a man who can't look another man straight in the eye is a thief. Sidi, of course, can look anyone in the eye because he half-scares them to death. But does Sheikh Bahram buy? Has he not met a thief greater than himself?

The deal is signed not in Kuwait but in Salzburg, no deal in Kuwait being worth signing. Dad always counts the spoons on his Gulfstream before leaving Kuwait. But the big end-money comes in at last for our steel deck and getting into the space discs. We rub our hands and get pissed on cognac topped with Dom Perignon. *In'sh'Allah!*

Awesome, Gong says. And Sidi is no pushover.

Insuperable salesmanship, I agree.

But I think it's time you tell me, when you say Dad more or less killed his father, what do you mean?

Why don't we stretch our legs? I saw some sweet little streets out front. Pretty chestnut trees and windows with flowerboxes.

You want to see the road? All right.

As we go round the house, she calls indoor to Helga that we'll be back shortly. Lakeside villas line one side of the road while on the far side steeply terraced villas rise heavenward, deck over deck. Greta barks from Otmar and Lisa's, begging me to visit.

Let's not go up there, I say. So, where were you born?

At the stove.

What!

Well, Gong says, my mum had six children on the family farm. The first, a boy, her mum helped her deliver at home. He later died and so she had five more babies until another boy arrived, her sixth child. She hoed vegetables and cooked right up to the delivery. My older sisters were born in the cow barn or out in the field while Mum was picking green peppers. I was the fourth girl and born at the stove. There was a heavy storm that day and she was inside with my three older sisters and had boiled some water and scorched a pair of scissors and did the entire delivery on her own. My father was always in the barn, shaping wicker furniture, and never helped. He grew faint at the sight of blood anyway.

Born in the den! I say.

No, the kitchen.

Right. But your mother was daring or very resourceful.

Solo home delivery is not unusual in our province, Gong says. But by Western standards she had mental problems. Well, even by my standards. And then my sister Poppy came down with puerperal fever when she tried to imitate Mum's self-reliance.

How do you mean she had mental problems?

Oh, she took it to heart when vicious neighbors ragged her for not having a living son. They scorned daughters. My mum cared more for the pigs and chickens than she did for us. The animals got her full attention. By three I was milking the cows before dawn. You have no idea how painfully hard it is for a child to stay awake by lamplight while giving cows their first milking. And I had to boil all the family's drinking water for the day. By five I had a boy's muscles. Shall we not talk about me?

What did your father feel about having girls?

His feelings were of no importance. My mother made him march off and pay the fines for each additional child until she was vindicated by a boy. We all had to help plant extra corn and vegetables and cure meat to pay each fine and support her need for a son.

So when she finally had a son? I ask. It was boundless joy?

Not quite. She'd been so beaten down by the fines, which grew larger with each child, and by the neighbors, that she paraded about the village each day, showing him off, and neglected work. She retired. My dad and sisters took over. We very nearly became beggars until the town leaders got after her, made her write a ten-page self-criticism, and more or less brought her back to her senses. She had no more children and after that never spoke unless forced to.

I love these little cobblestone streets, I say. The bypaths and gardens.

Gong looks upward. I'm not fond of all these deep steps. She nods toward the shore. Shall we sit?

I see. You're not the typical Swiss hill climber?

Not Swiss at all.

No, you're not.

We sit somewhat far from the road, below some big rocks, and then simply lie side by side on sedge in the afternoon stillness. She cups the back of her head in her palms. I rise onto an elbow and hang over her. Her beauty tugs like the midafternoon Moon.

Do you want to know the truth? she says.

Which truth?

I'm not sure I can help you. The more I listen to you the less I know.

I'm leaving something out?

Something very important.

That's true. Probably the most important things of all. And it's something I can't tell you.

You've told me some pretty awful things, Billy.

This isn't awful. It's just something I can't tell you. Maybe The Spear will tell you.

Then I must wait. So, how did your grandfather die?

I'll tell you. Dad knew that the time would come when the prince must kill the king. As I've said, it underlies all father/son ties among Bihusi. Grandfather knew this as well, having in his own way killed his father, who was still with him, smiling benignly in the Bihusi Wreath of faces.

She turns on her side, facing me, fiercely intent.

Well, Dad went to Christie's Auction House in London to unload some Fabergé eggs and watched a salesman lift up the *only two copies* of an African stamp with the erratum of an inverted biplane, perfect, pristine, and uncancelled, the rarest, most valuable stamps on Earth. He saw the owner step up, grasp one of the stamps with a silver tweezers, pull out his Zippo, light it, and burn the stamp. As assembled collectors watch in horror, he announces the basic rules of economics. By halving the world's inventory of this stamp, the surviving piece has quintupled in value. This strikes Dad as a paradigm for boosting the value of art. He thinks about his salt mine with the Nazi loot. Might something be plucked from that horde and boosted in value? Before he can act on this exciting view from the hilltop, which refreshes his greed at depth, Grandfather calls him to the family compound on the Jungfrau. In the library, overlooking monstrous deeps of ice and the fall of far-distant slopes of cow-pastures like uncancelled green and brown stamps, Grandfather instructs Dad about trading on the diamond market while echoing cowbells tinkle faintly upward. Meanwhile, he switches on the dimmers for his two favorite pieces of art, the only two that he prizes above money: a pair of great bronze hands by Rodin called The Hands of God. These rough fingers could easily slap the Earth together out of mud and with leftover clay people it with mankind and beasts of the field. The hands rise side by side, each on a wide column and big as an overstuffed chair. Dad thanks Grandfather for his instruction about boosting the value of diamonds. Then he says, I will now instruct you on boosting the value of a great work of art. Dad strokes The Left Hand of God, lifts the massive object, carries it about the room, and stops at the French window looking out over the West Face of the Jungfrau. Lazily, he tosses The Hand off the balcony, and waits, and listens as The Hand falls into a huge crevasse a half-mile below. Now, you see, he tells his father, you hear nothing and yet in that silence the value of The *Right* Hand of God, sitting here, has gone up beyond belief. Grandfather says, That was the single most loved thing in my life, for The Left Hand of God sees into the darkness of Creation and is wise about all mysteries. Dad asks, You loved it more than me? Grandfather says, I had meant to leave it to you. I treasure you as much as you treasure me. So I will now take from you what you just took from me and boost *your* value beyond belief as greatest living Bihusi. And Grandfather slowly rolls over the balcony rail, following The Hand.

Now it has come home at last. The death that he has sent to so many has struck Dad. Absolute danger and the sense of falling roar in upon him from the alarmed Wreath. He turns to ice. His father's body striking the bright ice slope below and bounding downward explodes in Dad. His heart cracks. He stares at the empty balcony and finds himself screaming. His own body bounces down the floe and into the crevasse. He sees The Left Hand of God clutching for him from icebound darkness, Granddad's body already gripped in its fingers.

All he knows next is that he sits in the library staring at The Right

Hand of God. This hand cups Grandfather's spirit. Dad fades utterly, sucked empty. His mind dances in brilliant static along his nerves and flutters without logic about his brain. The room impresses itself on him, stamps his eyes with the ox-blood leather divan, and above the fireplace the Shield of Genius bearing only the slant eyes of a Bihusi, below it in an ancient leather rack The Spear of Ahuramazda That Sees Everything. The rug runs red with late afternoon Sunlight. Dust rises in cosmic swirls. The dark bronze Right Hand of God fills blood-red with the setting Sun.

How can all this sensuous room be here, and its owner not alive?

But now The Right Hand of God calls him. The Sun-glowing hand pulls at and tugs a large supersensible bubble out of his breast. He delivers himself of the most pregnant light he has ever known as his spirit floats dancing through the room and slips into Grandfather's spirit in The Right Hand of God. If Dad has earlier thought himself possessed of the Wreath of Bihusi Genius going back to prehuman times, now he knows he has been but half-awake all his life. Grandfather floods in upon him. Dad gags, breathless. Something has happened. He feels both chained to Earth as never before and yet bounding madly and fluidly through black forests of the night with a sensorial forevision more keenly aware of things to avoid than he has ever known. Fresh power fills his fingers. His legs shiver. His father's great hands that have pulled many handcarts grip his shoulders and squeeze hard, shaking him. You, Alexandru, his father says, are now King of Bihusi, and we expect greater things of you than from any earlier Bihusi, even Genghis Khan or Attila. We offer you all the riches of the planet. I shall guide you, my son, and you shall own the Earth.

How did your father feel about that? Gong asks.

Grandfather is right. Dad prizes him above all things in his life, not just for being his father but even more for the bottomless rapacity he awakens in Dad's bowels. Dad sits about the chalet, shattered, a hollow shell, unable to know himself as King of Bihusi. He recovers Grandfather's body but The Left Hand of God has fled the Earth and, for all Dad knows, gone back to its Owner in the Upper World, or more likely to our own dark angel of the Lower World. He buries Grandfather on the very peak of the Jungfrau, himself packing the body up the highest slope and digging the grave with an ice ax. All Interlaken trembles below when from miles above on the first clear full Moon the howl of Bihusi is heard for miles, flooding up and echoing down the prickly fresh pinewood darkness of Lauterbrunnen

Valley, along winding streets and into bedrooms where a pining and horrid yipping seem, as Dad pays homage to Grandfather's grave, just outside the window! Fools who sneak outdoors and, piercing the night, shake at his shadow against the Moon will strangle in the crushed pine branch of his heartbreak.

And the world stands still, as the hands of every clock in Switzerland freeze at midnight. For what does it profit a wolf to gain his soul but lose the whole world, as Dad loses in Grandfather Bihusi?

So now Dad lies deadfallen and cured to the heart in wolf-mourning. Magda, threatens to divorce this wandering soul if he doesn't shape up, and cries, *Gain, gain! for the night comes wherein no wolf can gain! Incorporate! Beef up your bankroll, compound your capital! Where is your child's heart, Alexandru?* But no Moon-chill can shake, no warmth of Sun rub him awake. Even when the brightest Sun cries, *Make hay! Make hay!* he flees his own shadow and is obsessed with knives, razors, open casements. He turns from blood-meats, feeds only on nuts and berries. He who has lived for the Moon becomes a fallen thing, his sick nose dry as wood rot. He nurses a cyst on his prostate? No, he stares at the open French doors from which his father fled, the balcony where time turns to stone and will not go backward. He dwells on the layers of pack muscle crossing his chest, the tendons strapped upward from heel to hip. His Genius enters and twitches the dense neural fibres and riches of the corpus callosum, to no avail. His hypothalamus has shut down the motorworks, sludged up the whole Brazilian adventure of his brain. The fine-tuned refinery of greed goes to gum. Now sleeps the Wreath at midnight, the heartleap at the scent of weakness. No sense of self awakens. Intelligence shrinks to that of an orangutan as he reads empty rooms. He flinches at incoming signals of birdsong. He drools. His dick lies starved even of piss.

Then one day he trips on a library rug and falls on his muzzle. The pain crucifies him. *Pick up your feet!* he screams. He rises and stamps about until the flames fade to a stupor. His senseless eye falls on a huge bronze hand. He wipes his wet mouth and weighs what to do with The Right Hand of God. Now that it has risen in value beyond even a Bedouin's maddest dreams, should he sell it to the Japanese consortium of art buyers, well, billionaires, who want it at any price? Should he be a sentimental idiot and keep it? But the shape of the dark bronze hand, the gouged and scraped roughness of the fingers and the power of the palm and deep thumb-bed, seep into his dreams. Day and night he dwells on The Hand. Is it not his father's hand? Doesn't it show the strength of his hatred? Dad recalls childhood evenings with Rodin himself, a big hairy creature prowling about Paris, and feels not only an amused fondness for the artist, a rare sensation for Dad, but also overcome by a hunger and greed in the hand, a rapacity made to measure for his Bihusi soul. And now he misses The Left Hand of God intensely. Who knows what stumbling it might have spared him? He foresees a false start leading into a great bloody blot, an assurance of his own death. I, too, I the King, he thinks, must someday join the Wreath of Bihusi. Where? When? He watches fall leaves burn to gold in the valley below Interlaken. A maroon mortality spreads through the September twilight.

Later he takes me to Zürich to inspect the drug trade on the Platzspitz, then buys us a box of fresh Monte Cristos and we go out motoring on Lake of Zürich. We pass a drifting cabin cruiser with a bare Swiss blonde tanning herself on the prow, her pubes crowned with wiry, glistening curls, then on a raft topless girls push each other about and giggle in the water as their breasts rise and float before them, and somehow between the cigars and glitter and lapping water his appetite springs back to life. And his mind bolts from its darkness, a spider after the winged thing trembling before it. We are off to Salzburg to suck up a bank wriggling in our sticky lies and then to weave its losses into a vast new web of credit. *Hurrah!* Dad is on the loose. No dollar on the planet is safe. Bank vaults are mere piggy banks to his fingers. He laughs at mattresses where your savings are hidden. Did you expect a dime from the Tooth Fairy? Forget it.

For you see, there is the Dad of legend, the black figure run together from ten thousand fugitive shadows where he is seen lurking, and then there is the Dad who rubbed my head as a child and called me, My little pisser. There is the Dad pasted together from the letters of the great losers who have known him, the Synoptic Dad of the four massively inflated biographies testifying to his hatred of mankind and insane greed for getting his own, all of them filled with faded, falsifying, fourth- or fifth-source collections of the Sayings of Dad and written from outside the family. There is the apocryphal gospel of Dad put to verse by Sheikh Sidi bin-Bahram, *The Bad News for a Bad World*, for which he received the Nobel Prize for Literature, though I admit that for a human Sidi is a poet of molten power. There are dozens of false letters to the Swiss, the Austrians, the Liechtensteinians, none of them exactly showing Dad dancing in Loveland. Coverage of his travels in

Japan and Africa has faint historical accuracy. It's a surpassing wonder that historians even spell his name right, for many call him Alexandru Beshua and trace his forebears to Gitano Gypsies in Persia, horse thieves and fortunetellers of the first millennium Anno Domini, not sighted in Western Europe until the fifteenth century. The world's greatest linguist, Higgins of London, author of *The Rain in Spain*, places Dad's Rumanian accent among the Indo-Iranian family of languages called Romany that stems from South Himalayan tribes in Northwest India. Nothing, of course, to all these seekers of Dad would be so precious as one drop of his blood, which should it fall from heaven into one of their test tubes would lift whole worlds of Dadology and their foolish, weak canonical scriptures from a foundation in fantasy to the strange new ground of Superwolf DNA.

No, Dad did not give fishes and loaves to the Africans, well, anchovies, yes, he *gives nothing back:* that is our family motto. No, "Beshua the Butcher of Bucharest" did not turn wine into blood during a "Festival of the Beshua" or jubilee of "spirit-creatures" in the Carpathians. In all of these fancies in search of the historical Dad, it is crucial that there are angels and emissaries of the Almighty, the leading one being Sheikh Sidi bin-Bahram, who allegedly went down into hell on the West Siberian Plain to free the frozen and starving slaves of Bihusi on the oily deck of Baxter's Buster—actually he went only into the Kremlin War Room, Gong, as you'll see. The false writings on Dad depend without fail on Sheikh Sidi bin-Bahram to carry the weight of himself as angelic protagonist. The story of the sheikh's temptation in the pool by Dad and his franchises of Bihusi Beds is too famous to squelch, since Sheikh Sidi at no time said, Get thee behind me, Bihusi, but in fact bought into the scam. What can I say of the story of the dove descending to Dad through the New York Stock Exchange roar and thunderously declaring itself to be the voice of Grandfather, saying, "Thou art my greedy son, in whom I am well-pleased," an announcement that stifles the exchange, strikes to its heart, sends stocks soaring, and starts the mutter that Dad truly is the Son of Satan. Then comes the epic of Sidi bin-Bahram digging up the crevasse under Dad's chalet and uncovering The Left Hand of God, actually a bronze fake he's planted, which Sidi offers to the Japanese for half of Japan. What divine drama! Sidi against Dad. Among historians on each side, rubies of cosmic revelation become ever more finely cut jewels and flow back and forth on black velvet display cloths increasing false provenance and value. In triumph Sidi reduces me to impotence. As

Dad's secondary demon I fly about the globe looking for relief from Sidi's curse on my penile potency.

This is new! Gong says. You can't have erection? A hardon?

Ah ah ah! Of course I can. That's all baloney from Sidi. Sidi's greatest feat is destroying the Bihusi financial empire, that great squid gripping the Earth, its beaklike jaws ripping the mantle to pieces and despoiling the seas and forests. Nor, dear doctor, have we spoken of the glib histories of Grandfather's wife and Dad's mother, The Virgin, Maria Elisabeta Magdalena Giurgiu, who was herself immaculately conceived, and following an announcement from the Carpathian demon Nicodemus found herself heavy with cub though never having known a wolf, then married Grandfather, gave birth to Dad in a goat stall outside Bucharest and was given gifts of gold by Three Wise Wolves from the Gold Coast of Ghana who had followed a star rising over Bucharest and knew that the Devil's Own Son was about to be born. Can you believe it, Gong? People filling libraries with tomes attesting to my father's virgin birth? What's more, they have Dad marrying his niece, which is true, who is also his half-sister in the Giurgiu clan, which is true, who was herself an issue of virgin birth. Both my mother and my father were born of the same virgin, with *my* mother Magda "sired" spiritually by Grandfather's twin brother, Robert Cecil Rhodes Bihusi. Following Dad's birth, legend says, his mother, Maria Elisabeta, was revirginized by Satan. Pagans, doctor, pagans! Suckled on a creed outworn! Can't these historians see how this damages their whole fantasy? Well, they must not. For next they have Dad die on Baxter's Buster, go to hell in a coma for three days, and be raised bodily from the dead to rule by thought waves from a wheelchair. At which point Sheikh Sidi bin-Bahram has his greatest victory, which as you will see hinges on his famous verse about honor among thieves, "Trust."

Did any of this happen? Well, yes, but only in bits and pieces. And not as they tell it or have put it together from fragments of the Salt Lake Scrolls of Dad's Mormon followers who trace his superhuman lineage back to an attractively well-governed, small, monastic sect in Little Egypt, the Essenes. Doctor, theirs is a story much like Scheherazade's, much too marvelous ever to end, with marvel upon marvel. Much more marvelous is the true story, my dear, about how through the Wreath of the Bihusi mingling its blood with the Wreath of the Giurgiu, Grandfather Alexandru, Senior, while still in the womb of his mother, Anna Maria Iona Giurgiu, spoke to his son,

Alexandru, Junior, or Dad, in the womb of Maria Elisabeta Magdalena Giurgiu. John the Baptist in the womb of his mother speaking to Jesus in the womb of his mother, as has been reported, could not be as marvelous, since my father had not yet been conceived when this speaking-through-wombs occurred in the mingled Wreaths of our two clans. And yet, it happened, and if Doctor Jung himself were here I would have him put it in his pipe and smoke it.

Why? Gong asks. I think your story in particular would appeal to Jung. He loved myths about mortal women like Titania married to gods or half-gods like yourself. And he would enjoy disentangling all this virgin birth and revirginizing and the fables composed by Sheikh bin-Bahram. Heredity and race were very important to Jung. He thought his own grandfather the bastard son of Goethe, which made Jung himself not only the great-grandson of Germany's greatest poet but also, as he would himself suggest, the reincarnation of Goethe. Jung believed in eternal recurrence, ancestor possession, and the passing on of hereditary units, so the Bihusi Wreath is something he would take very seriously. Almost all you've told us falls into patterns of myth and symbol that were his daily meat and drink, archetypes of the highest order and to him the dishes of the gods. In Jung's eyes, as with Dad and the Bihusi through many earlier existences, the German folk-genius converges on Jung.

Believe me, he'd have been spellbound by the crossover from half-god to human by Dad's three daughters by Magda, the dress designer, the dancer, and the celebrity novelist. Did they give up extreme longevity as well? I take it that these vital, energetic she-wolves, like you, also want to submerge themselves in the human character. All your father's wolf progeny have slipped out of his grasp. True, the daughters seem fixed simply on being racy ladies, while you flee familial horror. When you speak of your sisters' virgin births, do you mean parthenogenesis?

Oh no. Dad is their father. I've undersold my sisters to you, by the way. Each defies Dad and leaves him stonewalled as she goes her own way. By human standards they have monstrous intuitional intelligence and humans in their presence learn quickly that these three women are mystically brainy realists, whatever their other traits might be. Fearful, blocky headed creatures, staring right through you, when not sparing you by looking aside. You think you're looking into the maw of death.

But, Gong says, they were all—

All virgin births, I say. As is attested to by both the Harvard Business School and the Harvard School of Divinity, who for once are in divine agreement. The Stanford Business School has abandoned its position on virgin birth among Bihusi, although it still maintains perpetual virginity in the case of my own mother, Angela Magdalena Giurgiu Bihusi, who has insisted upon it and made large donations to all three schools.

This defies common sense, Gong says. Are *you* of virgin birth?

I haven't asked. It'd be pointless. My mother is a renowned virgin. That's a subjective truth in the family lore, so let's not pursue this subject. I am "Magda's boy" as well as Dad's son and in the tangled tails and rump sniffings of Bihusi dens certain things are none too clear. I am surely my father's son, although I know my mother questions a certain failure of rapacity in my character. And I've married a human! This excommunicates me from the Giurgiu clan's rigorous morality, although I am still Prince of Bihusi and my mother Queen of Giurgiu. If I paint this over with a baleful light, so be it. I could put some bright, distracting colors over the whole mix-up, to throw off historians, but that would be blindfolding the blind.

Let me be clear, Gong. The whole public version of my father's life focuses on the idea that he is the Son of Satan, a thought so firmly held by the mullahs that in the Middle East one can be executed or hunted down by assassination squads for denying it even once, while rewards are offered for turning in such infidels. It makes a good story and it makes Dad's resurrection transcendent. For isn't evil still with us, despite Sheikh Sidi bin-Bahram's verses about the Satanic Messiah and the financial Apocalypse Dad brought about? So inventive of Sidi, the Kingdom of Bihusi being opposed to the Kingdom of Allah. The Middle East has long known that you can't have a Paradise in your racial myth without a Hell to give it force. Thus the blacker Sidi paints Dad the greater prophet Sidi becomes. Some say the kingdom of God is within you, as then must be the kingdom of Hell. And that makes sense. But the thought that there is a Hell worse than life makes Hell-to-Come anticlimactic. Do you really think Hell can get worse than what happens here? If so, could it possibly matter? The same is true of Heaven. Can there be a Paradise in the future more rewarding than a good life in the here and now? Those glories-to-come only devalue the good life here and now. Hey, you think life is good now? Wait'll you see what's up the road! Really? Then could a Paradise to come really matter, after we have enjoyed what love we enjoy here and now? Heaven is meat and potatoes today, not cotton candy with no suffering later, and Hell is *no* meat and potatoes today and *nothing* down the line.

What counts are ancestors, forebears who feed us spiritually and lead us to the good life now. They are the God-image within. But Sidi's ideas are simple. To sell his postmortal program Sidi must have Dad resurrected, must have the Hell to come, must have an apocalypse that raises us physically from the dead so that the Almighty can hold his final judgment of us and sort out the worthy from the unworthy, and must have Dad come back as herald of the Apocalypse. Like the Messiah, Dad too must overcome death or the story falls apart and one's followers disband. These banalities are the story according to Sidi and to the critico-historians of the Life of Dad. But this stupefying nonsense is also the art of storytelling at its highest level for, as you must know, Sidi touches all the bass notes in our lives and strives to carry us upward beyond our power to hear.

But what about the dark angel? Gong asks. Doesn't his existence support Sidi's beliefs?

Yes! But not Sidi's versions of Hell and Paradise. I'll tell you about the dark angel in a moment. Did Dad think himself the Son of Satan? Yes and no. When he talked with me about the space discs, he became eloquent. It's true that he was in the disc program for the money, and for the charged spirit that would be his for having the very largest possible controlling interest in the world, which the sale of light and power would bring. That holy project shrinks even the Bihusi Bed and Baxter's Buster. When he thought of the Sun discs, and saw them orbiting the planet and beaming down their laser energies, he'd grip my hand and, honoring Grandfather for hopes placed in him, he'd sigh and whisper, not just as King of Bihusi but with ecstatic passion, turning his soul over to the little folk peeping about his feet, *I am the light of the world; he that follows me shall not walk in darkness, but shall have the light of life.*

That's Jesus! Gong says.

Well, there you go. They both said the light of life, not of the world to come. Dad offers no one a life to come. He can't. For humans this is it. You are not going anywhere. You want to reject the Wolf Force in you? That's your loss, and you will never enter the kingdom of heaven on Earth, or any kingdom, for the other kingdom is not coming for you. You must struggle along without rapacity, which is barely to struggle at all, and a feeble attack on life. Among humans, I like a man who tears a big bloody chunk out of life. There is no dark angel? Let me ask, how can you force rational order on a mystical experience? Can you bind the sea of life with a net of virtue? Life is desire, rapacity, excess. It's not some weak little idea of everything working toward a final goodness. That's idiotic.

And I give Gong a double snap of my jaws.

Snap at me and I snap back, Gong warns. If you think I'm so feeble, let me ask you something. Do you really want to give up your bad old ways, which you see as evil? Aren't you simply bound up in some metaphysical bullshit and this unexamined, extremely abstract need for a daughter to save you? Not for a daughter from Titania, then from whom? What is it you want to detach yourself from? Your father or evil itself? Is evil a self-governing force with its own momentum? If so, then is it a biological force or even plague endemic in higher forms of intelligence? Is it an animating force, like your Wolf Force? Is it some demonic undersoul in whom evil below mirrors evil above? Is it illusion? What in Dad's spirit do you want to detach yourself from? Do you even know?

Well done, doctor! I think I can answer that. But first let me tell you what's happened, then we can go on from there.

Baxter's Buster is in full swing. But now Greenpeace gets really serious, Gong, and mounts heavy weapons against us on Lake Bolshoi, Kamikaze raids of high-speed ships exploding against our pontoons in hopes of tilting the gyro compasses that keep our pipes aligned without cracking. Dad says, No way will I put up with these monkeys. He phones Saddam for a shipment of Lafayette nerve gas bombs and shoulder weapons to fire them. He will show Greenpeace what real destruction is and orders our security to keep the media away.

Dad stands at the rail watching a Greenpeace vessel bear down on us and fire its deck cannon at our derricks. He himself raises the gas rifle and fires a bomb at figures running about the Greenpeace forecastle. The bomb hits their bow and a burst of steamlike vapor washes over the enemy. Suddenly no one is alive on board and with no one at the wheel the zombie vessel heads straight toward us. The Greenpeace boat plows through the pontoon below Dad and me and splinters like a teapot. I'm knocked back twenty feet, with debris falling everywhere. Crawling forward, I see Dad stagger and fall.

What is it? I cry, lifting him.

I'm sick, he moans. I've never felt like this before.

He grips his stomach, then feels his neck and face and skull. Something rises within him. Tears stand in his eyes.

Billy, the Wreath!

Thousands of wolf-heads back to our earliest generations leap sharp and clear into his mind. Billy, I see our family! All of it!

This is a dizzying overload even for Dad, who struggles for breath.

It's the nerve gas, he says. I must have got a whiff of it.

Nelson and Truesmith lift Dad into their Marine chopper and we take off for Doctor Zeitgeist aboard Bihusi One at the Bolshoi airfield. An immediate transfusion of my own plasma stored aboard the 747 saves Dad's life. But his brain races.

My mind, my Genius! The virus is eating my brain, Bobby.

Again my dead brother's name! You'll make it, Dad.

But delirium spreads over his face.

I see the space discs, Bobby, I see Ahuramazda! And she tells me, Whatever happens, we must not abandon our quest. Bihusi must still conquer the Sun! I'm sorry, Bobby, I'm sorry. But our marriage to Ahuramazda now rests on your shoulders. Promise me! Promise you'll not give up, even without me.

Magda, asleep on Bihusi One, gets danger signals. She wakes for a last talk with Dad before his brain creams out.

You are strong, Alexandru!

Oh, yes, he assures her. Don't think I won't always be with you.

Babayaga, beloved, you will beat this.

Whatever happens to Dad's body, I know for a certainty he will still be with us. And with that Dad dies. Well, his heart stops and he drops into a coma for three days. His body heat plunges to a death-chill. He stiffens in rigor, his wrists locked half-raised. He is a dead beast passed along the highway or come upon in the woods. During this coma, his body utterly still and without a heartbeat, his slant amber wolf's eyes follow me wherever I move, warning me against premature burial or cremation, or else they fix on Magda hovering over him, telling her he will rise from the dead. If she moves from his line of sight, a pressure builds to a rumble from his chest, like a long death-rattle, and calls her back. Even in death he carries the flame of Ahuramazda which cannot die.

Don't you worry, Alexandru, Magda says. I see you in the Wreath, warm under this blanket of snow.

We fly him home to the Jungfrau and gather the whole Bihusi clan about us in his bedroom where he lies in state. A small band of world-shakers, they fill the bedroom as Assad, Saddam, and the President of Serbia, abandoning his slaughter of the Albanians, lead us in a nightlong howl as loud as Verdi's *Dies Irae*. The resurrection comes after Dad, having already been scourged by Greenpeace, descends into the *Ünterwelt* and in penance for the sins he bears of his followers, and for his own unheartfelt but mischievous good deeds with anchovies and krill among the Pakistanis, for a time finds himself abandoned by and parted utterly from his dark angel, himself now low as a simple jackal as he pays for the iniquities of all wolfen. Grandfather spiderdances over the Styx and absolves him. Then Dad bids for the souls of his plasma gatherers, frees the bound bankers, lawyers and accountants stuck ankle-deep in baked shit and roaring and groaning under heavy chain in the fiery furnace, brings usurers prancing out of Shadowland, assigns fresh forests for trashing by the he-monster Behemoth, fresh waters and shipping lanes to befoul by the she-monster Leviathan, sets aside the bleakest mountain and coal-heavy clouds for the end times, prepares a judgment table for his enemies, signs contracts freeing up large financial cornerstones for ever-richer churches, temples and mosques, is now anointed by Grandfather, and after three days is sent back above to do more good works, his star-bright cosmic tail granted to him at last. I am to be his golem, the agent of his horrors.

But Dad's life now is limited for, as he catches his breath, gives a little yip, clears his throat and hawks phlegm off the side of the bed, he's only a ghost of himself. His eyes slyly take in the gathering. We await with wonder his first words, but they fail to come. Although he no longer speaks, we bear up as a brilliant glow inspires him. He gazes on Paradise, or someplace, pitying us that we cannot see what he sees. He has avoided the wolftrap and terror that spring by night in the darkest depths of the forest, flown over them fluidly, and returned, speechless with joy, his eyes dancing with Moonlight. His star-blue tail swishes in and out under the sheets, shocking all with its beauty and bushiness. But last memories of flesh and bone can bear only so much and he grips his ribs. His black lips form the words, *Bring The Spear!* Magda brings The Spear of Ahuramazda That Sees Everything and he points to his fourth and fifth ribs. *Here!* he groans, and Magda carefully runs the Spearhead into him between his fourth and fifth ribs. Blood gushes from the psychic wound he now bears as The Spear conquers the virus and flushes Dad's system by emptying his ghostly lungs. He points to his head and she cuts him across the brow with The Spear. A martyr's tragic vision shines in witness through blood seeping from his brow and carrying off viral brain tubercles. Through thorns of pain his eyes roll upward toward Grandfather. *We feel the dark angel himself in the room, invisible though he is, and hear his kiss on Dad's eyes.*

His ecstatic tail, thrashing and shuddering, quivers under the sheets.

We hear unseen birdwings flap through the bedroom and a voice much like Grandfather's fills us, saying, Is this the Wolf? This is the Wolf.

The bed sheet strips backward of its own will. The cosmic force of the Superwolf lies revealed for all to see, bloodless and drained blue. The President of Serbia steps forward and touches Dad's spearhole, then tastes his fingers to be sure this is not mere food dye or stage blood. Doubt fades. He radiates belief, he dances and shouts, *It's no phantasm crying wolf, it's him! It's him!*

A shaking grips Dad, then his bones lock as a howl winds from him, freezing us all, and he throws off mortality altogether, lies there in spirit, speechless, beside himself in the Divine Will, flensed of flesh.

And all the Bihusi enter the Wreath of Bihusi and hear Grandfather in the womb of Anna Maria Iona Giurgiu speak to Dad in the womb of Maria Elisabeta Magdalena Giurgiu and it is borne in upon all that the Wolf Force that has carried Dad to this crucifixion and the rising of his Holy Ghost was written into his being and stamped onto his soul before he was born and that his death and resurrection follow the wolfen's karmic path of least spiritual resistance and greatest physical reward. Waves of sound come from his breast, teaching his disciples:

I, Alexandru the Risen, speak. I come with a sword that all may bear in my Father's name. By my example you shall know Him. I have led you to the Promised Land and it lies before you. Now go forth and eat of the feast I have laid there, for this Earth is my body and my blood. Take my message into far places and other wolf tongues so that all may eat of me. But, my brethren, my cubs, before you go downstairs and with fresh spirit feast on my Earthly Body now being lightly roasted for the celebration of your Covenant with my Father, who expects to see each of you with a clean spirit washed in blood seven times over when your time may come, one by one, each of you, come unto me and let me hear your Confession, for I will bear all your iniquities, absolve you of all jackals saved and good deeds you could not resist commit-

ting, and award each of you a long woolly sheepskin with which to clothe
yourself in my image and to curl up in while chewing over conquests to come.
Remember this day with mingled heart as both your day of atonement and
the time of your passing over into the Promised Land.

And His spirit holds us all in thrall.

We wolfen surely are lower than angels, Gong, but we do think like them, by light-flow along the Wreath of our clans. Bodiless angels, we charge scent with radiance and think in a synergy of scent and light. As soon as it was said, Let there be light, we came into being, not physically, of course, but in immanence. We were, you might say, touched by the Moon and brought up in lunacy, or in a kind of twisted and reflected light. So we swear our ties to the Moon and are children of the Moon. Somewhere in the night a dark angel came to Earth and from his own ribs fashioned two of us, saying, This is bone of my bone and flesh of my flesh: he shall be called Bihusi; she shall be called Giurgiu; they shall be called Wolf and She-Wolf; and Giurgiu shall be the mother of all Wolves and She-Wolves. And they shall have one tongue and one speech. And when the dark angel saw all the wolves in their dens living at peace with one another, he said, These creatures are not yet in my image. I will confound their tongues and stir them to hatred, greed, and rapacity, so that they may become superwolves, more like myself, and not waste away in sloth and harmony. And the dark angel scattered them abroad on the face of the Earth. And the balefulness of a divine malediction fell upon the Wolves and would not be lifted until the Son of Wolf came to be martyred and paid for the faintheartedness and good deeds of the First Wolves, who were without hatred, greed, and rapacity. The dark angel was never a reasonable being. Something in him, a yellow fire in his eyes, remains forever beyond reason, and has been passed on to us. We are suprarational, a Genius race that lives by scent and intuition. Like the cloud-soaring, far-sighted eagles that can see a mouse breathe far below, we fall into fits of excitement by the smell of blood even on the far side of the Earth. Today we seek the return of our sacred tongue, the Original Light our dark angel gave us to think with. Our actual speech among ourselves is far from human, doctor, it is mental and its grammar, or ordering of ideas, follows no syntactical parallels with human tongues. Wolves speak in first principles, the first being *Strike!*—but we have learned to baffle our feelings and speak as humans to carry on our businesses, for every wolf has his business. We have forgotten the speech of Original Light, though not the historical events that happened in those first days when Magda, the first she-wolf, failed to kill the serpent Sidi but instead engaged it in talk, fell to trusting it as it lured her into a compassion against her nature, and outwitted her with its false eloquence and gift for verse, offering her love of family and the joy of sexual submission to her mate. We know the serpent won then, and has won many times, but we know also that one day the karmic wheel will give us the victory, when we bite his neck and shake him dead.

I would find these fears and feelings quite disturbing, Gong says. Just as you do.

Well, enough ancient history. I'm sure it bores you.

Isn't all this quite recent?

Yes, but I've been worried for years about taking Dad's place. And who knows what one of my hotheaded sons might do? Would you bear with me while we explore for a moment my Oil Emirate education, which leads to my present status as Sidi's Filipino.

I stand at the bar in the Interconti Hotel in Manila. It's a big circular bar. Across the way stand two rich-looking middle-aged Brits. One walks around the bar and speaks to me, quite politely. Excuse me, could you tell me where you got your shirt? I'm wearing a pearl-silk Guayabera. One of several I've had made and picked up that afternoon. So I give him the tailor's address in Tagaytay, a Manila suburb. He asks me what I'm doing in the Philippines. I tell him I'm a traveler who moves from place to place, doing first-hand observation of crop conditions for my personal commodity investing. Most of the time when someone asks you what you do, it's a creaky ploy to strike up a conversation to sell you something. It's Insurance Sales Technique 101. They ask what you do in hopes that you'll ask what they do. I said what the hell. What do you do? He said, My associate and I give physicals.

Physicals?

Yes, all day long, seven days a week, we give physicals to Filipinos looking for work in the Middle East. If they pass the physicals, they sign employment contracts. By this time, his friend has joined us. Employment contracts, Harold, bullshit!—they sign indenture agreements. Well, the first Brit says, it makes me a little uncomfortable to use that term. But that is what they are. Let me tell you what I learned from these two doctors, Gong. Here's how it works. The healthy Filipino signs the contract. Now to us in the West it looks like an employment contract. But let me tell you, when that poor bastard sets foot in Dubai, Abu-Dhabi, Bahrain, Kuwait, or any of the other emirates, he finds he's agreed to become a slave. Their laws require that he work only for the family that owns his contract, which usually runs three to five years. He cannot change employers. If he leaves he's automatically a wanted fugitive wearing a price. His picture will be published in the Arabic- and English-speaking press, with a reward offered. Runaways don't last very long in the streets. They get picked up and thrown into the second-worst prisons on Earth for a very long time.

For what crime? Gong asks.

Quitting the job.

Have they *no* rights? Can't the local courts help?

Understand the local courts. First, even if servants had standing before the local courts, and I'll get back to that, there is no law in the Muslim world as we understand law to be, there are no statutes, there is no precedent, there is no history of common law. There is the Koran. And its interpretation by the mullahs. Most judges are Islamic clergy. They interpret the Koran to fit the crime. As to standing, if an infidel, that's you and me, has a legal difference with a local, well, technically we don't exist. So the resolution is simple. Find for the local. This is why any savvy Western company does its Middle Eastern deals with paperwork executed in European cities, with financial guarantees deposited and present in the European cities. Say a Saudi wants to buy a hundred thousand shares of Texaco. He deposits the price with the broker in cash, letter of credit, or check drawn on a Western bank. No problem. If the Western brokerage or bank accepts payment to be made in, say, Abu-Dhabi, and the customer doesn't like the deal because the stock goes down, he stops his check or in some other fashion refuses to pay out of his Middle East funds. The Western mark takes the loss. And there's not a damned thing you can do about it. Players think this to be one of the world's great financial secrets. Believe me, Washington fully helps in hiding it.

Novices victimized in the financial world cry foul in the Middle East so often it's boring. You just can't talk the eager, money-blinded European or American into saving himself from getting burned. Get it? Screwing an infidel is no crime. You gain the foreigner's *trust. Trust* first of all. Once you can fake trust, like faking sincerity, you can do anything. I remind you: My brother and I against my cousin, my cousin and I against the world. Trust a

Kuwaiti and you become his Filipino.

I keep a villa on the Persian Gulf. A neighbor couple, she's British, he's Arabic, they take their two kids and fly to their flat in Paris for two months, leaving behind for maintenance a Filipino couple with a baby. One night the mother gets sick. The father borrows his boss's cheapest car and looks for a pharmacy. The cops stop him. He has no registration for the car. They telephone his employer's local number, and with the wife too sick to get up, there's no answer. They throw him in prison and await the return of his employer from Paris. His owner, really. Days pass. The little guy pleads, begs, cries. He's hysterical, bad things are happening. His sick wife, their baby! They ignore him. He's gotta get home, but he's livestock. Three weeks crawl by. At last my neighbor returns. As I've noticed, his villa reeks. Mother and baby? Long dead. My neighbor finds his car in the pound but his man is missing. He contacts the law. They talk. He explains that he's been away. The police remove the bodies. At last they find the Filipino half-dead behind bars. They take him to the airport. Put him on a plane. He goes back to Manila.

I don't believe it. This is the twentieth century, Gong says. Why would you tell me such a story? It's like the tales of mass murder of girl babies in China.

Because of what eventually happened to me. As for this, I saw it. He was *my* neighbor. Do you know what these Middle Easterners do with their dead? They dig a shallow grave, anywhere, wrap the body in a sheet, throw it in, cover it with rocks to keep the jackals out, and leave it. Can you imagine doing that with your husband or wife? They are not all mausoleum-builders like Sidi. When you look out your hotel window and see them dig a hole and drop a body into it, that's memorable. Even to a well-fed wolf.

I'm sure you know that almost all the young Middle Eastern men were sent by their families to Europe during the Gulf War while the Westerners fought it, and then returned after the war. Almost all.

Why do I tell you all this? To understand the poet of *The Profit*, our Boardroom's Wild Ass of Kuwait. When Sidi comes to his home in Paris, he has already had his filed teeth capped and his pockmarks abraded, to look less Bedouin. He also brings his fattest wife, who replaces the late wife who tipped five hundred pounds before she went into the mausoleum. Fat wives show how wealthy Sidi is. This fattest wife stays childless, and to keep Sidi joyful becomes as fat as possible, like a French goose stuffed with food all day, its liver growing for paté. His second traveling wife, kept thin, is brought along to start his car each morning.

Start his car?

When I was their guest, I would watch her raise the garage door, go in and start the car. No explosion? Fine. She comes back in for breakfast; we go on with our day. Hey, she *trusts* him and knows this is his big joke each morning. Sheikh Bahram, you see, is not yet ready for Johannom, known to us as Gehenna, the place where the tormented dead, whom he has blandly sent there, wait to pluck out his eyes, chew on his heart, and tear his soul to rags. He raises great medical centers to ensure his long life on Earth. Such a great heart. And poet? This is how poetic he is. Back home his Lamborghinis, his Rolls, and his Ferraris are parked on Persian carpets. It's true. If any oil or grease drips onto their fabric, the mechanic charged with the cars' care loses his profession along with any ability to handle tools or chew food. Sidi's given his security chief the most beautiful set of Swedish dental tools. Sidi likes me to pass these little torture tidbits on to Dad. I can be a wolf, too, this little old man says gently. To the Wild Ass, Dad and I are still nonbelieving offal and beyond all human regard. But he adores our money, which practically leaks out of the world's banks. And as you know, Dad thinks this way, too, about jackals. I was in the lobby of the Connaught in London one night, with a Lebanese politician, and we were greeted by a titled Englishman and his wife. The Lebanese embraced both with greetings and cries and dove-cooings of love and affection. When they walked on, the Beiruti grinned at me, saying, That man thinks I'm his friend.

Dad's like that, no question. But there's something wrong with these sheikhs, Gong. They do these things and think we'll never learn.

But, to go on. The time comes when we must meet with the Boardroom of the Sun for an update on our two projects. We gather in the former War Room four levels beneath the Kremlin, which we use with Russia's courtesy. Our Zoroastrians sit with heads covered at a huge, oval mahogany table under a gigantic flat map of the globe's surface. We now have a big Russian association and pay them a commission of fifty cents on each Lake Bolshoi barrel that leaves Russia. This is the first time the Boardroom has met since the Greenpeace fiasco and probably the last time that we'll be able to use this room. When we finally put the disc program in play, Siberian crude will drop to two thin dimes a barrel. I wheel the Spirit of the Risen Dad into the Boardroom. With my great ears I hear Sidi whisper to a Persian sheikh,

We can't work with a president like that. Not in a wheelchair, no, no.

You toy with your life-span, Sidi. My father hears like a wolf.

But does he sleep in a Bihusi Bed? Sidi asks.

Do you really want to know where he sleeps?

Well, he and I had a long talk in my wife's pool and it was all about the *everlasting* comfort of a Bihusi Bed. Sidi's eyes widen, all white and starey. I could buy one for him if he really needs it.

My father sleeps by the fireplace on a woven-gold rug that was once Nebuchadnezzar's own prayer rug. So he can stay warm, thank you.

If he needs a Bihusi Bed, just ask me! Sidi says.

These bad guys do not get excited, Gong. They never get excited. Even the falling in of Sidi's world-wide Bihusi Bed franchise pyramid scam does not excite or spur him to vengeance.

We have problems to solve, I say, parking Dad at the head of the table. I sit at the far end.

I begin, Now the problems are—

But Sheikh Sidi bin-Bahram, known throughout Kuwait as The Mighty Hunter but in Baghdad as The Wild Ass, stops me. Why doesn't President Baxter himself tell us these problems? I know he speaks like an angel when he wishes. Especially about my late wife.

This supremely dangerous jackal, the richest royal in Kuwait, does impress Dad with his wealth. No mighty hunter, or even wild ass, Sidi, to us at least, is an unsmiling, skinny shriveled up little shit with, however, one cancerous germ of compassion, that same touch of heart with which his serpent forebear seduced the first Magda in the garden. He has declared all citizens of Kuwait to be members of his royal family, so that by his fiat all Kuwaitis are princes and princesses. He has his own ravishingly beautiful but veiled food taster who follows him about, cuts his food for him, butters his rolls, and often chews his food before spooning it into him who needs then only swallow. My spoon-counting Dad never trusts this Kuwaiti, nor will he ever deal with him on his own turf, except to sell him a bed. Sooner or later, Sheikh Bahram thinks, this stupid Bihusi Westerner will make a mistake and *trust me*, and then I will take all his money. Being even more toweringly rich than the sheikh, Dad knows a financial assassin when he smells one, and the only way around this stinking thief is to have him join Bihusi Sunbeams and take a chair on the Boardroom of the Sun. As Dad's old associate, Don Corleone, an olive oil importer in lower Manhattan, often warned him, Hold your friends close, hold your enemies closer. We know as well that the last step in financing our disc show must be to take this bastard before he takes us, steals our wealth, and either foregoes the whole project or drinks it up as his own, with the Sun as his natural possession. Is this coyote keen? Is he wily? He has already formed a consortium for selling rights to the Moon itself, first to the Azerbaijanis, Kazakhstanis, and Turkmenistanis, so that he can mount a fresh and cleansing onslaught against all Christians in the region, with further sales to Muslim nations elsewhere. How did Sidi come to own the Moon? He leased it from Allah. He promised Allah mosques as great as the Taj Mahal, each with its own fragment of the black Kaaba stone from the Great Mosque in Mecca, in every country on Earth, which will then allow Hajj-pilgrimages worldwide by Muslims in every nation, in return for rights to the Moon in all its phases, starting with the crescent, its tear-drop star, and all the light the Moon reflects. Charging for Moonlight is a project already underway. If Dad can own the Sun, Sheikh Bahram can own the Moon. The charge on Moonlight is by degrees. No Saracen blade ever devised a more finely honed division of the degrees of Moonlight than that outlined by Sheikh Sidi bin-Bahram's Decree of Lunar Ownership. As everyone knows, the Moon is a woman and rests on a huge red crab standing in mud. Long yellow rays stream out of her that attract moisture. Payment for Moonlight is thus based on the weight of moisture collected on a glass slide set in a scale held by a veiled and blindfolded live woman in each country of the Middle East. Thus there is no question about the absolute value of the Moonlight collected, since it is by the mercy of Allah that any dew at all exists in the Middle East. All this, of course, Dad sees as a variation on the thousand-year-old Vatican scam of selling to Catholics True Pieces of the Cross and papal dispensations forgiving mortal sins and other guilts. But he says nothing, knowing that you set a thief to catch a thief, while he and the sheikh plan behind their smiles to leave each other poor as churchmice with beggars bowls. Now only I know that Dad is creamed out, cannot speak, perhaps cannot hear. Yet I must admit that he is still with me, like El Cid, dead in the saddle but riding out in the dawn to conquer the Moors.

Not really in our world, Dad's smile beams about the table, then he laughs silently at the boardmembers trapped in his monkey cage. Lightly, a palm beats on a wheel with pleasure. He glows and raises a finger in delight at Sheikh Bahram's shrunken cheeks and scary white eyes, seeing perhaps his favorite dish of roast wild boar's head.

I'm not sure, the Persian says to Sheikh Bahram, but I think he wants to eat you.

Ahh! nods the sheikh, weighing the pain of his own death, his face blank but for a hint of curiosity.

So I ask the Board, The Lake Bolshoi mission moves forward with great success. But how did we fight the Greenpeace devils? I'll tell you. We hired a team of French frogmen who wanted to get even for a lad murdered in Australia while trying to sabotage a Greenpeace vessel. When that story hit the papers, France had to cancel, deny the Australian underwater mission. When we offered these frogmen the technology and explosives, they jumped at the chance and took them out. No media. Semtex is Yugoslavia's gift to civilization.

I would like to know, sir, Sidi says to Dad, not to me, now that we are spending everything we've harvested from around the world, *sir? sir? are you listening?*—do we really have enough money to fulfill *both* of our projects? I try to add it all up on my pocket calculator but the zeroes go crazy. *They go crazy!*

With an admiring brilliance that lights up the Boardroom, Dad gazes at Bahram and seems amazed by joy. Has The Prophet himself descended to *The Profit?*

Dad thinks we have enough, I say. If we don't, we just buy what we need.

Sheikh Bahram the Unsmiling turns to my end of the table. Buy *wha-at?*

As my father has explained, Sheikh Bahram, four percent of the big bills in all world currencies, the hundred-dollar bill, the big pound notes and large francs, are made in Syria, which turns out tons of fake cash daily. We have only to ask the good Syrians.

That is so comforting, Sheikh Bahram says. No, the Syrians are not Samaritans, but we can always depend on our Middle Eastern brethren. Yes? Of course we can.

His lips purse into a killer smirk. He sees me as a babe in the woods. I see tiny Sidi as a full-sized python crossing the cool morning sand and leaving no track.

Yes, he says, someday soon the Sun will rise on our little family and we shall own all its light. All of us, Allah be praised. *Trust!*, trust in Allah, who gives us the Moon, who gives us the Sun. He is so merciful. And what is our deserving? We have only to trust his mercy. Must we be treated like thieves when all has already been given us? Does bin-Bahram not already own the Moon? I do, I do. And Bihusi Sunbeams, gentlemen, does it not already own the Sun? Well, practically. At least it's within our grasp, we all know that. I ask, what in Heaven must we steal, when all has been given? We will be lower than dogs and the shame of Islam if we fail Bihusi Sunbeams.

He crinkles sweetly, hopeful of having tempted Dad to reply about Islam. But Dad only brightens, speechless with accord. I ask myself, Is this truly not El Cid in the wheelchair?

Sheikh Bahram's withered little fingers bloom with joy. His mad white marble eyes take us all in. What a relief, he says. What joy in Paradise!—to see that you agree. That we shall all share in this legacy President Baxter brings us, gifts we shall use to lighten the burdens of nations heavy with grief. *Trust us!* we cry to the world. *Trust us!* There shall be Sunpower for all, for a slight charge. And not just for money. No, no, no. Respect! We shall demand respect. I kick the dog who fails to give his trust, who fails to give us *absolute* respect, the only true possession a man of honor can have. *TRUST!* Forgive me for going on like this, but President Breedwolfe Alexander has soothed me just by his appearance, and left me consoled, completely consoled, about our expenses in Siberia that so burden and terrify my heart and make it flutter with fear. But, Sidi whispers, I *trust* him. Aren't all Bihusi Sunbeam investments *indemnified* by Baxter Inc.? Who of us at this table can lose a penny in this venture? None. Not a sou, not a halala!

The demon dips his bulbous white eyes and tiny black irises in a girlish flutter.

I often wonder how this skinny, shriveled up little prick climbs aboard his latest extrafat wife. If she sat on him, she'd mash every rib and his pelvis. I won't tell you, by the way, what I know of her bathroom habits. That's not repeatable even between adults. Well, little prick, that's untrue. By his father's order, his uncircumcised penis had been oiled and massaged and sucked for hours daily since his pure silk swaddling clothes, by his mother, his older sisters and his father's other wives, and since youth by male adepts in the household, resulting not only in a once world-class swollen organ of deep girth but also now in a long, lifeless, rubbery and ever infirm soldier, out of the battle!—a state beyond all chemical repair and worsened by his present nervous tremble, weakened life functions, and wrinkled, fleshless, sucked-dry and skeletal body. Neither woman nor money can pleasure him, only torture and murder. Oh hell, Sidney must know all this?

A finger to her lips tells she's sworn to silence about Sidney's clients.

Dad's hatred of Bahram adds up almost to love. A bond of cruelty unites them, as does Bahram's massive dismissal of almost all human feeling from business. Bahram gazes out over mankind with cobra eyes looking for the slightest movement in world currencies. This is a monster after Dad's own heart. Dad hates and adores the puny little pup, applauds the figure the Wild Ass cuts, and has said of him, It's a wonder he doesn't slip into the toilet. This bandit is the first Mexican Bedouin, such a great human being. He almost makes sense when he talks, Billy. You want to pet him. And his pupils, have you watched how the eyes open and close like a paranoid parrot's? Sometimes I want to lick his face all over. Stop me if I get too close!

But as I've said, Sidi has this lone hopeless germ of compassion. Like Dad, he looks at any deal without measuring social consequences and is endearingly immoral, saying, in his baby tones, If *I* don't take this money somebody else will. It's just *lying* there. Somebody's got to pick it up. But after Sidi does pick it up, he goes and funds another cancer research program and buys a Bihusi Bed for every citizen of Kuwait. He won't miss the money. If it weren't for his spendthrift way with hospitals and medical research and bed-buying, Sidi would have been adopted by Dad as an honorary Bihusi.

Dad often would sigh, telling me, We just can't have softhearted dupes in our clan, Billy. Sure he's trying to beat cancer and senile dementia and a lapsed prick, but harboring a philanthropist would just give us a bad name. Double doors open and flanked by Steele and Truesmith, her Marine honor guard in white gloves and dress blues who bear Bihusi Medals of Honor and carry the Flag of the Bihusi and the Bihusi Sunbeam Pennant, Magda enters the Boardroom of the Sun for the first time, her figure stately, bearing The Spear of Ahuramazda That Sees Everything, and robed in a Unicorn Tapestry she has had cut down for a long coat, with a blue-eyed, chaste, white silken unicorn dancing down her spine, the horn sprouting from its forehead the sword of God in an impure world, and beneath the coat a gown of green silk with the bright red blood drop in the Bihusi Rose glittering on her breast. Her throat rises from a cowl that curls into a hood over her thick, low, virginal hairline as shock fills the Boardroom. A woman in this palace of thieves! And somehow she carries about her the soft, small tink of wind chimes, as if walking on stars or steeped in tiny bells ringing in what can only be a spiritual wind or breezes from above. Her mercurial eye darts about and declares at once that this unicorn is all business, virile, manly, and seeks out the mysteries of this church fathered by her invincible husband.

And are there no gentlemen in this room? Steele roars. Rise when the Queen enters!

All the Zoroastrians rise, as do I. Dad looks about in gay wonder.

Ahh! Ahh! sighs Sheikh Bahram. We are honored to see you, Madame Bihusi.

Will no one get Mother Bihusi a chair! Truesmith asks.

I will stand for now, Magda says, then barks at the Board, *Sit!*

Standing by Breedwolfe she throws back her hood, revealing the starburst superabundant power of her risen hair with its white waves streaking from each temple, then draws back her head for a great, loud goose hiss, nailing everyone's attention, and declares, I am she who lay down a virgin and arose a queen. This is the warrior who opened my womb and brought forth the Word of Ahuramazda. She grips her pelvis as a sign. I bring the pure Sword. I am He Who Is the Sun Force and Must Be Obeyed.

She rules the room. But at last Sheikh Sidi bin-Bahram speaks.

But, madame, you are clearly a woman.

She bears on her cheeks, though, a very thin but joyous, slightly golden beard, a kind of Sunstruck trim about her jawline, proper to a female demon in Arabic countries. Her eyes burn at Bahram. She is all energy. She has hit the Boardroom at a very high level, a figure hard to hold in check by human hand.

But Sheikh Bahram, barely human, whispers, *A woman, and so thin.*

Magda looks about the Kremlin War Room with its vast flat wall map of the globe and at the huge oval table. Gentlemen, she says, this is war. She points at the table, telling Truesmith, Put it there.

Truesmith puts a large, heavily strapped package on the Boardroom table.

This is my portfolio in Bihusi Sunbeams, she says, then smiles about the table and cries, *HA!*

She adds, The good always laugh. Ha ha ha. Her eyes weigh the intelligence of the assembled Arabs with their wrapped heads as her chest and wide mouth issue a deep rich purr. She tells them, I am here to help you. . . because. . . all good things. . . approach their goal. . . *crookedly.*

This thought the Boardmembers grasp at once and feel at home with.

She looks about the walls and tells Truesmith, Hang it there.

Truesmith taps a nail into the wall, unwraps a large framed blowup of Magda and hangs up this desk shot of Magda seated in her library at Chalet Bihusi on the Jungfrau, the Bihusi and Sun Company flags standing behind her, her brow crowned with the Bihusi/Romanoff tiara, her eyes starred by an evasive glint (infinite pity? *lust?*), a gyrocompass and a Persian astrolabe on the desk and a large world globe beside her, flanked by a Cray computer screen, swank telephones, piled glossaries, calendars and timetables, behind her a wide screen running stock figures, and at the open French window a powerful telescope pointed at Heaven. She holds upright in her left hand The Spear of Ahuramazda That Sees Everything, the relic that to the worthy eye turns all things to a world of glass.

Up and running, Mother, Truesmith says bashfully.

Thank you, my son.

Dad glows. He rocks lightly and grips his knees with pleasure.

Magda leans her ear to Breedwolfe's mouth. What's that? she asks him. He says nothing, but she rises, telling Truesmith, Alexandru says bravely done. Gentlemen, let us bow our heads as the threshold of a new day dazzles us.

Sheikh Bahram smiles, chin high. You speak well, dear lady. Now shall we get down to business? He glares about for support. Will you have a seat, madame?

You are still asleep in bed, Bahram, Magda says. None of this is happening. A bad dream has come your way.

Wonder strikes him. Madame Bihusi?

The Moving Finger writes, Bahram, and having writ, moves on. They say the lion and the lizard keep the courts where Bahram gloried and drank deep.

Too much wine has gone to your head, Madame!

And your extravagant monasticism has done *you* in, she says. I fear you will awake and find yourself in a Turkish bath, still rubbery and all adangle, if one can believe reports from your harem.

His jaw yawns.

Surprise fills her. You look wounded! What are these black looks?

Wounded, madame? Black looks? These are but smiles I would give a clumsy child who has dropped her milk! I am excited by your presence and offer a thousand pardons that my fattest wife isn't here to greet you and take you to the snack bar.

Do not haggle, Bahram. It does not become you. I am not the one who has spilled his milk.

Bahram hardens into pasteboard compassion. A wild kindness drips from his eyes as his arms fly to Allah. I bow to your Balkan wit, O Queen of Bihusi!

Rumanian, she says. Do not confuse the Bihusi with Hungarians, Albanians and other Central European riffraff. Do I call you Iraqi?

Forgive my offense, Madame. I am unpardonable.

Oh, no offense. I pardon you. And she turns a circle. How do you like my coat?

A very pretty scarlet horse, Madame, Bahram says.

Unicorn.

Truly a unicorn.

Yes. It's a Gobelin. It used to hang at Versailles, then at the Cloisters in New York. I thought tapestry would make a nice coat. You see the horn? That is the Sword of God. The unicorn itself can be tamed and ridden only by a virgin. As a consolation for the unfortunate death of Billy's twin brother, God has made me a virgin again. Since only a virgin can bear the Word of God, I am, revirginized.

The Zoroastrians sit back, shocked breathless.

Smiling, Bahram asks, Do you speak with Allah?

I allow Him in at times. When I'm not too exhausted. She waves at the blowup of her labors at her desk. I even call on Him for help.

Does He answer you, Madame?

He does, with grace, charm, and severe truthfulness.

What does He tell you, O Queen?

He says that unless I take my husband's place at this table, there will be fewer but better Arabs on His planet. Do you think this gown goes with the coat?

Bahram reads the heavens. Allah could not have chosen more wisely. When does He visit you, Madame?

We have supper together. Magda dusts her husband's shoulders. He owns a chalet in Provence and often, on Friday nights, He rides over to the Jungfrau for coffee and a napoleon. Sometimes He stays for brandy, if not feeling utterly grief-stricken about certain peoples.

That is a very long ride! Sidi says. And what does Allah wear for this ride, O Queen? A simple robe, perhaps?

In Provence and Interlaken? Don't be foolish. Le Seigneur wears riding boots and a cape.

Bahram shares his joy with the table. A cape, Madame!

A rather *Lordly* lionskin, with the head intact on His brow. Otherwise, He's nude, as on the Sistine Chapel ceiling.

Her look strikes him dumb. Can it be true? She speaks with Allah?

I am spellbound, he says. In what tongue do you converse?

I wouldn't know, Bahram. It's not human, I assure you. And she rubs Dad's shag. Not human at all. Do you doubt me, Bahram? After all, you yourself have spoken with Him, have you not? When you closed your Moon Deal?

Bahram scratches his cheek, then rubs an eye, then clears his throat and turns about in his chair. Blasphemy comes hard for little Sidi.

You did, didn't you? she says. You may speak freely. Bihusi Sunbeams has no interest in acquiring your Moon rights. Not when we have the Sun. You understand, of course, that when the space disc program is complete, we will have to charge you for Sun Light reflected from the Moon? Something minimal. Our engineers are devising Sun meters as we speak, to place beside your dewpoint Moon scales. It's only just. We can discuss this later.

Bahram shows no shock.

I see, he says. Madame, I am thinking of buying the Lamborghini Company. Does He perhaps drive a Lamborghini?

A Lamborghini? Why not a turtle, for heaven's sake! He rides a large scarlet stallion, Sheikh Bahram, much faster than any Lamborghini.

But of course. Forgive an old man, Madame Bihusi.

Next you will be asking if He rides a Schwinn. Do you want the Schwinn Company as well?

No, I am sure He does not ride a bicycle.

He does not, sir. He does not.

Sheikh Bahram points at a sideseat across the table from him. Madame, we must get underway. Will you have a seat?

Is that where Alexandru sits? No, it's not. I should be sitting here. At the head of the table. You see my portfolio?

Sheikh Bahram nods at the fat, strapped portfolio and says, You won't have to trouble yourself in the details of running the Ultimate Fund, Madame. We will take good care of you.

Listen, Sidi. I've been to this little gabfest before. My husband tells me everything when he comes home. So as far as this board is concerned, think of me as Alexandru Bihusi Baxter. Right, dollingk?

Dad glows.

Let me speak to you a moment, my son, she tells me. Grasping The Spear she takes me aside.

She picks lint from her sleeve. Kill him. Kill him now. Have Truesmith and Steele take him out and send him to Paradise. We'll punch his ticket.

Now? What's the hurry?

He's after your father's seat. Isn't that enough?

But we need his money, I tell her, or the space disc program can't go through.

And we need to kill him. Finish him. Quickly. He's approaching us in power. Cut his throat!

I don't think Trueblood and Steele will do that.

Then kill him yourself! Take The Spear and do it. Right where he sits.

I look at Sidi who reads his Charte Astrologique from an Orly Airport vending machine.

Now!

Her neck tenses. Back hairs stand with danger.

Prick up your ears. Listen! Can't you hear how slow and unaware his heart is?

I watch Sidi point out something on his chart to the Persian beside him.

Magda grips her muzzle in thought, weighing my strengths. Or you jump onto the table and distract him while I run him through.

I want to do it, I need to do it. I must do it. . . I can't do it. I ask myself, Should I just *bite* him? I get a whiff of bliss imagining this. My head swims. Something sick inside me wants Dad to lose. Where does it come from? Is this the time to kill the king and take charge? Must I use the sheikh to do it? Will I never sing over Sidi's bones?

I am at war with myself.

Let's talk with Sidi, I say. Maybe he'll fold.

Magda spits. Don't talk, don't talk. He screwed me in the garden with his snaketalk. That tongue of his could bamboozle Allah. Kill him!

I grab The Spear of Ahuramazda That Sees Everything.

Now, she says. Yes, now.

I look into her eyes. Mother, I can't lift it.

You will regret this, she says. This is no gamble. By not killing bin-Bahram, you bring us to endgame with our King mated in one more move. Or do you want to kill your father?

I turn to stone. Kill Dad?

She clutches The Spear as well. The world turns to glass before her. She sees the karma of Bihusi through glass, filled with infinite genealogies of Bihusi and Giurgiu.

Fate grips The Spear I can't lift.

You can't do it. Her voice drops. We'll do it next time.

We read each other's soul.

Well, I wouldn't have it any other way, Billy. I am proud of you. You had to run The Spear through Sidi or let Sidi spear your father *for you*. You choose as a good Bihusi prince must.

Wisdom floods her eyes. She is focused on Nirvana.

The wheel will turn again, she says.

The wheel?

We shall see the sheikh again. Another lifetime. It was not meant to be in this cycle. She gazes at Dad, who smiles just past us, not knowing us or perhaps looking slightly aside at us as if we are Hungarians or gluey aliens who have struck his interest but whom he will not challenge.

Wolf this down, she whispers at Sidi.

Her guttural yowl curdles the room. Raising overhead The Spear of Ahuramazda That Sees Everything, she charges the table. The sharp stone point whizzes by Sidi's nose and splits the table before him. The Boardmembers' elegant granite faces, each man an Oxford or Harvard graduate, wait for chips to fall where they may.

Sidi looks up sweetly, his heart still slow and normal, and points at his Charte Astrologique. My time is not yet, Madame! You're upset, O goddess?

Not at all, Sidi. We will meet again.

Magda yanks The Spear from mahogany depths. Turning, she says, By the way, Sidi, I loved *The Profit. A dollar on the wind, beloved, and then no more of thee and me.*

She walks to the door. A clear film like a shark's lid shuts on her eye.

Then no more of thee and me, Sidi.

All watch The Virgin of the Scarlet Unicorn leave the room.

I sit at the table beside Dad. Through the corner of my nose I scent Dad's power beside me. My father stares at my fiendish Hungarian hand that has failed in its duty and listens to Sidi's still beating heart.

TWILIGHT BREAKS OUR SILENCE. The absent Moon has gone into its dark phase for three nights and strong starlight brightens the evening. A summer wind off the lake lingers about us as we walk back, time aflow on our cheeks while Sidi, finding Rani Gupta a heartening companion, gives her a tender tour of his Swiss banks before they dine at the Dolder. Sidney has returned, alone. We sit on the lakeside porch and sip a tangy, slightly bitter green tea brewed from gingko, our bodies light and minds clear as Gong fills Sidney in about the boardroom. The evening waters lisp onto the sedge. A sigh gnaws at me. I feel my parting from Gong draw near. Ding dong, ding dong.

Sidney stirs. And then what happened?

We lost, I say.

You lost! she says.

Yes, we lost. Kismet, madam. *In'sh'Allah.* Whatever God wills. I became bin-Bahram's Filipino.

That sounds *awful*, Gong says.

Sidney waves this off. Oh, Sidi's not the horror he's made out to be, Gong.

I'd say he was, she says.

Well, I drawl, there are certain advantages to being Sidi's Filipino. Which I won't go into here. Doesn't Jung have anything to say about Kismet?

You feel locked into "karma"? Sidney asks. You said it's disintegration of your personality that drew you here.

Parting from my father and my people, as well as the threat from my foolish human sons, I say. Yes, my holdings are all up in the air. My luck has faded. I feel fate closing in on me. I want to fight it. What does Jung say about resisting destiny?

I think he'd go along with Herodotus, Gong says. Character is fate.

No, no, I say. Character can change. It's the genes that are irreversible.

But can *you* replace the character you were born with and the tradition you were born into and that grips you? All these are rooted into you as strongly as the sexual instinct. Or the instinct for self-preservation.

He knows all that, Sidney says. It's the feeling-tone his life has taken that stifles him. The underworld has risen up to swallow Billy. About predestination Jung has little to say. About rising above weariness of spirit, poor health and worn-out ideas and sentiments, he suggests rebirth through *intention*. The force of this virtue lies in guarding against generalization. You draw into yourself the flavor of your goal. *Your* goal is rebirth as a human and bringing a regenerative energy to mankind to absolve you of what you now see as your sins, just as Faust cleans out the swamps for penance. If that's what you aim for, you might take heart from the feeling-tone such a future success would bring you. Focus on your intention. Suck on it! Take hope from your goal. Sense the energy that repairing a damaged past will bring you. You love the Sun? Look to the Sun within you. You resist becoming the alpha wolf of the Bihusi? Your defection brings unbearable sorrow? For this you must somehow sacrifice your father. But he is, you say, already gone. So you're in standing water and locked into a depression coming from loss of the parental staff that has held you up all your life. But your greatest strength still lies in your wolf nature. Somehow you must bring that to bear on your rebirth. They seem antithetical? They are. But only their marriage will make you whole.

Yes, Gong says, her eyes rich with far-seeing. You smell the winter wind coming for *you*, not just your father's parting. But what about your sons?

Door chimes sound.

Ah, I say, Titania. With the family heirloom.

Sidney rises and goes into the house. I hear Titania say, Well, we meet again! You must be Doctor Chang. Is my husband still here?

Yes, indeed, Madame Baxter. How do you do? I'm sorry I didn't recognize you this afternoon. Please follow me. We are enjoying the evening air on the back porch.

Thank you. Actually, I keep my maiden name. Titania Tintagel.

Gowned for dinner, Titania bears a long leather case taller than herself, her aging eyes still half-lidded with girlish stargazing.

Wolfy, she says. How's it going? Nearly done?

Not quite, I say. I think my doctors are giving me a summary analysis. Sit down, my dear.

Eager Gong stares at the ancient leather case. *Is this it?*

Oh this? This clunky old thing, Titania says, and hands me The Spear as she sits. Look at this relic. They want me to be Keeper of the Spear. But how can I be? This is no spear from the kingdoms of elfin I know about. It's a hand tool for planting potatoes. I mean, I know what it's supposed to do, but it doesn't do it for me.

I unwrap leather thongs binding the halves of the long case together and slowly draw out The Spear of Ahuramazda That Sees Everything. Its heavy spearhead is two long heart-shaped and sharpened stones bound into a blade by gold, copper, and silver wires. The blade halves hold a rusted, five-inch, wavy iron nail lodged in a hollowed out stone bole.

Look at this old nail, Titania says.

What about it? Gong asks.

It's not useful. If it at least stuck out it might punch a hole in someone. But buried down in that bole, it's just a cheap decoration. If you want to see a spear you should see my father's old cavalry lance from the Danish hussars, with its glorious regimental pennon. Now that is an object of beauty. One look at that and your mind goes flying over the hills, puncturing Poles.

You have wonderful imagination, Madame Bax, uh, Mistress Tinta, Sidney blunders. How shall I address you?

Why not Titty?

How bewitching. Sidney laughs.

I hope so. Are we through, Wolfy?

Not quite. I believe that Gong is about to summarize my case. Try this, I say, handing her The Spear.

Gong rises. She grips The Spear and steps aside, facing us on the porch. A blue aura rises from her crimson shoes to her dark psyche knot. Her dark eyes widen, then dim and simmer with invasion as the world turns to glass. I am seeing. . . I see someone watching over us!

She walks about, her voice crossing the lawn, perhaps crossing the ages. A flashing quickens her as she digs into my state. Clouds part on a glass world. Dark eyes shine with truth and courage. All time pivots about her, tragedy upon tragedy, karma upon karma as genes shuttle and join.

She smiles through welling eyes.

Children! I see children! They laugh. And so beautiful. Whose are they?

Shock catches her throat. She shouts a warrior shout and raps the deck with The Spear. She catches up her breasts and clutches her heart. She peers toward the great unconscious body of the lake.

He's here! He's here! she whispers and steps backward. Her eyes fasten on the hammock. My God, he's in the hammock!

Her breath comes faster and faster. She watches something from the hammock approach her on the porch, and stiffens as divine force enters force. Her voice deepens and now speaks in the warmly commanding English of Dr. Carl Gustav Jung, psychopomp of the collective unconscious, sifter of darkness for world archetypes and wizard of analytic psychology.

You are Ahuramazda's child, Billy Baxter, states Jung-Li. But you are also the offspring of a seriously disturbed pair of psychotics! From a human viewpoint, that is. You no longer fit into their purposes. In this you are the most interesting patient I've ever had. Your lupine mind has been forever infected with compassion by Steele and Truesmith and the food kitchens in Pakistan. Your wife Titania hopes to join her energies to yours as a she-wolf. This delusion can have no peaceful outcome, since she can never achieve the hatred, greed and rapacity of a true Bihusi.

Oh, balls, Titania says.

Nor can your sons, despite her hopes, and theirs as well, become true Bihusi.

Gong stares blankly as Jung gathers his thoughts.

Let's be clear, though, Jung-Li says, that not killing Sidi bin-Bahram was not an act of compassion but rather the necessary deathblow to your father as imprinted on your wolf genes. That restraint in turn seemingly killed Bihusi Sunbeams and its benefits for mankind. Having surrendered to the altruism of Steele and Truesmith in feeding the Third World, you also wish to atone for your father's misdeeds by creating pure energy for mankind from the Sun. In abandoning your true nature, *your religion, you little pisspot*—you've gone way-y overboard. There is no way back to your pure wolf being. You are down and out. Your only hope of recovery lies in becoming human.

A jackal! I cry.

Yes, Jung-Li says. As a wolf the only way to work back to wholeness is with pain, cunning, and widespread death and terror. In your abandoning your wolf nature, as you have, the Bihusi line must fade. In fact, with your human wife you can no longer bear wolfen. The wolf carries his heart in his balls and shows a side of the world-soul given to growth through thievery, greed, and savage aggrandizement. You no longer have the balls to cheat, steal, and rob without mercy.

Tears stand in Gong's eyes. *The Bihusi must die!*

Die!? Titania says. This isn't analysis, it's Halloween on Elsinore. Wake me up when this old fart leaves!

But Sidney brims with wonder. Please, Madame, let Doctor Jung speak.

And the line *will* wither without your blood filling its veins, Jung-Li says. What does your dark angel say to that? Does he not watch in that cruel silence all Bihusi cherish. Well, dark angel? I ask you, What kind of an angel are you? Not caring for your legions, just watching to see how they stumble? He helps or handicaps his followers all by whim. Some angel! But he watches you, doesn't he, and pricks your heart, for there *is* individuation, or a rich new self, even on the dark side—but he wants you back instead. Wholly his. You still miss a heart compacted of darkness. Does not the shaken wolf face three nights a month in deep black horror, with his dark angel completely gone from the heavens, no Moon!—before the angel slips back into sight with the very slimmest of crescents, the faintest of hopes, before he once more slowly moves you toward wholeness and at last draws your heart up into the nightshout of his full glory bursting over hill and forest? It's the same old story, the struggle for wholeness, and never more crucial than in your present dark of the Moon.

Sidney, frozen by the voice of his prophet coming from Gong, breaks with a sob, *But what about the souls in hell!*

Oh, you're worried, are you, Sidney? Jung-Li says. You driven lump of ice, do you think souls in hell don't have a rapacity and greed for wholeness? I speak from direct experience! Hell is going through life again and again. Am I not here speaking through this big stick?

With that Gong raps The Spear against the deck.

Crushed by Jung's criticism, Sidney sits splayed. His arm fends off further blows.

Take a lesson from the Bihusi, Jung-Li says. Bihusi know they can not suffer for those born infirm or retarded and trod under. They turn from suffering just as they would hide weakness from the pack. To humans, suffering for others is the crucible in which they are purified. But the nightfolk howl a different music, blacker, cathartic. They live with a pack-intelligence unknown to man but which holds and fills them all with one harmonious whine of happiness, all the organ stops pulled out at once. Only the death-religion of the Egyptians granted a uniting darkness like theirs when millions died raising the great stone tombs. But where those millions had no hope of joining Pharaoh on his solar journey, the Bihusi when they have crossed the night sea will join Ahuramazda.

I cry out. And yet my blood! My human side streams through me like a cancer! I have mingled my soul with the jackals. What will happen should I change utterly?

Silence when Doctor Jung is speaking! Sidney tells me. But then he asks Jung-Li, Doctor, will you tell me? Is there really transmigration of soul?

It's something like that, Jung-Li says. And like reincarnation. Who can say? Such terms mean nothing over here.

Each time we live, I tell Sidney, we are more able, more fit.

This is true, Jung-Li says. I see newborn wolves with absolute memory and able by smell alone to follow a finger held before them.

That's wonderful for wolves, Sidney says to Jung-Li. But is it true for humans, Grand Wizard? Must we transmigrate?

Why should I answer that, you little conference addict? Jung-Li asks. You're so boring. Sidney, you should be certified. *Auf weidersehn*, wolf! I'm leaving. See you on the wheel.

But what should I do about my sons? I cry.

Jung's grip loosens from Gong's mind. She faints against the porch rail and I catch her and The Spear. Her body fills my arms. Her face lifts to mine. Our eyes trade beings. I am transmembered into Gong and sway with her longing for what she sees in me even as she knows my longing and sees herself through my eyes. Our beings breathe to and fro between our bodies.

Titania awakes. Did he finish? Is he gone?

Yes, Sidney says. It was amazing!

What happened? Gong asks.

Carl Gustav Jung! Sidney says. He came! He spoke through you! Oh my God, the prophet has spoken to me.

I tell Gong, All told he was rather harsh.

No, no! Sidney says. Just *crusty*.

He spoke through *me?* Gong says. I saw him in the hammock. And that's all I remember.

If only he'd answered me more fully, Sidney says. Transmigration? He was very interested in it for decades. But what did we just see?

My God! Titania says. Remind me never to get analyzed. I don't know how anyone could bear a whole day of this. She gazes about. Have you been telling them all your stories? How they could sit through it I'll never know. My mind just tunes out when he starts. I can't help it! The wolf I used to know has softened like warm chocolate. Melted! The big softy's practically human. I hope these doctors have put some gumption back into your—well, I don't know what he's told you about his lovelife. It's not the divine affair it once was. He must be in mourning. I don't know. Maybe he's seen all there is to see in women and we're just not enough. I suppose when you've got it all, you've really got nothing. When he met me he'd been depressed for years and then married me to come in out of the rain. All the money in the world couldn't make him happy, but maybe a wife and kids could. But then he went on chasing deals with Dad. Left me home, spinning books. I think his mistress is depression.

Perhaps things will be better now, Gong says. I am a great admirer of your stories. Might you sign your books for me?

Titania winks greedily. I'd be delighted!

But something has left Gong withdrawn. May I show you our library? she asks me. You'll never guess what we have. One of those little wolf statuettes your father makes.

Not any longer, I say. But I'd like to see them.

I hear her heart suddenly thrum.

Gripped by fate, I follow Gong's severe black pants suit down a hall and into a high-ceilinged and crammed library. Every bone in my body sings.

She laughs nervously, pulling out Titania's four books. They look well-read.

I'm afraid Sidney never reads fiction.

That's makes two of them, I say. Titania never reads either. She only writes. Let me carry these.

Our hands touch. I grip hers.

It's over here, she says, nodding toward a small bronze statuette on a book shelf. Isn't it exquisite? So fierce!

She smiles, half-sadly. Her eyelids charm me.

Wait a minute. Gong, your eyes simply amaze me. You must hear this a lot. Mostly I can't look anyone straight in the eye. But it's like Titania says. I've melted. With you, I'm human! I'm not a monster. I'm sure you have this effect on all your male patients. Am I right? Please. Never close your eyes when you're with me. I may kiss you.

I beg you, don't talk to me like this.

Her eyes well. She turns aside.

I take her hand. What's wrong?

I can't tell you.

A deep sob and she hides her nose. I draw out my handkerchief and dab her face.

Yes, you can, Gong. Tell me.

I must fight the stars! Agony fills her. What do you ask of me? Do you think I'm not moved by our meeting? I'm someone without a heart to lose? I have taken a holy vow to speak only in truth and courage! I cannot speak otherwise. And if I speak my heart, you won't respect me.

A vow to whom?

To one who has the right to ask it of me.

To Sidney?

No, not to Sidney. To one who stands on the highest peak. The great guide of my life. Carl Gustav Jung.

I know you mean that. But just because I always lie and cheat doesn't mean I can't respect an honest woman. Here I've been a monster all morning, afternoon and evening and you've seen only my worst side.

No, no! I've seen your best side.

I drop Titania's books and take Gong's shoulders. She's somewhere far ahead of me in this moment. She hears my every word with a touch of wildness and fear.

I'm married, Gong, but I'm lonely as rain falling on the sea. I have no right to say such things. But I want to see you again. I must see you. I don't mean as a patient. I see something in you that a Buddhist spends decades trying to find.

Her eyes shut, head raised, her shoulders sink. I am helpless before you. I have heard your heartbreak, Bihusi, and you have drawn me in half.

Then look at me. I've lived my life to arrive at this moment! Be honest. What did you see when you held The Spear?

I saw what I cannot speak of and keep your respect.

Gong, tell me. What did you see?

I saw a happiness unknown to me. I saw children. My own.

Yes? Don't stop.

—and *yours*.

Thank you for telling me. If you hadn't, we might both have gone on half in the dark. I'm married. You're married. How can we have children?

Must I tell you?

Well, you must!

Gong draws me to the empire sofa and pulls me down beside her. Lamplight from a rosy glass shade softens her. She can't speak. Large frank eyes from the world of China search my character at depth.

If I don't know you after this long day, I never will, she says. You've hidden nothing, have you?

Only that I'm half the wolf that I used to be.

No, no. You are half the man you could be, if you go away without hearing me. If you go, I'll understand. But first, please hear me out. Do you love your sons?

Of course.

I've learned some things about you not just today but also in researching The Spear. Here's my advice. What you must do is this. Tell your sons that you were born and raised as one being and have become another. However, aside from Bihusi Sunbeams, of which you will retain control, you have surrendered all other business ventures of yourself and your father to your mother, Magda. You must keep control of Bihusi Sunbeams, should it ever come into being, so that your sons or even Sidi, should he snatch it from them, don't bleed the planet dry through overcharging for solar energy. The day will come, of course, or so they'll think, when they inherit Bihusi Sunbeams from you. But long before that happens Ahuramazda has told me to tell you that you must turn Bihusi Sunbeams into a public service owned and operated by the world's governments, thus bringing not only cheap power globally but a major step toward world peace as well. Of course, there will always be sociopaths who take over governments. That's understood. But you will have done as much as is possible for you to do. Then you must also warn your sons that, being human whether they like it or not, their Grandmother Magda will tear them to tatters if they even think about taking her place. Explain this to them. She might welcome being overthrown by a Bihusi, but she will not stand for overthrow by human grandchildren who don't have the genetic blueprint for parricide. They can forget that.

I'm following you.

No. I'm following you.

I say nothing.

I must leave Zürich, Gong says. *Oh, I've said it!* Her eyes well. She grabs my hand and crushes it. I *can't* raise children in this stuffy Jungian atmosphere. I am not a Jungian.

You're not? But you swore a holy vow to Carl Gustav Jung.

She studies the doorway. Billy, I am a lapsed Jungian. I am a closet Freudian, if anything. I have no practical faith in Jungian analysis. And Jung was a terrible man—a womanizer like Sidney who takes him as his model. Like him, Sidney is fixated on his mother and has no room for a strong woman, only for replacement mistresses. You no doubt heard him today try to dismiss my comments, while I have the good sense to stand up to him at every turn. Well, when necessary. He is doomed to endless license and despises me for not being even stronger than his mother and crushing him underfoot. And Jung's own behavior in tramping all over his submissive wife, seemingly justifies Sidney's, at least to Sidney.

But Jung spoke through you this evening!

So? I didn't hear it. Was it helpful?

He said that if I'm to be made whole, the Bihusi must die. The clan will wither without my carrying on the royal line.

Do you agree?

I do agree. I take her hand. You know that I have never had a wolf-child. So the clan must wither. Now that my father is retired, I must turn a corner in my life. Do some thinking. Start over in your world.

She sits tall but her face flies between relief and fear.

This is no honeymoon, she says. But I know you will still respect me when I say what I must. Let me strip this to the bone.

Her eyes drill into me and I can't believe my good fortune to be sitting here alone with this wildly intelligent and warm creature reading my soul and pouring herself out to me.

Our mates are not satisfied with us. My husband denies me the children I must have for my physical health, if for no other reason, and I am not growing younger. My golden moments are going. We have not made love for over two years, and never will again. I cannot submit my body to mere pleasure for Sidney. I *must* bear offspring. He finds satisfaction in a number of gosling Valkyries, or *Jungfrauen*, who follow him about and, frankly, we now live in a *ménage à trois* with his latest *femme inspiratrice*. Rani with her fear of abandonment has really dug herself in with Sidney. Her father abandoned her before birth, her mother is mentally incompetent, her husband divorced her, she has a background of prostitution to earn tuition for her education, and she has a history of suicide attempts. She adores and reveres Sidney and she's as beautiful as any woman on Earth and we both love her, but if Sidney withdraws from her it may be the last straw, the abandonment that ends her life. He knows that and she has him handcuffed. This is a tragic situation he's dug himself into. But all of his women have mental problems they sublimate as analysts under his guidance, and I can't see that they are greatly helped when they find they are not the incarnated goddesses he first tells them they are. He justifies all this by calling women the Dark Continent whose emotional riches need much greater exploration than men. He's self-indulgent and self-righteous. And yet a Don Juan whose magic touch opens buttons on any blouse. Sitting next to him, you find his charm stalking you and ready to spring like a lion. You can't believe the hunger he has for you. He faints onto your bosom. Sidney the Infant has just shot from your womb and is dying for the nipple. He needs you like a raging tooth needs a dentist. You are the keeper of the nerve drops, the love-balm that his pain begs for. And yet he is reading your soul as you soothe him. You have never seen such love-charms as his eyes, eagerness to have you, you alone, a god's hunger for you, unlike anything you've ever known or seen, not in books or in the movies. He has the uncanny ability to make you feel seventeen. Years melt away. He strips your resistance bare. You *are* seventeen and his eyes eat you alive. *But,* he knows nothing about women and is obsessed only with capture, phallic performance, and domination. Not warmth, not heart, not soul. And yet this penile icicle—who focuses on himself alone and thinks nothing of the bewildered woman beneath him— sees himself as a great lover. At this moment he is seducing your wife and quite likely has already fondled her breasts. Does that bother you?

I suppose it should but it doesn't. I hope she enjoyed it. But he may find he has truly met an incarnated goddess who is more than his match. Titania masks a dragon with her fairy tales and she's at least ten years older than Sidney. She can handle herself. And he's not telling her anything she doesn't already think about herself.

I have a loveless marriage, Billy. And by your own admission and your wife's complaint, you have failed her. I'll tell you, you are a being I could easily *mingle* with. That's your word. I'm asking you. Am I a jackal you could mingle with, until the end of her days, and help raise her children?

My God, yes.

That's good. Because when I held The Spear and the world turned to glass, I saw our fate. Very clearly. Her eyes shut. And I've been fighting to keep my happiness in check. I ask you, how can we fight The Spear when it shows me that I am destined to be Keeper of the Spear?

Then, I say, The Spear is drawn to your hand by Ahuramazda herself. I learned long ago not to fight The Spear.

Billy, can you help me through this night? I must leave Sidney. Sidney and I can never return to a married state. We already go our separate ways. But why am I torn when I foresee what must be? Why do I feel evil?

My darling, I say, all things truly good start from wickedness.

And I hug her among the books and say, I love you. Of course I'll help you. Leave Sidney tonight. I'll reserve a room for you at Les Armoire. I know you have a number of things to clean up. Come to me at my father's chalet on the Jungfrau when I send for you. We are having a great unveiling for Dad and you must be there. What I plan may send him into the Bihusi Wreath. And it may not. But this is not as you might think. I hope to give him the greatest gift of his life—or maybe afterlife. And he may need your help. He'll be your patient. As of this moment, I am no longer your patient.

I will come. You won't phone me?

I couldn't bear to hear your voice without holding you. But I may.

We must go back.

May we have one stolen kiss?

No, not stolen, she says. *Lost!*—and we have found it together.

Her kiss rises like fresh bread. I stand drunk with yeast.

Smile, I say. Our eyes trade kisses and time-to-come. Keep smiling.

We go back down the hall, breathlessly alive.

Your wife! Sidney cries, has been telling me the most fabulous story.

She warns Sidney, Wolfy wouldn't care about that story.

Which story is this? I ask. Or is it a new one?

About your wedding night, Sidney says.

But I already told you that, Sidney.

Oh, no. No, no, no. Not this story.

It's from my side of the bed, Titania says.

I have not been so stimulated in years, Sidney says.

Then you will have to read her books, Gong says.

Sidney frowns. But this was not fiction.

With Titania, I tell him, you never know.

Do you know, Sidney asks Gong, that Titty's first husband was Chinese! Of course I know that.

Two Chinese, Titania says. Twins.

A most unusual case, Sidney says. I would love to write it up. Or we could write it together from two viewpoints, analyst and analysand. If only you had a neurosis or psychosis of some sort, ha ha.

That can be arranged, Titania says. Perhaps I should make an appointment?

I would not charge you!

Very well, she says, we'll get together. She gives him her Queen of the Fireflies stare. I've never had a co-author.

Have you read Bettelheim's *The Uses of Enchantment?* Sidney asks her.

I don't read. I write.

Well, he was a greater monster than the ones he wrote about.

So am I.

Oh ho! And what do you eat?

What are you offering?

Hansel and Gretel!

Oh, I baked them up long ago.

Gong nudges me. This is going just where you think it will.

What? her husband asks.

I say, Gong wants to know what happened with Sidi this afternoon.

Sidney's self-assurance glows. Oh, I detected a certain romantic urge in him.

You see, I tell Titania, Sidi is Sidney's patient and Sidney has been treating Sidi's impotence.

Small world, Titania says. And who was that Indian woman I saw Sidney and Sidi with at Les Armoire today?

Rani Gupta! Sidney says. She lives here. She's my student.

Titania stares at Gong, but says nothing.

Quite a beauty, she says at last.

Catnip for Sidi, I say.

Sidney glowers in silence.

My problem with Sidi, Sidney, I say, is that I made a naive error which became a tiny loss leading to an awesome mistake.

And what was that? Gong asks.

I trusted Sidi. Breaking off an infinitesimal part of my spirit, he squeaked his way in, cracked me entirely and then went whole hog for Bihusi Inc.

I know all this, Sidney says.

But not from my side of the bed, I say.

Gong eyes me compassionately. How did he do that?

He saw that the space disc program would eat up his Moon Deal. He knew we needed his wealth for our final assault. When he would not give it up, we collapsed, and went under.

Gong's wonder rises. You trusted him in what way?

He opened our very next meeting with some old Babylonian verse he'd unearthed. He said in a whisper that it had moved "this old bandit" profoundly. He looked stricken, almost cancer-ridden. I swore he'd had a change of character at depth.

Oh? What was this verse?

Well, it was "Trust," written in the Akkadian dialect of Old Babylon. But he'd had it Englished especially for me:

My hanging gardens are gone, but still too much with me.
Getting and spending, I lay waste my powers.
Little I see in Nature but that it flowers
And dies, my barren petals fallen beneath the Moon.
Allah be merciful! I'd rather be an infidel suckled
In a creed outworn, so might I return and swoon
To childish things and to a heart unbuckled.
O from low to high my dissolution climbs,
I sink from high to low a million times,
So that now I seek through trust transcendent power,
Trust in Allah, trust in close friends, and surcease from crimes.
No more do untrustful notes, those discords dour
Steal from me each beauteous evening, calm and free.
Praise be Allah, who lets my very heart now creep
Through Paradise, whose mighty hills lie fast asleep.

I must say, my friends, he is a great reader of his own verse and spoke it softly, almost timidly, with heartbreaking, eloquent, whimpering sincerity.

Yes, yes! Sidney says. I love his readings. The old bandit reads marvelously.

Must be nice to have a Nobel Prize winner as a patient, Titania says. Even when it's all in strictest confidence. I pass on confidentiality. My life's an open book, if you know how to read it.

What happened with Sidi? Gong asks.

I agreed to loan Sidi's cousin money in a joint venture with me, a loan that Sidi and his brother guaranteed. When Sidi and his brother first come to me about this loan to their cousin, I cannot resist the terms. But I am troubled. Haven't I long seen Bahram's and his brother's ill will toward his cousin? The cousin begins making some payments. I stupidly lower my guard. For six trillion they give me twenty-five percent of the cousin's scheme. Now they offer me thirty percent more for five trillion. I never see it coming. Like a moron standing before a three-card monte box, I miss the hook. All I see is control coming to me in the second loan, giving me an additional thirty percent, for a total of fifty-five percent, at much more favorable terms. And that's what I watch. Even now I can't believe that I'd go for this. Dad and I have done this so many times to others. Building our obligations until they are so huge that the lender can't afford to let you default. I'd been hustled. I knew what would happen next. The cousin fails. The guarantors stall. And I'm short of the cash needed. The only play left for me is to entreat Bahram to take over Bihusi, Inc. and give me a contract for a management position, and as I go through the motions I know what he's going to say. And I know how much he's going to enjoy saying it. Bihusi Sunbeams' Ultimate Fund collapses, as does the space disc project. Had I tested that first loan to his cousin with The Spear, I would not have been suckered. It sees Everything.

Well, that's sad, Gong says. I know you'll weather this. But how did your father hold up, may I ask?

Titania covers her ears. Wake me up when he finishes. Money talk kills me. And that's all he and his father ever discuss: Analysts, bankers, share-holders.

Dad has achieved the perfection of the alchemists. He has been burned black in the athanor of Greenpeace and sent back from the underworld pure as salt by the dark angel. He and Magda, who failed to become two in one flesh, have become two in one spirit. Like desert winds, Magda has joined him soul to soul in One Self. I'd tell you more but this is a private, most mysterious marriage, whose inmost nature takes place subliminally, below even wolf consciousness, and is denied me.

How nice for your mother, Sidney says. I saw her at first only as a saucy little minx with a psychic whip.

Now, I say, she is Queen of Giurgiu and Queen of Bihusi.

Ahh! Sidney says. I wish I'd met her.

No, you don't, Titania says.

IN BALLGOWN AND DINNER JACKET for the great event, Gong Li-Chang and I enter the library of Dad and Magda's Jungfrau chalet. My parted wife Titania now rooms here along with my sons. I hear Gong's heart thump against her breastbone in the broad unfamiliar room where Grandfather rolled off the balcony and followed The Left Hand of God into the crevasse. She will meet Dad—at last! Well, more or less.

Her breath heaves and breasts sway in an ankle-length strapless sapphire slit gown I helped choose on the Bahnhofstrasse—along with brilliant sapphire earrings and a Nile-blue semi-secret engagement ring studded with diamonds. I have despite her modesty led her to wear and swim in a wildly heavy smell of money. Maybe this will rake Dad's nostrils and wake him up.

White bolts of late afternoon Sunlight crush the blood-red rug. Dad sits in his smoking jacket of blue silk with the Bihusi crest, his red cordovan slippers waxed with Sunlight, and sees God knows what as he stares past us. But Bihusi rarely look anyone in the eye anyway. Magda, breathtaking in The Bihusi Rose and an antique purple Fortuny, lies on the Sunstruck big ox-blood boat of a divan, flanked by stacks of philosophy. She keeps her faint beard in devilish trim and grapples with karma in Shaw on *The Wolf Force* and Nietzsche's *Wolf und Überwolf*. By the lighted fireplace The Spear rises from its ancient leather case.

I've warned Gong about the psychotic musk that clings to the bookcases—an evergreen delight of jojoba oil stirred with sex juices, though every binding reeks of damp wolf hair as well. The Holy Ghost of Bihusi never bathes and usually sleeps on the golden fireplace rug once graced by the sandals of Nebuchadnezzar. I'd earlier sprinkled some Malaysian Lime about but the overrich room still shocks and charms my firefly-soon-to-be-ex-wife. In this room Titania's eyes glitter with an exalted blue hysteria and mysticism that leave her spiked and half-drunk. She's on top of the world.

What are you doing here, Doctor Li-Chang? she asks. Oh, what a nice ring—and great smell!

Thank you. I am a compassionate physician, Gong says. I hope to help Dad and want to be here when he goes through something this important, this critical. I've been thinking about Billy's story. To me he did not lose to Sidi bin-Bahram. But Sidney thinks he did.

Sidney may be right, Titania says. By the way, Sidney's on the balcony watching the sunset.

What a pleasant surprise. I haven't seen him since we parted.

Again I hear Gong's heart thump and scent the heat racing over her skin as she trades words with Titania.

Titania glows with news. We're writing a book together!

Oh? What about?

My Wedding Night. Mine, not yours and Sidney's.

Gong laughs. Yours will be much more interesting. I look forward to it.

Oh, that's right. You're a fan. Titania casts a lovelook toward the balcony. Well, Sidney's quite a wolf these days.

That's nothing new.

He's like a young Billy. And, maybe he's told you, we're co-authoring in more ways than one.

Titania pats her tummy, smiling darkly.

We slipped this in just under the wire, she says.

What wire? I ask.

The wire, she says.

She slinks away, sits on Dad's chair arm and fearlessly takes his hand. He turns to her, a question flickering. She lifts her arm for him to sniff.

I'm in season again, Dad, she whispers. Smell my musk, lilla father! Do you understand? I'm baking twins in the oven. Chinese! She places his palm against the small rise of her belly. Nice, huh? Will you help us with the names?

The ghost studies her.

I hope they have big teeth like yours and chew their food good. I'm only sorry they won't have tails! Now, Dad, are you awake? Really? Because we're throwing the switch on Ahuramazda. And we want you to do it!

Sidney in from the balcony nods coolly at his wife, and sits by Titania and Dad.

I want to ask you, sir, Sidney says, what your thoughts might be on transmigration? Sidney lights up with childish eagerness. Do you believe in it? I know Billy does. But I'm wondering about you. The horse's mouth, so to speak. You who have come back from that undiscovered country!

But Sidney leans too close to Dad. Dad's jaw suddenly lowers and his great teeth clamp onto Sidney's face, or would, but they go right through harmlessly and Dad snaps again and again, then stops and sits back in wonder that his victim is still unbloodied.

Sidney leaps up. I'm sorry I've bothered you, sir. I must get a drink. He looks back at Dad. This is the great Trickster himself!

I lead Gong to my father's ghost.

This is my future wife, Dr. Gong Li-Chang, Dad.

Gong digs up a breath and a deep smile, saying, I am so happy to meet you at last, royal Bihusi.

Dad sits smiling, speechless as ever, unable to fight her superhuman wash of money and compassion. She draws even nearer. Her beauty and corner-lidded dark eyes hang before him measuring out joy. Surely hers is the first human face he does not at once want to snap into his great jaws.

How are you feeling? she asks. I hope this event won't be too great a strain on you. I am here to help should you experience discomfort.

He draws closer to her bright human force. Drawing close is one of his very limited vocabulary of signs. Does he smell the money? Surprise fills her. She senses agitation in the ghost.

I'll leave if I make you uncomfortable.

Dad's teddy-bear smile says nothing.

Titania breaks in. You look terrific, Dad! I swear you are the handsomest wolf on Earth. I want to eat you up.

And she puts her face near his, licks his muzzle and thrusts her hand down into his lap for a rub. He lights up, purring. The old wolf has not felt like this for a long time.

He likes that, she tells Gong. If you want to get on his good side, this never misses.

I glance at Magda. Jealousy of humans is beneath her. She calls to Titania, You've got to rub hard or he forgets.

Titania pats his lap. Now that's enough. We don't want you getting too excited.

Gong's eye catches The Right Hand of God dancing with firelight and calling to her. As she stands over the great bronze, the aura of its magnificent rough fingers encloses her. Magda joins Gong, The Bihusi Rose aflame on her purple Fortuny.

It was a great tragedy, Magda says, when Alexandru threw The Left Hand of God off the balcony. That casting which Sidi recovered, and is now enshrined in Tokyo Art Bank, is a fake. The Japanese would not know a Hand of God from a cornflake. It's still down there in the crevasse! So I think, though Billy thinks it has gone home to the dark angel of the Bihusi.

Something moans.

Gong asks, Royal Giurgiu, do you hear something?

I do! Magda says. I hear whispering. You hear it too?

Gong puts her ear to the palm of The Right Hand of God.

It's coming from here.

She draws back. They gaze into a bush of firelight in the great palm.

Magda whispers. What's it saying?

The Spear, Gong says. It says, Bring me The Spear.

It wants The Spear? Billy, bring us The Spear! At once! At once!

I unsheathe The Spear. Before I can hand it to Mother, an iron force enters my arm and draws The Spear to Gong. Surprise dances in her. Yes, she says firmly, give it to me. She grips The Spear. At its touch a trance settles on her.

Her voice deepens. *I am lonely!* she says.

That's Grandfather! Magda says. I'd know that voice anywhere. Alexandru, Alexandru, your father is here!

Titania groans. Oh my God, Gong's done it again. Another one!

I call, Titania, bring Dad over here.

Titania wheels Dad to The Right Hand of God.

Magda says, Grandfather's here, Alexandru! Listen!

Gong's mouth falls open like an adolescent's. She clutches The Spear. Her dark eyes dazzle, reading the vivid air, and go blank.

Gong-Grandfather says, I am lonely, Alexandru!

Dad's smile fades. He leans forward in his wheelchair, gazing at Gong.

I am lonely, my son, for my Left Hand. I know where it is. You must bring back The Left Hand of God and make me whole again.

I ask, How can we do that, Grandfather?

Grandfather-Gong says, Hold The Spear over the balcony. The Left Hand of God will come to you!

I will, I say.

Gently, I lead Gong bearing The Spear to the blood-red Sunset balcony where Grandfather, following his beloved Left Hand, jumped into the beyond.

Grandfather-Gong says, Rest The Spear on the railing.

The Spear juts like a flagpole over the crevasse. Gong and I brace the bottom half. Together we feel magnetic power pour from The Spear into the abyss. A marlin-like tug strikes The Spear. It bends!

Somewhere below, ice cracks. Lightning bolts down the Jungfrau and echoes throughout Lauterbrunnen Valley. The crevasse splits, a frigid womb under burning force. A dark thing buried far below the West Face cracks free, splits and bristled with ice crawls upward through a shag of diamonds.

My beloved's arms strain with mine.

Hold tight, hold tight! Grandfather-Gong commands.

Grandfather, I'm holding!

Splintering upward, something breaks into the fevered Sunset and, palm down, creeps skittering up blood-colored ice.

Magda gasps. It's The Hand! It's The Hand!

Hang on! Grandfather-Gong cries. Pull, pull!

The Left Hand of God spiders up The Spear's invisible force. It crawls over the railing, drops thunderously onto the balcony, chipping the stone floor, creeps across the red rug to its mate and climbs the empty pedestal awaiting its return. I scent rich currents flowing between the huge bronze hands.

Sidney reels back from the superhuman *thing*, crying, Am I mad? What did I just see? Did I just see that?

Dad leans over the great hands. He reaches out to touch the force flowing between them.

Now, Grandfather-Gong says, The Left Hand of God that knows all mysteries has rejoined The Right Hand of God that makes all things, and I forgive you, my son.

A sob from Dad shocks us. Iridescence from his left eye streams down his cheek. We stand awed by his passion.

It's so moving, Magda whispers.

Gong bearing The Spear moves into the current between the hands. As Grandfather-Gong speaks, her beatified face burns pearl and pale-green.

Magda, my daughter, Queen of Bihusi and Queen of Giurgiu, hear me out. The golden days of our clans are gone. Your son has left the arms of the dark angel. We are seedless. Without an heir the dark force withers already. We are left only with pip-squeaks like Saddam, Assad, and Milosovich. As for Sheikh Sidi bin-Bahram, the Mighty Hunter of Kuwait and Wild Ass of Baghdad, that would-be wolf, contrive no more against him. At our picking his pocket with the Japanese and Canadian banks, I am overjoyed. *WELL DONE!* I could not have improved on it—although it was my idea. Some of you have not heard of this but now it can be told that many years ago President Reagan came to me, saying, The Japanese have overestimated their markets and are going under. So he asked me to come in. I did, on the guarantee of a later tax break. Hate to tell you this, Reagan said at the same time, but the Canadian banks are going under too. Will you come in on that? We'd like to buy the Canadian banking and investment system but the

Canadian people will never stand for it. There's only one guy I know who can do it *under the table* and with ready cash. I lie and say I can't do the whole bolus but that I know an Austrian bank funded by the Royal Family of Arabia. Here's the prince's number who handles investments. Phone him. So Ron calls what he thinks is the Austrian bank funded by the Royal Family of Arabia, but actually the call goes to me. I do the deals, obligate the President, and am quite merry about my tax advantages. So I tell my son Alexandru about these two dying Japanese and Canadian shells, and with his Bihusi Genius all these years later he now unloads them on Sidi. Poor Sidi, ha ha ha, who thought Billy his Filipino! I visit that bandit often and leave his hair standing on end. May Rani Gupta comfort him in his last days. His final verse approaches when this little sheikh joins his fattest wife and lies down in their pool. Under the stars and rain. Forever. Leave him to Allah.

I draw a chair up to Dad.

Dad, did you hear that? We have great news.

The ghost shows a spark, just a spark.

You have screwed Sidi!

He smiles on.

Do you remember the Japanese/Canadian deal we set in motion before the Greenpeace disaster? The money we applied before Sidi cleaned our clock? Well, it has come through. We have suckered Sidi for half of his wealth and doubled our own. You did it, Dad.

Sidney edges near. What is this news? Can you say?

It's no secret now. And I'm sure Sidi will be in to see you very soon.

Magda asks, What has happened, Billy?

Just before his illness, Dad allowed it to get out that he was looking into two big, hugely profitable deals. One was with Japanese banks and brokerage houses, and one with Canadian banks and brokerage houses. When Sidi heard this, he knew these deals must be good or Dad wouldn't want 'em. Dad and the Japanese and the Canadians were about to close the two deals. The Japanese deal now is for one point one trillion. The Canadian deal is for eight hundred billion. Sidi moves in with his brother and his cousin and steals both deals from us. Pulls the rug from under Dad. He's nasty, a cheat, unfair, and so are his cousin and his brother. They do this by paying a hundred-million-dollar premium to each deal's shareholders. Dad has looked close to closing both deals, so Sidi's in a huge hurry. Piggy-back-ing his deals on what he thinks is Dad's research, speedy Sidi doesn't do his due diligence. Once Sidi owns the companies and puts his accountants in, he finds that the Japanese lose six billion a week, and that the Canadians have a potential of only five million investors and can generate less than one percent on their assets. Sidi's been screwed. Robbed twice at once. The real kicker is that Sidi once owned and sold that Canadian group to investors for thirty billion, and now has bought it back for eight-hundred billion. The truth is, we were the secret owners of the Japanese and Canadians and wanted to dump those losers. For a while we'd been picking cherries with the Japanese. Then things soured. So we created interest, set baits, and lured Sidi. We were actually pretending we were going to buy what we already owned and, boy, did we not want it.

Sidney implores, But can't he sell them!

Japan is an investment graveyard, I say. Sidi *can't* sell his Japanese white elephant, and Canada has nobody big enough to buy, so he's going under. Even Sidi can't swallow a two-trillion-dollar loss. Dad has just picked Sidi's pocket for over two trillion—*sold Sidi two empty bags!* We're back in business, Dad. *Big.* How's that!

The ghost sparkles.

Sidney asks, But why didn't the sheikh's spies see the balance sheets?

Because Sidi was too greedy. And relied on *Dad's* phony research— *because he trusted you, Dad!*

I am proud of you both, Magda says. She leans over Dad. *I'm proud of you, Alexandru.* And I am so happy, Billy, that I saw the outcome so clearly for you with The Spear.

I hope you heard all this, Dad! By God, you look almost alive.

Grandfather-Gong says, It will take more than money to bring Alexandru back.

Titania says, If money can't bring him back, nothing can.

We'll see, we'll see, I say. Don't forget my big surprise.

I glance at Mother. Amazement sits on her.

The Bihusi cannot die! Magda cries at Grandfather-Gong.

Do not fight my words, Magda. The Moving Finger writes! Even as *The Profit* laments, My hanging gardens are gone, it may also be said of Bihusi: *They have licked the blood off the grass and gone their way.*

Magda's foot stamps. I am a Giurgiu, Father Bihusi. I have carried the cubs of both clans. My seed cannot wither. I'll see you on the wheel, old man.

The wheel, yes. You are right. And I glory in your great heart, Angela Magdalena. But, my daughter, you no longer own the power of The Spear. I declare a new Keeper of The Spear: *Gong!* this handsome young human through whom I speak. From her alone you must take truth and courage when The Spear turns the world to glass and foresees all works and days.

Bowing over and over, Sidney breaks in on Grandfather-Gong.

Oh, Grandfather Bihusi, what is the answer to the eternal question?

Which eternal question?

Why, about transmigration!

Why do you ask, legendizer of symbols?

Sidney turns aside shyly. I dream of a book that will show all people the road we must travel.

Yes, I see. But that book is already written. You turn its pages daily and are a character in it. For your own good, I cannot reveal the solution to a mystery you will unravel by your own deeds. I see that you have won many maidens. Perhaps too many for a human who gropes through the Dark Continent of female emotion, where even I have trouble. I see you leaving Zürich and establishing the First Jungian Institute of Budapest. You shall be joined by Titania Tintagel and have the twin sons she already bears. The Hungarians will love you. Their sophisticates offer such a fertile field for a legendizer. They need you, Doctor Chang, to straighten out certain warpings of their unconscious. Do not fear parking your car on the street in Budapest.

By day? Or overnight? It *is* a Lexus, revered Bihusi.

The Hungarian auto thieves will find it anywhere. Now I must leave. But before I go, I must speak to my son.

Something wonderful is about to happen to you, Alexandru. Do not fight it. You are about to enter the great god Ahuramazda who will swallow you even as you swallow the fire of his great Eucharist. You will be transubstantiated into the primal element of fire. The Divine Cannibal will eat you even as you eat Him. You will be the first Bihusi to rise above the Wreath of Bihusi. Even above the great wheel of karma. By the purity of your rapacity, greed, and hatred you have achieved Nirvana. Never having done a single good deed, my son, yours is a holy state unknown to any wolf before you. Ahuramazda welcomes you to supreme liberation and bliss. Your flame will be swallowed up in the greater Flame. You no longer need fear the unconditional suffering of wolfen whose limbs and lungs and blood and bone howl for the dark angel because Ahuramazda is too powerful to pray to—beyond even the howls of great packs of wolfen singing in the dark. To bear us up we have only the dark angel before his deep lavender light—the burning filament at the core of being—burns itself black and is swallowed up in Ahuramazda in time-to-come. You go to Ahuramazda before the dark angel himself achieves annihilation. Your coming enlightenment cannot be described. You will be attached to nothing and above ignorance. You will have swallowed the Sun That Powers All Things and Sees Everything in All Directions at Once. You will never know darkness again.

Billy, yours is a different path, no longer attached to Bihusi. With this woman who is the Keeper of The Spear you will attempt the golden road of truth and courage in broad daylight, a life never before undertaken by a wolf. Be brave! To rise above the wheel on this semihuman path is even more arduous than the way of the wolf.

Gong, through whom and to whom I now speak, admitting that you are a lapsed Jungian is a giant step out of illusion. You come to my grandson divinely gifted by your ancestors and stripped naked of analytic fuss, fluff, and feathers. Awaiting you is a God-image you alone can give birth to, a passionate resplendence and blood-warmth at your life's end you cannot yet imagine. For this path you are well-chosen by your ancestral spirits. You will begin a tutorial on practical compassion which will be beamed about the planet from the space discs when they come into being, as they will come. You shall climb more Alps than a mountaineer but they are all within. Into great old age you shall be the mother otter who dives and swims and teaches her cubs, coming up always aglow with morninglight.

Well, *I'm* waiting, Titania says.

What, are you still awake?

Well?

O Queen of Fireflies, you are far too fey for an old codger like me to make sense of. You will have many grandchildren and never lose your sense of daily wonder. Even in Budapest you will root yourself in the irrational and bring forth fairies caught up in violent thunderstorms. And books, books, books!

Dad leans on finger and thumb listening to his father.

Good-bye, Alexandru. In Nirvana you will have no chance to be *my* father in the next turn of the wheel. Farewell, Magda. Fight it as you must, you rule over the waning of Bihusi and Giurgiu. Good-bye, Billy. You need no words from me. You already have the undimming heart of your new mate.

Gong relaxes, hanging on The Spear. She looks about.

He's gone? she asks.

I nod. Do you remember anything?

Yes! He took me into The Left Hand of God to show me the five mysteries.

He did? Magda says. And what were they?

I read the book of losses, the book of balances, the book of hearts, the book of clouds, and the book of darkness. And he said I would remember some things later.

But you are glowing, Gong tells me. I like this. Are your fortunes restored?

I am no longer Sidi's Filipino, my dear. Or leading his spies into our big Japanese and Canadian rat trap. I have my balls back.

Well, this has been marvelous, Sidney says. Even though I did not learn all I wish to know, I have enough material for several conferences.

In Budapest, Magda says. Where you will be received with open arms.

Yes, he says. Zürich will just have to get along without me.

I must rest a moment, Gong says. That was very exhausting.

She goes out to the balcony and looks through the roomful of Bihusi lighted within. Nothing can spoil her great leap forward from Beijing to the Jungfrau. I sleep with the wolves, she tells herself aloud. And one even has a tail. What would her parents back on the farm think of all this? She'll never know. She's not going back and soon will no longer be a Chinese Swiss but rather an American. A pang stabs her as all China melts off the planet as she will know it hereafter. She sees herself in her teens, on vacation, bicycling fifty miles home from the university. She sees the big bath pan in the kitchen in which she'd sit and bathe. She hears the melodious racket of the Beijing Opera on the radio whenever the family had a full set of tubes. Early piano lessons and Debussy before she gave up music for science. All gone. Will People's Republic allow her return even for a visit, perhaps for a funeral? After she's lived in Montana with Billy? Not bloody likely. Not welcome, even by her parents. Too disturbing. Does Billy know what she's sacrificing? He's no dunce. Nor will her life go to waste. Will she ever come into a religious or political belief to replace state socialism? Certainly she is no visionary of Ahuramazda, though Ahuramazda now feels her out with spirits speaking through The Spear. She cannot live but by her true beliefs. But these are all used up. Or hanging in the air? She lies awake nights, going through a sea-change. I am drowning now so that others may live later.

Will her daughter have Western eyes, Western dolls? Chinese dolls? Does it matter? She'll marry a Westerner and her children will be only half-Chinese? Shuffling the genes. The inner fold on her eyes will disappear in Western grandchildren. Smells, textures, flashes of walls and alleys in Beijing, fade, though she knows they will come back full force late in life. She sees her daughter in a brick house in the States, closets stuffed and shelves of shoes. Central heating, running water, flush toilets. She sighs, again seeing Beijing's overpacked streets as well as the American brick house. Clearly, memory is timeless, all memory, concurrent, before and after forever now, a heart tug empowered by yearning, forged of yearning.

Wooden alphabet blocks with Chinese characters? No, her kids will most likely speak English, French, Swiss Deutsch. They sit conjugating verbs, the little marvels. Homework. Human genes, since Bihusi are only by Giurgiu females. She *could* get a set of basic Mandarin alphabet blocks mailed from Beijing. Offer them piano lessons longer than her own. Her daughter will play perfectly. If this Bihusi marriage doesn't take, she'll quit. What does Billy want from her? Sticky rice in banana leaves?

And someday. Shroud. Fire. Ash.

We'll all go. Everyone here. Unbearable that all these nicely lacquered library facings, these great bronze Hands of God can't save us from vanishing from our flesh. Not all the Baxter wealth can buy off that final harshness. The last mask. Stillness. Will I be still alive somewhere, or simply gone? Actually, I can never be gone. All my life long I will know only life. In that sense I live forever. A grey gaiety in that thought. Sly death, catching us up like children at the amusement park. Will I speak to someone in that silence? Even to myself? An ancestor. A voice? What an eloquence to lift the heart! Any voice at all would be greater than all the music you've ever heard. One small voice, even a whisper. My God, how the heart would burst. The relief, the joy. To know that your loved ones, still alive or now dead, would also vibrate to the voice. You'd be afloat on a chorus of cellos. The afterlife, a woman's heart.

But first I will be forty-five. I will be fifty-five. I will be sixty-five. I will be seventy-five. Barring cancer, car accident. Something failing me. Myocardial failure not likely. Billy's three sons, so wryly set on being on top of their businesses, masters of finance, and my children—at the crematorium to see me off? To set forth in flame. Clean. Hard to accept. Even if there were consciousness, which there isn't, it would be better to be ash than to be drying in a box. Fire is so final! Makes a clean sweep of it. Just go. No burial. Scatter me somewhere in Montana. If there *were* an afterlife, you'd simply slump out of your body and be elsewhere. Entering the Wreath of Bihusi must have its own strange, breathless uplift, a flying dream the wolves have some control over. A dark alley emerging into light? I'll never know.

She sees Billy's three sons, Vincent, David and Val, arrive. Pushing, shoving and laughing loudly, they are soon guided toward her by Billy and Titania.

Do you mind, Billy asks her, if we have a little sit-down out here? The boys haven't really met you, Gong.

All three sons, as Gong knows, attend Harvard Business School. Their ardent wolfhood, as pumped into them by Titania, saddens and dispirits Billy, since they adopt a false heartiness in imitation of Dad's friendly good cheer, and walk and style themselves as dandies in tailored denim.

Your mother and I are parting, Billy says. Amicably. She's decided to partner up with my analyst, Sidney Chang, whom you've met, and as it happens I hope to marry Sidney's wife, Gong, who is also an analyst. She's Chinese-Swiss like Sidney.

The three lads look palsied.

You and your analyst are trading wives? Vincent says. That's a laugh!

I suppose it is, Billy says.

I don't think I like you putting it that way, Vincent, Titania says. It's not like we're swingers.

Hey, I have nothing against swingers, Vincent says.

Gong weighs the angled set of her stepsons' eyes, a slant mix of wolf and human, blue as Titania's, and only David's Bihusi amber like Billy's. The human accent in the wolf slant gives them a glancing oddity. Billy tells her he finds fatherhood hard, and yet she sees staring at her three images of her lover's face. Val has Billy's cheekbones, David Billy's eyes, and Vincent Billy's refined stance and walk. The youngest, Val, is a lumbering adolescent and already taller than his brothers, though Vincent and David are tall indeed, Titania being nearly six feet.

Vincent, still a student, has moved into the health food business with a vengeance and, set on making his mark early, has mastered herbal science and aligned himself with the biggest East Coast distributor of gingko biloba, yohimbe, billberry, saw palmetto, echinacea, and dozens of other tonics, remedies and herbal tinctures, extracts and elixirs. The middle son, David, the wildest, most mysterious, unreasoning and short-tempered of the three, wants to be an environmentalist while earning enough money to rebuild the US wolf population nationwide. He has a languorous smile, in tune with God, as he and God both damn well know. Val slips and slides unsurely toward his future. Kids. They're all three kids with a great secret: they're half-wolf, or so Titania would have them believe.

The Spear, Billy tells them, has chosen Gong as its new keeper.

When will we finally have access to The Spear? David asks.

Probably never, Titania says.

You're not in the Bihusi Wreath, Billy says.

Well, shee-it, Val says. Who needs that stupid spear anyway? I piss on The Spear from a great height.

Right on, Vincent says.

Good, Billy says. I'm glad you feel that way. However, I know you may feel your world tip over on its axis, with your mother and I marrying others.

Oh sure, Val says, turning away. It's like living on a laugh track with you two and all your phony feelings.

Shut up, David tells him.

What phony feelings? Titania asks Val.

That our dad isn't a wolf and that you are. A pair of loopy kooks in rose-colored glasses, it's no wonder you can't get along. But you're well-matched, both lying to yourselves. Deliver me from such nut-cases.

Just in case you're being frank and not cynical, Billy says, your mother and I remain quite amicable, Val.

I've heard that before.

We're hopeful that none of you will feel you have to choose between us.

Choose for what? David asks. Loyalty? You want to know whom we're loyal to? Grandfather Bihusi! But he's not his old self, is he? He never talks to us anymore.

Dad died, Billy says.

We've heard all that, Val says. Then who's that guy in the wheelchair?

What's wrong with you? Vincent asks. That's Grandfather Bihusi, isn't it, Dad?

Val says, Yeah, but why does he hang around like a pet dog?

It's hard to explain, even for me, Billy says. My father is undergoing a spiritual sea-change.

Sea-change? Val says. You're over our heads, Dad.

Billy reads their faces. Your Grandfather Bihusi has become the Holy Ghost of Bihusi.

Awe fills his sons.

Are you serious? Val asks.

Never more, Billy says.

I don't—Vincent begins.

You don't what? Billy asks.

I don't believe in ghosts, Vincent says.

David turns on him. Oh, what do you know? You *see* him sitting there, for Christ's sake. It's Grandfather Bihusi plain as day.

Young Val groans. And with a tail! Where did that suddenly come from? Or has he always had it?

The boys turn to Billy.

That's hard to explain as well, he says. When Dad died he entered the Bihusi Wreath, descended to the underworld, freed all sinners who had done good deeds, was anointed Savior of the Bihusi for having lived a spotless life, and then was sent back to us by the dark angel.

Their faces are warm taffy, falling.

That is *so hard* to believe, Val says.

David asks, How do we know that all happened?

Because I went with him, Billy says. All Bihusi did. When Dad entered the Bihusi Wreath all Bihusi wherever they were entered with him and went through his agony. He has taken all sins of the Bihusi upon himself and been scourged. The Bihusi have been purified.

Val shakes his head. This is too much to take in, he says. They never told us *anything* about this at B School!

Billy grips Val's shoulder. That's all right, Val. I wouldn't believe it either if all Bihusi hadn't entered the Wreath and gone with him.

Vincent says, I still don't believe it. Of course, I see him sitting right there in his wheelchair. But it all sounds so—so—

Fictional! David says. Here we have a savior and he's—he's fictional!

Gong says, All saviors, even the once real ones, eventually lose reality.

I want to beat him up! David cries. I want him to do it all over so I can see it.

Of course you do, Davey, Billy says. But you really can't ask him to go through his crucifixion and scourging twice.

Well, when you went into the underworld with Grandfather Bihusi, Vincent says, did you see the dark angel too?

Yes, Billy says.

Val asks Titania, Did you see him too?

I'm not a Bihusi or Giurgiu, she says.

But then why didn't we see the dark angel too? David asks.

You don't carry the wolf gene, Billy says. That can come only from a Giurgiu mother.

The three lads' faces stiffen about their hard luck on the wolf gene.

I don't know if I should tell you, Billy says. It's a great Bihusi mystery. But if I close my eyes I see the dark angel instantly, right on my retina.

David insists. Dad, you can't stop there. Tell us!

The dark angel is shaped just as you shape him. He is a shape without form and each Bihusi shapes him in the image each Bihusi finds most supernal. At heart, he is a massive dark blue blotch, like filament in a dark blue bulb. He's actually Power, cleansing, ecstatic, dark power. I saw him through Dad's eyes and felt a damp cold wolf shape of pure purple light, a huge swollen throat and head without detail, no eyes or teeth, just a pulsing shapeless light I knew was pure wolf, the most fearful experience in my life. I was in a cold sweat the whole time. My hair stood on end—not so uncommon for a Bihui. I wanted to faint or wake up, anything but be there. My whole body felt scraped raw. It was pure fear. I shook for days afterward. I can't tell you much more—your mother should have gone, she has the fancy words, not me! Believe me, when you see him, he's the joy of every wolf's desiring. Pure power!

But he's not your angel? Vincent says.

I renounce him.

The lads take this in uneasily.

Then he'll whip your ass! Val says.

I'll take that chance.

What do you mean, David says. You renounce him? You can't renounce your birthright.

I have already.

But you're a wolf! David cries. Why would you renounce that?

Because I must. If being a Bihusi means I must follow my father's path, I renounce my birthright.

Titania's face says, This is so sick.

I don't like to hear this, Vincent says.

Val agrees. Sounds wimpish, if you gotta know.

You can't do it, David says. You should be breaking your ass to spread the Bihusi pack. We're part Bihusi, we know we are, whatever you say! We want to grow up straight and tall as Bihusi, just like mother has always told us.

I'm sorry we ever told you about any of this, Billy says. But you had to know where all our money comes from. I sold you a bill of goods about my happy business deals—and your mother did even worse.

I'm proud, Titania says, of anything I've ever told you about your grandfather's family.

Believe me, Billy tells Val, renouncing the dark angel is not wimpish.

Vincent reddens. I don't want to live a bland human life!

I can't imagine anything sweeter, Billy says.

Well, I love my wolves, David says.

So do I, Billy says.

You're abandoning God, Val says.

The dark angel isn't Ahuramazda, Billy says.

What is he then? Val asks.

He wants to eat up Ahuramazda. The dark angel wants to be Ahuramazda. He split off from Ahuramazda long, long ago and became a free spirit with free will, but ruled by bottomless hunger and absolute greed. And what is the biggest thing he can find to eat and that will sate his fury and rapacity? His parent force, Ahuramazda. And Bihusi follow suit, with murder of the alpha wolf as their first need to keep the line strong with an even more powerful alpha wolf.

Did he have a tail? David asks.

Who?

The dark angel?

He was all tail. His light wagged through and through.

To have a tail like Grandfather! David says, his eyes ringing with pride.

Well, that's it, Billy says. Let's go back inside.

He knows all three will side with Titania, for whom the Wolf Force is sheer heaven.

Did you tell them what I suggested you tell them? Gong asks.

Not altogether. They can only take in so much at once.

Don't underestimate their resilience, Gong says. May I say something, gentlemen?

Her chest constricts as Billy again turns to his sons. They look away, over the Sun-reddened valley, then eye her sapphire twilight gown, a heart-shaped turquoise pin at her throat, dark hair drawn up into a liquid pile showing off her rounded perfect ears, her thoughtful and welcoming shy, gay smile.

I'm so delighted we're getting all this off our chests, she says. Billy tells me you all think for yourselves. That's wonderful. And that's what he wants too. But he's undergone big changes. I hope you'll understand.

Which big changes? Val asks.

Well, Gong says, you fellas will have an extra mother to come to for advice. If you want it.

Gong is a trained advice giver, Billy says.

Yeah, but I don't mean that, she says. And, of course, your dad will always be there, as well as Magda. Your grandmother, Queen of Bihusi, Queen of Giurgiu, can give you guidance nobody else can give you. You have a whole backup team in her. And you shouldn't fear coming to either of us. I mean, fear that we won't take you seriously. But it's Magda who knows all there is to know about everything.

That's right, Billy says. Your grandmother is the top authority in the family.

But with Grandfather out of the picture, Vincent asks, why aren't you King of Bihusi?

How can I be king if your grandmother is queen? I'm her son, not her husband.

I certainly hope you're not sexists, Gong says.

Sexists? David asks.

Who think women can't rule, Gong says. European males lock their women into second-class citizenship. Everything is race, class, and masculinity with these modern-day Neanderthals who are a half-century behind the times. Even the Swiss didn't give women the vote until the nineteen-seventiess. She turns to Billy. Can you imagine Emma Jung not having the vote until her last days?

Who's Emma Jung? Val asks.

Her husband founded Jungian analysis, Billy says. Sidney and Gong are Jungians. Though Gong is changing fields.

All that aside, Gong says. Your grandmother is a bloody owl who can see in the dark and fears no man. I'm sure you know that. Keep it in mind when you plan your futures. She will steer you right to your targets. She's not one to be trifled with. Titania and she will make sure you're not trifled with either. Any problem at all, see Magda.

She'll tear the facts off by their legs and hand 'em to you, David tells his brothers.

Vincent agrees. She's all wolf.

Billy nods. That's my mom.

Val says, But it's Dad who really knows how to stick it to 'em.

But he's dead, Billy says.

No, I mean you, Val says. We'll nail that Kuwaiti sonofabitch somehow, someday. Won't we, Dad?

We'll see! Billy says. I think we already have.

I know we will. Val smiles hugely at Gong about Billy, then draws in a big smell of roast boar and of life itself, saying to his beautiful Chinese stepmother, Give us a kiss, Mum.

Suddenly, she is Val's and touches cheeks with all three sons. Soft, gentle, just what they need from this bird of sapphire twilight. Vincent, the last to exchange kisses, stares at her thoughtfully, drawn to the piercing beauty of her eyes, the mystery and allure behind their corner fold. He sucks from her full breasts and strong shoulders the breath of life. Youth courses through his blood, a wine that only makes him heavy with hunger and sensible of the absence from his own life of a plenteous spirit like Gong. Even the blue veins of her hands attract him unbearably.

Titania watches Gong's conquests then sees Sidney within talking with Magda.

I think we've said it all, she says, leaving. And I think Sidney needs me.

Gong's warmth still works miracles on all three sons, awakening them to a transfiguring gaiety, wisdom and femininity each now wants for himself. Their hearts shift. She clearly hasn't an ounce of wolf in her, only a spinal humanity that gazes out at them and reads their souls. They are not the same sons they were before meeting her. And such hair! Those ears! One wants to finger her head's erotic mystery, probe her bosom in the dark of night, and the soft, supple curls of Persian lamb below. Each lad foresees a hardship in curbing fantasies about his future stepmom. Their dreams rise to a high place as her fresh new chinadoll womanhood invades them with her weighing eyes. They find in her a hug of compassion they have never known in Titania. Here glows a woman in her sexual prime, thirty-five, perhaps, and stunning power flows from her, a sapphire-silken beauty that leaves them famished to the bone.

David melts to a dreamlike vagueness.

Where's that lovely pin from? he asks.

Gong fingers the turquoise heart at her throat.

I don't know. Billy gave it to me just this morning.

Oh? from the Bahnhoffstrasse? David asks him. I'd like to get one for someone I know.

I'll have one delivered, Billy says.

Actually, David wants it for himself, to keep in his wallet. To remind him of her gift, the second chance she's given him to be more than wolf.

She'll think it's smashing, Gong tells David.

Her warmth seeps through him. He wipes his chin with joy.

Splendid, he says, at once atremble, and whispers, *Smashing!*

Gong senses an opening. You're into health food sales?

He lifts a finger. Big time, he says. Well, on the East Coast.

So I hear. Have these been tested?

Tested?

What are the side effects of St. John's wort?

There aren't any, Vincent says.

Oh, everything has side effects, she says. Even salt. I mean, why would you take St. John's wort for depression when there are more effective anti-depressants?

Oh, those! They *do* have side effects.

And St. John's wort doesn't?

I don't think so.

Or it just hasn't been tested? she asks.

Hmm.

I mention this because I am a doctor and I prescribe antidepressants. If you could give me a good reason to prescribe an herb rather than a drug, I'd be very happy. This is an avenue for you to look into. You could go nation-wide.

But herbs can't be patented, Vincent says. That's why drug companies don't spend money testing them.

Oh, but they can be, if you have the right process. You should do double blind tests and publish your results. Start early because they take a while. A gingko biloba process has recently been patented after small tests in Germany but not here. And what have they patented? Only a standardized extract useful for jogging the memory and in large doses for Alzheimer's— though they don't claim that yet. If they can go nationwide with gingko, so can you, using your own process for a standardized extract—or even a tincture. Do the testing. Pay for it. A hundred thousand dollars worth of tests can bring you back tens of millions—*and* you'll have patents. If you can make a strong enough extract of St. John's wort, maybe you could cut into the Prozac market. Or a strong enough yohimbe extract might replace Viagra. What's the active ingredient in yohimbe that helps with a hardon?

Her frankness brightens their nerves.

I don't know, Vincent says.

Think about it.

I will.

Talk it over with Billy, she says. He'll be happy to back you.

Val says, A prosperous beginning, Vinnie.

Vincent nods as Gong tells Val, in a whisper, I'll be talking to The Spear about you. You can't badmouth Ahuramazda and get away with it. But I'll stand up for you.

I'm not really a full Bihusi, Val says.

Don't worry about it, Gong says. I'm even less, and I'm Keeper of The Spear.

That's terrific! Val says.

Well, your great-grandfather appointed me.

Mother turned down being keeper, he says.

Her loss is my gain, Gong says. Anyway, I think The Spear may be afraid of Titania's vivid imagination.

Well, yes, Val says. And she glows in the dark.

Surprising him, Gong runs a finger down his cheek and arm. Her fingers curl about his hand in passing.

I'll bet you do too, she says.

I'm afraid I don't.

Maybe you just haven't tried, Gong says. Maybe you should all try. I should think that's an inheritable trait. Why don't you three have a blood workup at Wolfington Labs? They should look for a high luciferin count. Wouldn't you like to glow in the dark?

Rather a smashing idea, David says.

Sure is, Gong says.

Vincent says, You know, Dad, Mother was brought up with the wolves at Stargarden. You'd think she'd want to be keeper.

Gong is silent.

If only The Spear thought so too, Billy says.

Gong's hand rests on Vincent's. The Spear has a mind of its own, she says.

It's true, Gong is much older than Vincent, but in his mind none of that matters.

You're damned right, he says with a worldly swell. And that's the way it is. Do you ever think of living in China again?

Back to family planning? That's a national policy I can do without, but it's what they would have me doing. If your family had been raised in China, there'd only be Vincent. After Vincent, Billy might well have had a vasoligation. No David, no Val. Sad thought, huh? Despite what you may think, sexual ignorance in China is widespread. Couples have no idea that their domestic disputes arise from sex. They really do think it's about money and the grocery bill. Sex education is abysmal. Married people literally sit about quarreling in the dark. I mean with the lights still on. It's dreadful, people dying of fright because they're at absolute zero about sexual physiology. Frigidity's rampant! You boys don't know how lucky you are having Western girlfriends.

Their eyes pop as the sapphire vision lectures them. They see a face rich with inner shadow and sunshine.

Of course, she says, I did write the history of The Spear. It's on the shelf in there. Maybe that's why I was chosen.

You should read it, Billy tells them.

Lightly flushed, Val tells her, I will. I think I see what you mean about standing up for me. If anyone can, it's you. His slant eyes glisten. I mean, it makes sense.

Now I want to ask something of you three wise Rumanian-Danish-Swiss-American businessmen. I take it Val *will* be going into business. Do you have a minute?

We're in no hurry! David says.

You may have heard that China is a sinkhole of civil rights and it is. But Europe as well is a bastion of backward ideas. When you three are running your businesses, and you have an opportunity to make an equal rights decision for a woman, don't hold back. Make it. You three can help make a great advance in equal rights. This will all be to your honor and make your family proud of you.

Except for Granddad, Vincent says.

And he's dead, David says.

More or less, Val says.

It's your decision. Make the world a better place or let it keep floundering. I'm not saying you should do anything outlandish, like seriously take up philanthropy. After all, the Bihusi motto is TAKE EVERYTHING, GIVE NOTHING. I couldn't expect you to dishonor a thought that has been the backbone of Bihusi.

The three lads say nothing. Thinking.

Of course you three have minds of your own and think for yourselves. It's not as if you're chained to the past. New ideas have to come. If I had the money I know a few programs that I'd fund. I could do a world of good.

She stares at the world of good, measuring it.

She wakes up. Well, you've heard enough from a Chinese world suffragette like me. What could be an odder creature? Now you know my big secret. I'm a freethinker. Keep it under your hats. My family could get into big trouble back home. Try to understand. Lives could be lost.

The lads stand speechless.

Anything good you do, she says, do it on the quiet. Don't let it get out that we're related. Will you promise? You three are my silent soldiers.

They stare in wonder.

You swear? she says.

Slowly, they swear with rapt fervor.

I think I've scared you, she says. Believe me, I'm scared even worse.

Vincent whispers, We're not scared!

Just don't let it get out what you're doing. She waves at the red heavens and salmon clouds, then grips Vincent's hand. This far corner of the sky is ours. We've made a pact. Put your hands on mine.

The three lads pile their hands on Gong's.

Keep it in your heart, she says. Swear it?

Wonder and desire feed greedily on them.

We swear!

Now go get some roast boar.

Val stands spellbound.

Val, she says, won't you be the good spy for me? Stand tough for your stepmum?

He nods and, whispering, the three stepsons go off muttering, conspiring, crossing bridges to a new world. She watches them as Billy grips her shoulder. His eyes shine with water.

I love you, he says. How did you do that?

She looks about, sure they're alone.

That's charismatic analysis. It's all my own.

I'll bet you could find underground springs, he says.

You just want to get on my good side.

I'll take any side I can get.

The setting Sun blisters the abyss below. She feels a heavenly hunger to hold this moment forever, the hot red light, Billy's warmth blushing through her, beading her bones with pearl.

She holds Billy and cups his face, his breath on her, and remembers their cries together, the rush of lust. He is so in love. Does love last? The Spear has shown her a long life and her eyes brim. Gong has no close women friends. Well, Annette Gunthardt, perhaps, her Berlitz instructor. At first she was too exotic to attract friends, then Sidney took up her free time. She turned to writing and does not miss friends. And at the institute she appears as too much the prima donna who needs time for research and overseeing her publications as they pour out. Each book is subsidized by the Bollingen Foundation in Switzerland and distributed in America by Princeton University Press as ancillaries to Jung's work. She will have to find a new publisher and break entirely from the body of longwinded Jung studies. Charismatic analysis for children draws her interest.

Yes, that's it, Gong tells herself. I must find a new religion. I absolutely never dreamed I'd be where I am today. Wherever I am.

Did you say something? Billy asks.

Yes. I said. What a bloody beautiful Sunset. I want to jump out of my own skin and fly into it.

He studies her a long moment. You are experiencing the momentum of life, my love.

She grabs his arm. I want everything. So badly.

Do you? And when did this come over you?

She turns solemn and begging. Emotionally, I am eighteen years old. I've been only half-alive with Sidney. Now I want to live.

He drinks in her sapphire gown and turquoise heart-pin and the youthful dark new fringe she allows on her brow.

Give me your hand. I think I can help you. He leads her in, saying, Well, according to Credit Suisse, Jung's down twenty-six percent and they're laying people off. Charisma's the hot new stock. Good news, huh? Time to buy, sweetheart!

She smiles at his poor stab at humor and fingers a wound.

You don't think much of charismatic analysis?

My God, he thinks, this Chinese has been raised to be dreadfully solemn. He glows at her.

Honey pie, I'm sure your analysis will pump the breath of life into any poor beggar, and I'm behind you all the way.

She returns a dark, silken drunken look, the physical ache of love. She's a poppy in the wind beside this tall, tall creature, and surprises herself at how drawn she is to the way his lips shape certain vee sounds or sidewise d's for a wry phrase. His presence beside her burns like cognac and leaves her strengthless, something she never felt with Sidney, her only other mate. In private Billy usually kisses her but at times gets carried away and falls to lapping, which she has come to enjoy as if being preened with chamois or stroked with fur mittens. The experience drives every fear or twisted feeling out of her as a laying on of hands heals the mad or ill. She feels explored, opened, filled. The bird-spirit once broken by Rani Gupta's moves on Sidney feels restored and pinned all over with gifts from Billy. She sleeps on silk sheets of love. Oh God, what an appetite she has these days and must rein in. It's him, he fills rooms. He fills her. She wants to die like a moth. Her heart dreams big, rustling dreams. When she lies alone on the bed, her bare white toes yearn for him. When the lovers make love his long slender organ blows up with blood like a small balloon and can't be withdrawn for a quarter of an hour after release of his sperm. Flesh to flesh, nothing can part them. Her afterglow, leaving her loose as freshly upturned garden earth, dazzles with red, yellow, blue and white tulips that sway in a breeze and swag with dew. In her languor, cruel little ripples surprise and eddy. She swallows tiny shrieks, her sex a split peach lying open to the hot Sun. And at last, when withdrawal nears, she watches crisp hands unlock from autumn maples, fall slowly and make a bed of rust around the trunk and roots. Red leaves at rest.

He's not sure why she gives him this drunken glow but a smile fathomless as flame holds his heart for ransom and he's not getting it back without paying.

NOW, MY FRIENDS, I say, shall we give Dad his great present? Gong, bring The Spear.

I punch on the holovision. The large cube of light pops up, half-filling the library, and hovers midair. In it hangs an array of space discs, like the silver dust ringing Saturn, circling what we see of the blue and white planet below. But does this upward step in wolf Genius even register with Dad? Perhaps not.

Spear in hand, Gong stands beside Dad.

When you punch this button, Dad, I say, holding up a punch pad, the whole Christmas tree will light up.

Dad stares at Gong from whom his father's voice had come only moments ago.

I tell him, Ahuramazda awaits the touch of your finger.

Wh-wh-wha-wha-who-who-who?

It's the space disc program, Dad. Push the button.

T-t-t-t-to-to-to . . .

Magda watches us silently.

Toast, she says. He wants some toast. He likes that nutty-tasting seven-grain bread.

That's fine, Mama. But we've got to do this first. Dad, the whole world is waiting for this Sunrise. Punch the button.

Dad's hand rises, finger outstretched. But he can do no more. At last, Gong leads his finger—warily—and pushes the pad against it. His ghost finger goes through the pad. But he has picked up enough current from the two Hands of God to make a connection. Suddenly the holocube lights up with a thousand laser beams trained on receptor dishes below. White light bursts the walls.

Ah-Ah-Ah!!! Dad cries softly, staring at the global flood of white beams. He turns in mild amazement, hinting at a smile and begging something of me.

Dad, I tell him, your whole chalet is now being lighted by the space disks.

Magda rises from the divan and, trailing swirls of cosmic radiance from the Sunlit rug, sits by Dad and takes his hand.

So you've done it, Alexandru. You promised when we married that you'd honor me in a way you said only I deserve.

She grips his hand and gives his lap a hard rub. His eyes roll up and he yips softly.

Do you remember our wedding, Alexandru? She turns to me. We were married in Bihusi by Alexandru's beady-eyed little great-great-grand-mother, Maria Ouspenskaya Bihusi, who warned us, *Even de wolf who is pure in heart and says his prayers by night must beware the desert jackal when de fool Moon and de jackal look trustful and bright.*

Dad paws at the intense Saturnian brilliance ringing Earth. Bolts of Sunset outdoors fall straight into the holovision and mix like red paint.

Your father wrote our wedding service, Billy. He's quite a poet. Someday I'll show you his love letters. Well, perhaps. *I was just a child from Turda,* she sings, *when you chose me as your bride.* Can you still hear the service you had Maria Ouspenskaya read, Alexandru? I remember it, every word.

In winterlight all starvation leads to Ahuramazda. We shall send upon the jackals arrows of famine and we will destroy them. We shall increase the famine among them and break their bones. And so on. That was your father's song to me. Didn't that big bad wolf open his greedy heart? Completely! Didn't you? You withheld nothing. I had no idea what he was saying! Then you gazed into my eyes, and you nipped my neck and shoulder, Alexandru, and licked my muzzle all about, over and over, and dug your tongue into my ears and could not get enough of me. Now what is all this nonsense about you leaving me and going off to Ahuramazda?

Dad sits as stone-silent as the Great Statue of the Sun-god Ahmunhotep at the Temple of Luxor in the Valley of the Kings.

Well, now! I think he's ready to eat, Magda says, and uncovers his cold dinner of half-cooked birds. A fresh paprika smell rises. His long black lips fatten and gleam with drool. She tears off a thigh and he bites through it, bone and all, then sits fumbling with his napkin and chewing and grinding far too long before Magda reminds him to swallow. As a ghost, no longer chasing companies, he seems to have grown quite fat.

Where does the food go? Gong asks me.

I have no idea.

And as Dad stares at Earth's laser light whitening his face, a fragment breaks loose from below consciousness and lifts a last spark of wolf Genius into his goldglowing eyes. His cold nose, now sharpened to a pen point, broadens. He raises his napkin and sniffs his fingers, then slowly falls to rest, more and more sparklingly, all teeth and chicken back to his ears, his eyes glaring from a Carpathian forest and aflame with the amber fire of Bihusi. He sits in bliss, then turns to me, to me Sunny Jim, his long lips heavy with foam, and gurgles, *The light, the light! The light, the light!*

Yes, Dad, you did it. You chained the Sun.

But down in the corner of the holocube I see the Industrial Light and Magic logo, the company which teamed up with Jet Propulsion Lab to film this illusion for which I paid many millions. A yipping and a soft howl rumble in Dad's chest. Glee lifts him. His hands clench. He would yip and hop in circles if he still could. My father is a great oak never felled in battle before the North Wind on a distant mountain in the dark of winter. And now, how can a risen wolf be felled who has already thrown off his mortality and been eaten by his apostles in every land?

Oow, oow, oowww, ooowww, he whines, his tail aboil with the dark bliss of Bihusi. *Ooooowww! Ooooowwwww!*

Mother feeds him half-raw chicken wings that he crushes joyfully and with her fingers slips into his mouth small, juice-red cuts of breast. This wolf weeps not but gulps down everything and licks his long lips clean, and then leans his scenting nose and risen ears straight into the glowing cube. Though he's still seated outside the cube, his pale, golden eyes pulse as his brightened skull sweeps about outer space within the cube. He gasps as the nutmeg and cinnamon of Ahuramazda shock his muzzle. His nose nerves quiver, awash with freshly split apples and green-pepper flesh, perfume of sugary dates and fig-flesh, and as he drowns in paprika and garlic, light bursts, all his sinuses prickle with crushed pine needles out of Carpathian darkness as his lost Genius floods upward from the Wreath of Bihusi layered in a soft garden of fur and humus going back to the First Day's Original Light. He beats his knees at new beginnings. *Oooooowoooo!*

Red gold Sunlight runs in blood down the blue planet. We sit in Ahuramazda and glory in stolen fire. Magda rubs Dad's back as he rolls about and dances in his chair, his head in the heavens inside the cube.

By slow degrees the view swivels from the blue planet toward the Sun itself. The cube turns golden, more golden, and into a bubbling rage of gold as Ahuramazda comes forth in all Her Glory, a ball of bolting solar forces that form the oceanic fertility and sacrifice at the heart of life, what is born eating up what is, as the heroic horses of Ahuramazda haul her raging joy through black deeps of nothingness. Ahuramazda! Mithra! Yahweh! Helios Apollo! All-Seeing! All-Knowing! Eye of the Universe! Eye of Varuna! Of Ra! Of Allah! All-Mothering Ever-youthful Goddess at our Heart's Core! Pumping, pulsating bloodfire of life! Left Hand that Sees into All Mysteries! Right Hand that Makes All Things! All-Warmth Flooding All Greenery! Ice-Gripper! Power that binds! Love sword and Love sheath! Hunger of Sperm for the Spirit-Egg! Sun of Egypt! Sun of Mexico! Sun of Peru! Sun of Rome! Ahuramazda who rules all Suns of Man! Heartbuilder Sun! White Sun! Red Sun! Force reborn! Invincible! Whose Moon Magnifies and Suffers All Waning and Waxing! Hear us Your Children, O Queen of Light, Splendor Resplendent, as our golden eyes sing back the hymn of your light! Hear us, O Heaven, as our Heartbreak Howls Our Love of All Sun-built Particles on the Face of Night, even as you Soothe Us with the sultriness of your Sunset Glow, and Wake Us with Sun-fire on Snow and the Firelight Trembling in Winter Ice.

With a shout, Dad clutches his chair arms and bounds upward. Gong beside him stands stiff with The Spear of Ahuramazda locked upright. The smell of money money money flows from her glowing sapphire gown in flashing waves whose blue depths drown Dad's senses.

Clanging, The Left Hand of God that knows all mysteries falls from its pedestal, skitters across the room, climbs up Dad and clutches his chest.

Hoooooooooo! Dad howls in the bronze grip of mysteries. His ears prick high, his tail stiffens to starlight. Then the Hand that holds him drags Dad against the cube. Dad's jaw drops and gulps in greed at the Eucharist flaming before him. His great jaw swallows Ahuramazda as Ahuramazda gulps him down. With only a staticky crackle, the Hand flees into the Sun and Dad's starblue tail fades utterly.

Gong raises a farewell with The Spear and grips my hand. We stare at the dumb ponderous plasm of Ahuramazda whose birthmatter eats its own being and floods forth from the egg-bearing cleft of creation. It bursts and falls in its everlasting toil of bloom and blossom. O font of touch and whisper, bring us back again. Let bright new creatures of light arise on your hot breath, Great Maker. Bring us back rosy ripe and violet with blood and let us fall from our mother's lap and surge with breath as we reclaim your caress and taste your salts anew. Amaze us with your energy and strength, scorch us with joy and kisses, then send us forth hungering for your love.

Magda wails. *Babayaga, Babayaga beloved!*

But paradise claims the Holy Ghost of the Bihusi. His chair sits empty. He has swallowed the Sun. He is the Sun.

THE END

Cape Cod, Greenwich Village
1998–2014

ACKNOWLEDGMENTS

Profound thanks are extended to the following for their generous financial support which helped to defray some of this book's production costs:

Kevin Adams, E.R. Auld, Thomas Young Barmore Jr., Andrew Bissaro, Brian R. Boisvert, Matt Bucher, Jeffrey Canino, Dave & Joan Carr, Tobias Carroll, Scott Chiddister, WD Clarke, Seth Coblentz, C. Colla, Joshua Lee Cooper, Michael Corkery, Nike Cosmides, Sheri Costa, Devin Curtis, Isaac Ehrlich, Margaret J. Evans, Luke Frazier, Nathan "N.R." Gaddis, Stephan Glander, GMarkC, B F Gordon, Richard L. Haas III, Mark Hartman, Erik Hemming, Aric Herzog, Adam Hetherington, Morgan Hobbs, Per Kristian Hoff, Erik T. Johnson, Haya K., Tom Kiefer, Jesse Knepper, M. E. Lis, Jim McElroy, Brendan McGrath, Sidney McMahon, Mark S. Mitchell, Steven Moore, Geoffrey Moses, Gregory Moses, Michael O'Shaughnessy, Danny Paige, Marshall Parks, Ry Pickard, PK, Poems-For-All, Pedro Ponce, Pops, Kristjan Ross, George Salis, Frank V. Saltarelli, Spike Schwab, Connor Shirley, Joel Stimpson, Tanveer, Desiree Troy, Cato Vandrare, Jack Waters, Justin White, Karl Wieser, Stephen Williamson, Michael Zhuang, znf, and Anonymous

Rick Schober
Publisher
Tough Poets Press